Praise for

FOREST
of SOULS

"Non-stop action, political intrigue, and dark magic are woven into this silky-yet-fast-paced daydream of a fantasy. Lori M. Lee casts the perfect web of unforgettable characters and an intriguing plot—you won't want to escape."

—Sarah Henning, author of *Sea Witch* and *Sea Witch Rising*

"Imaginative [and] action-packed . . . this engaging title will leave fans eager for the sequel."

—*Booklist*

"Lee is a masterful world-builder, creating intriguing scenarios and a compelling cast of characters, anchored by the strong portrayals of female friendship."

—*School Library Journal*

"A refreshing fantasy for readers looking for more friendship and adventure, less romance."

—*Kirkus Reviews*

"A classic fantasy rooted in self-discovery, death-defying friendship, and political intrigue, *Forest of Souls* spins a tale as lush as its world. You can't help but want to see this dark journey through."

—Linsey Miller, author of the Mask of Shadows duology and *Belle Révolte*

FOREST of SOULS

Lori M. Lee

PAGE STREET
PUBLISHING CO.

PAGE STREET
PUBLISHING CO.

Copyright © 2021 Lori M. Lee

First published in 2020 by
Page Street Publishing Co.
27 Congress Street, Suite 105
Salem, MA 01970
www.pagestreetpublishing.com

Distributed by Macmillan, sales in Canada by The Canadian Manda Group.

25   25   23   22   21   1   2   3   4   5

ISBN-13: 978-1-64567-337-8 (paperback)
ISBN-10: 1-64567-337-5 (paperback)

Library of Congress Control Number: 2020945232

Cover and book design by Laura Benton for Page Street Publishing Co.
Cover illustration by Charlie Bowater
Author photo by PrettyGeeky Photography
Treeline and spiderweb vectors from Shutterstock

Printed and bound in the United States

For everyone who's ever wondered
if they were enough.

GLOSSARY

THIY (THEE): Continent consisting of three kingdoms: Eveywn, the Nuvalyn Empire, and Kazahyn

THE DEAD WOOD – An ancient forest of dead trees possessed by vengeful souls

DRAGULE – Species of drakonys native to Evewyn, reserved only for royalty, nobility, and the Queen's Guard

DRAKE – Most common species of drakonys, large and sturdy, used as pack animals and for transportation by humans

DRAKONYS – Large bipedal lizards. Strong backs and short clawed hands; large heads balanced with long tails. Their sizes and the shapes of their heads differentiate between species. They come in all colors.

FALCON – Messenger bird trained to deliver short and/or urgent correspondence between various points in Thiy. Managed by a local Scholar of Falconry.

HUMAN – One of the three dominant races on Thiy, they do not possess the ability to perform magic. It's said that humans were born from the bones of the fallen sun god, leaving them too solid and making it impossible to access the magic in their souls.

SHADOWBLESSED – One of the three dominant races on Thiy, with the ability to manipulate shadows. It's said that the shadowblessed were born from the blood and ichor of the fallen sun god, gifting them magic over the darker elements.

SHAMAN – One of the three dominant races on Thiy. It's said that the shamans were born from the fragments of the fallen sun god's soul, gifting them power over the elements and the ability to touch other souls.

EVEWYN (EVE-WIN): Kingdom ruled and predominantly populated by humans

BLADES – Evewyn's warrior elite

BYRTH – Major port city on the western coast of Evewyn

THE DEMON CRONE – The eldest of the Sisters. She is the keeper of the earth. Depicted as extremely old, to reflect the ancient world, and hideous because she grants all her beauty to the earth and keeps none for herself. Brown skin like the trees, with hair fine and pale as spider thread. She is celebrated on the first day of spring.

THE FALCON WARRIOR – Third eldest of the Sisters. She is the protector. Pilgrims and travelers often pray to her for safe journeys, and soldiers pray to her when they seek victory in battle. She is celebrated on the first day of winter.

HATCHLET (QUEEN'S COMPANY) – A first-year in the Queen's Company. Their hair is shorn so that their heads are bare like a newborn hatchlet. They wear yellow sashes.

MONKS – Keepers of the temples and devout followers of the Sanctuary of the Sisters

THE MOTHER SERPENT – The second oldest of the Sisters. She is the guardian of the faithful. She nurtures belief and rewards the devout. She is celebrated at midsummer.

Prince's (Princess's) Company – Mandatory preparatory school where all children, peasant and noble alike, aged eleven to thirteen live within a restricted compound in Vos Talwyn for three years. They are taught general subjects like history, medicine, and other electives in addition to how to fight and use a weapon. The second child born to the ruling monarch oversees the Company.

Queen's (King's) Company – Voluntary military finishing school for graduates from the Prince's Company who wish to join the Royal Army or Royal Navy. Four years of training, in addition to history, math, tactics, and other subjects. Each year, they earn a new name: hatchlets, weans, wyrlings, and wyverns.

Queen's (King's) Shadow – A master spy, employed by the Queen/King of Evewyn, who delivers secrets abroad and within to the queen/king. Sometimes, the Shadow is also an assassin.

Reiwyn – Evewyn's nobility

The Sanctuary of the Sisters – The dominant religion in Evewyn. Typically shortened to the Sisters: the Demon Crone, the Mother Serpent, the Falcon Warrior, and the Twins.

Shamanborn – Shamans from Evewyn; no other distinction from Nuvali shamans

The Twins – The youngest of the Sisters. The Bright Twin (good luck) and the Pale Twin (ill luck). They appear as young girls with skin pale as the moon and hair dark as the night sky, and one can never be sure which is the bearer of ill luck or good luck. But the Bright Twin is most commonly depicted wearing stars in her hair. The Pale Twin is depicted with a silver moon. Her sister keeps her in line, but when the Pale Twin is depicted alone, it's a bad omen.

Vos Talwyn (VOHS TAHL-win) – Capital of Evewyn

Wean (Queen's Company) – A second-year in the Queen's Company. They wear green sashes.

Wyrling (Queen's Company) – A third-year in the Queen's Company. Their hair is long enough to be tied back into a wolf tail. They wear blue sashes.

Wyvern (Queen's Company) – A fourth-year in the Queen's Company. Their hair is now long enough to earn the right to be braided with feathers, which flap behind them like the tail of a wyvern. They wear red sashes.

THE NUVALYN EMPIRE (NEW-VUH-LIN): Kingdom ruled and populated predominantly by shamans

Breathsipher – A windwender who can suffocate a person by stealing the breath from their lungs. They can also steal a person's voice, perfectly mimicking it.

Brumys (BROOM-is) – A windwender who can conjure fog or create creatures out of storm clouds. They can also siphon a magical attack or spell, allowing the magic to pass through them, leaving them unharmed; doesn't work against physical attacks.

Burner – A firewender who can summon and manipulate fire. The most powerful can create creatures of fire and brimstone to fight for them.

Dragokin – A species of drakonys that lives only in the Nuvalyn Empire. Tamed and ridden by the shamans as life partners. Opalescent scales that vary in shades, four ivory (or black) horns, powerfully fast runners. They are able to spring into the air in battle, clawing down at their enemies while their riders attack with weapons.

Earthwender – Shaman with one of three earth crafts: forger, terranys, and stoneskin. Eyes the color of emeralds.

Familiar – The souls of beasts made physical again by the magic of a shaman. They're sometimes called Little Gods. When a bond is formed, they possess the ability to channel a shaman's magic, giving them a corporeal form. In exchange, the shaman uses the familiar as a conduit to perform magic.

Firewender – Shaman with one of three fire crafts: burner, wyrmin, and flame eater. Eyes the color of rubies.

Flame eater – A firewender who can transform into smoke and flame

Forger – An earthwender who can shape and bend metals. Expert smiths and craftsmen.

Lightgiver – A lightwender who can steal the "light," or life, from one person and transfer it to another person or themselves

Light Stitcher – A lightwender who can gather and create light even in the darkest of places. They can also use their magic to stitch the light within other people. They're renowned healers.

Lightwender – Shaman with one of four light crafts: light stitcher, lightgiver, soulguide, and soulrender. Eyes the color of topaz or amber yellow.

Mirrim (MERE-im) – Capital of the Nuvalyn Empire. Only shamans can enter due to a spell cast about the city.

Shamanic Calling – The five elements of magic, to which each Nuvali shaman is sorted: fire, earth, wind, water, and light. Each Calling has three (or four) crafts.

Shamanic Craft – The specific talent a shaman possesses

Soulguide – A lightwender who can shepherd souls, guiding them to the afterlife or back to life. There has never been a soulguide in living memory. The only one recorded was the founder of Mirrim, who created the spell allowing only shamans to enter.

Soulrender – A lightwender who can rip the souls from animals; extremely rare that a soulrender can rip the soul from a person

Sower – A waterwender who can magically assist in growing plants and helping seeds take root

Stoneskin – An earthwender who can transform themselves into stone. They can still move while transformed, making their skin nearly indestructible, and they possess super strength. The length of time they can remain transformed is limited.

Suryal (sur-YAHL) – The sun god, from whom it is said all the races were born. Worshipped by the shamans.

Tempest – A windwender who can summon gentle breezes and howling gales. The most powerful can summon tornadoes.

Terranys (TAIR-ruh-nis) – An earthwender who can move earth and rocks. The most powerful can create earthquakes or create beings of stone and earth to fight for them.

TRUTHSEEKER – A waterwender who can use water as a means of divination. They can also divine whether a person is telling the truth.

VORTYS (VOR-TIS) – A waterwender who can move and manipulate water. The most powerful can create tidal waves or create creatures of water to fight for them.

WATERWENDER – Shaman with one of three water crafts: sower, vortys, and truthseeker. Eyes the color of blue sapphires.

WINDWENDER – Shaman with one of three wind crafts: tempest, brumys, and breathsipher. Eyes the color of violet amethyst.

WYRMIN (WEER-MIN) – A firewender who can increase the temperature of objects, air, and people. Could boil a person's blood or melt an opponent's iron weapon.

KAZAHYN (KAH-ZUH-HEEN): Kingdom predominantly populated by shadowblessed clans

DOOMBRINGER – A shadowblessed who can summon complete darkness

ENCHANTER – A shadowblessed who can imbue the properties of a gemstone into a weapon, such as the strength of a diamond and color of a ruby. Can also pass certain qualities, temporarily, into people and animals.

FIREBORN QUEENS – One of the most powerful clans in Kazahyn. Their High Queen's magic smells of brimstone and is said to emit heat.

FLESH WORKER – A shadowblessed who can manipulate flesh and bone. Renowned healers and deadly warriors.

GATE – A shadowblessed who can create doorways through shadows, moving great distances instantly

HATCHLET – A newborn wyvern

HLAU – A Kazan prince

NECROMANCER – A powerful shadowblessed capable of commanding a dead body to rise (without its soul)

PENUMBRIA (PE-NUM-BREE-UH) – One of the largest cities in Kazahyn; location is hidden and can only be reached through Shadow magic

SHADOWMASTER – A shadowblessed who can manipulate shadows

WEAN – A young wyvern that cannot yet fly

WYRLING – An adolescent wyvern that has learned to fly but is not yet fully grown

WYVERN – A winged creature native to the mountains of Kazahyn. Although they are scaled, they have long whiplike tails ending in brilliant feathers. Also feathered around arm/leg joints and sometimes around the head. Strong fliers and fast runners. They are also the companions of the shadowblessed. Among certain clans, it is a rite of passage to catch and tame one. They become companions for life, even going into battle with their riders.

ONE

The earth is black with last night's rain—a perfect morning for shadows.

When I arrive at my mentor's tower door, my damp gloves barely brush the heavy wood before it flies open. Its half-dozen locks jangle and clack noisily. For a blind woman whose eyes are always concealed behind a scarf, Kendara's face can convey an impressive amount of disdain.

"Sirscha Ashwyn, you thoughtless dolt," she says, her voice low and gravelly. "Took you long enough." She used to speak more gently when I was younger. Maybe that's why the sound of it still makes me smile, even when she's insulting me.

"I was only gone for an hour," I say, shutting the door behind me.

Kendara snorts as she returns to the chair by the open balcony. There's a white circle painted into the balcony's floor, large enough to fit two battling opponents. I've earned more wounds than I can count in that circle, but this tower is the ideal place to conduct our training, high away from the watchful eyes of the palace. A dagger lies on the seat of her chair, and she picks it up as smoothly as if she can see. Sitting, she tests the blade's edge with the thick pad of her thumb.

To a stranger, she is a woman descending into old age, her hair gone white save for a few stubborn streaks of black. Age spots speckle the deep bronze of her skin, which is a couple of shades darker than my own. But she is far from infirm. The dagger she handles and the weapons that hang from her wall aren't decorative. She is the queen's Shadow, and for the past four years, my secret mentor.

"Would have taken me half the time," she grumbles, reaching for the whetstone that rests on the floor. "And *without* the need to show off."

My nose wrinkles as I remove my gloves. Opening my satchel, I dig inside for the banner I appropriated from the city's southern watchtower. I *may* have also waved at the tower guards while scaling the walls.

"I wasn't showing off." I've learned to stop being surprised—and to stop denying—when Kendara knows things she has no business knowing. "I was just having a bit of fun."

"The Shadow does not reveal herself for any reason. What would be the point, then?"

I hold out the banner. "I'm not the Shadow yet," I say with an emphasis on *yet* and the hope that she'll take the hint.

"And you won't be if you keep behaving like a compulsive twit." The whetstone clatters to the floor as she snatches the banner out of my hand. She stalks across the room, weaving neatly around a table, and flings the silver moon of Evewyn into the flames of her hearth.

"What are you doing, you daft hag?" I shout, dashing after her.

The flames take a second to catch, the banner still damp from the rain. But quickly enough, fire sears through the thin fabric, sparking blue from the spidersilk threads of the moon. Dark smoke billows up the chimney. The smell singes my nostrils, and I try to wave it away, toward the open balcony.

"Idiot girl," Kendara mumbles as she sets down the dagger. She opens a cupboard that hangs skewed on the wall. "I don't want that thing in here." Cursing me under her breath, she rummages through the cupboard's overflowing contents.

I glance back at the hearth and the ruined remains of the banner. Grudgingly, I see her point. Once, Evewyn's banners had flown a white falcon clutching a branch of plum blossoms. But when the queen succeeded the throne eight years ago, she changed the emblem to a silver moon, the symbol of the Pale Twin, harbinger of ill fortune.

"Then why did you send me to retrieve it?" I ask. Smoke lingers in the room, a dingy haze that stings my eyes and tickles my throat. Kendara is still preoccupied, so I move toward the balcony where the air is clearer.

From this height, the capital of Vos Talwyn is an enormous

sprawl of stone, statues, and curling green rooftops. Beyond the city's walls, the land extends south like lush brocade stitched with the golden threads of morning. A shadowy ribbon against the horizon draws my eye eastward. Even from this distance, a shiver slithers down my spine. The Dead Wood mars the eastern border like the puckered, blackened edges of burned fabric.

"I told you to steal the banner from the watchtower," Kendara says, drawing my attention again. I return to sit near the hearth as she withdraws something small from the cupboard. "I didn't tell you to bring it to me."

"Well, now I can't even put it back," I say, but our bickering is forgotten when she places a bracelet on the table before me. With a quick glance at Kendara, who nods to confirm that I can touch it, I trace my finger along the designs carved into the jewelry. The smooth texture glistens like white jade. "What is it made of?"

"Troll bone."

My finger stills on the bracelet. Intrigued, I lean in closer to examine it. The bracelet can't be thicker than the width of my little finger. "I would've thought troll bone would be bigger."

Kendara grunts, a noise I've come to recognize as scorn for my imagined ignorance. She has a wide array of such sounds.

Lifting the bracelet, I turn it toward the sunlight that streams in through the open balcony and diffuses into the smoky air. The polished surface gives off a beautiful sheen, and the color transitions from a warm butter to the burned yellow of old parchment. The jeweler etched a curling design into the bone that lends it an elegant quality. A metal fastener fashioned to look like tiny lotus petals allows a section of the bone to be removed so that the bracelet can be worn. It's lovely but somewhat grotesque, given its origin.

"For you," she says.

I almost drop the bracelet. But I recover quickly, clutching the troll bone in my fist. "I . . . um. Thank you. It's very . . . thoughtful." I narrow my eyes. "And unusual. Why are you giving me this?"

Kendara is many things, but thoughtful is not one of them. It's part of what I admire about her. She never pretends to be anything other than who she is.

She turns away, but not before I notice the slight purse of her mouth. It's not a smile—Kendara does not smile—but sometimes the muscles around her mouth spasm and twitch, like she's trying to imitate the motions. It's just as well. An actual smile might break her face.

"Trolls are slow creatures but wickedly strong," she says. So I'm to decipher the bracelet's purpose on my own. "Anyone with the misfortune to be caught by one isn't likely to survive long enough to speak of it."

"But you speak as if from experience." I pop open the segment of bone fastened to the metal lotus and fit the jewelry around my wrist before snapping the piece back in place. I barely feel its weight.

"I've had a great many experiences, none of which are any of your business." Kendara flits restlessly around the workroom, returning vials of unknown substances to cupboards and books to shelves.

"Fortunately, you're not likely to encounter any trolls in Evewyn. Nor anywhere else in Thiy. The last colony died out some time after the shamans claimed the eastern lands for their own."

How old must the bone be if no living troll has existed in Thiy for nearly a thousand years? It must be extremely rare as well. "I suppose that means you're not sending me out to bring you a fresh rib for a matching necklace."

"Trolls were known to be highly resistant to magic," she says, completely ignoring me. Another of her many talents.

Although I've no idea what use she has for books, I've read every volume she's crammed into her numerous shelves. I recall a passage that explained how the remains of powerful creatures, such as trolls, retain certain magical properties that the creatures possessed when they were alive. Shamans often fashioned the bones of such creatures into objects like this bracelet. But not as jewelry.

"It's a talisman," I say, twisting the bracelet around my wrist. It's still cool, despite that it should have warmed from my body heat.

Depending on the creature a talisman is made from, the bones not only protect against outside magic but dampen one's own magic as well. Or amplify and change it. Those sorts of talismans are rare.

But a troll's bone? "Protection against magic." My smile broadens and my heart sings with a longing bordering on desperation. "Will I need such protection?"

Has the moment I've longed for these past four years finally arrived? Will she at last name me as her apprentice?

"Most of you do," she mutters. I mentally curse at the way I flinch—not only for the implied insult that I should need protection beyond my own abilities but also for the reminder that I am not her only pupil. The knowledge—the *fear*—that I could so easily lose all I've worked for to some other nameless competitor is never far from my thoughts.

Kendara scratches at the bottom of her handkerchief. For all that she's taught me, she's revealed almost nothing about her past. I don't know if she has family, where she grew up, if Kendara is her real name, or even what the upper half of her face looks like.

But I've come to know her in other ways. Although she demands the respect and honor owed to her as my elder, she loathes mindless obedience. She encourages my curiosity even as she insults my intelligence. She constantly challenges my limits, but only ever within the parameters of her rules.

Her fierce independence and abrasive honesty are what first convinced me to trust her those years ago, qualities that would have offended others but to me were admirable. Something to aspire toward.

In the four years I've been her pupil, her training has been harsh and unforgiving. I've stolen fruit from the queen's orchards. I've been shackled and dropped into a flooded well. I've crept through a den of sleeping rock scorpions with bells woven in my hair.

Every assignment tested my skill and my resolve. After all, a Shadow is tasked with whispering to the queen the secrets of allies and enemies alike, and with quietly extinguishing any powerful opponents. Kendara has never underestimated me. She is one of the few people who do not equate my upbringing with my worth. And when I am the queen's Shadow, who I was will matter less than nothing compared to who I will become.

"I heard you're to accompany the hatchlets to the Valley of Cranes today." Her lip curls. It isn't the first time she's expressed disgust with the prison. While I agree with her, I'm not bold enough to say so. It would mean criticizing the queen, and no one except Kendara would dare.

So I only say, "I am."

She makes a shooing gesture. "Get going. They've already gathered in the Company yard."

The disappointment strikes swift and brutal, as all her blows do. I've less than a month in the Company before graduation, before the Royal Army ships me off to who-knows-where. Less than a month to prove to Kendara that I deserve to remain here and to study as her official apprentice. Every day that passes without her decision is a kick to the gut.

Swallowing back the protests that crowd my throat, I push to my feet, my braid swinging against my back. I tug the sleeve of my gray uniform over the bracelet and ask, "Where did you even get this?"

Kendara retrieves her dagger and whetstone from the floor, but rather than reclaim her seat by the balcony doors, she settles into a rocking chair before the fireplace. "A Shadow must keep her secrets."

"Only some."

"But all of them today. Now get out, witless child." She sits so close to the hearth that I worry she'll catch fire. But she seems to cow even the flames, which don't dare do more than lick at her toes.

My steps are silent as I cross the room. A single creak of the floorboards, and she won't call me back for days. In her presence, to be anything less than what she has made me would be an insult.

"Thank you for the gift." I reach for the door, scratched and marred by the heavy locks. Before leaving, I grin and toss over my shoulder, "Ill-tempered crone."

TWO

Saengo is waiting for me. She sits astride her drake, beside where I left my own mount. When she sees me, her dark brows crash together in a scowl.

"Do you know what time it is?" she snaps, already turning for the gates. "They're about to leave. Do you *want* to be punished?"

"Sisters, save me. Not you, too," I mutter. I greet Yandor, my drake, with a firm pat to his neck.

The huge lizard gives a pleased shake, the motion rippling through his dark-green scales. Gripping his saddle, I pull myself onto his back. The old leather groans. I brush hair from my face, inky strands that have come loose from my braid. My fingers trace the thin scars that line the top curves of my ears, a mindless action born of repetition.

With a flick of my reins, Yandor's powerful legs take off running after Saengo's drake, who's already halfway down the path.

"I only have enough patience for one relentless grouch today," I say. Despite Kendara's nature, I'm always reluctant to leave her.

"And I've used up all *my* patience waiting for you," Saengo calls over her shoulder.

The path takes us around the Outer Court before exiting the palace grounds. Within minutes, we plunge into the winding, cobbled streets of Vos Talwyn. We head eastward, away from the Grand Palace with its tiered roofs and sharp spires, dipped in gold leaf and sunlight.

I fell in love with this city from the moment I arrived seven years ago. It had been like diving into cold water, a breathtaking shock after the drab orphanage. Houses capped with curling clay tiles huddle together like hooded old men, exchanging secrets through traceried windows and paneled doors. Our mounts weave through gilded carriages clattering along on oversize wheels and laden carts pulled by teams of drakes. We skirt around some reiwyn lady's palanquin draped in turquoise silk. Patrons crowd outside a popular noodle shop, and raucous children gather excitedly around a theater cart on the street corner.

The sights of the city don't hold my attention for long today. My hand finds the shape of the troll-bone bracelet beneath my sleeve. Soon, Kendara will name me as her apprentice. *Soon.* My fingers tighten over the talisman, clutching it close, like a promise.

We turn onto a private lane, lined with buildings belonging

to the Grand Offices. It's quiet here, only a few soldiers chatting off to the side. The lane leads first to the enclosed grounds of the Prince's Company. We pass it by, continuing along a shaded path lined with plum trees. The path ends at the doors to the Queen's Company. The gates open directly into a sizable training yard. Long two-story buildings enclose the yard on three sides. Those are where students sit for lessons on subjects like history, religion, and military strategy.

Currently, students fill the yard in neat rows. They move in synchronization, shifting through the familiar forms of the Wyvern's Dance, the fighting style of our armies. Near the entrance, already divided into two lines, are the first-year hatchlets. They're always easy to spot because of the yellow sashes around their waists and their shorn hair. Was I that small at fourteen? I remember wanting to cry tears of self-pity every time I looked at my bald head in a mirror.

"Wyverns! You're *late!*"

My spine snaps straight at the voice. Dread spills into my ribs. *No, no, no.* I dismount and drop immediately into a deep bow as Officit Boldis breaks away from the supply wagon.

He isn't supposed to be leading us today. His name wasn't on the duty report. There must have been a last-minute change. The officit he replaced is one of the few who likes me. She would have scolded me for being late and, at most, assigned me to cleaning after the drakes during the trip. If I'd known Officit Boldis would be here instead, I would have endeavored to arrive early.

"Our deepest apologies, Officit Boldis," Saengo says, her voice pitched low, appropriately contrite. She hates him as much as I do, but she would never publicly disrespect an officit. "I was delayed by one of the falconers, and Sirscha was good enough to fetch me. It won't happen again."

Officit Boldis eyes me with suspicion. Saengo comes from one of the oldest reiwyn houses in Evewyn, House Phang. They're renowned for producing the best falconers in the kingdom. Saengo is often approached by the capital's falconers to discuss some matter or another about the messenger birds.

"Even so," Officit Boldis says, sneering. "Your tardiness has cost us time. As penance—"

There's a light cough from behind us. Saengo's eyes go wide as we both turn to see who's dared to interrupt an officit. I'm unsurprised to find Jonyah Thao climbing off his drake. I clasp my hands behind my back, fingers clamped tight together, as Saengo and I share a glance.

Jonyah bows first to the officit and then to Saengo. Saengo is Jonyah's cousin and the future leader of his House. Although he doesn't spare me even the vaguest acknowledgment, as he is my elder in age and my superior in station, I'm still expected to show respect. My head twitches in what could arguably be a bow.

Jonyah says, "Officit Boldis, it is my duty to inform you that Phang left the Company grounds a mere half hour ago. My friends and I witnessed her departure."

Saengo's gaze darts to mine, her nostrils flaring. I imagine the look on Jonyah's face if I punched him right now.

The corners of Officit Boldis's mouth pull downward as if

imitating his drooping mustache. His heavy brows hang low over his eyes, his expression thunderous. "Lying to an officit," he all but spits out. "*Cane!*"

I tuck in my chin, lower my gaze, and mentally swear in three languages. My legs just finished healing from an encounter with a thorneater last week when Kendara sent me north to retrieve one of its tusks.

Saengo tries to catch my eye, but my gaze remains firmly on the ground. Neither of us speaks. Our pleas would be useless. As the child of a reiwyn lord, she is above physical penance from even the officits of the Company.

I am no one, the child of nameless people who left me at an orphanage when I was two. Whatever memories I might have once had of them are long faded. This will hardly be the first time I'm punished for something involving us both, but as I'm the reason why we were late, it's my fault, anyway.

Officit Boldis says, "The penance is usually fifteen lashes. However, as you've already caused us delay, I will allow five strikes to the legs."

I wait, knowing there's more. He isn't the merciful sort.

"Thao," he says, addressing Jonyah. "Would you administer her penance?"

My eyes close to conceal my murderous thoughts. At my side, Saengo gasps. Even Jonyah can't hide his surprise. This breaks protocol. To be punished by a fellow wyvern is a grave insult, especially in front of nearly the entire Company. Kendara will hear of this within the hour, and she will scrutinize my every action, my every response. So I allow myself only a heartbeat to control my face, and then I nod.

Jonyah and Officit Boldis march me past rows of students who continue to shift from one fighting stance into the next. Their eyes follow us. It never gets any less humiliating.

A single wooden pole stands ominously at the front of the yard, visible to everyone. Public humiliation is only effective when witnessed, after all. Without having to be prompted, I lift my arms and wrap my fingers around a rope knotted to a hook that's been driven into the wood. I grip it tight and stand so that I'm facing Jonyah.

Officit Boldis steps away to give us room. "Don't break anything. She still has an assignment to complete."

"Yes, Officit," Jonyah says. He slaps the bamboo cane lightly against his leg, testing its weight and where it will fall against my skin. And then—

I inhale sharply as the first strike finds my left thigh, sharp and sudden. I hold Jonyah's gaze, taking what satisfaction I can in the curl of his lip. His next strike falls harder, the pain brilliant, streaking up my hip. I remain silent although my fingernails nearly tear through the rope. I don't cry out, and I don't allow my legs to fold. I am used to pain. I have lived with it for four years, sometimes delivered at Kendara's hands, sometimes by the Company's.

When another student suffers penance, I always avert my eyes out of respect. Many students do the same now, continuing in their stances. But plenty pause to watch as well. I can stomach the pain, but the sense of helplessness, of being exposed, never becomes any more bearable.

The third strike nearly takes out my knee, but I wrap the rope around my wrist and shift my weight to my other leg. Kendara's words repeat like a mantra in my head: *"Bite your tongue. Play your role. Do not lose your place in the Company, or you will lose your place with me."*

Less than a month, I tell myself. Just a few weeks more, and maybe not even that, if Kendara makes her decision before the month's end.

The fourth and fifth strikes fall in quick succession, nearly in the same spot. My lips pinch, jaw clenched. The bruises will be impressive. As Jonyah steps away, I release the rope, willing my legs to hold. When our eyes meet, I lift my chin in triumph over this latest attempt to break me. Jonyah's nostrils flare with rage.

"Good," Officit Boldis barks. "Let's get going. You've wasted enough of our time."

Jonyah backs me against the pole as he returns the cane to its usual place on the hook. He's an entire head taller, and his height is another tool he uses to intimidate. As he shifts on his feet, close enough that his breath falls sour against my hair, something crinkles lightly in his pocket. He jerks on my braid, forcing my head back so that I have to look up at him.

His voice is a growl. "You should give up. You are a pebble beneath my boot, annoying but insignificant enough to be crushed."

I allow the venom in my eyes to answer for me. Although I'm

hardly his only target at the Company, I'm his favorite. Hatred roils between us, so fiercely palpable that I wonder if he'll strike me again, just to prove that he can. But then Officit Boldis makes an impatient sound. Jonyah releases my braid before stalking away. As soon as Officit Boldis passes her, Saengo rushes forward to offer me a shoulder.

I shake my head, waving away her help. Instead, I grit my teeth and place one foot in front of the other.

Officit Boldis is already astride his drake, alongside the hatchlets who will make the trek on foot. Although my legs burn, I refuse to limp. It's a relief when I finally reach Yandor and take hold of his reins. Yandor nudges my shoulder with his head. I lean into him, accepting his support.

"You will walk," the officit says, which makes me pause with one foot in the stirrup. Slowly, I turn to look at him. He smiles at me and then shifts the smile to each of the wyverns, six in all, including Jonyah. "You will all make the journey on foot, with the first-years. You may thank Ashwyn's disregard for her duties."

My fellow wyverns shoot me glares as they dismount. The journey to the Valley of Cranes is an entire day's march. I fall into position at the rear with Saengo, leading our drakes along by their reins as we at last file out from the yard. We head for the nearby gate kept exclusively for the use of the two Companies. It's purely functional, free of the ornate carvings and brushed gold that accent the public gates into the city.

There are two sets of doors, the first an iron trellis that can be raised and lowered like a portcullis and the second made of wood and iron that can be swung shut and locked with a series of heavy deadbolts. Currently, both are open. Outside, a dirt road cuts through a stretch of grass that dips downhill and then curves into the woods.

The welts on my legs have settled into a steady ache. I always carry medicinal herbs with me, but I don't know when I'll have the opportunity to apply them.

"Are you all right?" Saengo murmurs. Her drake tries to lick her hair, and she swats at it.

"I'll be fine," I say.

A fourth-year wyvern walks on either side of the marching hatchlets. Two more are stationed at the front with the officit. Leading our whole party are four soldiers and a large wagon pulled by four drakes. The wagon is filled with supplies for the prison: simple but clean clothing, bushels of herbs and vegetables, sacks of rice, and even a couple of pigs that snort merrily as they jostle along.

When we reach the bend where the path passes through the woods and joins with the main road, I turn to look over my shoulder. The walls loom, green-clad sentinels patrolling behind the crenellations. Beyond, peering out over the stone are the shining marble domes of the Temple of the Five Sisters and each of their massive statues—the Demon Crone, the Mother Serpent, the Falcon Warrior, and the Twins. But they all cower beneath the spires of the Grand Palace. The structure rises from the city in gilded tiers of sculptured jade roofs and ornate gables, its towers and extravagant finials like lances that spear the clouds.

With ease, my eyes locate Kendara's tower and the wide lip of her balcony. It's one of the tallest among the dozens of towers throughout the Grand Palace. Is she still tending to her weapons? Sometimes, I'll return to her workroom to find her in the exact position as I left her days prior.

I joke that she survives only on the crushed hopes and tears of her pupils, which incenses Saengo. Kendara's age and high position warrants that she is spoken of with respect. Normally, I'd agree, except . . . well, she's Kendara. As Shadow, she doesn't just exist outside of Evewyn's entire social structure; she exists *above* it, answering to no one but the queen. I've always found her remarkable for that alone.

"Hatchlets!" Officit Boldis barks, falling back to speak to the first-years. His voice is grating. "You'll do well to remember that the Valley of Cranes is a prison. There is to be no interaction with the shamanborn, and I would advise against straying from the group."

The first-years shift uncomfortably at the warning. These hatchlets would have been no older than six or seven when Queen Meilyr rounded up the shamanborn for imprisonment.

"I'm sorry," Saengo says.

"For what? Lying?"

She winces. "I thought it would help."

I paste on a smile despite that I'd like nothing better than to lie down, in the middle of the road if need be. Saengo is my best friend, and I value her as I value no one else save Kendara. The guilt will bother her all day if I don't alleviate it.

"I know, and we'd have gotten away with it if not for Jonyah, curse him." Besides, I could have avoided all this if I'd been on time.

She looks away, a line between her brows. Even despondent, she walks like reiwyn: chin up, shoulders back, impeccable posture. Her long braid, with its sleek black feathers, swings between her shoulder blades. We have the same midnight-black hair, but where my eyes are gray, hers are light brown, and where I was born to nothing, she was born to all the privilege and self-assurance of a reiwyn house, members of court. We are opposites in nearly every way, and yet I can't imagine a life without her in it.

"You know, you're actually a very good liar," I tease.

Saengo rolls her eyes. "A skill that's sure to come in handy in the Royal Army."

"Every talent has its uses."

"Unlike you, I don't need such talents."

"Right," I say, "because your winning personality is enough to get you by?"

She angles me a haughty look through catlike brown eyes. "I am *delightful* company."

I choke down my laughter, but it's enough to soften the stern set of her mouth.

Aside from the occasional stray puddle, there's little evidence of last night's rain on the open road. Farms and orchards stretch eastward, broken up by patches of woodland. To the west, the Coral Mountains, named for the plum trees that thrive in the higher altitudes, are a vibrant, blushing procession. The serpentine segments of rice paddies, with the fields prepared for the start of the rainy season, transform the mountainsides into a sinuous painting.

Something sharp strikes my cheek. I flinch, instinctively ducking as another small projectile soars over my head. I quickly find the culprit. One of the other wyverns carries a handful of small pebbles. She launches them at me when the officit's back is turned.

Saengo's cheeks flush. "Ill-mannered boar—"

"She's just angry." I swat down a pebble before it can connect with my temple. Most of the Company students are content to ignore me and I them, but those like Jonyah certainly make up for that.

Around noon, we're at last allowed a break to eat and relieve ourselves. The girls head into the trees first. When Saengo and I return to our drakes, I find the contents of my satchel spilled across the dirt road. Yandor is eating what's left of my dried mango.

"You can share with me," Saengo says quickly as we kneel to return my blanket and other supplies to my satchel. A light gust scatters the herbs I'd planned to apply to my legs tonight. A mixture of anger and frustration claws through my gut, but I only press my lips together, jaw tight.

I leave the remains of my food. There's not much I can do to recover them, not even the sticky rice wrapped in banana leaves, which someone had taken care to step on. Officit Boldis sits on his drake nearby, eating his lunch and pretending not to see.

Behind me, one of the other wyverns approaches. Judging by the faint crinkle of paper tucked inside a pocket, I assume it's Jonyah. He always carries paper money, which reiwyn prefer over coins. He thinks it makes him more important. He sneaks up quickly enough to snatch the feathers from the end of my braid.

"You're a disgrace." Jonyah flings the feathers into the dirt.

Saengo stands, fists balled. I straighten alongside her and place my hand on her forearm, stalling whatever she means to say.

Jonyah sneers and doesn't back away as I step close enough for my fingers to dart along the pocket of his uniform pants. For a tense second, we only glare at each other. Then his gaze flicks to Saengo.

"You dishonor our House by—"

"If I want your opinion, I will ask for it," Saengo says.

His lips compress, but he backs away with a curt bow. Once he's gone, I slide my hand into my pocket along with the paper money pressed into my palm. Then I kneel again to finish gathering my scattered supplies. Whenever we're assigned the same duties, he never fails to make them more difficult for me. After seeing Jonyah's name on the duty report under the list of wyverns assigned to this supply delivery, I'd groaned and then asked Saengo to shoot him with an arrow and plead that the sun was in her eye. I would gladly have taken the penance.

"Swine," Saengo mutters. She retrieves the gray feathers and blows gently against the soft edges. "Here, let me."

Although my legs scream in protest, I remain crouched over

the small pile of my things in the road as she returns the feathers to my braid.

The privilege of a feathered braid is one only given to fourth-years, when our hair has grown long enough. The style and adornment are meant to represent the tail of a wyvern, one of the most fearsome predators in all of Thiy. Of course, they're not real wyvern feathers—wyverns are native only to Kazahyn, a mountainous kingdom to the southeast.

To Saengo, the feathers are a mark of achievement. She wears them proudly. Even I'd felt a tiny spark of pride the day we became wyverns and earned our feathers, although the feeling faded quickly. I'd chosen gray ones to match my eyes. Kendara sometimes has a point when she calls me vain.

Now, though, I sometimes hate the sight of them and what they've come to symbolize. My place in Evewyn. My place in this Company. The insults I've had to tolerate, the penance I've had to endure, every slight the officits and people like Jonyah believe are my due because of my low station.

We stuff my things back into my satchel and secure it to Yandor's saddle as the others ready to leave. The hatchlets re-form their lines, and everyone returns to their positions. Saengo offers me one of her rice balls, but I shake my head. I'm not hungry, and her food will have to last her through tomorrow when we make our return journey.

The cry of a falcon sounds overhead. Instead of up, I look at Saengo. Her eyes search the clouds, her brows pinched together. The tightness around her mouth relaxes when she spots what she's looking for—Millie, her pet falcon. Pets are prohibited within the Queen's Company, but Millie isn't truly tame so the officits can only do so much.

Officit Boldis casts the sky an annoyed look and then barks, "Back in formation!"

The wyverns farther ahead quickly correct the lines as we begin to move again. Beneath their anger with me lies a barely contained restlessness.

For the last few weeks, all the fourth-years have shared a jumble of excitement and uncertainty over our upcoming graduation. Students like Saengo are usually posted within their own lands. Saengo actually received her assignment last week, to join the royal ranks stationed at Falcons Ridge, her family's ancestral home. She submitted a request to have it changed.

However, students like me, with no allegiance to a particular lord, take a little longer to receive our postings. If the decision were up to Officit Boldis, he'd probably put me in the east. I've heard other fourth-years say that's where the troublemakers get assigned.

Evewyn is a small kingdom, long and narrow like a sword blade. Two kingdoms lie east of us—the shaman-ruled Nuvalyn Empire to the northeast, and Kazahyn, home to the shadow-blessed, in the southeast. But soldiers assigned to the eastern border are met only by the Dead Wood.

The Dead Wood is a growing swath of impassable darkness that separates us from the other kingdoms, leaving open only the stretch of the northern grasslands between Evewyn and the

Empire. According to other fourth-years, soldiers have been known to go mad staring at those cursed woods day after day.

Every so often, some thief or drunk farmhand gets it into their head to brave the woods. But the trees have a will of their own, and no one survives them without the protection of the Dead Wood's ruler, Ronin the Spider King. Rarely, someone foolish enough to enter the woods comes clawing their way back out, broken, hollow, and barely human, only to seize anyone close enough to offer help and drag them into the darkness with them. Soldiers who've witnessed what the trees do to their victims are never the same again. At least, that's the rumor.

I've seen my share of dangers since becoming Kendara's pupil, but she's never sent me near the Dead Wood. I can only assume the rumors are true.

"What are you thinking about? You've a look on your face," Saengo says, nibbling primly at her rice ball. I make a quick gesture, like I'm about to shove her food into her face, and she dodges, snickering.

"What look?" I say as she shifts her food to the hand farthest from me.

"Like you're imagining something unpleasant."

"I was thinking about how Officit Boldis would probably assign me to the eastern border."

She groans. "If I were a vengeful person, I'd ask my father to have him removed."

"Well, I *am* a vengeful person, so you could do it for me?"

Rolling her eyes, she says, "If you're assigned to the east, maybe you'll get to meet Ronin."

She sounds intrigued. As the enforcer of the peace between the three kingdoms of Thiy, Ronin's power is immense. That would intimidate most people, but not Saengo, heir to an ancient Evewynian House. I, on the other hand, have no desire to meet the Spider King. If there's one thing I don't need, it's more people to lower my head and play subservient to.

Anyway, I prefer to believe that the real reason I haven't received my posting yet is because my place is to remain in Vos Talwyn with Kendara as her official apprentice.

I hold Yandor's reigns with one hand and stuff the other into my pocket. My fingers touch the money I'd lifted from Jonyah. I pull it out.

"What is that?" Saengo asks.

"Jonyah's. I was being petty." I don't care for his money—I just wanted to retaliate somehow.

But when I glance down at my hand, I'm surprised to see crumpled parchment instead. I frown. My gaze finds the back of Jonyah's head at the front of our party as I smooth out the crinkled note.

My feet stutter at the neat, precise handwriting. Only Yandor's forward momentum keeps my legs moving because my mind has gone blank with confusion. Why in the names of the Sisters would Jonyah have a letter from Kendara?

Tonight. Talon's Teahouse. Wait for the man with crossed swords. Commit his words to memory. Return by dawn. Burn this upon reading.

The words tumble through my skull, upending all logic. The world goes suddenly loud, every sound magnified: the shuffle of tired legs, the plodding of boots through dirt, the wind raking over the grass. My breath falls quick and harsh through my nose as my fingers tighten around the paper, nearly tearing it.

"Sirscha?" Saengo asks, uncertain.

"He's a pupil," I whisper through my teeth. I shake the paper at Saengo. "He's one of her *pupils*."

Saengo is the only person with whom I've shared my secret. It was impossible not to, given that she is my best friend. As she takes the paper and skims the words, another realization strikes me, even more shattering than the last. Kendara's notes to me have only ever been instructions for mundane assignments, like retrieving an object, overcoming a mental test, or hunting some obscure beast.

Never assignments like rendezvousing with an informant or relaying back a message. This . . . this is not training. This is Shadow business.

My fingers grip tightly to Yandor's reins, a paltry anchor as the true meaning of this letter hurls against me. If she hasn't already, then Kendara plans to name Jonyah her apprentice. For long seconds, I can do nothing, letting the impossibility tear through me. Every part of me screams in denial even as heat rises from my chest into my cheeks. I curl my fingers around the troll bone at my wrist. Kendara wouldn't choose *Jonyah* over me.

I scowl at the russet dirt that passes beneath our feet. How *dare* she not tell me this morning? I clutch the troll bone so tightly that my palm aches.

It occurs to me what the talisman might really be: a parting gift.

My anger suddenly drains, leaving me swaying. Only the shreds of my pride keep me from tumbling to the ground and ripping into the earth at the unfairness. Somehow, in some way, I was not enough.

That has been the constant of my life. Not obedient enough. Not clever enough, except maybe in languages, and what use is that? Not humble enough to suit my betters.

Not enough for the parents who abandoned me, or the monks who raised me, or the officits who trained me.

Although I met Kendara when I was eleven, the first time I fought her was at thirteen, during my final year in the Prince's Company. By the time graduation neared, not even the officits could best me in the sparring circle. Kendara found me training alone, and when she stood opposite me in the sword ring and ordered me to attack her, I laughed, thinking she was joking.

Blind and weaponless, she defeated me in less than two seconds.

This, she said, meaning her own skill, was what I could achieve if only I stopped pitying my circumstances and started *demanding* that I become more. That I *deserved* more.

Kendara always believed I could be something great.

But I spent the last four years devoting myself toward this single goal, and now? I only joined the Queen's Company because Kendara required it of me—a test of my dedication, she said, of what I would endure to win my place as her apprentice. And I have endured. Oh, but I have endured.

Perhaps my pride was my downfall. The Shadow must not draw attention, must allow herself to be underestimated. For the sake of securing my future at her side, I could lower my head and swallow my pride—except in the sparring circle. Not there, the one place where I'm allowed to fight back, where I can bury my fear of worthlessness beneath the proof of my strength.

What was it all for?

Up ahead, a path cuts away from the main road, heading west. Until now, we've been on Keistra's Flight, which stretches from Evewyn's southern shores, through the capital of Vos Talwyn, and north to the port city of Byrth. But the path that leads west is little more than a couple of narrow depressions in the grass formed by the passage of wagons and drakes.

The hatchlets grumble beneath their breaths when the guardsmen veer off Keistra's Flight onto the narrow, uneven trail. I glare at the back of Jonyah's head and jerk Yandor's reins, bringing him to a stop. With a worried glance at the growing distance between us and our party, Saengo pauses as well. No one has noticed our departure.

Saengo clutches my arm hard enough to regain my attention. "Sirscha, talk to me."

I take the note from her, glancing at the words again before crumpling it in my fist and shoving it back into my pocket. To reach the teahouse by tonight, Jonyah will need to leave soon. He's likely already invented some excuse to gain Officit Boldis's permission.

When I trust my voice not to break, I say quietly, "I'm going to the teahouse first."

In less than a month, we will graduate. I will be cast about the kingdom at the whim of the Royal Army, left to rot in obscurity at an outpost for six years until my required service ends. And what then? I have no family, no home, no talent other than fighting.

If I'm not to be the Shadow, then I am nothing.

I am *tired* of being nothing.

THREE

We remain on Keistra's Flight, hoping to put as much distance between us and Officit Boldis's party before we're missed and someone is sent after us. I briefly consider turning back for Vos Talwyn to demand an explanation from Kendara, but she would never tolerate such impudence.

"You should go back," I say when Saengo glances over her shoulder for the dozenth time in as many minutes. "I don't think you're going to get out of penance this time."

Saengo's cheeks flush at the reminder that I'm the only one punished for our shared transgressions.

"It's possible," she says, sounding almost hopeful. "But someone has to watch your back. What are you planning to do when we get to the teahouse?"

"Take his place, of course." Talon's Teahouse is about a half day's ride south, directly along Keistra's Flight. We've got a head start. With luck, I'll have whatever message Kendara wants from "the man with crossed swords" before Jonyah even catches up.

In the past, fellow pupils were known to either sabotage or eliminate one another to thin out the competition. Kendara herself had killed two of her competitors when she'd been in training beneath the previous Shadow.

For her own pupils, she'd chosen to keep our identities hidden. She disliked how the practice drew unwanted attention, especially when the dead pupil turned out to be someone of influence. She also preferred her pupils focus solely on their training and not on one another. However, she implied that should one of us expose ourselves, another pupil could capitalize on it. From Kendara's mouth, it is all but permission.

But my concern is less about whether sabotage or interference is allowed and more about the repercussions.

The Queen's Company is run far more rigidly than the Prince's. The first time I spoke out of turn—a simple, honest question—the officit struck me hard enough to knock me off my feet. He'd wanted me to wear the shame of my disrespect on my face until it healed. After that, I quickly learned my place, for what little good that did. Students like Jonyah delighted in reminding me of their power, cornering me when I was without Saengo or spinning lies that would earn me all manner of penance.

Abandoning our posts, however, is a worse offense than anything Jonyah's ever concocted. The Prince's Company is compulsory for children eleven through thirteen, but continuing on to the Queen's Company is voluntary. When I enrolled—

at Kendara's bidding—I committed myself to the service of the Royal Army and all the consequences therein.

If I'm not outright expelled and branded as a deserter, I will likely have my feathers stripped and my braid cut, demoted to a previous year.

But if I do nothing, then I will lose Kendara, and with her, my entire purpose. There is no punishment the Company can bring down on me that would be worse than that.

Stealing Jonyah's mission is a dangerous gamble, but it's one I have to take. I must prove to Kendara that I am the better choice. My entire future depends on it.

By the time we spot the red shingles of the teahouse's roof, the day has almost ended. A crescent moon hangs low, a silver scythe to cut away the light. The teahouse is a small two-story building with dark columns and a dramatically curved roof ending in splayed talons at each corner. It's impossible to miss, even in the dark, and a popular stop for travelers in need of refreshment.

We agree that Saengo should remain outside with the drakes to keep an eye out for Jonyah. Unless he took a different route, we should have beaten him here. Before dismounting, I brush my fingers along Yandor's jaw. He's panting heavily, but he still leans into my hand.

With the heavy flapping of wings, Millie lands on the nearby hitching post to keep Saengo company. She sets about watering the drakes. I tear the feathers from my hair, along with the distinctive red sash of a Company fourth-year from around my waist. I stuff both into my satchel and retrieve a long gray scarf

I'd brought on our journey to shield against light rain. My legs are stiff, and my bruised muscles sting fiercely. But I bite my tongue against the pain as I head inside and send a prayer to the Bright Twin to keep luck on my side.

I wrap the scarf loosely around my hair and neck, taking care to conceal my face and the collar of my uniform. Inside, the low light of a single fireplace and several oil lamps cast the room in flickering shadows. The teahouse is nearly empty. Tables are arranged in a square around an empty platform where the entertainment would perform, likely a musician with a two-stringed lute or a storysinger, who relays old tales through lilting, rhythmic songs.

The earthy scent of firewood is ruined by the curdled odor of the day's unwashed patrons. A trio of hooded men sit quietly at a corner table, sipping tea or perhaps something stronger. As far as I can tell, none wear crossed swords.

As expected, Jonyah isn't here. I release a slow, even breath. He won't be far behind us, though. Hopefully, Kendara's mystery informant shows up soon. I choose a table with a clear view of the entrance. A short woman with dark brown curls and a round face emerges from a door that I assume leads into a kitchen. She presses her palms to her floral apron and dips her head in a polite bow.

"Anything I can get you?" the owner asks.

"Some hibiscus tea, please."

She returns a moment later with a tray bearing a steaming ceramic teapot, a small saucer of honey with a dainty spoon, and an upturned cup. Once she's filled my cup, she leaves the tray and disappears again into the back. I spoon some honey into the aromatic tea and then take a light sip.

Someone jerks my scarf off my hair. I'm instantly on my feet, the dagger hidden within my wrist guard sliding into my hand. I freeze at the sight of Jonyah. How had he sneaked up on me?

"It *is* you!" he snarls. He would be handsome if his face weren't always twisted into an ugly sneer. The firelight from a lantern casts copper tones in his dark hair, which he has freed from its usual braid. "Pray the Twins favor you, if you're here for the reason I think you are."

When I don't shrink back, the muscles in his neck go taut. His hands lift, fingers flexing as if he'd like nothing better than to throttle me.

"And what reason is that?" I ask coolly. We're far from the Company and anyone who knows who we are. Since he's hardly going to report my disrespect without giving away his own little adventure here, I can speak to him however I wish.

When he doesn't answer, I lean my hip against the table and ignore the way my thighs protest. I pretend to study the blade of my dagger, which glows faintly orange from the firelight. I stole it from the armory two years ago. Kendara doesn't always warn me when she's sending me off into danger, so I try never to be unarmed.

Jonyah grips my forearm, yanking me far too close for my comfort. His grip is bruising, the only sort of grip he's capable of, I suspect. I almost smash my fist into his face.

Instead of replying, he spits out, "What are you up to?" His reluctance to name his task irritates me, because it proves he did learn something from Kendara.

"What do you think? Work it out yourself," I say and then casually withdraw the note from my pocket.

Jonyah goes still. The brief flash of alarm on his face is almost comical. But then he laughs, the sound abrupt and harsh.

"*You're* one of her pupils? She must have been desperate. You've lost, Tshauv Taws. She's going to choose me." He spits at my feet. "Because I'm better than you in every way. My name, my station, my skills."

My nails bite into my palms. *Tshauv Taws.* In old Evewal, which is taught only to reiwyn, it means "ashes." Saengo told me after the first time he'd called me that. It's a translation of my last name, Ashwyn, which isn't a true Evewynian surname. The monks gave it to me at the orphanage as an unsubtle way of saying I come from no one and nothing.

Despite the insult, he's unwittingly revealed what I've been desperate to know since reading the note—Kendara hasn't yet named him her apprentice. I haven't lost everything. Not yet. "She doesn't care about any of that."

"Doesn't she?" He looks me over. "You're a skinny bit of noth-ing with no true name and no future. I've been trying to get you to do everyone a favor and turn that dagger on yourself for seven years. When will you understand? No one will miss you."

My jaw feels like it might crack from how tightly I'm clenching my teeth. I remain still because if I don't, I'll stab my blade into Jonyah's thick neck. While he helps himself to my tea,

I exhale slowly through my nose and consciously relax my body, muscle by muscle.

Chairs scrape over the scratched wood floors. My gaze lifts to the corner, where the three men are now standing. They pass in my periphery, their heads bowed. The last one looks up, and his eyes, beneath the heavy folds of a scarf, find mine. I stiffen. He has the luminous scarlet eyes of a firewender, a fire shaman.

Sparks dance around his fingers. Instinct takes hold, and I vault over the table as my chair erupts into flames. I hit the ground and then dive behind the center platform.

My pulse races. Shamanborn roaming free in Evewyn? Impossible. The queen imprisoned them all. But if they'd somehow escaped capture, they would be in hiding. These have to be Nuvali, shamans from the Nuvalyn Empire. What in the Sisters are they doing in Evewyn?

Everything turns red and hazy. The pain in my legs becomes secondary as I brandish my dagger and survey the damage.

Flames engulf the room. Tables and chairs glow like kindling. I cover my mouth with my scarf as smoke stings my eyes. The front door bursts open. Plumes of smoke escape into the open air. Saengo stands beyond the threshold, shouting muffled words, arms raised to ward off the heat. Streaks of fire shoot straight for my feet. I run, ducking beneath a table and colliding with Jonyah as the back door and part of the wall explode.

Flaming wood chips fly through the smoke only to be engulfed again by fire. I've confronted this brand of chaos once before, when Kendara tied me up and left me in a hut full of burning thatch. But this fire is different. This fire spreads too quickly, too controlled, raging through the teahouse in seconds.

Jonyah shoves me away with a curse as we both stand. Flames snake across the floor. Jonyah whips out a dagger twice as large as mine, although I don't know what good it'll do. His back hits my elbow as we grip our useless weapons and watch the fire encircle us, trapping us inside a burning ring. Beyond the circle, one of the shamans steps into view.

Not the firewender. The dancing flames paint highlights across his face, but his eyes glint purple, brighter than any human eye color. His arms lift. A sudden wind gusts around me, tangling my scarf and snagging my braid around my neck. The flames roar higher, twisting into an inferno. I recoil, pulling my limbs in tight to keep from being incinerated.

Then the tempest falters, and the man shouts, dropping to his knees. Millie, who must have swept in through the open door, flaps madly above his head, raking her claws against the back of his neck.

I've lost track of where the third shaman is, but I leap over the flames that singe my boots, heading toward Saengo, who's made her way inside. There are too many burning obstacles between us. The fire bounds up the walls, smoke tumbling across the ceiling like a boiling cauldron.

"Saengo!" I choke out her name, but I can barely hear my own voice. There's no way through, so I double back toward Jonyah. He's grappling with the firewender, who wields a short sword. Smoke thrashes around them like something alive. I can tell

Jonyah is holding his breath.

I crouch low, aiming my dagger for the firewender's unprotected back. Before I can strike, Jonyah's blade whips the sword from the firewender's hand and then immediately slashes down his middle. Blood spatters the floor, sizzling in the heat. The firewender stumbles, clutching his chest where blood pours through his fingers. The roaring flames suddenly shiver and dampen.

Jonyah drags in a wheezing breath and his eyes catch mine. He lunges for me.

I block, but his strength shoves me back until I collide with the edge of a table. Pain shoots up my spine, echoing in my legs, and it takes all my strength to keep Jonyah's dagger from piercing my chest. With a ferocious cry, I crush my knee into the vulnerable spot between his legs. His attack instantly falters. He staggers away. It only takes a second for me to leap onto him, my legs trapping Jonyah's meaty neck as I twist my body and drag him off his feet.

He lands on his back with the crash of shuddering floorboards. I kick his dagger out of his reach and straddle his chest, pressing my blade to his neck.

"What are you doing?" I shout, my voice hoarse with smoke.

"Getting rid of my competition," he snarls through his teeth, "which you'd do, too, if you had any sense!" His hand snaps up to grab my throat, but I jerk away and his fingers clutch my braid instead.

Fire explodes between us. My body flies off him. I hit the ground hard. Air rushes from my lungs. I can't breathe, but I roll across the floorboards, my hands slapping away the flames that lick up my arms. Nearby, the firewender collapses, having delivered his final attack. But the teahouse is already engulfed, and without the shaman's control, flames tear through the building.

Jonyah is screaming. Half his body is on fire. His shirt peels off, melting into the skin that bubbles and blisters beneath. My breaths are loud and fast in my ears as something rises in my stomach. I force it down.

Sisters, protect us. I smack frenetically at the last of the embers crackling through his hair. The smell makes me gag. He's still struggling and screaming, but I can only grab hold of the waist of his unburned pants and heave him toward the door.

The sound of squawking and flapping indicates Millie is keeping the windwender busy, but I still don't see the third one. A dark shape materializes from the fiery haze in front of me, and I almost cry in relief to see Saengo break through the smoke.

"Help me!" I shout, my voice raw. Together, we manage to haul Jonyah's considerable bulk out the door, escaping at last into the open air.

"Are you okay?" Saengo asks, taking in the state of my uniform.

"Fine," I wheeze between coughing. Against my flushed skin, the troll-bone talisman Kendara gave me is startlingly cool. Protection against magic. It must be the reason I'm not lying unconscious and half dead beside Jonyah.

We lower him onto the dirt. He is a scorched mess, and he's neither screaming nor moving now. I kneel beside him, uncertain where to even touch him without stripping away more of his flesh. Steam rises from his chest, face, and arms. Gently tilting his head, I find an unburned spot beneath his chin and press my fingers there. His pulse flutters weakly.

"He's alive." I breathe, and then, "He's lucky I don't finish the shaman's job. *Bastard*."

"We need to get out of here," Saengo says. Her voice doesn't even waver. How she can sound so calm when everything has gone so terribly wrong?

Why would Nuvali shamans attack a teahouse in Evewyn? Saengo has told me of skirmishes between Evewynian and Nuvali patrols in the northern grasslands near her family's home, but the threat of the Spider King's wrath always kept the skirmishes from escalating into something else.

Something like this. Ronin's influence over the kingdoms should have prevented this from even happening.

Millie shoots out the front door, now spitting black smoke, and she swoops up into the night sky. The windwender stumbles out after her, shouting curses, his hands and neck a bloodied mess of raw skin. I grip Saengo's wrist, pulling her with me as we back away. With a glance at the stables, which have yet to catch fire, I gauge how quickly we can reach our drakes.

We can't leave Jonyah behind, though. Cursing, I lift my dagger again just as the third shaman spills out from the teahouse.

"Which one is it?" he shouts, voice ragged. He tries to spit the bitter taste of smoke from his mouth.

The windwender grimaces with pain as he says, "Who cares? It's got to be one of them. Just kill them all."

"Works for me," the other shaman says. Then it strikes me what he's wearing. His clothes are singed and darkened by smoke, but the light from the burning teahouse illuminates the brooch pinned at the collar of his tunic. Two crossed swords.

Kendara's informant. But that would mean this isn't a random attack. This was a trap. They came here looking for the Shadow. For Kendara.

I nudge Saengo behind me and set aside my confusion. Even amid the heat pouring from the teahouse, a cold stillness spreads through my arms, my legs. Every bruise and abrasion fades. The chill of battle, Kendara calls it, when the mind and the heart go quiet and the body's instincts take over. I hadn't understood what she meant until now. My heartbeat stops trying to shatter my ribs. Everything becomes very simple.

Us or them.

I hurl my dagger. It strikes the third shaman in the throat. The windwender startles as his companion's blood spatters his face. With a gurgle, the shaman crumples. Before he even hits the ground, the windwender wrenches the dagger free and flings it back. I duck the blade easily, diving for his legs. With a cry, he topples over, his cheek hitting the ground with a crack.

I climb onto his back, trying to get a grip around his neck to snap it. His skin and hair are too slippery with blood from Millie's attack. He bucks and rolls, his fist glancing off my jaw before I can dodge. I shake away the pain, but then I'm suddenly weightless. Wind hurls me through the air. I shield my head as my body slams into the dirt. I curl onto my side, stiff and hurting.

Through the hair that's come loose from my braid, I see him heading for the stables. My nails claw through the dirt as I pull myself up.

"Saengo," I shout, struggling to my feet. "He's getting away."

When she doesn't respond, I look for her. She's lying on the ground. The dagger hilt juts grotesquely from the center of her chest.

I open my mouth, but my lungs are unable to draw air. She'd been standing behind me when the windwender flung the dagger.

"S—Saengo," I gasp as my body trembles with a sudden horror that cleaves through me like a storm. I forget everything: the pain, Jonyah, the shamans, becoming Shadow. There is only Saengo as I scrabble through the dirt and collapse at her side. My fingers search for a pulse, but there's nothing.

The pain in my chest sharpens into a smoldering rock. It scorches through my ribs and then bursts outward, stealing what breath I have left and forcing it out of my mouth into a scream that echoes down the stretch of Keistra's Flight until there is nothing but blinding white and agony and grief, and then blessedly, nothing at all.

FOUR

"*Sirscha?*"

Her voice sounds in the dark. I reach for it, sinking into the blackness where I might still find her, but her voice flits away. When I give chase, hands emerge from the abyss. They grasp my arms, my hair, my neck. Clammy fingers wrench open my mouth, worming inside, choking me. Jagged nails tear at my lips and my cheeks and gouge my eyes. I can't breathe. I can't move. I can't—

"Sirscha."

I shoot upright, gulping in air. Light spears my eyes, and I flinch at the remembered pain of fingers digging behind my lids.

Several things register at once. First, I'm outside. Grass prickles my palms and the scratchy wool of my blanket covers my legs. Second, it's morning. Sunlight streams through the branches above my head, bright and bold.

Lastly, and most pressingly, Saengo is sitting beside me in the grass, blinking at me with an expression of stunned amazement. I can't imagine why my waking up is so shocking when she's the one who'd died.

I lick my dry lips and, uncertain, look around at the trees. The sound of water rushing over rock pulls my gaze to a creek burbling nearby. My clothes and hair smell strongly of smoke, and my legs still ache, so I doubt it, but . . . "Are we dead?"

Saengo's astonishment transforms into confusion. "I don't think so. But your ey—"

I throw my arms around her shoulders, which seem suddenly small. Her breath against my neck grows thin, hitches once. The memory of the knife in her chest makes me wince. "What happened?"

She pulls back, clasping her hands tightly in her lap. "I wasn't sure what to do when I woke up. You were lying there and . . . and Jonyah and the shaman." A tremor runs through her. "I panicked. So I took you and ran."

The entire evening rushes back in a single nauseating wave. Sisters, save us. We left Jonyah to die. I killed a shaman. And Saengo . . .

I push to my feet and stumble the few steps it takes to reach the pebbled sand at the bank of the creek. I drop to my knees. Stones jab my skin, but I barely feel them as I plunge my hands into the icy water. The shock of cold makes my breath catch, but the icy prickling quickly sets into numbness.

My distorted reflection stares up at me. My face is filthy with smoke and dust. But that's not what stands out. At first,

I don't understand what I'm seeing.

My eyes, which should be gray, are an impossible crystalline amber.

I drag in short, stuttering breaths as my arms sink deeper into the chilly water, my sleeves soaking through. Those unfamiliar eyes remain, bearing the jewel-bright irises of a shaman. That's not me. It can't be. The sounds of the creek grow muffled. The world tilts.

Hands grip my shoulders and yank me away from the water's edge. "Sirscha—"

"I'm fine," I breathe, rolling onto my back. Frigid droplets spatter my face as I throw my arms over my head. Feeling returns to my fingers in near-painful tingles.

"Yeah," she whispers. "I'm fine, too."

We remain there for some time, me on the bank with pebbles stabbing my back and Saengo sitting beside me, boots burrowing into the loose sand. We don't speak. My mind remains blank, refusing to process what's happened. I listen to the water swirl and rush by. The leaves shake at me, green satin with shimmering silver undersides.

Finally, when I can't bear the silence any longer, I reach out and touch Saengo's wrist. She laces our fingers together.

Despair catapults into me, flung from the connection of our joined hands. I wrench my hand back and stare uncomprehendingly at my palm.

"Sirscha?" Saengo asks, looking first at her fingers and then at me. Had she felt it too?

Shaking my head, I can only repeat, "I'm . . . fine."

I am, in fact, the opposite of fine, but I don't know how to fix it.

"You were defending yourself," she says.

I marvel that after what happened to her, she still thinks to comfort me. I trained with Kendara for four years. The Shadow is a spy and an assassin. I would have taken a life eventually. I know I should be more disturbed by how easily I killed that shaman, but how can I when Saengo was dead? She was *dead*, and now she's not, and I don't know what to do with that. Or with *any* of what's happened.

"I'm sorry." My throat still hurts from all the smoke. "I should have protected you better."

Saengo shifts so that she's on her knees, facing me with a fierce glint in her eyes. It's a welcome alternative to the haunted way she was looking at me before.

"You reacted to the shamans' threat exactly the way I expected you to," she says. I frown, but she's not done yet. "When you fight, you . . . you don't hesitate. You react. Danger—it makes you deadly. Seeing you fight those shamans, and *Jonyah*—"

Her mention of Jonyah surprises me. She must have been watching through the flames when he attacked me.

"It made me realize what Kendara saw all those years ago when she took you on as her pupil."

My capacity for violence? I want to ask.

"I'm not . . ." Her brows twitch together. "I'm not like that. For all my training, when those shamans meant to kill us, I froze. I should have been more help."

"You're alive. That's all that matters." I clear my throat, wincing at the soreness. "How, though?" My question is a whisper; I'm afraid anything louder will make it untrue again.

Her smile becomes a grimace before wilting. Shrinking back into herself, she touches her chest, directly over her heart where the dagger struck her. I brush her fingers aside. There's a tear in her shirt, the edges dark with dried blood. Slowly, I slide two fingers through the tear and touch the center of her chest. She's whole. Nothing but the slight ridge of a scar, as if the wound were an old one.

I pull away and look down at my palm. I remember the blazing heat that tore through me before I passed out. And now my eyes . . . I couldn't have done this. It's not possible.

Years ago, we'd promised each other that when we died, we would sing the other's lifestory to the Sisters. The song is how the Sisters know to open the gates to the spirit realm for those who've passed. I'd also made a promise to myself: that the day I sang Saengo's lifestory would be a distant one. Last night, I'd nearly broken that promise.

My fist slams into the dirt. "The shaman who did this. He got away. We have to find him."

"The magistrate will have sent a falcon to the Grand Offices by now," Saengo says. She sounds much too reasonable for someone with every right to be raving at the sky. Or at me. Part of me wishes she would. "They'll have sent soldiers to the teahouse. If they haven't caught him already, they will soon."

I dearly hope so, but if the authorities are focusing their

search on a shaman, not two wayward wyverns, then we need to take advantage of that.

Saengo bites her bottom lip. "Did you know?"

I sit up, angling my face away to hide my eyes. Did I know that I'm . . . I can't even think it. I don't know anything about the people who left me at the orphanage, and the monks certainly couldn't have known, either. They would have gladly given me up to the Valley of Cranes if they had.

How is any of this real? And why *now*, when I'm so close to achieving my goal? I half expect Kendara to appear and confess that the entire past day has been an elaborate hoax, an outrageous test to assess my mettle.

But while Kendara can perform feats unimaginable, she can't make Saengo's heart stop beating. Nothing will ever erase the memory of Saengo's sightless eyes, her blood darkening her shirt, every excruciating detail seared into my consciousness.

If I can't seek vengeance for Saengo, then I need to speak to Kendara. I have to explain what happened and tell her about the ambush. I have to fix this somehow.

But how can we return to Vos Talwyn? Queen Meilyr makes no secret of her hatred for shamans. The former king and queen, along with a dozen other Evewynians, died when a firewender lost control during a performance of his magic and burned down half the festival grounds. The firewender hadn't survived, either, but that hadn't been retribution enough for the new queen. She was barely seventeen when she took the throne. She outlawed all shamanborn, regardless of the fact they were innocent

Evewynians. She also forbade Nuvali shamans from stepping foot in Evewyn, renewing old tensions with the Nuvalyn Empire.

Some shamanborn fled to the Empire or sought the help of the Spider King. But Ronin turned them away. He enforces the peace between the kingdoms; he does not interfere with how the kingdoms choose to rule their own.

My clearest memory of the shamanborn is also the one I try never to think about. There's a town near the orphanage where the monks go to purchase supplies. I'd accompanied them that day along with the other kids bound for the capital and the Prince's Company. The monks claimed they wanted us to get used to busy streets, but that was far too considerate an excuse. Soon enough, their true purpose became clear.

An execution had been scheduled for that morning. Two shamanborn, a woman and her husband, stood on a hastily erected platform outside the town. I don't remember their crime. Perhaps nothing. Perhaps resisting capture. The monks had forced us to watch.

That day, I had understood the finality of the queen's power, and that I would never dare to cross it.

Returning to Vos Talwyn now would be dangerous. But I have to speak to Kendara. Not only to warn her of the attack but to seek her aid. As the heir to Falcons Ridge, Saengo has the protection of her House. I have no such protection. Kendara knows me better than anyone, aside from Saengo. Surely she'll help me, or at the very least, vouch for me? She answers to no one but the queen, who values Kendara's counsel.

There is no better person to speak on my behalf.

I press my palms against my eyelids, but I can't block out the image of my reflection in the water. For a moment, with my eyes closed, I feel almost like I'm falling. My pulse races, my stomach climbs up my rib cage, and the sheer unknown of what awaits me now that my entire world has been upended fills my mouth with the sour taste of fear.

Saengo touches my shoulder. Emotions simmer through me at the contact, none strong enough for me to name. All too aware of her watching, I take several deep breaths, grounding myself with reason and strategy. Lying here feeling sorry for ourselves isn't going to change anything. We need to keep moving before we're discovered.

I stand and look around, trying to gauge where we might be. Tied to some low branches nearby are our drakes. Yandor is asleep.

"Yellow means lightwender," Saengo murmurs.

I wring out the water in my sleeves. "What?"

"Your eyes," she clarifies, dusting sand off her fingers as she stands.

I frown, because I don't know what she wants me to say to that.

There are five Shamanic Callings: fire, water, earth, wind, and light. Within each Calling, a shaman can possess one of three possible crafts. The firewender who attacked us was a burner, a fire summoner. But firewenders can also be flame eaters, who can transform themselves into smoke and flame, or wyrmin, who can raise the temperature of objects or liquids. Powerful wyrmin can kill their opponents by making their blood boil or disarm them by melting their iron-forged weapons. I doubt we would have fared so well against one of those.

I'm unfamiliar with the three crafts within the Calling of Light. What knowledge I possess beyond the Company lessons was gained from Kendara's books, and very few of them are about magic.

My satchel hangs from Yandor's saddle, and I yank it open. I have only a second set of Company uniforms to change into, but it'll do. Smoke-stained clothing with not a few scorch marks would make anyone we happen across immediately suspicious. Aside from her clothes, Saengo looks relatively clean. She must have washed while I was still out.

"Where are we?" I toss my ruined clothes into the grass, glad to be rid of them and the stink of fire. I want to wash the grit off my face, but I can't bear seeing my eyes again in the water.

She points downstream. "If we continue that way for a few hours, we'll reach the Stone Serpent."

The Stone Serpent, a slender bridge connecting opposite sides of a gorge called the Hollow Sea, is a half day's ride southwest of the teahouse. We must have ridden all night.

I tell her that we need to return to Vos Talwyn so that I can speak to Kendara. Saengo warily concedes that if anyone can help us, it's her. It's probably a terrible plan, but I don't know what else to do. If we had more time, maybe I could think of a better one. Maybe I could stop feeling like I've been taken apart at the seams and put together again into something unrecognizable.

As I'm securing my bedroll to Yandor's saddle, the sound of

trampling feet breaks through the forest. Saengo and I dive for cover behind the trees.

Tipping my head, I close my eyes and listen. Judging by the pacing of their footfalls, there are three of them, and their noisy arrival means they want to be heard. My lip curls as I glance around the trunk and take quick stock of our opponents.

Three Evewynian soldiers have emerged from the forest. They spread out wide to close us off. Two look barely out of the Queen's Company, but the third is older.

"Come out, come out," the older one calls, caressing the hilt of his sword.

I have no idea where my dagger is, but I've no stomach to use it after seeing it embedded in Saengo's chest. Behind a nearby tree, Saengo gives a slight nod, having come to the same under- standing: if we're to escape, we'll have to deal with them first.

Only a day ago, I wouldn't have raised my voice to a soldier. Now I will have to raise a weapon. Kendara will understand—I must do what's necessary. In fact, as my fingers attempt to gouge the smooth tree bark, I find I'm all too eager.

I step into the open. Saengo follows my lead. At the sight of us, the two younger soldiers lift their swords. The third one cocks his head.

"What's this?" he says. Black tattoos that resemble lightning bolts stretch from the outer ends of his eyebrows across his tem- ples and into his hairline. "I thought we were looking for a pair of deserters, but it seems we have us a shaman!"

"Maybe we should wait," says one of his companions, his

earlier keenness flagging. The third soldier nods. "We weren't supposed to find—"

"Don't be such a coward," Eyebrow Tattoos spits out.

If they're looking for us, they must have found the shaman already. Why waste time on two wyverns when there's a Nuvali assassin on the loose?

Eyebrow Tattoos's companions exchange a look, their hands flexing around their swords. They've never fought a shaman, I realize. Well, they're in for a surprise, because they're about to learn what it's like to fight *me*.

Saengo sounds offended as she says, "We're not deserters. I'm Saen—"

Eyebrow Tattoos charges me at the same time one of the others swings at Saengo.

I duck the swipe of his sword before delivering a kick to his side. My thigh stings at the impact, but the pain only helps to focus me. He groans and shuffles back, surprised. My teeth flash in a smile. His brows narrow, making his tattoos look like bizarre horns, and he comes at me again. Although I have nothing to defend with, I trust my feet and the speed of my own body to avoid the bite of his sword. My knuckles easily find his flesh, every blow building my frustration rather than alleviating it.

The relief I'd felt in the teahouse when I learned Kendara hadn't yet named an apprentice is impossible to recover. I've more than enough standing in my way without these soldiers adding to my troubles.

My opponent grunts as I land a vicious kick to his ribs. It's not the soldiers I'm furious with; they're just unlucky enough to be here. My fist connects with a meaty gut, my elbow with his jaw, a flurry of attacks the opposite of the battle calm, all rage and fear and resentment.

If I don't prove to Kendara that I still deserve a place with her, then I not only lose my future as Shadow, I also lose Kendara. I lose Saengo. I lose Evewyn, my home.

I sidestep his thrusting sword, clap my hands around his wrist, and twist his arm back. With a shout, he drops the sword. His other hand immediately seizes the dagger sheathed at his waist.

Locking his arm behind him, I press my thumb against his middle finger, bending it back against the knuckle until he cries out again.

"Drop the knife," I demand with a quick glance at Saengo to see how she's faring. She's found a sizable branch and is deftly applying it to her attacker's ribs. I don't see the third soldier.

"You're dead, shaman," Eyebrow Tattoos growls. His lip is bleeding, and half his face has already begun to swell.

Part of me recognizes that I was unnecessarily brutal, but most of me doesn't care. Not anymore.

"I'll tear those disgusting eyes out! I'll cut your—"

I bend his finger a bit farther. His threats dissolve into mindless shouts and curses.

"Drop it," I say again. My voice somehow sounds calm. It's a lie.

Instead, he stabs blindly at me. The bone of his middle finger snaps. Screaming, he drops the dagger.

"Agree to let us go, and I'll let you keep your other fingers intact," I say, twisting his arm enough to get his attention again. Naming Saengo's House might persuade them, but the Company might yet find a way to shield House Phang from disgrace, and I'd hate to risk exposing Saengo's involvement if I can help it.

"Release him, shaman!"

I look up. The third soldier must have fled to retrieve a bow, because he has an arrow nocked and fixed on Saengo. Saengo, about to deliver a kick to the other soldier's face, freezes. The archer's cheek is mottled and bleeding, cut open where Saengo must have struck him with the branch. The other soldier stands, panting and red-faced, favoring her right leg. Her arm shakes as she points her sword at Saengo.

If they hurt her, I decide, then Evewynian soldiers or not, I'll kill them.

Saengo's eyes fix on the archer's weapon. She could disable all three within seconds if she had his bow. But she doesn't, so I release Eyebrow Tattoos with a shove. He trips away, cradling his broken finger to his chest. Then he snarls and rounds on me.

"Tie her up!"

The archer keeps his arrow trained on Saengo as the other soldier disappears into the trees. Their drakes must not be far off, because she returns before long with a length of rope. I sneer as she approaches me, taking satisfaction in the way she hesitates, but I allow her to yank my arms behind my back and bind my wrists together. The rope pinches my skin, and the troll bone digs into my forearm.

Nearby, Yandor stomps and snarls. His clawed feet rake the dirt, tearing up earth as he tries to break free from where Saengo tied him. I hope the reins hold. While drakes are as vicious in battle as their riders, that archer could easily shift targets. I couldn't bear it if Yandor were shot.

"You're going to regret this," I say lightly, at odds with the way my heart wants to fling itself against my ribs.

"I doubt that." Eyebrow Tattoos bends over so that his hot breath assaults my cheek. "Shamans and deserters all deserve to meet the end of a blade."

The soldier behind me gives the knot a final, spiteful tug. Then she plants her boot into the back of my knee. My legs fold, and my knees strike the ground hard. Eyebrow Tattoos glares, probably hoping I'd fall on my face. He holds his bad hand tight against his side. The broken finger sticks out at an unnatural angle.

I smile, and he backhands me. Pain bursts through my jaw. The blow nearly knocks me off my knees, but I recover my balance.

"You should be begging me for mercy," he growls and then backhands me again. My teeth cut the inside of my cheek, and I taste blood. I pretend to sway to disguise the movement of my wrists against the rope. I've gotten far worse than this.

With a jerk of my head, I toss back the loose hair that's fallen across my eyes. I spit blood onto his boots. His face goes tight with fury. There's a kind of freedom in defiance, in being released from every restraint, every expectation. But I would gladly embrace those restraints again if it meant having my place with Kendara back.

He bends over and snatches his dagger from the ground. He presses the dagger to my throat, beneath my left jaw. "Where's your familiar, shaman?"

"Probably dead from the rot," one of the others offers. "She hasn't used any magic yet. No familiar means no magic."

When I don't respond, Eyebrow Tattoos's gaze flicks back to me. "I should kill her. Queen Meilyr might grant me a title for it."

The soldier who tied my hands snickers, but the archer looks uncomfortable. I hold Eyebrow Tattoos's gaze, unblinking. I wonder what he sees in my eyes, now amber like gemstones. Whatever it is, it unnerves him, because his hand quivers. My neck stings as the blade breaks skin. I grin, baring my teeth, which are bloody from my split cheek.

Fear glimmers inside me, startling the smile from my face. Yet somehow, I know it isn't *my* fear. I'm not afraid. I'm bitter, determined, and *enraged*. But not afraid—at least not of these soldiers. The sensation is more an echo of the emotion, not strong enough to truly take shape inside me.

Saengo calls out, "Leave her alone!"

All three turn to her. Although I'd prefer their hostility remain directed at me, I immediately resume the work of freeing my hands. I've lost count of the number of ways in which Kendara has tied me up and left me somewhere highly questionable.

Although Eyebrow Tattoos watches his companions circle Saengo, he keeps his blade against my neck. The archer abandons his bow for closer torment as he fingers the feathers in Saengo's hair. Her lip curls in disgust as the third soldier coils

Saengo's heavy black braid around her hand and jerks her head back sharply. Rage—and that inexplicable echo of her fear—brightens inside me.

"Wyvern, is it?" the soldier says. "Once my friend there finishes with the shaman, you'll be coming back with us to be tried as a traitor. You don't deserve a braid." She steps away, but only far enough to slice her sword through Saengo's hair.

Saengo's shock ripples through me as her mouth opens on a soundless gasp. She reaches up, her fingers stiff with horror as they touch the blunt ends of her hair.

"You didn't need to do that," the archer says, grimacing. Eyebrow Tattoos throws his head back with a guffaw.

A chill spreads through me, all the fiery tumult of my emotions icing over.

The rope binding me falls away. I grab Eyebrow Tattoos's wrist, yanking his dagger a safe distance from my neck. His head whips around in time for me to bash my forehead into his face. His nose cracks as he falls. I wrench the knife from his slackened fingers, slam his good hand into the grass, and stab the knife through it, pinning him to the earth.

The whole thing takes only a second. As he screams, I advance on the other two. The one who cut Saengo's braid rushes me, drawing back her sword. I smash my knuckles into her throat before she's even swung. She makes a harsh choking sound and instantly drops. Too late, the archer scrambles for where he'd carelessly tossed his bow. I beat him to it, stomping my boot against the wood and snapping it in two.

I retrieve the sword Eyebrow Tattoos dropped. My eyes pass over the stump of Saengo's braid. That braid, and the attached feathers, meant more to her than mere rank. It was evidence of her defiance, her refusal to bow to her father's demands and the duties of her station. With one cruel act, they stripped her of everything she accomplished these last four years.

"Stop!" the archer shouts, glancing wildly from me to his incapacitated companions. "Queen Meilyr will have you locked—"

An arrow strikes the earth between us. I startle back, recognizing immediately the silver and black plumage on the arrow. The Queen's Guard.

"Hold your fire!"

I jolt at the voice, sucking in my breath. A company of Blades bursts through the trees, led by a familiar figure—Prince Meilek Sancor, captain of the Queen's Guard and the queen's younger brother.

FIVE

In moments, we're surrounded by a half-dozen riders, their arrows drawn.

Prince Meilek breaks away from his circle of Blades. I immediately drop to one knee, bending low so that my forehead brushes my pant leg. His mount's clawed feet sink into the soft earth as he approaches. I risk a glance up through my lashes. The triple-horned stag of House Sancor is emblazoned across his black chest plate. An embellished gold pin secures his black hair at the crown of his head, the ornament indicating his royal blood.

He takes in the scene, making me excruciatingly aware of how this might look. How are we to get out of this now?

Prince Meilek nudges his mount forward, his expression unreadable. The soldier I punched in the throat is similarly bent over one knee in deference. She's still wheezing, which gives me a small measure of grim satisfaction. As does Eyebrow Tattoos lying facedown in the grass, whimpering.

To the soldiers, the prince says, "Pick yourselves up and get back to the Valley. I'll deal with you later."

They rush to obey, pausing only long enough to unpin Eyebrow Tattoos from the ground. He screams pitifully.

When they've gone, Prince Meilek glances at the top of Saengo's bowed head and then to her braid lying nearby. Finally, his brown eyes settle their full attention on me. I quickly lower my gaze again. It would be inappropriate to meet the eyes of a royal.

"Stand," he commands.

Tensing against the pain, I slowly rise. I keep the stolen sword lowered at my side. His Blades' arrows are still trained on me.

With him on the back of his pearl-scaled dragule, I'm eye level with his hip. Two sashes are cinched around his waist in an elaborate Evewynian knot denoting his rank.

Prince Meilek says nothing. I don't know this version of him, the captain rather than the prince. Although he's only two years my senior, as overseer of the Prince's Company, he was a common presence during my years there. I can still recall the light pressure of his hand guiding mine through a difficult sword form, or his encouraging nod before an exam.

Besides Saengo, he is also the only other person who knows I am one of Kendara's pupils. After I graduated from the Prince's Company, our paths crossed primarily outside Kendara's door.

Still, in all the brief moments in all the years that I have known him, I've never stood before the captain of the Queen's Guard. I have little idea what to expect.

"An officit reported two missing wyverns yesterday," he says at last.

I don't respond to this. We can't exactly deny that we abandoned our positions with the supply delivery, but neither will I blithely confess guilt. I rub my tongue against the cut on the inside of my cheek, tasting blood again.

"In addition," Prince Meilek continues, "a falcon arrived late last night with troubling news. A teahouse burned down, reportedly due to an attack by shamans."

To have reached us so quickly, he must have ridden out from the Valley of Cranes. He was meant to be there when our party arrived with the supplies.

Nearby, Saengo stares down at her feet. Her nostrils flare with each inhalation. She's wary of him as well, but beneath the wariness is concern.

Although I don't understand how I can possibly know this, her concern is only for me. I know it in the same way I know that the sun will set in the west, the leaves will fall in autumn, and that Saengo died last night. Before, with those soldiers, I thought maybe these remnants of emotion were from seeing Saengo mistreated, but that's not the case. Her emotions burn low like a candle flame. I feel its heat, the way it sputters and flares and sways, without needing to see or touch it.

This new connection alarms me, possibly even more than the

fact we're surrounded by Blades ready to kill us at a single gesture from their captain.

"Saengo Phang," Prince Meilek says, to which Saengo can't help but stiffen her spine. "Your cousin, Jonyah Thao, was found near death outside the teahouse." His gaze shifts to me. "And the owner reports a girl matching your description, Sirscha Ashwyn, arriving shortly before the attack. Yet rather than return immediately to Vos Talwyn to report the crime, you fled. What am I to think?"

It sounds like he's already decided. I wish I could see the expression on his face.

"I'll need you to come with me for questioning."

"Those shamans attacked us," I say, flushing at my boldness. "We barely made it out alive." I point to the clothes I discarded earlier, lying in a pile near Yandor. "Your Highness," I add hastily.

Prince Meilek speaks gently. "If that's true, then you've nothing to fear."

I have *everything* to fear, but I only make a jerky motion at my face. He must know what I mean.

I would prefer the officits' malice to his pretty promises. At least at the Company, I knew where I stood. There was honesty in their cruelty. With Prince Meilek, his manner grates because I know better than to trust his words. He has a way of putting people at ease, but I'm familiar with the tactic. I was never very good at it.

Prince Meilek dismounts. On reflex, my fingers tighten

around the hilt of my sword. I force my arm to relax, for the blade to remain firmly pointed downward. As Shadow, I would lay down my life for him. After all, he is still my prince. But to die in defense of him isn't the same as bowing my head and handing over my life.

"No harm will come to you if you're innocent." He gestures to my sword. "So long as you give me your word that you won't impale any more soldiers."

"Why would you trust my word?"

"Because you trusted mine once."

My chest tightens in remembrance. In my second year at the Prince's Company, when I was twelve, an officit took a switch to my hands for the perceived indignity of defeating him in a spar. I couldn't carry a sword for days. Prince Meilek found me nursing my hands in the garden fountain. He'd taken the washcloth, mottled with blood, and tended to my knuckles with a gentleness that I have never forgotten.

"I'll have the officit replaced," he'd promised.

With five arrows aimed at my heart, the prince could easily order us trussed up and delivered to the queen. Instead, he chooses diplomacy. He might present himself as a man of honor, but experience and Kendara's tutelage have taught me that *everyone* has an ulterior motive.

Still, I don't know what to do besides concede and wait for the right opportunity to present itself. The sword slips from my fingers, hitting the ground with a dull clang of metal.

He snaps his fingers at his Blades, who promptly put away

their bows. "They won't run," he says, and the edge of warning in his voice is very much the captain's. "Will you?"

I cross my arms. "Nowhere to run."

"Good. A chase would have ruined both of our mornings."

Prince Meilek allows us to finish gathering our things. The Blades crowd in, giving me no opportunity to speak with Saengo. As soon as we're saddled, we set out through the trees, riding two abreast.

Although Saengo rides at my back, I don't need to see her to reassure myself of her safety. That connection between us lingers even now, the flame of her worries a constant heat at my back. My hands tighten around Yandor's reins. What did I do to her? To us?

Yandor makes a deep, grumbling sound, sensing my anxiety. I pat his neck in reassurance, although the contact helps to soothe my distressed thoughts as well.

Now that I'm not at imminent risk of being shot, I consider the thick growth in this part of the forest, which could be to my advantage. Unfortunately, so long as Prince Meilek remains with our party, my options are limited. And I can't risk Saengo getting caught in the cross fire. I won't make that mistake again.

I mentally sigh and take stock of my captors and their mounts. I've never seen dragules this close before. Dragules and drakes are both bipedal species of drakonys.

Every part of Prince Meilek's dragule proclaims his status. Its scales are white with an iridescent pink shimmer. Its head is wide and thorny, its snout shorter than a drake's. Gold-plated armor molds to its body from above its flat nostrils, over its brow, and all the way down its neck. Four shining black horns curve out from its head, tipped in gold and painted with beautiful designs to accent its custom armor. Savage companions in battle and symbols of high status, dragules are reserved only for reiwyn and Blades, Evewyn's warrior elite.

I wonder if Yandor would be able to outrun it. Drakes are larger, not as lean, but he also isn't weighed down by absurdly elaborate armor.

"Blades," I murmur with a soft snort.

Prince Meilek glances at me and then back at his Blades. "I agree they can be rather sullen, but what specifically has you irritated?"

I lower my head. I hadn't intended for him to hear.

"Is it the capes?" He flips back his own, letting the material catch the air and billow out behind him. "Rather inconvenient, really, but they're excellent for making dramatic exits."

In another situation, I might have laughed. Now I only glower at the trees in our path. "Forgive me, Your Highness. I was making an observation."

"Please enlighten me."

"The owner of the teahouse would have told you there were three shamans last night, and only two were accounted for. With a company of five Blades and three soldiers, your main objective would have been the shaman who escaped, not two fourth-year students."

He cocks his head at me, appraising. "I see now why

71

Kendara speaks so highly of you."

At the mention of Kendara, I stare stonily ahead. "Does she really?"

The thought fills me with joy and a dangerous, fragile hope.

"Constantly." He sounds almost embarrassed by the admission, although I can't imagine why. "I feel as if I ought to know you already."

"*I* don't know me," I say softly, remembering my reflection, wearing a stranger's eyes. For Kendara to speak so freely with him, she must trust him implicitly.

I'm unsurprised, though. When they're together, Kendara's face and voice soften in a way they never have for me. I've seen enough mothers speak to their children to recognize that Kendara and Prince Meilek share a similar connection. He was only two years old when she first joined the Evewynian Court as Shadow to his father, so it makes sense that they would form such a bond.

I've always envied him for having Kendara's love, when I could barely earn a kind word. There've been times when I thought she might love me, but she was always quick to dispel the notion. The day I began my training, I gifted her a bouquet of flowers in what I hoped was a gesture of my respect and gratitude.

"*We are not friends,*" she told me, tossing the flowers over the edge of her balcony. "*We are not family.*" I was no longer a child, nor a student, nor even a girl. If I was to succeed, I must become a shadow stretching unseen into the descending night. And when necessary, to be a knife in the dark.

From that moment on, every step I took was to bring myself closer to that goal.

Now, unless I find a way to restore my place with her, I will be none of those things. Not a soldier. Not the Shadow. Just a girl, once again, with no true name.

"Since you've proven to be sharp as well as observant, tell me: What did you gather about the attack?" asks Prince Meilek.

I press my lips together and consider what, if anything, to say. Given his relationship with Kendara, I can't come up with a good reason not to tell him the shamans had been targeting the Shadow. Besides, it's in my best interest to gain his trust and prove that I wasn't involved.

I tell him about the shaman with the crossed swords. "She needs to know it was a trap."

"I'll ensure she's informed and that measures are taken to protect her."

I nod, reassured. Kendara will be fine. In addition to the arsenal in her tower, she never goes anywhere without her favorite weapons at her waist—two dual swords that she's never allowed me to touch. She's even named them: Suryali and Nyia, after the sun and moon.

"The shaman either stole the brooch from the true informant or deceived the queen and planned the meeting as an ambush all along." Probably an attempt to weaken the queen's power by taking out her master spy and assassin. "Were you able to question him yet?"

When only silence sits between us, I glance over, keeping my gaze on the prince's chin. He has warm, lightly bronzed skin, a strong jaw, and full lips. Back in the Prince's Company, those lips had nearly always been curved into a smile. Now, although his expression remains neutral, his hesitation sparks a realization.

"You haven't caught him." An angry knot of disbelief forms in my gut. My hands clench around Yandor's reins. Why would Blades be south of the teahouse if the shaman hadn't been caught yet? Assuming he intends to escape into the Empire, north is the only direction he would head.

"I sent a search party of Blades north," Prince Meilek explains. "But I couldn't disregard the possibility that he'd go south to Vos Gillis. A large port city makes it easier to disappear. I sent others ahead without me, but once you and Saengo are seen to, I'll continue that way. It's possible he's already been apprehended."

But not guaranteed. The idea of him getting away is intolerable. Even worse, I can do nothing about it.

Ahead, sunlight narrows to bright flecks stippling the forest floor. The ground began to incline some time ago, indicating how closely our path hugs the outskirts of the Coral Mountains. My thoughts grow darker the farther we travel. I don't know how I'm going to get out of this.

"Are you injured?" he asks abruptly.

My shoulders bunch. "I'm fine, Your Highness."

"There's a tightness about your neck every time your drake jostles you," he says. I wonder at why he's paying such close attention. He probably knows I still plan to escape. "You hide it well."

I've been consciously keeping my expression as impassive

as possible. He must be especially skilled at reading faces. I don't appease his concern, whether real or calculated, and he doesn't press me further.

After what feels like hours, he glances over his shoulder and shares a look with his Blades that I can't decipher. A moment later, our path turns, making a sharp descent. I can't help the sudden catch of my breath. I jerk on Yandor's reins, coming to a stop. Instantly, two Blades circle forward to close me in.

I know this place, although I've only been here once before. Even the surrounding wilderness can't mask the pungent smell of the prison and the reek of misery. Spread out below us is the Valley of Cranes.

"Why are we here?" I ask quietly. Anything louder and I worry he'll hear the high note of my voice. "I thought you were taking us back to Vos Talwyn."

He reaches out to grip my reins. "My sister doesn't allow shamanborn into the capital except for one reason."

Public execution. My dread grows, heightened by Saengo's apprehension, which I can't shut out. Her emotions transform from heat into flame, trying to scorch away my own. It's oppressive, and I want to snap at her to stop it, but I don't know that she even realizes what she's doing.

I lower my chin and close my eyes, breathing deep. Again this creeping panic sits in me as comfortably as a bed of nails. Kendara's voice rings in my head. *"Discipline always. Stay your hand. Play your role."* I release a slow, steady breath.

"You will have to remain here for questioning." Prince Meilek sounds irritatingly reasonable. "And until we determine what happened at the teahouse."

Play my role. Very well. I can do that. For now. Let him believe he's gained my trust. Once he hands me over to someone else, maybe I can devise a proper escape. I lift my chin and nod curtly to indicate I won't fight. Prince Meilek releases my reins.

Nestled at the feet of two mountains and enclosed by steep cliffs, the prison camp is supposed to be inescapable. We'll see about that.

From this vantage point, the valley spreads out before us. Tiny cabins squat in rows on the far end of the grounds. The earth is dry and sparse, packed down by the feet of hundreds of prisoners, possibly thousands. Distant figures push carts in and out of a hole in the mountainside. Working alone or in clusters, they haul lumber from the forests, water from the stream that trickles through, and rocks cleared from the mines. Everything from the buildings to the people is coated in tawny dust.

Uncertainty digs talons into my stomach, but I force myself to keep looking. The only bits of liveliness in the whole place are the gardens beside the cabins, rows of sowed earth that have just begun to sprout. A low stone wall forms the base of the prison's enclosure. Above that, thick iron bars rise to twice my height.

Prince Meilek leads us toward a drab-looking building with a large gate, outside of which I'm horrified to find the party Saengo and I abandoned yesterday. The hatchlets are already lined up, their satchels at their backs. The wyverns haven't mounted their drakes yet, still clustered behind the now empty wagon and Officit Boldis. Beside him is a guard dressed in the dark green and silver uniform of the Evewynian Royal Army, but they've abandoned their conversation in favor of gawking at our arrival.

Upon recognizing me, Officit Boldis's surprise transforms into smug satisfaction. The urge to kick him in the face almost wins out against my better judgment. Anyway, the satisfaction is ultimately mine when I pass him on my drake and he meets my changed eyes. His ruddy face pales, and his mouth drops open.

I grin, relishing his shock. At least until my gaze passes over the hatchlets and their accompanying wyverns. They've noticed my eyes as well, and their expressions are a chilling reminder of how things have changed. They shrink away in fear and revulsion. I'm relieved when Prince Meilek leads me inside the building.

We enter a large courtyard. At the opposite end sits a closed iron gate topped with spikes—the only entrance into the prison. Through it, the grounds are a filthy brown stretch, the mountains a beautiful but jarring backdrop. The shamanborn shamble about their work, wearing their exhaustion like weights around their necks.

They're a reminder of what happens when the queen decides you're an enemy. My stomach turns in dismay.

Prince Meilek pulls his dragule to a stop in the courtyard and dismounts. Warily, I do the same. Instantly, two guards are at my side, securing my wrists in iron shackles that wedge the troll bone into my skin. I clench my jaw and suffer the restraints in silence. My only consolation is that Prince Meilek cuts them off with a look when they attempt to do the same to Saengo.

"How long are we to stay here?" Saengo asks, her misery evident even without our connection. But with it, I'm being dragged underwater, chains wrapped around my ankles.

"Until I can address the matter with the queen. Although Sirscha will need to remain here, I should be able to relocate you to Vos Talwyn soon."

She sucks in her breath, eyes darting from me to the Blades as she wages some internal war. Then she scowls and pushes her drake forward before dismounting at my side. "I won't leave her."

"That isn't your decision to make," Prince Meilek says, that edge returning to his voice.

Her anger builds inside her, a storm gathering size, speed, and devastation. I've always known that she presented a front, that her deference and obedience in the Company was as much an act as mine. But to feel it there, the great depth of her resentment colliding and breaking against me, makes me realize how much she's kept hidden.

I raise my hands. The links in my shackles clank together as I place one palm on her chest, directly over the scar that rests above her heart. "It'll be fine." I wring every drop of conviction I have into the words so that she might believe me. "You'll have your father's influence to protect you."

Saengo pulls me into a hug. I squeeze my eyes shut as we

clutch each other, surrounded by the scents of dust, smoke, and despair. The deluge of her emotions crashes into me, rushing into my throat and clogging my lungs. I try to focus instead on her arms around me, sucking in air to remind myself that I can, in fact, breathe.

"Come on," I say thickly. "You're not going anywhere yet. Pull yourself together, Phang."

One of the Blades places a hand on her shoulder, forcing us to part. Two other Blades flank me as they lead me toward the back of the building. Already, the reach of Saengo's candle flame grows faint. I'm ashamed that a part of me is relieved to be alone with my own emotions.

SIX

My cell is a small metal room with a barred door and nothing else, save for old scorch marks that indicate a firewender had been kept here once.

When I grow tired of sitting, I prowl the narrow space between walls. My wrist shackles attach to a chain in the floor, which doesn't allow me to move more than a few paces in any direction. I tug irritably at them. Despite Prince Meilek's reassurances, these chains are proof he's equally wary of me.

I'm not even sure he has any intention of taking my case to the queen or if I'm to be left here until the fight has been bled from me through hard labor and starvation. I grit my teeth. I won't allow that. I'll escape well before that can happen.

If I focus, I still sense Saengo's presence nearby, a candle in the dark. It's unsettling, but given the circumstances, also reassuring. She's my only anchor in all this.

The irony is that I loathed her at first. We met in our first year at the Prince's Company, when we were eleven. She'd kept to herself and hardly spoke to anyone. I assumed she thought herself better than the rest of us. One day, after I'd bested Jonyah at swords, he cornered me in the armory. He would have broken my arm if Saengo hadn't intervened. Jonyah was a bully, but Saengo was the heir to his House, and he knew his place.

After that, Saengo always chose me for her sparring partner. I was suspicious at first, but she never seemed to resent losing. Instead, she liked that I fought her as an equal, and I liked that she treated me like one. In the years to come, I would learn that the only thing she truly resented was that she, too, knew her place. And she wanted nothing to do with it.

The longer I languish in this cell, the more certain I am that my window to sneak back into Vos Talwyn has closed. Queen Meilyr will be securing every entrance into the city, making it impossible to penetrate. I can't rely on Kendara to speak for me, assuming she even would.

Besides that, now that I've had time to consider the situation more fully, I realize I hadn't thought about the ramifications of the attack for Evewyn as a whole. The queen's treatment of the shaman-born might have sparked current tensions between the races, but the hostility goes back for centuries. Given this blatant attack by Nuvali shamans on Evewynian land, unless the Spider King can maintain the tenuous peace, this could very well mean war.

My muscles tense with dread. Evewyn's armies have always been a formidable force, even during times of peace. But would my fellow wyverns, who graduate within the month, truly be prepared? I'd wager the most violence they'll expect to meet as soldiers is from local criminals, maybe a pirate or a sellsword. War is a wholly different beast.

Without knowing what the shamans wanted, the queen might look to blame the whole Empire, the way she'd punished all shamanborn for what happened to her parents.

However, if I were to discover the true purpose of the attack and present that information to the queen, it could both prevent a war and win me back my place with Kendara. If I were the queen's Shadow, this would be information I'd need to acquire, anyway. What better way to prove myself?

I groan and cover my face. What hope do I have of accomplishing any of that when I couldn't even stop one shaman from hurting Saengo?

A door opens down the hall, beyond my line of sight. Curses and profanities taint the air in a voice I recognize as Eyebrow Tattoos's. A heartbeat later, the door slams shut with enough force that it reverberates through my cell. A girl limps into view, thin and disheveled, with an impressive red mark already darkening into a bruise across her cheek.

The guard outside my door unlocks my cell and gestures for the girl to enter. His keys jangle as he locks it again after her. The girl sets down a basket filled with bundles of herbs tied with twine. When she straightens, her eyes are the vivid emerald of an earthwender.

Those eyes linger on mine, narrowed slightly. An emotion

passes over her face, too quick to name before she looks away. Seeing as she's obviously a prisoner here as well, I don't blame her for being guarded.

"Are . . ." Something in the tremor of her quiet voice makes me wary. "Are you really—"

"Five minutes," the guard says, cutting her off.

She flinches, lips compressed. Her question is forgotten as she steps closer. "Before he left, Prince Meilek asked me to tend to your injuries."

"You're a healer?"

"Of a sort." She gestures to her basket. "I'm no light stitcher. And anyway, I don't have a familiar anymore." Her voice dips even lower, but bitterness saturates her words.

Shamans can't access their magic without familiars. Although I've never quite grasped how it works, I know that familiars begin as spirits, intangible and unable to communicate except through a medium, but only until they bond with a shaman. Then they become physical conduits, connecting shamans to their magic. I've no idea what any of it means for me.

Once, familiars would have been as common a sight in Evewyn as shamanborn. When the Valley of Cranes was first transformed from a lush mountain refuge into a harsh prison, familiars were either killed or imprisoned separately from their shamans. But those familiars soon died off from the rot, a disease born of the Dead Wood. The disease, which affects only familiars and possesses no known cure, first appeared decades ago, and neither king nor Scholar has been able to offer an explanation for why.

Whatever magic this earthwender possesses is inaccessible to her now. Part of me thinks I might understand the frustration of knowing what you're capable of and never being able to embrace it. But I recognize the lie for what it is.

I chose to restrain myself at the Company for the chance at something more. These shamanborn had no such choice. I haven't known their suffering. I haven't shared their loss.

I nod at her bruising face. "I'm fine. You should take care of your own injuries first."

She ignores me, her hands brisk and efficient as they move from my arms to my torso and then my legs. I immediately stiffen, and she makes a small knowing sound.

"I'll need you to lower your pants," she says.

I'm not used to having anyone else tend to my injuries, and I don't know where to look as I untie the laces of my pants and push them down to my knees. I grimace at the sight of my thighs. The bruises are nearly black, haloed by billowing red and purple discoloration.

She applies a thin paste I recognize as one meant to accelerate healing. I study the lines that form between her eyebrows and wonder at her age. She looks young. Maybe fourteen? Does she have family in the prison? Parents?

"Did that oaf with the eyebrow tattoos do that to you?" I ask as she places her weight on her left leg and winces. "I should have broken his arms altogether."

"You're the one who injured his hands?" A smile steals over the corners of her mouth.

"I'm sorry you had to tend him."

She shrugs, and the smile fades into practiced indifference again. She wraps my thighs in clean bandages so the paste doesn't stain my pants and then reaches inside her basket again. "Are you in pain at all?"

"No." I tug my pants back up over my drawers. I have a high pain tolerance. With daily doses from both the Company and Kendara, my relationship with pain is long and complicated.

She pauses, as if to ensure I won't change my mind, and then puts away the vial of pain reliever she'd withdrawn from her basket. From the courtyard come the sounds of drakes. There aren't many, maybe two. Too few to be an arriving prisoner. I can only assume the shaman who hurt Saengo continues to elude capture. He cannot be allowed to escape.

I add hunting him down to my list, even though it all feels so impossible. And yet, the fact that Saengo is alive is proof enough that I need to reconsider what impossible means.

That's something else I'll have to deal with in the near future—what I did to her.

But first I have to make sure I have a future at all.

The girl arranges her medicinal herbs and vials into neat piles, her fingers long and gaunt. Her small nose is slightly crooked, like it was broken once and wasn't set properly. Her tunic hangs off her thin frame, the hem frayed and torn in the back.

And yet, as the girl glances up at me from behind the knots of her hair, I glimpse the defiance in her. Despite the vast difference in our experiences, I feel a kinship with this ragged healer.

Back in the orphanage, the monks claimed I was a nuisance

from the moment I arrived. I'd been two, with no possessions save the clothes on my back and my name on a card. Overindulged and disobedient, they said, incessantly crying for a mother who had abandoned me. In truth, I'm not sure why they didn't throw me out. The scars on my body tell a very long story indeed.

Children are meant to obey those who raise them, but how can respect be born of abuse? Whatever manner of punishment the monks inflicted on me, they could not break me. I think, above everything else, that is why they hated me most.

"Miss." The shaman hangs her basket on the crook of her elbow. She's giving me the same look she had when she entered— one of tremulous uncertainty. With a glance over her shoulder at the guard, she dampens her lips and asks, "Is it true?"

She delivers the question in a quick whisper, as if the words are pebbles in her mouth, released quickly lest she choke.

Before I can ask what she's talking about, the guard abruptly straightens, drawing my eye. Then there's no time for explanations because Prince Meilek steps into view. I lift an eyebrow. He'd initially left hours ago. The shaman shrinks back, clutching her basket the way my fingers grasp the troll bone.

"Open this door and remove her restraints," he orders the guard, who races to comply.

The earthwender dips her head low to Prince Meilek, who thanks her for her help and then catches sight of her cheek. His eyes darken with anger.

"I'll speak to the guards," he promises her. "Please see to your injuries."

She nods and then disappears from view. Once my shackles are removed, I rub the chafed skin of my wrists and follow Prince Meilek out into the courtyard. He wears the look of the captain again, and his manner tells me I'm not being freed. I spot Yandor saddled for our departure, but my belongings are still in his Blades' possession.

More guards appear with Saengo. I'm relieved to see her, but this only heightens my confusion. Her own relief trickles through our connection.

"Where are we going?" I ask, fingers flexing at my sides. We'd already established I wouldn't be returning to Vos Talwyn except for execution. Prince or no, if he thinks I'll allow him to lead me to my death, he's mistaken.

With a glance, I count eight guards in the immediate vicinity, not including Prince Meilek's two Blades. The nearest weapon is at the waist of the guard to my left, which I could obtain in seconds if necessary. If Eyebrow Tattoos and his friends were an example of what I might expect from the soldiers here, I could tear through them in less than a minute. The Blades would present more of a challenge, but with only two, Saengo and I should be able to handle them.

Prince Meilek, however, is an unknown. At only nineteen, he isn't captain of the Queen's Guard without reason. And it's entirely possible that if I raise my sword to the prince of Evewyn, then it won't matter what information I bring back to the queen. It would be seen as treason.

Saengo seems to sense my dilemma. When I catch her eye,

she looks meaningfully across the courtyard. A bow and quiver rest carelessly alongside a rack of swords. The soldiers must use the courtyard to spar. They're out of reach of prisoners, but if I create enough of a diversion, Saengo could likely reach the bow.

I don't know what I did to deserve a friend who would commit treason with me at a moment's notice. But still, I give a slight shake of my head. Not yet. Not until I know what's happening.

"I'd barely reached Keistra's Flight when a messenger from the queen intercepted me," the prince says. He approaches his dragule and tests the straps on the saddle. "Early this morning, she received a falcon from Ronin of the Dead Wood."

For an excruciating second, all thoughts of escape are shoved from my mind. The implication of his words pulls me off-kilter. Just to be sure I heard right, I say, "What?"

"Ronin has summoned you to Spinner's End." His gaze flicks to Saengo. "Both of you."

Ronin has a permanent encampment called Sab Hlee at the western border of the Dead Wood, where we'll begin our journey. Spinner's End, Ronin's home, resides a half day's walk through the woods.

Prince Meilek explains that, as peacekeeper between the kingdoms, Ronin wants a first-person account of what happened at the teahouse. I find it curious, though, that he's already aware of the attack. For a falcon to have arrived in Vos Talwyn that morning, Ronin would've had to have sent the summons immediately after the attack occurred. Is he a seer?

As we travel, I consider that Ronin is the perfect person to help me uncover the shamans' motives. His summons drastically improves my chances of accomplishing what had seemed an impossible goal mere hours ago. If anyone can help me uncover the truth of the attack and win back my place with Kendara, it's Ronin. As intermediary between the three kingdoms, he must be the most well-informed person on Thiy. Still, I berate myself for the way my hands tremble.

Saengo shares my apprehension. The Blades don't allow us any time to speak, herding us along like cattle. But I sense her there, her fear a chill against the back of my neck. Although I'd planned to keep secret what happened to her, few people are given the opportunity to speak with the Spider King. I'd be a fool not to ask his advice.

The only craft I know of that can raise the dead is necromancy, which isn't a shamanic craft. Kendara has a book in her workroom about the Calling of Shadow, the magic of the shadowblessed, the peoples of Kazahyn. It's a slim volume, information about shadow crafts being so limited. But I've read about how, in the past, the shadowblessed raised the bodies of fallen foes to intimidate and demoralize their enemies. The bodies were nothing more than animated corpses controlled by the necromancer.

Saengo is no corpse, and I am not shadowblessed. I felt her heart beating against my palm and the warm aliveness of her skin.

But if anyone can explain what happened, it's Ronin. According to history books, he originally hails from the far north, where the Great Spinners build webs that span mountainsides. Not much else of his past is known, but one fact has never been disputed: he is one of the most powerful shamans in Thiy.

Some centuries ago, a shaman who would become known as the Soulless rose against the kingdoms. He had the power to kill by ripping out the souls of his enemies. The history books are always vague about what exactly happened, but not even the armies of Thiy could subdue him. He merely claimed their souls for himself, strengthening his power and his madness.

Then Ronin descended from the north with a massive spider as his familiar, one of the Spinners of his homeland. No shaman had ever possessed a Spinner as a familiar before. Only the union of two such powerful beings could defeat the Soulless.

After the Soulless's death, the souls he'd claimed scattered, taking root in the trees. Over time, the forest died and became a dangerous place for travelers. For whatever reason, Ronin made his home within the woods, using spidersilk spun from the bond with his Spinner to cloak the restless spirits. Not only that, but he convinced the kingdoms to sign the first and only peace treaty of its kind, one that would ensure peace for centuries to come.

And now, after all this time, the Dead Wood has begun to expand far more quickly than in the past, casting Ronin's power into doubt.

"Have you ever seen the Dead Wood?" Prince Meilek asks, breaking the silence.

"Only from a distance. Even Kendara didn't want me getting close to that place." That's saying something, considering all the ways I nearly died under her care. "She sent me mostly on tasks in the west, like in the mountains or to port cities like Byrth."

"Byrth," he says with a sudden smile. "Once, when we were children visiting with our parents, Mei and I sneaked off to watch a drake race, and I bribed the drake master to let me enter."

How strange to think of him and Queen Meilyr as children, misbehaving as children do. "Did you win?"

He shakes his head. "I fell off short of the finish line. Half my face was bruised for the rest of our trip. My parents were outraged. But Byrth's market was a wonder. Father bought us candied plum blossoms."

"Candied plum blossoms?" I've never heard of such a thing.

"They don't sell them in Vos Talwyn."

I look down at my hands clasped around Yandor's reins. I miss the busy streets, the statues of the Sisters, and the sense of history on every corner. Would I ever see Vos Talwyn again?

Reading my expression, he says, "You needn't worry. Ronin has granted you both safe passage."

"Can . . . can such a thing be guaranteed?"

"I know it seems unlikely, given how persistent the trees have become in recent years. The woods have always spread, just very slowly. Ronin's control isn't absolute, but it's always been enough to ensure the safety of his guests."

"Don't you think it's odd? After nearly three centuries, what's changed that he's only now . . ." I don't finish the suggestion that

Ronin is losing control. It's a dangerous thing to voice.

Prince Meilek opens his mouth but then pauses. I wait, wondering what else he knows that I don't. The prince of Evewyn is obviously far better informed about foreign leaders than I am. To my disappointment, he doesn't speak. Instead, he calls for one of his Blades to feed us, and we eat as we travel.

We've only a few hours of daylight left when the Dead Wood at last appears as a dreary bramble beyond the next farm. Fear rises within me, heightened by Saengo's alarm that presses, insistent, against my back.

Prince Meilek pulls ahead of me. Sab Hlee is little more than a smattering of tents and a few collapsible buildings. The Dead Wood lies beyond, crouched against the sky like a resting spider.

We pass through a brace of torches and guards. They bow to Prince Meilek before leading us through the center of the encampment. More soldiers appear to watch our arrival, curious. They wear simple leather armor with little adornment, other than a gray sash secured over a belt and sword.

Ronin's standard flies from the peaks of the largest tents: a skeletal tree, stooped and malformed. Its silhouette resembles that of a spider. Deliberate, I'm sure.

Prince Meilek pauses just long enough to speak quietly with two people. Their armor and the knots of their gray sashes indicate they're Ronin's officits. One is a shaman. The other has dark gray skin, and although he looks young and lean, his hair is completely white.

Shadowblessed, I realize. I know very little about them, even what they look like. I've heard that some shadowblessed live in Evewyn's port cities, but the clans rarely venture beyond Kazahyn's mountains.

I glance back at Saengo. Her gaze is fixed on the Dead Wood. She looks ill. I wish I'd had time to explain why going to see Ronin is, in fact, a good thing. But I'm not sure it would help much.

The Dead Wood terrifies me as well, because I cannot battle trees. I cannot win with fighting skills and weaponry. Ronin's assurance and our wits will be all that stand between us and the spirits' malice.

But if the Dead Wood is our only path to Ronin, then we'd best be about it quickly. We'll be out of daylight soon. Even after everything I have done under Kendara's tutelage, walking into those trees of my own will in the dead of night might take more courage than I possess.

SEVEN

We continue through the encampment. I spot a human, two shamans, and a shadowblessed sharing a wineskin around a cooking fire, all dressed in the light armor of Ronin's soldiers. It's bizarre seeing all three races gathered together like old friends. Before Queen Meilyr, such a sight might not have been so unusual in Evewyn.

We soon leave the encampment behind, my heart hammering against my rib cage. But as we near the tree line, the bare branches and the crooked trunks look less sinister and more forlorn. Perhaps my expectations colored my judgment, lending malevolence to the mundane. Perhaps the stories were exaggerated, tales to instill fear in children and travelers who might dare to venture into the Spider King's domain.

Saengo doesn't share the sentiment. Her fear is a knife lodged between my shoulder blades. I slow Yandor so that I fall into line with her drake. The Blades close ranks around us, as if they think we'll try to run with Ronin's camp behind us and the Dead Wood before us.

I take Saengo's hand, only flinching a little when her fear hurls through me. "We'll do this together."

She squeezes my hand, her fingers like ice. It's only through our connection that I can even tell she's afraid. Her expression is unreadable as she tilts her head back to survey the woods before us.

The trees are much taller than I expected, many nearly the height of Kendara's tower. The forest must have been old even before the souls took root here. A dusty, unmarked path leads into the trees, one I don't notice until we're standing on it. The path begins as a few cobblestones set into the dirt but quickly disappears into the gloom. There are no leaves, nor anything green at all. The branches twine and crowd into such a thicket that very little sunlight reaches the ground.

I draw a deep breath, rallying my courage. Then I release Saengo's hand and climb down from the saddle. Yandor grunts unhappily. He turns his head and nudges my arm until I wrap it around his neck.

"It'll be okay, my friend." I close my eyes and rest my fore- head against his warm scales. "We'll see each other again." When I lean back, his tongue flicks out, licking my cheek.

Prince Meilek pulls up beside me, his mouth set into a frown. "Are you ready?"

"Yes," I say before I can give the question much thought. Saengo murmurs her agreement, chin held high—ever the reiwyn lady, even now. "What will happen to us after we've spoken to Ronin?"

He looks troubled as he says, "I'm afraid I don't know. It depends on Ronin."

One of Ronin's soldiers withdraws a white cloak that seems to absorb the sunlight from a leather bag. He hands it to me. "Spidersilk. Sturdy and difficult to penetrate. It carries an echo of Ronin's power. It will help to deter the trees."

My fingers brush over the fabric, slick and light as air, the softest I've ever touched. I drape the cloak around my shoulders. It's like wearing clouds. I fasten the cloak at my throat and say, "Spidersilk is quite rare. Has he an army of Spinners at his command?"

Predictably, the soldier doesn't reply. He turns to Saengo to present her with her own cloak.

"You've traveled the path before?" Saengo asks him. "I didn't know there were any paths left."

"This is all that remains of the watchtower that once guarded Evewyn's eastern border. The Dead Wood claimed it some time ago. We've traveled the path before but not often."

If even Ronin's own soldiers are wary about traveling the woods alone, then that certainly doesn't bode well for us. Still, there's nothing to do but trust in his protection. I somehow doubt he extends such protection to just anyone.

I remove my satchel from Yandor's saddle and sling it over my shoulder, the strap resting across my chest. The troll-bone talisman bumps against my wrist. It helps if I approach this as one of Kendara's tests, many of which would have raised the brows of even the most hardened sellswords. We will survive the Dead Wood, because as with Kendara's training, failure is unacceptable.

"Keep your wits about you. Stay on the path." The soldier leans forward, expression grave. "Walk fast."

Prince Meilek swings down from his dragule's back. He reaches into his own saddlebag and then presents me with a shoulder belt bearing two short swords sheathed in leather scabbards.

"Your Highness?" I say, uncertain. Despite the unusual circumstances, I'm still a prisoner. Does he really mean to arm me? I could cut down all three of them and escape right now.

Then I really *would* be a traitor.

"What we spoke about earlier. Just in case," he says.

I dampen my lips. Just in case Ronin's assurance of safe passage is no longer a guarantee.

I accept the swords. Strapping on the shoulder belt, I already feel more in control, even though it's a false security. The prince nods to one of his Blades, who removes a plain sword and leather scabbard from his saddle. He hands them to Saengo. She wordlessly attaches the weapon to her belt.

"Weapons will not help you in there," the soldier says.

"Perhaps not," I say. "But better than nothing."

Prince Meilek nods his agreement. "May the Falcon Warrior protect you on your journey."

Saengo and I bow deeply in goodbye. When I straighten, I roll my shoulders, the swords resting comfortably against my back. My hand finds the talisman again. I look at Saengo.

She smiles back, betraying only the slightest tremor of her lips. "Together."

We face the Dead Wood, and together, we march forward.

A gloom descends with unnatural swiftness. The trees stand so close that we can't walk more than two steps without our shoulders brushing gnarled bark. The trees look stooped and frail, as if, rather than withering to dust when the shadows fell across the forest, they simply . . . grew old. The path we tread, our only guide, is hardly a path at all. The cobblestones are sunken, overrun with thick roots, devoured by the trees like everything else in this place.

Since the Dead Wood has born no leaves for so long, there is only dirt underfoot. Just as the branches shut out the sky, the roots overtake the earth. Some form strange jointed shapes, like deformed legs and severed arms. Only slivers of light penetrate the canopy. Dust motes dance in the tiny sunbeams and make those odd-shaped roots, muddy green-gray like the color of dead flesh, appear to tremble and strain away from the light.

Saengo glances over her shoulder. Prince Meilek and the soldiers have long since disappeared.

"Are you sure you wouldn't prefer to just escape now?" she asks in a whisper. There's no one to hear us but the trees, and yet . . . I can't deny it feels as though they are listening.

I shudder and adjust the shoulder belt, glad for the comfort of the swords' weight. Quickly, I explain my plan to her—that in order to prevent war and win back my place in Evewyn, our best choice is to secure Ronin's help in uncovering the purpose of the attack.

Saengo tugs the cloak tighter around herself. "I'd thought about that, actually. Almost every family at Falcons Ridge has a soldier in the army, and most of those families have been under the care of my House for generations. If we go to war with the Nuvalyn Empire, all those families could be torn apart."

"Not just the families. Falcons Ridge is too close to the northern border. Your lands would be devastated." I skirt around a thick nest of roots. They're so dense, the ground so uneven, I must take care where I step.

"I guess you're right, then. We'll have to see this through. And, Sirscha—" She rubs her hands down her arms as if she's cold. Her fear transforms into something else, something more fragile. I can't put a name to it, only that it feels like a breath of frost against the inside of my ribs.

Being privy to her emotions suddenly feels intrusive. I imagine a mental barrier between me and Saengo's candle flame, something I can open and close at will, like a window.

"When we get to Spinner's End, we should . . . talk," she says.

"I know." I've been a coward for not facing what I did—but Saengo had *died*. There hasn't been time to press her about how she's been handling it, and now, in this haunted place, we need to remain focused. "But maybe Ronin will know what happened."

She shrugs one shoulder and gives a low-hanging branch an uneasy look. "Maybe? Let's just get through this place first."

"We've been through worse. Remember that time when second-years poured cabbage soup down the latrines?"

Her lips twitch. Through our connection, a momentary

warmth flares through me.

"And it clogged the pipes, and the Company yard smelled like manure for a week?"

"See? What's a bunch of old trees compared to that?"

They're not just old, though. They're ancient, their surfaces drab and brittle, their decaying innards exposed where patches of bark have flaked off. And yet, they remain standing. It's peculiar how intact these trees are, given that they've been dead or dying for centuries. They should have collapsed long ago.

I lift my foot high to step over a raised root. It still bumps the heel of my boot. A minute later, I duck a low branch only to feel it brush the top of my hood. A chill races through me. I must have misjudged the distance. I continue telling myself that when I angle my body to slip between two trees, and the bark rasps against my shoulder.

"Maybe we could run a bit," Saengo suggests, her voice soft and high with alarm.

"My thought exactly."

We break into a light jog. The Company makes us run five laps around the Grand Palace every morning, so we won't tire quickly. Kendara often made me run twice that in half the time. Even with my injuries, I should be able to keep up.

There is magic here as old as the Dead Wood itself. The longer I run, the stronger a sensation grows in my chest. It's not the warmth of Saengo's presence, her candle bright and strong even from behind the mental window I've placed between us. This feeling burns from inside *me*, hotter, more effusive, and slightly painful. It reminds me of what I felt after Saengo died, moments before I passed out.

After jogging a steady pace for over an hour, we slow so that we can withdraw our waterskins from our satchels. We drink quickly. My legs ache, and although I should be warm from the steady movement, I can't shake the chill. A wrongness lingers in the very air; it seeps into my skin like a slow poison. A corruption beyond what can be seen. The sooner we get to Spinner's End, the better.

As I put away my waterskin, something brushes against the backs of my legs, cold even through the layers of clothing. I startle, spinning around. Saengo hisses my name. There is nothing behind me but the serpentine lattice of roots and the trees, rustling gently.

There is no wind.

My mouth goes dry, despite having just drank my fill. With a glance at Saengo, we continue on, increasing our pace again. The slender trees take on the shapes of broken men—roots like legs bent the wrong way, bodies torn in half, arms locked at grotesque angles. I look away. I focus only on where I place my feet, but even that has become difficult in the swiftly fading light.

Something snags my hood. I whirl back around, my hands half raised to draw my swords. There are only the branches, low enough to block the path when only a moment ago, they'd been well above my head.

My breaths come quicker, louder. I almost don't hear it. A high, hoarse wail, like when air pushes between the grooves of branches.

The trees are breathing.

"Sirscha, we can't stop." Saengo's fear bleeds into mine until there's no distinction between our feelings, only an icy certainty that we should keep running.

So we run. The shadows grow darker. Night settles into the woods. Our cloaks glow faintly, but it's a meager light.

My imagination can only be blamed for so much, because I'm convinced the trees are pressing closer. The branches shake and dip, reaching. The roots shamble after us. Saengo knocks aside a branch that drops into our path. It snaps, but not before ripping her hood off her head.

Something spindly snatches my braid. I yank my hair free, and we both dash into a sprint. My heartbeat drums in my ears. The wailing grows, rising up like a chorus of banshees. Skeletal fingers grasp at our legs, scoring the old leather of our boots and catching in the loose fabric of our pants.

The roots lift from the ground like risen corpses. Dead earth cascades from their pale, exposed flesh. Saengo leaps to avoid one and then gasps when it shoots out, catching her foot. She sprawls into the dirt.

"Saengo!" I drop beside her, pulling at her arms to get her to stand.

A branch strikes her temple. She flinches and scrambles back. Spidersilk tangles around her legs. Another branch whips across my cheek, stinging as it breaks skin. The pain sharpens my senses, cutting through my fear. Cursing at myself, my hands find my swords, and I stand. The roots unfurl, revealing sharp ends that strike out. I split them in two. Suddenly, the woods shriek, enraged.

The trees writhe, the bark buckling and cracking open. Faces emerge from within, straining against the decaying wood. Their eyes are wrinkled burls. Their mouths scream their anguish and outrage. I recoil, my own scream frozen in my throat. The faces twist away, sinking back into the wood, but they're quickly replaced with more—snarling, screeching, weeping sticky black sap from those horrific eyes. Branches like fingers grasp at our clothes, our skin, our hair.

Saengo draws her own sword and finds her feet. A trickle of blood slides over her cheekbone from her temple. With a fierce, shaking breath, she whispers, "Courage."

The heat in my chest sears as if trying to melt the skin off my bones. I gasp at the pain. Something cold wraps around my ankle. I slash at it, suddenly furious.

This is not how we die. Not here. Not in this wretched place, and not by the hands of creatures that should be long dead. Together, pressed back to back, our swords flash, severing branches and scoring trees. That scorching heat, a power that can only be my craft, blazes bright and pure.

Every branch clawing at us crumbles. The roots, too, scatter into the dirt like sand.

"What?" Saengo whispers, confused.

Panting, I slowly turn in place, swords ready for the next assault. Tiny orbs of light wink into existence all around me. Warily, I sheathe one sword before stretching out my hand, my fingers tingling with a sudden and desperate need.

Saengo reaches for me. "Wait, don't—"

The moment my skin makes contact with a glowing orb, they all brighten as one. They circle around me, spinning like a vortex of strung paper lanterns. Saengo gasps.

My eyes widen in wonder. Are these . . . ?

That power in me loosens its grip, and the lights disperse into the dank, shadowy air.

I release an unsteady breath. Darkness settles once again. The trees are still. Faces continue to press outward from within the bark, but the shrieking has stopped. The roots rustle and the branches vibrate, agitated. But both keep their distance.

Saengo whispers, "What just happened? Did you do that?"

"I don't know." A wave of exhaustion washes over me. I cup my head as my knees waver. Saengo catches me before I can fall.

"What's wrong?" she asks, frantic.

I try to tell her I'm fine, but I can't seem to speak. My heart thunders. The branches shake over our heads. The trees seem to press in again, but not with the same malice as before.

Then, all at once, the trees shrink away. Saengo's head snaps up at the sudden movement, and she reaches for her sword again. A tall figure emerges from the dark. I squint up at him, but he's difficult to make out in the gloom.

Ronin the Spider King says, "Come. The woods at night are no place to linger."

EIGHT

My head feels like it's been stuffed with feathers. I squint at Ronin's back, his broad shoulders, and the sweep of his gray robes. As much as I want to ask him questions, I'm more intent on not falling on my face in front of him. It would make for a poor first impression.

After a length of time that feels like ages, Ronin leads us through a gauzy white drape that hangs from the trees, and just like that, we stand before Spinner's End. I take in the impression of somber walls, curved roofs, and towers limned in silver moonlight before soldiers sweep Saengo and me into the castle. They usher us into a room where we're ordered to rest for the night. We're so exhausted that we don't argue. We merely seek out the bed and fall into it.

Thankfully, I awake clearheaded in the morning, despite disturbing dreams of grasping, broken hands and silent, screaming mouths. Saengo is asleep beside me, hogging the blanket. We're still wearing our clothes from yesterday. My nose wrinkles at the smell.

I sit up and take in my immediate surroundings. I'm in a bedroom with scrubbed wooden floors covered in plush rugs. Beyond a pair of glass doors lies a balcony. A mirror hangs on the wall, its antique copper frame flecked with green. The bed I'm in is large enough to accommodate both Saengo and me, although a second bed sits across the room. They're both framed in exquisitely carved oak and draped in curtains dyed the rich orange of persimmons.

"Good afternoon," says a voice.

I instinctively reach for swords that aren't there and then force myself to relax. Standing in the doorway is a woman in the crisp gray uniform of what I assume must be the castle staff. She carries a tray with a cup and pitcher.

"Afternoon?" I return warily, glancing at the light through the balcony.

"Indeed. It's past midday." She sweeps into the room and sets the tray on a desk.

I haven't slept past morning bells at the Company in years. Rising from the bed, I scan the room for my things. My boots rest against the wall beside the armoire, the last few days' worth of mud scraped off the heels. I pull open the armoire. My empty satchel is neatly folded on a shelf above the bare clothes rack.

"Where are my swords?" I ask, circling the room.

I peek into a door beside the armoire. It leads into a small bathing chamber, unfurnished save for a tub partly hidden behind a screen. My gaze falls longingly on the tub, lined with linen to prevent splinters.

"Confiscated, I imagine," she says dryly. I'm uncertain if she's teasing me. The servants at the Company never would have dared.

In the bed, Saengo mumbles something in her sleep and rolls over. Her newly short hair sticks up along the side of her head. I frown, an echo of anger tightening in my chest.

In truth, I don't understand how we're both not dead. Once again, I'd done something with no earthly idea how or why. But it wouldn't have been necessary if Ronin's promise of safe passage had been guaranteed. That he'd ordered us into the woods, knowing we might die, sets fire in my gut. I suppose I ought to be grateful that he came for us, but my store of goodwill has never been very full.

As I prowl through the rest of the room, I catch sight of my reflection in the mirror. My feet freeze. This is the first time I've seen my eyes since I glimpsed them in the water.

Hesitant, I approach the mirror. I raise my hand, fingers skimming over my reflection. My irises are a brilliant amber, startling and strange but no longer alarming. My gaze shifts to my fingers. I'm struck by the memory of light and heat, awe and horror. The extraordinary awareness of an entire being compressed into a tiny, brilliant sphere of light. What *is* this power?

"Some water if you're thirsty," the woman says. I drop my hand, glancing at the pitcher on the table. "And there's food in the sitting room. I'll be back in a bit to help you wash."

As she leaves, I approach the glass balcony doors, framed by sheer curtains. The balcony is a fraction of the size of Kendara's. It looks out on the remains of a garden, within sight of two guards.

From my view, Spinner's End is smaller and less opulent than the Grand Palace. The architecture is lovely in its simplicity, the clean lines of each level accented by gracefully swooping roofs. Curiously, white patches cover sections that have decomposed, holding the castle together like bandages stretched over a wound. I hadn't noticed that last night.

At the very border of the grounds, the gauzy white curtain that Ronin had led us through drapes the trees, separating Spinner's End from the Dead Wood.

I'm on the second of four floors. Leaning over the rail, I memorize the arrangement of the roofs and mentally draft three different routes to the perimeter before I'm satisfied that my only true obstacle to an escape is the Dead Wood.

A cushioned sofa the color of pomegranate seeds furnishes one half of the adjoining sitting room. There's also a table laden with several steaming platters. My stomach grumbles, reminding me I've had very little to eat these last few days.

"Saengo, food!" I shout into the bedroom.

Nothing quite motivates her the way the promise of good food does. She won't admit it, but I know she misses the meals at Falcons Ridge. For me, the Company had been an improvement on the orphanage.

Without waiting for her reply, I sit before the table and serve myself a bit of everything. I pile my plate high with stuffed chicken smothered in a sweet and spicy peanut sauce, fat mushrooms and seared greens with slivered ginger, and sticky rice stained a brilliant purple.

Students at the Company only eat this well a few times a year, when we're allowed to attend Vos Talwyn's festivals and during every Company end-of-year celebration. During the latter, Saengo and I plant ourselves next to the refreshments and stuff our faces until our sashes feel like instruments of torture around our waists.

Saengo appears in the bedroom doorway. Her clothes are thoroughly wrinkled, and her hair defies all logic. She blinks blearily at the table. "Did I hear you say 'food'?"

I refrain from laughing and pat the seat beside me. "A lot of it. Just the way you like."

We're both on our second helping before the servant returns and introduces herself as our personal maid. The idea both intrigues and confuses me. I've never had a personal maid. I suspect she's meant to report everything we do back to Ronin.

Saengo only spares her a brief glance, but I give her closer scrutiny. Her eyes are brown. Human, then. Originally from Evewyn, I'd guess. She has the light skin tone and black hair of the northerners, like Saengo.

Although I'll never know my blood family, my appearance— tawny skin, black hair, the shape of my eyes, and the curve of my nose—indicates I have ancestors from both the northern and southern regions.

There'd been periods in ancient history when the borders stood open, allowing free movement across Thiy. But that was well before the Dead Wood and before the shaman emperors conquered much of the continent to form the Nuvalyn Empire. With so much animosity between the kingdoms now, it's difficult to imagine how such a time ever existed.

Before the attack, I'd never even seen a Nuvali shaman, much less glimpsed the Empire. But the stories I've read and the tales I've picked up paint a strange picture—a land where the sun holds dominion, where magic lingers thick as dust in the air, and where the power of the shamans runs through the earth like veins, the very lifeblood of the Nuvalyn Empire.

The servant announces that Ronin will see us both, but separately. My stomach dips, making me wish I'd eaten less. Saengo gives me a small smile, but I can read her nervousness even without the connection between us.

I allow the servant to usher me away from the table to bathe. I've just finished changing when there's a knock at the door.

"That'll be your escort," says the maid. She rushes out into the sitting room to answer the door. I take *escort* to mean *guard*.

I'm proven correct when two soldiers await me in the hall: one, an older woman with the gem-colored eyes of an earthwender. The other is a human man with heavy brows and a thin mustache framing his mouth. The human man stays behind to guard Saengo, but the earthwender gives me a curt command to follow her.

She guides me through long hallways with floor-length windows and past columns inlaid with chips of crystal. I take in what I can of the castle and its layout. Closed courtyards with marble pools, long dried, whisper of a former grandeur. Given the castle's age, it's in remarkable condition. White patches speckle the stone, especially glaring against the more vibrantly patterned walls. As we round a corner, I peer closer.

Webbing. I realize it with a start. Whoever's castle this had once been, Ronin restored the ruins splendidly. Holes in ceilings and floors and crumbling walls have been filled by raw webbing—thick, fibrous, and remarkably strong. Maybe Ronin really did bring Spinners with him from the north. How else could this have been accomplished?

My guard stops outside large iron doors that stand open. Inside is a vast chamber that must have once been a throne room. A boy sweeps in the corner, the rasp of his broom's bristles the only sound aside from our footsteps. Glowing braziers hang at either side of the aisle, pungent incense curling around the broad metal bowls and their golden chains. A magnificent set of stairs leads up to a long dais where a throne would have once sat. It's empty now; the wall behind it that would have born the royal crest has been replaced by an enormous hearth.

Ronin stands from his seat at the center of a long table set before the dais. The sound of sweeping stops as the boy quietly takes his leave. I force my steps to remain even, to not stall. Unlike last night, I have all my wits about me this time.

The guard who escorted me drops her head in a quick, polite bow. Evewyn is ruled by customs and tradition, but Kendara never prepared me for what to do when faced with the Spider King. I err on the side of caution and greet him as I would a reiwyn lord, bowing deeply.

Ronin dismisses the guard, leaving us alone.

He gestures wordlessly to the chair across from him as he lowers back into his seat. He sits in an oversize, ornate thing. It's upholstered in black spidersilk with the wooden back carved into vines and broad leaves brushed in gold. The chair dwarfs every other seat in the throne room. Although he does not sit on the dais, neither does he pretend to be the equal of those who share his table.

I pull out a simple wooden chair and drop stiffly into it, looking only at his chin. He has a narrow face, lean cheeks, and an angular jaw. He's tall and broad-shouldered, with short hair the color of charred wood and a sturdy build that tells me he's as much soldier as diplomat.

"You seem recovered." His voice is quiet but deep, and his Evewal is flawless.

I mentally cringe and try not to feel mortified that the last time he'd seen me, I'd been stumbling after him like a drunkard. "Yes, my lord. I'm . . . sorry about that."

"You may look me in the eye. I do not hold to Evewyn's conventions."

Hesitant, I lift my gaze to meet his. Sapphire. A waterwender.

He folds his pale hands on the tabletop. His fingers are long with knobby joints. "I regret the difficulty you encountered getting here."

I'll bet you do. "You promised us safe passage."

When his lips compress the tiniest bit, I wonder if I've made a misstep. A knot forms in my stomach. Insulting the Spider King would be a grave mistake.

His lips relax, and one corner of his mouth curves up. It's wholly unnerving to have the full attention of a man whose name is only ever uttered in reverence or fear.

"I wanted to know if you could do it."

I frown, a spark of anger releasing my tongue. "You *let* the trees attack us? Because you wanted to see if we'd survive?"

"But you did."

He hadn't lost control over the Dead Wood. He'd allowed it to nearly kill us. My hands curl into fists beneath the table, but I relax my face so that I don't betray my anger. With Ronin, I must tread even more carefully than I had at the Company.

"So we did," I say evenly.

On the table between us, a silver tray holds a porcelain tea set. The teapot steams faintly. I don't lean back like I want to when he lifts one pale hand. But nothing happens except a door swinging open to our right. A servant hurries across the polished floor, pausing only to bow deeply to Ronin, before reaching for the teapot. He pours us each a cup, then bows again and scurries out as quickly and silently as he entered.

Ronin spends the entire time scrutinizing me. I give him as little as possible. The tea smells sweet with a dash of warm spices, but I make no move to drink it. I worry that my hand will shake.

"Tell me what happened the night before yesterday." He speaks with a poise that I recognize in many of the lords who've passed through Vos Talwyn. Yet his fingers that rest on the rim of his saucer are those of a soldier's, dry and roughened by work.

My anger with his manipulation aside, we still need his help. So I tell him about how unusual it had been for three Nuvali shamans to attack a teahouse in Evewyn. With hesitance, I force myself to also tell him about how Saengo had died.

"But I did something to her, and when I woke up again, she was alive with only an old scar to show for it." Saying it out loud for the first time makes my chest constrict.

He listens without comment, his expression one of keen interest. When I finish, he looks down at his untouched tea, contemplative. I rotate the talisman around my wrist, trying to find answers in the angles of his face. Even though he gave me permission to meet his eyes, doing so still feels insolent.

"Light magic is unique," he finally says. "All lightwenders possess the singular ability to touch the source of a person's magic. That is, his soul. But such an ability can come with a cost, which is why you were out of sorts last night."

I wince, but he continues.

"The awakening of your craft rippled across Thiy. It unsettled the spirits of the Dead Wood as well as many shamans and shadowblessed who are sensitive to the spirits. Within the Calling of Light, only one craft would be able to resonate that way with others. I knew immediately what you are, as did every lightwender and shadowblessed who felt your craft awaken."

My throat has gone dry. I lift the teacup and take a scalding sip. "Which is what?" I croak.

"Have you ever heard of a soulguide?"

"I might have seen it in a book once," I say, but I don't know its significance.

"A soulguide is a lightwender who can shepherd souls, guiding them either into the afterlife or back to the living. Or so the stories say. Only one soulguide has existed in the long history of the shamans. Sury lived long before Evewyn was even conceived as an idea. She founded what would become the capital of the Nuvalyn Empire, the shaman city of Mirrim."

I'm grateful I'm sitting because my legs feel weak. In the last few seconds, the throne room seems to have risen in temperature. My head swims. How could such a thing be possible? And yet, I had clutched Saengo's lifeless body, and the very next day, I had touched my hand to her beating chest.

"Is that what I did to Saengo? I restored her to life?"

"In a manner of speaking, although it wasn't a demonstration of your specific craft, not like what you did in the Dead Wood. What you describe sounds more like you made her into your familiar."

NINE

"Into my . . ." I think about the healer from the Valley of Cranes, her magic trapped within her without a familiar as a conduit. That Saengo could be my familiar hadn't even occurred to me. "I'm sorry, but I don't quite understand."

"Shamans cannot access their magic without a familiar, almost always an animal spirit. Being the remnants of souls, they're able to resonate with our living ones. Think of it like a song only souls can hear. The bond is an exchange. The familiar becomes the shaman's conduit for her magic, and that same magic allows the familiar to regain physical form."

And to become vulnerable to attack and disease. A smart enemy would target the familiar and render the shaman powerless.

"Normally, a medium is required to bond a shaman with a familiar. Mediums can see and speak to spirits. But occasionally, in situations of high stress, your magic can be unlocked by reaching for the nearest available spirit."

"High stress," I echo faintly. My pulse races. Confusion and disbelief war within me. Can this really be the meaning of our connection?

The light of Saengo's candle burns strong from behind my mental window. I resolve to keep it shut. Her emotions should remain her own.

"But she's human."

"Exactly." Although his voice is quiet, the word and all its implications spear through me. "No human familiar has ever before been recorded."

"Then how can you be sure?"

"You wouldn't have been able to perform magic last night without a familiar. It is the simplest explanation, and yet, not simple at all. It is unprecedented."

"Will she be okay? Is she . . . did I hurt her?" My chest aches with the possibility.

"She will be tied to you and your magic so long as the bond remains."

By racing after Jonyah that day, I'd upended both our futures. I rub my fingers, warm from the tea, over my temples. "This is . . . a lot."

"I can imagine." He stands.

I stiffen, but he only climbs the steps up to the dais and the enormous fireplace there. His clothes are simple but finely made, a floor-length black jacket with gray accents over a matching shirt and pants. He wears a gray sash knotted at his back and a second sash, embroidered with his sigil in black, knotted at the front. A sword is belted at his hip, the scabbard and hilt plain enough to indicate its presence isn't mere decoration.

His ears are unusual. The tips taper up into a noticeable point. Frowning, my hand wanders to my own ears. I don't recall if the healer from the Valley or the shamans from the teahouse had such a distinguishable feature. But then again, the healer's ears had been hidden behind tangles of hair, and I'd been too busy trying not to get killed by the other shamans.

"Many stories about soulguides, often altered at the will of those telling them, have been passed down from the time of Sury. That one should, at last, again appear can only be taken as an omen."

What kind of omen? I hesitate to say it out loud. Most stories are simply that—stories. Tales to inspire awe and nostalgia for the heroes of old, that such heroes might one day rise again.

A draft from somewhere in the large room rustles the hem of Ronin's robe and breathes life into the dying embers in the fireplace. With his dark hair and plain features, it's easy to imagine that I would have passed him by in Vos Talwyn, brushing him off as just another visiting lord or even a high-ranking soldier.

But that would be untrue. Something about him draws the gaze, demanding acknowledgment of his presence. He commands attention without speaking a single word.

He steps away from the fireplace and descends the dais. "There are some who will see your presence as a threat. The limitations of shamanic crafts begin to bend when shamans achieve a certain level of power. In the past, some continued to push until those limitations broke. Or until they did."

"Like you?" Apparently, I have a death wish. My breaths quicken, and I wonder if it's not too late to make a run for it. I don't know what possessed me to say that, except that Ronin must have pushed against the limitations of his magic—and broken them—when he sought to defeat the Soulless and tame the Dead Wood.

He rests his hands against the edge of the table and leans forward. I stare hard at the tabletop, regretting my brash words.

He speaks softly. "Yes. Like me."

At this, I look up. The sapphire of his irises and the black of his pupils seem to fracture, splintering into the many-eyed gaze of a spider.

The hairs on the back of my neck stand on end, and I stop breathing. Chills skitter across my skin like hundreds of tiny legs. I tear my eyes away, but fear spreads through me like venom.

He reaches for his neglected teacup and takes a languid sip as I try to recover the use of my lungs. The silence grows taut until he finally says, "The Dead Wood is growing."

I imagine the branches breaking through the ceiling, wooden beams crashing on our heads as roots erupt from the floors. The trees would rip Spinner's End apart.

"I've been able to slow its progress, but it's no longer enough. This is a problem for which there is no solution, not even from the vast knowledge of the Nuvali. The trees cannot be harmed by magic lesser than what created them. They can be cut, but even their severed branches can cause harm. They do not rest. They do not burn."

Every attempt to destroy the woods has failed, and yet I did something to them. The roots and the branches disintegrated. They *can* be stopped. But I'd rather crawl into a nest of wyverns than voluntarily step foot back inside that forest.

"There must be something else you can try," I say. "You're . . . Ronin the Spider King."

"I have never called myself a king. That title was not of my own design. Still, there can be power in names. What will people say of soulguides a year from now? Or a decade? A century? You freed the souls trapped in those trees, and you must do it again."

Before I can think better of it, my gaze shoots up to meet his. Thankfully, his eyes look normal again. "Me? I . . . but—" I pause to gather my thoughts. "Why are the trees growing at all? What's keeping the spirits tied to the Dead Wood?"

"It doesn't matter why." I think he's patronizing me. It's hard to tell, though.

"Of course it matters. Wouldn't it be better to figure out the true cause? Then you could just undo it."

There was a boy at the orphanage who spent several hours every evening before bed screaming in terror because he was afraid of the dark. The monks tried all manner of things to calm him—teas, then bribes, and then threats and punishments. At last, someone discovered that a year earlier, the boy's mother had led him into the night and abandoned him to the dark. The other children were able to find more tailored solutions to his fear.

Culling the Dead Wood would be addressing the symptom of a deeper problem. In order to truly understand how to control the woods, one has to know what lies at its roots.

I begin to tell Ronin this, but he interrupts me. "If only the solution were that simple. For now, what matters is that you can stop it. You're a soulguide. This cannot be taken lightly."

"But I don't know the first thing about my craft. I couldn't—"

"The growing trees threaten the kingdoms, but as a dividing force, it is also the best means to maintain peace. In order to remain effective, the Dead Wood must be brought under control. There is no other option."

Even knowing of the tension in the north between Evewynians and Nuvali, I'd scoffed at the idea of war, certain that Ronin would never allow it. But if he believes the Dead Wood is the only means of preventing war, then the kingdoms of Thiy exist in a far more tenuous peace than I believed.

This must be the real purpose of his summons, not to discuss the attack but to assign me this daunting responsibility. Even though I understand his reasons, anger hardens within me. By forcing me to come here, to this place that is merely a more opulent prison than the Valley of Cranes, I have no choice but to obey his command.

Still, I came here with my own purpose, too. I need to know why the shamans attacked us. But if what Ronin says is true, and I'm the first soulguide to appear since Mirrim was founded, then proving my usefulness against the trees could convince the queen I'm an ally. It might even earn me back my place beside Kendara.

"You're right. The Dead Wood needs to be controlled. However, there's something I need as well."

Ronin's eyebrow slowly raises. I wonder what he'd do if I told him no. It's probably not a word he hears often.

"Are you bargaining with me?"

"Yes."

Although his expression remains neutral, I have the impression he's amused. "What is it you need?"

"That attack at the teahouse. One shaman got away. First, I need him caught. Then I need to know who sent them and why."

One corner of his mouth twitches upward into the barest of smiles. "Your queen readies for war. She has sent falcons, demanding answers, to Mirrim. She will not easily forgive this attack. Her accusations have angered the Yalaengs, who already mistrust her for her treatment of the shamanborn."

The Yalaengs are the Nuvalyn Empire's imperial family. "Why would they care about the shamanborn?"

"They don't," he assures me. "The shamanborn are not Nuvali, and the Empire will not rise to protect them. But the Empire takes offense at her hatred of the shaman race. Evewynian shamanborn or Nuvali, they are all shamans."

"But if Queen Meilyr is truly ready to go to war with the Empire over this, then all the more reason to seek out the truth."

"I've managed to placate both sides for the time being. We will meet in two weeks' time at my northern holding to discuss a diplomatic solution. Therefore, I agree to your terms. As you say, I must know the truth of the attack."

I'm so overwhelmed by his agreement that I'm momentarily at a loss. When I collect myself, I ask, "And the shaman who escaped?"

"I've already sent my own soldiers to assist in the search. In the meantime, you must begin learning to summon your craft immediately."

"I'm afraid I don't know where to start," I admit. "I don't know anything about, um, summoning my craft."

He sets his teacup on the saucer, gently enough that it doesn't make a sound. Then he rests his fingers on the tabletop. From beneath the table's edge, a white spider crawls out. It climbs onto his finger, long legs moving over his knuckles to rest on the back of his hand. I watch it, half afraid it'll leap across the table and land in my lap.

"You are inexperienced and untrained. We cannot possibly evaluate your capabilities until you learn to use your craft." He leans over to peer more closely at the spider perched between his knuckles. The angle makes his ears more pronounced. "Would you measure the capacity of a swordsman by their first fumbling duel?"

The first time I tried to wield the dual swords, I nearly cut off my own foot. The other students had laughed. Jonyah, whom I'd only just met, declared that a talentless orphan without a proper upbringing couldn't be taught.

"No. I would not."

"Your powers are a question that must be addressed. *Much* relies on the answer."

The spider crawls over and down his wrist before disappearing beneath his sleeve. He makes no move to dislodge it.

Before I can respond, he turns, striding the length of the table. "I have arranged for you to meet with one of my guests—a Kazan Hlau. Shamans learn to summon their magic by dueling with their elemental opposite. This normally can't be done for lightwenders, since your natural opposite is shadow, which isn't a shamanic craft. But the Hlau has agreed to try and invoke your magic. This is a rare opportunity."

"Invoke . . . what?" I shove to my feet. He's already halfway to the door, apparently finished with me. "Wait!"

To my surprise, he does. He stops and turns, looking infuriatingly patient. "As I said, you disturbed the Dead Wood and all those sensitive to the spirits when you awakened your craft. As you can imagine, this did not go unnoticed by Thiy's leaders. The falcons have been arriving in casts. Leaders and heads of Houses from all over the kingdoms have already begun journeying to my northern holding to seek my counsel. In addition to the peace talks between Evewyn and the Empire, I hope to present them with a solution for the threat of the Dead Wood. We have a deal, Sirscha Ashwyn. You have two weeks."

TEN

Out in the hall, my guard awaits me. She's dressed in the same gray sash and leather armor as the soldiers from Sab Hlee.

Although the prospect of meeting this Kazan Hlau, the equivalent of a prince, intrigues me, it's hard to focus on any single thing after everything I've learned. Mostly I just want to speak with Saengo.

I follow my guard, assuming she's delivering me back to my room. But the corridors remain unfamiliar. "Where are you taking me?"

Without looking at me, she says, "To meet the Kazan Hlau."

I pause before a mezzanine that overlooks the front of the castle. There's a courtyard, some miscellaneous buildings, and a handful of soldiers and staff going about their business. For a castle of this size, I've seen hardly anyone.

Beyond the courtyard, there again is that gauzy white curtain stretching from tree to tree, somehow keeping the Dead Wood at bay. And trapping us all inside.

"I need to go back to my room."

The guard gives me an annoyed look. "The Hlau is expecting you. Lord Ronin gave me specific orders."

It irritates me that he'd arranged all this before even speaking to me. "Well, then where is your Lord Ronin so that he can un-order you?"

Her lips pinch. Those vivid green eyes flash with derision. I'm well familiar with the look. "He is meeting with the other girl, the human you arrived with, in his study."

My stomach drops at this news. Saengo should hear what I did to her from my own lips. I can only hope Ronin will consider that. Guilt and worry rush through me, bunching the muscles in my shoulders and back.

I linger at the balcony, my fingers tightening against the cold stone. For the first time, I consider abandoning everything—culling the Dead Wood, regaining my place in Evewyn, stalling war between the kingdoms. Spinner's End is close enough to the eastern edge of the Dead Wood that it wouldn't take long to reach the Nuvalyn Empire. If, by some miracle, Saengo and I managed to escape without being maimed, we could find our way to the coast and board the first ship away from Thiy.

And then what? We would be free, but at what cost? I could never ask Saengo to leave behind her family and home for me. Besides, Evewyn is my home, too, one of the few things I've ever been able to lay claim to. I've always been prepared to defend it.

Fleeing could never be an option for either of us. If Saengo is now tied to my magic, then I have to make sure we still have a home in Evewyn. I'll have to meet this Kazan Hlau and learn how to use my craft against the trees.

The shamanborn probably studied under mentors who shared their craft, but there's no one like that for me. How do I learn a craft that no one knows anything about? And how do I do it in *two weeks?* My failure with Kendara is still a fresh reminder that I am only a girl with no true name, and I have never once lived up to anyone's expectations, except in disappointment.

"Give me a moment," I say to my guard. My nails scrape against the stone as I turn away from the balcony, heading for the stairs that will take me down into the courtyard.

There's a rudimentary palisade up ahead, little more than misshapen posts running the perimeter of the castle grounds. I hadn't noticed it when we arrived. An open gate leads to the white drapery that shuts out the trees. On closer inspection, the gauzy material is exactly what I suspected: more webbing. It circles the entire castle.

Spinner's End resides within an enormous spider's nest.

I dance my fingers over one of the white posts that form the palisade and then pause. The material is neither stone nor wood, but it's quite smooth. Leaning closer, I rub my thumb along the side of the post. A faint vein-like texture ambles across the surface, bearing a striking resemblance to the talisman around my wrist.

They're troll bones, I realize, taken aback. I finger the talisman, more curious than ever how Kendara came by it. Drawing a deep breath, I nod at the guard glowering at me.

She leads me back inside and then down several corridors and a set of stairs. At last, we stop at an open set of double doors with ornate silver knobs.

I suck in my breath, pausing at the threshold. Shelves jammed with books cover the walls from floor to ceiling. More shelves run parallel through the considerable length of the room. A single traceried window rises the height of the left wall, its shadow casting complex patterns against the hexagonal floor tiles. The ceiling soars above us, what isn't patched in white revealing a faded map of ancient Thiy.

"He's usually that way," my shaman guard says. The corners of her mouth turn downward as she nods at the middle aisle, braced by lanterns. Then she retreats to the door. "If you need me, I'll be outside."

I plunge down the center of the library. All manner of tomes line the shelves, from books bound in leather, cloth, and wood to scrolls of parchment, papyrus, and vellum. This library must be a dozen times the size of the throne room.

The shelves aren't as fastidiously clean as the occupied parts of the castle, but they look routinely dusted. The scholar in me rejoices at so much knowledge kept safe. Some of these books must predate Ronin's arrival here.

The lanterns are lit farther apart the deeper I delve, and the shadows grow darker. I wonder if I've been misled when I spot a square table and two chairs occupying a small space between shelves. A lantern rests at the table's center, the golden glow illuminating a man sitting with a stack of books.

My feet haven't made a sound against the faded tiles, so he hasn't noticed my approach. The fine silk of the jacket draped over the back of his chair indicates he must be the Kazan Hlau, a fact further proven by the style of his clothing. He wears a black tunic, embellished with turquoise embroidery that adorns the collar before racing down the front in two ornate stripes. The detailing repeats around the cuffs of his sleeves. A broad strip of turquoise cloth circles a trim waist, knotted at the front and overlaid with a beautiful belt of interlocking silver links.

His hair is the perfect white of fresh snow. I assumed he was an old man, but I recall the shadowblessed in Ronin's camp. They all possess the same brilliantly white hair.

I lightly clear my throat.

His head snaps up. As I suspected, his face is young, and his skin is a solid gray. He can't be more than a few years older than I am. A silver circlet with pure white stones rests across his brow.

"Rather rude to sneak up on a person," he says in Evewal, closing his book. His voice is low and clipped.

"I'm sorry. I didn't mean to startle you," I say.

He turns in his seat to face me. "You must be the lightwender shaman."

"My name is Sirscha."

His mouth curves, but the smile doesn't reach his eyes. "Everyone has been buzzing about you."

"Oh?" I say, wondering if it's appropriate to show too much interest. "And what are they saying?"

"That you're either the Soul of Thiy or the Ruin of the West."

I stare a moment and then let out a short burst of laughter. *"Ruin?"*

"Not everyone stands to benefit from what you can do." He looks me over, and the way his lips compress and one eyebrow lifts tells me well enough what he thinks.

Ass. I lift my head, meeting his eyes and abandoning my attempt at deference. "How would you know what I can do?"

I am not beholden to this prince. No one will chain me to the stocks or force me to haul barrels up and down the tower for a misplaced look or speaking out of turn. I've not yet been able to shed myself of habits ingrained into me by the Company, but as long as I'm here, I won't stand for humiliation or ridicule. Although I yearn for the life I'd lost mere days ago, I hope never again to be made small to appease someone else's ego.

"Because I know what a soulguide can do," he says.

Such knowledge is probably why he agreed to help me in the first place. "Do you mean to introduce yourself, or will I have to guess your name?"

He stands. Although not nearly Ronin's height, he's still very tall. With the lantern at his back, shadows steal across his face as he bows. "Hlau Theyen Yee of Penumbria, seat of the Fireborn Queens."

Penumbria is one of the largest mountain cities in Kaza-hyn, its exact location unknown to outsiders. The Kazan don't acknowledge a single monarch. Instead, each clan has its own leader and customs. One of the oldest and most powerful among them are the Fireborn Queens, a matriarchal clan. What reason would a Hlau of Penumbria have to be here?

He takes his seat again and flicks his hand at the chair opposite his. "Sit, if you must." When I don't move, he adds, "Or stand there and gawk. The view must be far more magnificent than what you're used to."

My brows twitch together. I'd prefer to leave, but we haven't yet spoken about my magic, and he might know more about the gossip beyond Spinner's End.

I sit. "They're not really calling me those things, are they?"

When he answers, he keeps one finger slowly moving across his page as if still reading. "They are, although I doubt any know what they're talking about. Most who might have heard the word *soulguide* would have acquired the knowledge through superstitions and folk stories. Next thing you know, they'll be claiming to have seen you take flight and disappear into the sun."

I look up at the ceiling draped in shadows. "If only I could."

"Yes, you're utterly ordinary after all."

"I understand now why my guard didn't want to join me. You're insufferable."

He finally looks at me, his expression bored. "So I've been told."

That's not at all the reaction I was expecting. Annoyed, I reach for the top book in his stack. "Ronin says you agreed to invoke my magic."

"I did. Do you even know what that means?"

I reluctantly shake my head.

"You don't know a thing about magic, do you? Typical Evewynian ignorance. But I suppose you can't be blamed for the faults of your upbringing."

I narrow my eyes, uncertain if he's insulting me or Evewyn. Probably both. "And I suppose you know all about the Callings of Magic."

"Of course. I'd wager you didn't even know you were a shaman until . . . well, until everyone else learned as well."

"I had no reason to suspect."

"No?" he asks archly. "What about your ears? The tops are shaped a bit funny, and they're edged in a pale scar, like they were cut when you were a baby."

I frown as I reach up to trace my finger along the top curve of my right earlobe, feeling the faint line of the scar. "How—"

"I have excellent eyesight."

No one has *ever* noticed the scars before. In fact, I've never even *told* anyone about them, not even Saengo. That someone mutilated my ears as a baby isn't exactly something you just bring up in a conversation. His vision must be exceptional, indeed, to pick out such a fine detail in the library's dim light.

"I couldn't have known about shaman ears," I say. The shamanborn were imprisoned right before I left the orphanage. On the rare occasion I'd been allowed to accompany the monks into town, I'd been too taken by their eyes to notice their ears. "I didn't really have the opportunity to interact with the shamanborn before they were imprisoned."

I've always wondered at the scars, though—if my mother was the cause and why anyone would do such a thing to a child.

He looks down his nose at me. "As I said. Typical Evewynian ignorance. *Both* races of magic possess a slight point to their ears. It's actually not very noticeable. It's only in highborn shamans and shadowblessed that the difference is dramatic enough to be noted. Like Ronin's." He sweeps back his white hair, tucking it behind his pointed ears. "Like mine."

Whoever abandoned me to the orphanage cut away the evidence of my heritage when I was a baby. They didn't want anyone to know I'm a shaman. They didn't want *me* to know.

A startling possibility occurs to me—what if my parents are in the Valley? The thought is alarming. If they are, I don't want to know. They gave me up when I was a child, and I returned the favor a long time ago.

"And your eyes," Theyen continues.

"Well, they're obvious *now*."

"What color were they prior to changing?"

"Gray."

His smile is patronizing. "All shamans are born with gray eyes."

I'd known that shamans weren't born with jewel-colored eyes, but I hadn't known they were all gray before changing. I rub my fingers over the raised lettering of the book cover in my hands. The signs were there all along. I just hadn't known what to look for. Hadn't known to look at all.

"It's a common-enough color in Evewyn," he says, flipping a page. "But for all those born of shamanic blood, they possess gray eyes until they obtain their first familiar. When the bond is formed, they awaken their magic and learn which Calling they've been gifted."

By which color their eyes turn. Nuvali customs aren't taught at the Company nor in *any* Evewynian school, I suspect. And after Evewyn's shamanborn were imprisoned at the Valley of Cranes, no one dared mention them beyond mumbled reiterations of the queen's hatred. Threat of retribution silenced those who remembered their shamanborn friends and relatives, but for everyone else? The ignorance bred fear.

The Scholars point to the Nuvalyn Empire as proof of the shamans' violent nature. The Empire's history is fraught with blood and death at their attempts to conquer the continent. But how much of what we've been taught is based in fact, and how much is the invention of a fearmonger's hatred?

He reaches for the book in my hands. "That one is outside your level of comprehension."

I move it out of his reach. The book's title is in Kazal, the letters embossed in gold. Beautiful metal rivets decorate the corners. Lifting my chin, I angle the book so that the candlelight illuminates the cover. I read in Kazal, *"Beasts of Earth and Wing: Twelfth Edition."*

Theyen's eyebrows rise. He runs his fingers, the color of pale ash, through his snowy hair. "You speak almost as well as a Kazan."

"I have an ear for languages." I return the book to its pile.

He makes a pensive sound and then lifts his own book, showing me the cover, which depicts a man wearing a crown so heavy that he stoops.

"*Myths and Legends of Thiy,*" I read. "History or fiction?"

"Bit of both. I just finished 'The Tale of the Woodcutter.' It's about a lowborn earthwender who, upon witnessing a grand procession through the forest, wishes he could instead be a king. And the gods, hearing his wish, grant him a crown and all that comes with it. But he wanted only the riches and the adoration, not the responsibilities of running a kingdom. Being ignorant in such things, his people fell to ruin and starvation."

"Pleasant," I say, but Theyen isn't finished.

"He begs the gods to reverse his wish and return him to his humble position as a woodcutter. But the gods refuse, proclaiming that he should live with the consequences of his greed. In defiance, he condemns every temple in his kingdom to fire. When the gods fail to respond, he then puts to death a hundred newborn babies. When even such a heinous act does not move the gods to reverse his wish, he orders a hundred shamans to consume their familiars so that they might claim the power of the gods for themselves. But such a monstrous act drives the shamans mad, and they overrun the castle, killing the king and all within it."

I lift one eyebrow. "I don't suppose that was a children's tale."

"It's a cautionary tale, actually," he says, watching my reaction, "about what happens to those who claim titles that they've not earned."

My fingers itch to punch that smug look off his face. How arrogant of him to believe he can wound me. It's the same arrogance I saw in the officits and every person who believed me their inferior.

I push to my feet. The chair scrapes loudly across the tiles. "Titles *should* be earned. As should respect, which makes it hilariously ironic coming from someone like you."

"Someone like me?" he echoes, mouth stretching into a smile.

"An ass," I clarify, striding away.

This was a waste of my time. But as long as I'm here, I might as well look up some reference books. In a library this size, there has to be something about the Dead Wood. Or soulguides. Or a practical guide to learning one's craft, hopefully with step-by-step instructions accompanied by illustrations.

Theyen stands, snatching up the lantern as he follows me down an aisle I pick at random. "You should learn how to speak to royalty before you insult the wrong royal. I've punished people for less."

Spinning on my heel to face him again, I dip into a mocking bow. My braid spills over my shoulder, nearly touching the floor. "Oh, forgive me. An extremely rude, self-important ass."

His lips quirk. "I can't tell if you're fearless or stupid for disrespecting a prince."

I allow him the same disdainful appraisal that he gave me. "You're not *my* prince."

"And yet you need my help."

"You're not the only shadowblessed in Spinner's End."

At least, I hope he isn't. "I'll find someone else to help me."

He looks amused and lifts the lantern higher for better illumination. "Are you looking for something specific or just enjoying the identical rows of shelves? Seeing as you're not familiar with the library's layout, it'll take you weeks to browse everything."

It irritates me that he's right. While perusing the books to my heart's content would be ideal, my priority is to learn as much as I can in the brief time Ronin has allotted me.

I look around the shadowy aisles, wondering if I should return in the morning with Saengo. My stomach dips as I wonder if she's returned to our room.

"History," I say reluctantly. "I think."

Theyen turns away, not even looking back to ensure I'm following. I entertain the idea of letting him saunter off on his own and seeing how long it takes for him to realize and double back. But I can't waste any more time. So I sigh and hurry after him.

We weave through the shelves, at last stopping before a row of old books and loosely bound manuscripts. "These are Scholar archives of various points in Thiy's history. You'll find them organized by kingdom."

"Thank you," I say slowly, suspicious of his helpfulness.

"Tomorrow morning." He hands me the lantern.

"What?"

"Before dawn. Shadowblessed are at their best in the dark."

"You still want to help me?" I ask, dubious.

"I don't see why not. Besides, Spinner's End is sorely lacking in people who can hold a conversation for more than two sentences."

"Maybe that's because they're in a hurry to rid themselves of your company." I pull a book titled *Early Evewyn and the Age of the Drake Queens* from the shelf and settle it into the crook of my elbow.

He sounds amused. "Must be how 'insufferable' I am."

"Must be," I echo lightly as I crouch to look at the lower shelves.

Without a word of farewell, he turns away. His footsteps are silent as he disappears into the dark.

Thank the Sisters. What an excruciatingly unpleasant man, and I've known many. At least he was of use. And although I'd like to pretend I've no intention of meeting him in the morning, it would be a lie. I'd be a fool to reject the opportunity.

Once I've acquired a few more books, I gather up the stack, balance the lantern on top, and make my way out. Fortunately, I don't run into Theyen again.

I find Saengo in the bedroom, standing before the glass balcony doors. She's dressed in the same simple shirt and loose pants as I am, and her ragged hair looks roughly brushed. The day's last light illuminates her silhouette against the darkening room. For the briefest of moments, the light appears almost to shine *through* her.

My gut clenches. I set the books on the desk and join her by the balcony. After a moment, I take her hand. Her skin is warm.

"Are you angry with me?" I ask quietly. I can easily find the answer for myself, but I resist the temptation to crack open that mental window between us. I still feel her there—I always feel her there—but the glow of her emotions is easier to ignore when it isn't so intense. If Saengo doesn't wish to share how she's feeling, then it's not for me to know.

A faint line forms between her brows. She lifts her other hand, extending it palm up to the sunlight. "I don't know. Ever since I woke up at the teahouse, I've felt . . . strange. Not unpleasant, just weird. Like I'm being held together with sunbeams, and I could dissolve at any moment. Like those souls in the Dead Wood."

The idea sends panic shooting through me. "What did Ronin tell you?"

"A number of things—what kind of lightwender you are and how shaman magic works. I thought maybe he was trying to put me at ease about you being shamanborn." She drags her fingertips against the glass door, watching shadows chase the light across her knuckles. "But the more he talked about familiars, the more I began to wonder."

Ronin didn't tell her, then. My stomach weaves itself into knots. "About that . . . I have to tell you . . . when I brought you back, I—"

The words stick in my throat, thick enough to choke. Saengo's fingers still against the glass.

She looks at me, her eyes dark and intense. "Am I your familiar?"

My heart races. I want to fall to my knees and beg her forgiveness. Instead, I force myself to hold her gaze and say, "Yes."

She draws a slow, deep breath. I squeeze her hand as she struggles to control the way her entire body trembles, just faintly. Her jaw clenches tight, as if the truth is a poison curled against the cage of her teeth, and the moment it reaches her tongue, she will forever hold its bitterness in her mouth.

"I'm sorry," I whisper, heart aching. "I didn't know."

She tries to smile, but it wilts as soon as it forms. "How could you have?"

Silence weaves between us. It feels fragile, held together by the threads of unraveled dreams.

When she speaks again, it's in a near whisper. "Ronin says a familiar can't be apart from their shaman for more than a few weeks. Anything more than that, and the familiar begins to fade. Not completely, not as long as the bond remains, but they . . . *I* will need to be near you to be real."

"You *are* real," I say fiercely. "You are Saengo Phang, heir to Falcons Ridge. And you're my best friend."

"He also says familiars don't age. How can I be any of those things when you'll continue to grow and change, and I . . ."

"Saengo." My voice breaks, but nothing I say or do can repair this. So I say nothing. I only hold her hand in both of mine, willing my strength into her.

"It could be worse," she says, although she doesn't sound like she believes it. "You are my sister, Sirscha. And now we're bound together." She reaches up and wipes from my cheek a tear I hadn't even felt. "Tell me what Ronin said to you? He alluded to a deal of some kind."

That's the last thing I want to talk about, but she's clearly finished speaking about her own somber situation now that she's gotten her answer. So I don't press her and instead relay the bargain I made with Ronin.

"This soulguide thing is probably just an old story. I'm not sure how much of it I believe. But what matters is that I prove I can help control the Dead Wood. It might be enough to convince the queen that I'm not an enemy so we can go home."

Saengo looks down. "How can I possibly go home?"

"We'll figure something out." I can't promise her that things will work out, not when everything feels so hopeless. But for her sake, I try to sound optimistic. I gesture to the books on the desk. "I'm hoping something in there will mention how the Dead Wood was created or tell me more about the first soulguide. Culling the trees only works if I know what I'm doing."

Saengo moves away from the balcony for a closer look at the books. Her hand slips from mine.

"*A Chronicle of the Yalaeng Conquest*," she murmurs, reading the first title.

The Yalaeng Conquest is how Scholars refer to the period in Thiy's history when the Nuvalyn Empire set out to expand its borders by conquering smaller neighboring kingdoms. It culminated in the rise of the Soulless, which effectively ended the conquest.

Before I learned exactly how the Soulless fit into Thiy's history, I knew him as a figure of nightmares. At the orphanage, the monks would warn of a shapeless shadow that swooped down from the night sky to swallow unruly children the way the Dead Wood swallowed its victims. In my head, he became the source of all evils in Evewyn's folktales. He was the one-eyed serpent who hissed from dark corners, or the winged crone with wooden hands that snatched you from your bed if he peered into your window and found you still awake.

It wasn't until I entered the Prince's Company and had more extensive history lessons that I learned the true origins of the Soulless. In some ways, his real story—or at least what the Scholars know of it—is more terrifying than the folktales.

"Do you think Kendara will take you back if the queen allows it?" she asks.

"She has to," I say, because I don't know what to do if she doesn't. I am meant to be Kendara's apprentice. I've worked toward that single goal for four years, and I'm damned good at it.

But something else I'm good at is surviving. I don't know how to be the soulguide Ronin wants, but if this is the path that will lead me back to Kendara, and Saengo back home, then I can adapt. As Kendara would want, I can play the part.

We take turns washing up in the bathing chamber, enjoying the novelty of having time to soak and enough hot water for us both. Our maid brings us a late meal of rice porridge and fish, and then she offers to assist us with readying for bed. I decline, but Saengo doesn't object or speak when she helps her change. I wonder if having a maid reminds her of her home at Falcons Ridge.

In the Company, we washed on a strict rotation with only a couple of buckets of water and a bar of soap. You *really* didn't want to be the last person in line. The last time I had a bath was a year ago—ten minutes in a hot spring to soothe fresh bruises.

Earlier that day, I'd trapped an enormous zaj serpent that lived along Evewyn's southern border where the Black River emptied into the sea. Kendara wanted me to retrieve a handful of its iridescent scales.

Zaj serpents are native to Kazahyn, but the Dead Wood's expansion stranded a colony of them in Evewyn a decade ago. I recall, with an echo of irritation, that Kendara wanted the scales for no other reason than to decorate new sheaths for her prized swords, Suryali and Nyia. As I tie the laces at the collar of my new nightgown, I wonder if Prince Meilek has told Kendara that the attack was meant for her, and if she's tried to find her own answers.

Would he also have told her what I am?

I perch at the edge of my bed and try out the words in my head: *I am a shaman.* I wince. They don't fit right. Too tight, constricting enough to make my breaths grow shallow. That's not who I am.

Saengo is already in her bed, so I slip into mine, tugging the thick blanket over my legs. The maid blows out the lantern on her way out, leaving the room in darkness. The half moon outside the balcony doesn't offer much light.

After a while, a sound disturbs the quiet—short, muffled gasps. Her anguish echoes in my chest like a fresh wound. Silently, I rise from my bed. I cross the room and lift the corner of Saengo's blanket so that I can slide in beside her. She's curled on her side, away from me, her face buried in her pillow. Her body trembles faintly.

My heart breaks, the pain a knife beneath my ribs. I don't speak, but I put my arm around her, letting the force of her quiet sobs rock against me.

Saengo has always been meant for so much more than the life of a soldier. She's supposed to travel and have adventures and claim her own fate. And then if she wants, she's supposed to fall in love and get married and become the Lady of Falcons Ridge. She's supposed to grow old, happy, and content after a life well lived.

I squeeze my eyes shut and turn my face into the pillow as I listen to her mourn all the things she's lost. All the things that I've taken from her.

ELEVEN

Hands in the dark. Bones with too many joints breaking through skin. Nails splinter and peel, clawing, clawing—

My eyes open. The drapes enclosing the bed shroud me in darkness.

I rub my forehead. Why does my sleeping mind torment me? My throat feels dry, and my tongue sticky. Careful not to disturb Saengo, who is burrowed into the blanket, I slap the drape aside so I can sit up. Maybe the dreams are related to what Ronin said about how my craft can resonate with spirits. Evidently, I disturbed those in the Dead Wood when I awakened it.

Are the spirits trapped there trying to ask for help? If so, they could stand to be less creepy about it.

The fire has burned down to a pile of embers, their slight glow the only light in the room. Too sleepy to bother with the lantern, I open the armoire and find the black pants and fitted shirt that

149

I requested from our maid last night.

I yawn as I dress. My body begs me to crawl back into the warm blankets. My chest feels heavy with the evening's unresolved matters, although the thought of Theyen standing in the dark courtyard, growing increasingly annoyed, briefly amuses me. But I made a bargain with Ronin and a promise to myself. So I braid back my hair and splash water on my face until I feel more alert.

When I leave my rooms, the dozing guard outside my door jolts awake. It's the shaman from yesterday. She yawns and returns my smile with a slight narrowing of her eyes. It's half-hearted, though, as if she's attempting to make peace with being assigned to me. Well, I'm not thrilled about her assignment, either.

She falls into step beside me as I say, "I never got your name. If we're to be stuck with each other, I should at least know what to call you."

The shaman glances at me. Her black hair is cut short to her chin, streaked with gray at her temples. Her eyes are vivid green, and her lips seem determined to form a thin, unhappy line.

"Phaut," she says grudgingly.

"How did you come to be in Ronin's service, Phaut?" Are his soldiers here by choice? Or were they sent to Ronin by their respective leaders through an agreement between the kingdoms?

Phaut stands a good head taller than me, which makes me eye level with her jawline. Age lines brace her mouth and crease the corners of her eyes. Her sword is strapped to her right hip. She must be left-handed.

"I swore an oath to Lord Ronin when I was young," she says in accented Evewal.

"That's not an answer."

The lines around her mouth deepen as she frowns. "I volunteered. As we all did."

Does that mean she's loyal to him? From what I've seen thus far, the staff seem happy here, which surprises me a little. But I suppose people make their homes wherever they will, so long as the choice is theirs. And sometimes even when it isn't.

"Are there shamanborn here as well?" I ask.

Her eyebrows come together in confusion. "Shamanborn?"

"In Evewyn, we call our shamans 'shamanborn.' Their abilities aren't any different, as far as I know. It's just a geographical distinction between Nuvali shamans and Evewynian shamanborn."

"Ah. Then I believe there are a few shamanborn among the staff, yes. Are there many in Evewyn?"

"Not compared to the humans." Queen Meilyr had been able to force them all into a single prison, after all. At least those she hadn't killed first. "How many people live in Spinner's End?"

She takes her time answering, turning my question over in her head. Likely searching for an ulterior motive. I could reassure her that I don't mean to escape, but it's more fun to watch her second-guess my words.

She finally says, "Just over two hundred."

I frown. Two hundred people, the majority of whom would be soldiers and staff, in a castle that might have once housed four times that. From the courtyard yesterday, I'd noticed that whole sections of the castle had been left untouched by Ronin's webbing, abandoned to time. They must have been either impossible to restore or unnecessary, given the castle's small population.

"Most of Lord Ronin's soldiers are spread out among his various properties and encampments," she explains. "There isn't much use for soldiers here at Spinner's End, when the Dead Wood is all that's needed to keep intruders out. And prisoners in."

I make a face at her, but she doesn't seem to care.

At this hour, with the halls bathed in shadows and the silence and stillness absolute—not even the scratching of mice within the walls—the castle feels truly abandoned. It's almost like I'm still caught in a dream. Any moment now, hands will reach from the dark to grasp at my ankles. I suppress a shiver at the memory of being yanked down into blackened earth.

Minutes later, I descend the stairs that lead out into the courtyard. Theyen is sitting on the bottom steps, already waiting. Two blazing torches tint his white hair with gold. He wears all black, a simple combination of dark pants and tunic with a modest sash.

He stands at my arrival. "You didn't bring a weapon."

I note the curved dagger tucked into his sash. "I assumed we'd be using magic."

"I should have known you'd need detailed instructions. Invoking your elemental opposite works best with increased danger."

He addresses my guard in Nuval. I assume he told her to fetch me a weapon because she turns back to the castle. Kendara promised to teach me the language of the shaman empire if I became her apprentice. I haven't yet lost hope that it could happen.

As Phaut's footsteps recede, he continues in Evewal, "You can fight without a weapon, I hope?"

"I guess you'll see," I say as I join him in the courtyard.

Rolling his shoulders, he says, "The way you move means you've had some training. But Evewynian soldiers aren't trained for true battle—"

My foot strikes his stomach. He staggers. I grin wickedly at the stupefaction on his face. But his surprise lasts only a moment before he retaliates.

I avoid his punch, skidding back into the stairs. Then I slide left, dodging another punch. I block a kick, then strike out with my elbow. Our forearms meet with a jarring *smack*. I duck beneath another kick and drop into a roll, dirt flying into my face as my braid slaps the ground.

Theyen is impressively fast. Not as fast as Kendara, but he's a talented fighter and a fierce opponent. I've barely blocked his attack before the next one comes. His foot hooks behind my knee, forcing my leg to fold as his elbow nearly slams into my temple. I block in time, his elbow meeting my palms. But I can't stop his knee from jabbing my gut. I fall back and use the momentum to roll onto my feet again.

He smiles shrewdly as he looks me over. "You're better than I expected. But I somehow doubt all Evewynian soldiers are so well trained."

"I somehow doubt you know as much about Evewyn as you think you do." We circle each other. Shadows shift over our forms as we move past the torchlight.

Something catches my foot. I jerk my leg to shake it loose, but it won't dislodge. I have to look down. The moment I do, he attacks. I block as an invisible force wraps around my ankle and drags my foot out from under me. I go down, but not before my free leg whips up and catches him in the back. He topples over my shoulder as I land on my bottom. My fingers grope for whatever's snagged my ankle.

There's nothing. I press my fingers directly over that definite weight, but my hands touch only the worn leather of my boot. The shadows lurch around my legs.

I gasp, flipping to my feet, feeling that hold loosen and break. Dancing back, my eyes track the moving shadows. Quick as snakes, they converge on my feet. I kick and twist, but the shadows twine around my legs, rooting me in place. My fingers dig into the shadows, trying to claw them off. I'm shocked when my nails catch an edge. Somehow, Theyen has given the shadows movement and substance.

Theyen attacks again, but without my legs, I can only block in quick succession before he catches first one wrist and then the other. Theyen's arms circle me as he secures my hands behind my back. We're almost chest to chest.

"Shadow magic," I say, struggling.

"Your natural opposite." He lowers his face a mere handspan from mine. "Now, come on, lightwender. Impress me."

I suck in my breath and slam my forehead into his. With a grunt of surprise, he releases me. My hands whip up, grab two fistfuls of his hair, and give a vicious yank. His head snaps back. Before he can recover, I smash my knuckles into his jaw. He stumbles away, and the shadows loosen enough for me to untangle my legs and put space between us.

"You fight dirty." He rubs his jaw. He doesn't sound upset about it.

"Only dead men fight fair. Now, tell me honestly. Do you think invoking my magic will make any difference against the Dead Wood?"

The question seems to surprise him, because his eyes narrow. "How do you expect to prevent war between the kingdoms if you don't even have the conviction to summon your craft?"

It annoys me that he knows what Ronin wants of me. But I suppose it's not difficult to work out if he's aware of what a soulguide can do. "Make all the assumptions you want about my conviction. *I* assume the only reason you agreed to this is because you want Ronin's favor. You need something from him."

Footsteps rush down the castle stairs. Phaut pauses near the bottom, taking in the shadows writhing at Theyen's feet. She unsheathes my swords for me.

I extend my hands, and she tosses my weapons. I catch them both by the hilt. Brandishing my swords, I lower my center of gravity into the first stance of the Wyvern's Dance.

"You're not wrong," Theyen says. "Our motives aren't so different."

Shadows circle me again. Sharp steel slices through the shadow snakes, which snap like stretched leather. Theyen draws his own dagger and charges. He's even faster with his blade.

"I find that hard to believe," I say. Metal screeches against metal as I fend him off with one sword and the shadows with the other. They swarm around me, no longer merely snakes lying in wait.

Shadowy forms rise from the earth. They don't waver like flimsy, weak things. They're solid and sturdy, faceless bodies of black and nothingness. My sword arms tremble as I cut through them.

The creatures are unnerving. The warmth of magic ignites inside me as the predawn sky begins to chase away the night. Theyen slashes at my head, the tip of his dagger narrowly missing my cheek. He attacks hard, fast, and unrelentingly. His shadows continue to merge and multiply, moving in perfect balance to his strikes. Black fingers slither around my arms before my blade slices them away.

"If you knew anything about the politics between Kazahyn and the Nuvalyn Empire, then you would know that I'm engaged to the Ember Princess."

This surprises me enough that I nearly miss blocking his next attack. He's deliberately trying to distract me.

"The Ember Princess?" I echo, dubious. My magic is a hot stone in my chest, but I don't know how to push that magic outward.

"Surely even *you've* heard of her. Sister and future advisor to the Sun's Heir. Soon to be the second-most powerful shaman in Thiy once her brother takes the Radiant Throne. Et cetera, et cetera. They have a ridiculous number of titles."

I'm tempted to point out his lengthy introduction in the

library yesterday, but I valiantly refrain. My focus remains only on not letting him gain the upper hand. His shadows block me in, driving me backward until my heels bump the stone rail that braces the stairs.

"So," I say, grunting as my back hits the stone. "If you're already engaged to a Nuvali princess, then why would you need Ronin's help in keeping the peace between your kingdoms? Unless you want help getting *out* of the engagement?"

Theyen smirks and cuts upward. I slam my swords together, metal singing as the blades catch and lock around his dagger. The stone rail digs into my lower back, but I use the leverage to shift my weight and drive my knee into his gut. His grip slackens. I shove him away, plant one foot on his stomach, and flip backward onto the rail. My other foot smashes into his jaw, knocking him to the ground.

I'm on top of him before he can regain his feet. I stab both blades into the earth at either side of his neck, pinning him. A feral smile pulls at my lips. I know I've won as I straighten, backing off him even before his shadows leap between us.

"Am I right?" I ask, because I want to hear him concede.

He doesn't reply. He reaches up, grabs my swords, and gingerly tugs them free. Tossing them at my feet, he stands but doesn't attack again. We're both still, breathing hard. His shadows fade and dissipate, scattering like wisps of smoke.

He looks to where the emerging sunlight slowly edges away the darkness and then lowers his gaze to mine. "So much for your conviction."

In truth, the words sting because he's right—I didn't try hard enough to summon my craft. This match may have ended with my swords at his neck, but I didn't win. Not the way I should have. My shoulders tense with annoyance.

Outwardly, though, I roll my eyes. "We could try again." A single fight can't be indicative of much, can it?

Apparently, it can. Theyen shakes his head and sheathes his dagger. "You've been trained to rely entirely on your physical skills, something you can't easily unlearn. I suspect for this to work, you need to believe you're in genuine danger."

I snort and throw back my head. "It certainly felt like I was in genuine danger." Despite the physical activity, the failure makes me restless. What would it take to summon my craft if a dagger aimed at my face isn't enough? "What you did with the shadows—can most shadowblessed do that?"

"No. The Calling of Shadow isn't limited to only three variations of ability like shamanic crafts are. There are many different crafts the shadowblessed possess."

"Like giving life to shadows." I retrieve my swords from the ground, wiping dirt off the blades before sheathing them again.

"An imitation of life."

"Well, don't feel bad, Hlau Theyen. It's been years since anyone aside from my swordmaster has defeated me in a fight."

When I first entered the Prince's Company at eleven years old, I was a scrap of a girl, too skinny to lift a proper sword, which was why I chose the dual swords instead—two lighter, shorter blades that allowed for more fluid motion in combat. And despite that initial near-disaster, as training progressed, it became quickly apparent that I had an affinity for swordplay, which is why Kendara took notice of me.

"Perhaps you need stronger provocation, then," he says.

"Bold words for someone who ended this duel on his back. Were this a real fight, you would no longer have a head."

He crosses his arms. Dirt clings to his shoulders and hair. "I have many years left of studying the sword before I can call myself a master. Only a fool overestimates their own ability."

"I recall you saying something about not being trained for *real* battle?"

"You're good. Your swordmaster no doubt claimed you're a natural."

She didn't. In fact, she told me I'm overconfident and a show-off. Sisters, I miss her.

"But once you've truly seen death—"

I'm already annoyed that I didn't invoke my craft, and his condescension unleashes my anger. Before he's finished the word *death*, I've released my sword from its sheath and nudged the tip beneath his chin. He goes still but otherwise doesn't react.

"Don't speak as if you know me." Satisfaction rushes through me at the thrill of having someone with Theyen's power at my mercy. It's not something I've ever before thought possible. For a moment, I understand how Ronin might feel with his influence over three powerful kingdoms, and why he would want to hold onto it.

"Watch yourself, shaman. I am a Fireborn Hlau." Theyen

speaks softly but coolly. Now that the sun has begun to rise, his eyes are visible. They're a vibrant shade of coral blue, rimmed in lavender, a bright contrast to his white hair and gray skin but just as cold.

"What does that matter to me? Do you think imprisoning his soulguide will win you Ronin's favor?"

His gaze doesn't waver. "If you think Ronin can protect you from me, you're mistaken. Put away your ego and do your job. What do you think threatening royalty will gain you, other than a brief moment of satisfaction over your failure to summon your craft?"

My sword arm wavers. Anger vibrates through me. I sheathe my sword again in one smooth motion and turn away for the stairs. "We're done here."

TWELVE

Saengo and I spend the rest of the day combing through the library for books that might mention anything about soulguides. Or, failing that, the fall of the Soulless and the rise of the Dead Wood.

We sit on the hard floor, propped against the shelves, with books piled around us. It feels a little like we're back at the Company, studying for our next exam. I roll my shoulders to relieve the ache there and notice Saengo lifting a hand to her chest for at least the dozenth time today.

"Are you okay?" I gesture at the way she's rubbing the skin beneath her collarbones. An echo of pain pinches beneath my own chest.

She lowers her hand. "I'm fine. Just uncomfortable."

I close the book I was reading with more force than is strictly necessary. "This is useless. Why wouldn't Ronin focus his attention on *why* the trees are growing? It doesn't make sense. He's hiding something."

Saengo gives me a patient look. "Sirscha, he's a centuries-old shaman with control over an undead wood. Of course he has secrets. Everyone with power keeps secrets."

She tucks an uneven length of hair behind her ear. I'd offered to trim it this morning, but she'd refused. She'd barely been able to look at herself in the mirror.

"But to stop a weed from spreading, you tear it out from the roots. It's simple gardening."

"What would you know of gardening?"

I wave away the comment. I've never planted anything in my life, and neither has she, for that matter.

"Ronin's power is waning," I say. "Why wouldn't he explore every possible avenue for a solution?"

"What makes you think he hasn't? He's not going to provide you a list of everything he's tried and failed."

That would be nice, though. "Do you think he already knows why the trees are growing?"

"It would make sense. He's ruled the Dead Wood for as long as it's existed."

"So he doesn't want *me* to know, then."

"Think about this logically. Ronin knows how precarious his position looks to the kingdoms. The more the Dead Wood grows, the more Thiy's leaders will look for someone to blame, and Ronin *is* its self-proclaimed ruler. He *wants* to fix this. He wouldn't withhold important information if he thought it'd help you.

My father—" She pauses as the skin around her mouth tightens with pain. I look down; the guilt that always perches at my shoulder digs its claws into my skin. She clears her throat and continues. "My father says that there are some in each of the kingdoms who've tired of him reining in their ambitions."

That her father should know this makes me wonder if he's one of them. "When did he say that?"

"A few months ago, when I went home for my mother's birthday dinner." She says it casually, but only highborn students are given leave from the Company for something as mundane as a birthday. I certainly wouldn't have received the same accommodations.

Knowing this makes me more curious about Theyen's engagement to the Ember Princess. Why would the Nuvalyn Empire agree to bring a shadowblessed into their royal house? With the exception of a brief fifty-year period when they were temporarily usurped, the Yalaengs have ruled since the founding of the Empire, the longest dynasty in Thiy. And they've been enemies with Kazahyn for much of that time.

The enmity between humans and shamans is a childish spat compared to the feud between shamans and shadowblessed. It's difficult to believe that such a union was even considered.

But an alliance between the Fireborn Queens and the Yalaengs could be enough to renew the old peace treaty. The fact one should even be needed, however, indicates Ronin might no longer be able to hold the peace on his own.

The Dead Wood runs vertically down Evewyn's eastern

border and both the Empire's and Kazahyn's western borders. But nothing separates Kazahyn in the south from the Nuvalyn Empire in the north. Only Ronin's power and legacy—his defeat of the Soulless and the memory of that devastation—keep the two kingdoms in check.

Around midnight, we concede at last and agree to resume our research in the morning. But I don't want to return to our room with nothing to show for the day's efforts. I look down the empty aisles and then at a narrow window where moonlight spills over the frame into a silver puddle on the tiles. Not once has anyone disturbed us in here, not even Saengo's guard, who's even more rigid than Phaut.

"I want to look around the grounds without our guards hovering behind us."

Saengo follows me to the window, the only source of natural light this deep in the library. I rap my knuckles against the glass to test its solidity.

"What do you think you're going to find?" she asks as I search for something to break the glass. Books are all that's readily available.

I'm far enough from the doors that Phaut isn't likely to hear glass breaking, but in the utter silence, the sound could carry. "Not sure. You said Ronin's study is at the back of the castle?"

She nods. "Top floor."

"Then that's where I'll go. My gut is telling me that he already knows why the trees are growing. But he must not want anyone else to know. Maybe I'll find some answers there."

I'll have to risk the noise. Nearby, a narrow table is pushed up against the end of a bookcase. A strip of cloth runs the length of the tabletop, set with an unlit candle in a glass lantern.

I hand the lantern to Saengo, then gather up the table runner. Next, I search through the nearest shelf for the heaviest book I can find. There are plenty of options, but I want something that no one will care much about if it's accidentally ruined. I settle for a tome on the history of cutlery and napkin folding. That seems a useless-enough topic. Why would anyone care about the history of eating utensils, and why in the names of the Five Sisters is the book so *thick*?

Saengo watches, brown eyes caught between amusement and worry, as I wrap the book in the cloth. Then I heft the weight in my hands to get a solid grip. If I were caught, what would Ronin do to punish me? At the Company, I knew what was expected of me, what was allowed and forbidden, and how I would pay penance. Here, I have no idea how far I can push.

My fingers tighten around the book. I didn't excel as Kendara's pupil by playing it safe. I suppose I better not get caught.

I fling the book against the window. The glass shatters with little resistance. We both cringe. The book falls to the ground outside with a heavy *thump*. I wait a moment, just in case, but there's only silence. When I'm certain Phaut isn't rushing through the aisles in search of me, I use the tablecloth to break off any remaining shards clinging to the window frame.

"Keep watch," I say. "If Phaut comes to check on us, make up something."

Saengo gives me an irritated purse of her lips. But she doesn't stop me from shimmying through the square of space with a nimble ease that would make even Kendara snort in approval. The glass broke in large fragments, so I gather as many shards as I can from the ground, fold up the bundle, and hand it to Saengo along with the book. I scatter dirt over what slivers remain to conceal them from passing servants. An open window is far less suspicious than a broken one.

I flash Saengo a reassuring grin. Then I hurry along the side of the castle until I reach the perimeter of the bone palisade. I've seen very little of the rear half of Spinner's End, but it can't be that difficult to find Ronin's study. At this time of night, the grounds are deserted.

I follow the bones. Outlying walls and buildings stand a good distance from the palisade and the trees just beyond. I pass a large yard filled with animal pens. Most of the animals are asleep, but a few sniff and dig through the dirt. One rolls on its back in a puddle of mud. My nose wrinkles at the smell.

Past the animal pens is a high wall with drooping weeds half clinging to the stone. An arched doorway leads inside. What lies beyond surprises me. It opens into an enclosed garden overrun by weeds.

A cobbled path winds beneath a series of stone archways into another walled space and even more intersecting avenues. It's like a maze. Fascinated, I turn in circles, taking in the meandering pathways and secluded gardens. The arches are beautiful, the stonework chiseled into symmetrical flourishes and fantastical creatures. When these gardens were flowering, they would have been breathtaking.

Maybe I should return to the library and bring Saengo back here in the morning to explore more fully. I turn back just as an awareness awakens inside me. There's a presence somewhere in these gardens. It becomes an ache in my joints, a pressure building inside me like a scream that needs release. The skin on the backs of my arms and neck prickles, although the air is warm. Something about this presence feels familiar, although I can't place it.

Brushing the hair from my forehead, I stare in the direction of the path to my left. There are four paths in all, one leading back to the exit, and three more branching off into places unknown. But the arches over the left entrance are dressed in spiderwebs.

⁎ I haven't taken more than a step before I freeze. A clicking sound fills the silence—something heavy striking stone. The space beyond the arch darkens with an encroaching shadow. The clicking grows louder, more hurried, like snapping pincers or . . . numerous legs over the cobbles.

I spin on my heel and rush back the way I came. My face feels hot, but shivers creep across my shoulder blades and breathe icy plumes down my spine, urging my feet faster. Once I'm out of the gardens, I launch up the wall onto the nearest ledge, unable to shake the sensation of multiple eyes watching my retreat.

I'm halfway across the ridge of a roof when a quiet whistle sounds behind me. Dropping, I grip the ridge with one hand to keep from sliding and flatten my back to the tiles. A knife soars past me, moonlight catching the blade in a flash of silver. I've only a second to wonder if what I'd sensed in the garden followed me out before a shadow rises in my periphery and a sword swings for my neck. I roll, using the momentum to slide off the roof. The curling eaves slow my descent long enough for my fingers to catch the edge of the roof and swing myself over.

My attacker is fast on my heels as I shimmy down a corner column and drop to the ground. The moment my feet touch dirt, I shove away from the stone to avoid another swipe of a long blade.

I edge backward, toward the bone palisade, as my attacker lands in a crouch on the ground. As the figure straightens, his silhouette appears to be that of a man's. He's tall and wiry, concealed head to toe in formfitting black. I can't even make out facial features. He attacks again, shockingly fast, and I only barely dodge. The night helps to disguise his movements.

My neck stings as his blade kisses my skin. Then he grunts and staggers back. Embedded in his upper arm is a knife, the same one he'd thrown at me. My gaze flicks up to see Saengo crouched on the roof, braced against the side of a nearby tower. She slips behind the tower and out of sight again.

The darkness of my attacker's disguise wavers long enough to reveal luminous white hair. Shadowblessed.

He isn't wearing black. He is wearing *shadows*. They settle seamlessly over his form again as he fades into the shadows of the castle. Only his slight movements reveal where he is. Even his sword has been stained a dull finish that doesn't reflect the light.

It would probably be smarter to stay where I am, exposed by the moonlight, and force him to come to me. But while I don't have his abilities, I, too, have been taught to become a shadow—and I do not fear them.

So I step forward. I feel his gaze on me. It's a different sensation from the one in the garden maze, the one that tugged at my core to venture deeper, whispering of dangerous secrets.

I join him in the shadows of the castle, where even the walls become inseparable from the dark. I wait, letting the night wrap itself around me—the distant crackle of stretching trees, the satin warmth of air against my neck. The sharp smell of blood that closes in on my left.

I dodge, my hand shooting out to grasp his arm. With a sharp twist, I snap his wrist. He grunts in pain, his sword falling from his grip. I catch the hilt with one hand while the elbow of my other arm smashes into his face.

Dark-gray blood spurts from his nose. My knee meets his gut. He grunts again, stumbling. Another punch to his jaw, and he sprawls into the dirt. His shadows melt from his body, sinking into the earth like water. Beneath the disguise is the simple tunic that all the castle servants wear under their uniforms.

A quick scan of the area confirms our fight hasn't drawn the attention of any guards. That's good. Judging by his silence, he doesn't want the attention, either. Also good. I lift his sword, admiring its razor edge as he gawks up at me, bewildered, white hair mussed.

"You're good with this." He might have gotten in more than a small nick if not for Saengo. I twirl the sword. The blade sings through the air. He sucks in his breath as the metal stops a hair's width from his neck. "Who are you?"

His lips flatten, nostrils flaring as he draws a slow, deep breath. My mouth stretches into a smile that makes the blood drain from his face. His fingers flex against the earth.

"Just kill me already, shaman," he says through his teeth. "I won't tell you anything."

"Are you absolutely sure about that?"

"Inferni take you," he spits.

I lean over him, speaking low. "You must not have very much practice in this sort of thing. Allow me to explain. When I ask you a question, you answer. And when you don't . . ."

The sword stabs through the fleshy skin between neck and shoulder. His back arches as his mouth opens on a silent scream. As I expected, his control suggests he's had training not unlike my own. Blood wells around the blade, trickling down his collarbone and pooling at the hollow of his throat. Should it disturb me how easily I can hurt him? How his pain can move me so little?

"Why are you trying to kill me?" I suspect I know the answer, but I'd like to hear it from his lips.

"You bring nothing but destruction," he hisses. "You are a weapon of the shamans to be used against my people."

"Are you a servant here in the castle?"

The corners of his lips pull downward, and he doesn't reply.

I lean over, allowing my weight to settle on the sword. Pain tightens his face. "What am I to do with you? Do I kill you?"

"Sirscha," a voice hisses. I don't turn, but I hear Saengo sliding along the roof behind me.

His eyes close; his mouth pinches tight. The resignation there surprises me. I don't actually intend to kill him. I only want answers before I hand him to Ronin. Tears seep from beneath his lashes, sliding down his temples into his pale hair.

I startle back, confused by the anguish carving lines around his eyes. In a flash, he rips the blade from his shoulder and springs to his feet.

Saengo makes a strangled sound of warning. I curse and raise the sword to defend against an attack. Instead, he flees and launches himself over the troll bones.

"Wait," I say, but he's already scrabbling to get beneath the white drape that separates Spinner's End from the trees. My heart hammers in my chest. "Wait!"

I gape, jaw hanging loose, as he vanishes into the dark. Should I go after him? What was the fool thinking? I wouldn't have killed him, but the trees certainly will.

I look up at Saengo. She stares dumbstruck at the place where the shadowblessed had vanished.

"Damn it," I whisper fiercely, stabbing the sword into the dirt. I approach the palisade, fingers gripping the troll bones. My stomach churns at the idea of entering the trees, especially now in the dead of night, but can I just leave him to die?

"Don't," Saengo calls, her voice high and frantic. Her fear rises inside me, even with the barrier between us.

"Damn it," I repeat, just as the trees groan. I freeze, chills racing down my arms despite that I'm still warm from the fight. I swallow thickly, perfectly still, listening.

Something almost like a scream pierces the night before it's abruptly cut off. I release the bones, backing away as I slap a hand over my mouth, panting against my damp palm. My heart races; my legs tremble. The trees shift again.

Grabbing the sword, I spin and vault up the wall to where Saengo waits for me. We don't stop until we're slipping back through the window into the gloom of the library.

THIRTEEN

The next morning, Saengo and I go over the details at breakfast. Our maid sets for us a meal of spongy rice cakes, bright fruits shaped into whimsical beasts, and a steaming pot of chrysanthemum tea scattered with petals. It's a bit surreal, like if I rub my eyes, the bounty before us will ripple and vanish.

But even in the bright light of day, my belly full and warm, I shiver at the memory of the trees and that lone, strangled scream. Although I pity his death, I can't summon any remorse. He did try to kill me, after all. I only wish I'd gotten more answers from him.

"Why would someone try to kill you?" Saengo asks, scowling down into her tea. Last night, she'd grown bored alone in the library and followed me out the window in time to witness the attack. Thank the Sisters no one besides Ronin knows she's my familiar.

"He mentioned me being a weapon against the shadow-blessed, which doesn't make sense. Controlling the Dead Wood benefits everyone, not just the shamans."

"I don't think he meant the Dead Wood. As a shaman, you're an enemy by default. The Empire once tried to conquer Kazahyn. Think about what it must mean to shamans that another soul-guide has appeared after so long. The last one was the founder of their kingdom."

My nose wrinkles. I don't like the reminder of expectations built around preconceived notions of who I am. I've been contending with such notions all my life, namely that I will never attain anything because of my low birth.

"Imagine what would happen if the Yalaengs got their hands on you," Saengo continues. Her voice grows hushed with worry. "Or me. If they think you're a threat to their power over the Empire, then they'll kill us. Or just me and use you as a powerless figurehead to—"

I toss a chunk of mango shaped like a bird at her. It splashes into her nearly empty teacup, spattering her pale cheek.

"Sirscha! Really?" she says, exasperated. But the dark cloud over her eyes clears and a smile pulls at her lips. "How did Kendara ever wring any discipline out of you?"

"Focus on the problems we have now." I reach for more mango. "Not the ones you're adding in your head."

She grabs for the grapes just as I lob another chunk of fruit at her head. We're both laughing, juicy ammunition primed for attack, when the door opens. Saengo slams back into her seat, grape-filled hands hidden in her lap. She'd be the picture of decorum if not for her twitching lips and the way her hair sticks straight up in the back. Neither of us had bothered to wash up before breakfast.

Unlike Saengo, I don't hide the beast-shaped fruit fisted between my fingers. Instead, I pop a papaya-drake into my mouth.

Our maid sweeps into the room, ignoring our antics. Her arms are laden with layers of sheer golden fabric. I catch a glimpse of Phaut out in the hall. Her short hair is tucked behind her ears, which are only slightly pointed. She looks like she's just arrived to join Saengo's guard, who'd been on the night shift. Then the maid swings the door shut with her foot.

"Come see!" The maid rushes past us into the bedroom. I fling one more piece of fruit at Saengo and then follow after her.

In the bedroom, the maid is shaking out a stunning wine-gold gown with matching robes. I suck in my breath.

The style is a little outdated but certainly Nuvali. Intricate gilt embroidery decorates the high collar and either side of the sleeveless bodice, a shade darker than the flowing skirt, which falls loose and airy in a stream of pale gold broken by panels of gossamer lace. A carmine sash embroidered at the ends in shimmering thread provides a bright stripe of color. Without even touching it, I know it's spidersilk.

The maid beams as she spreads the lush dress across the foot of my bed. "Isn't it beautiful? Oh, and this one is for Saengo."

She rushes over to the second pile of fabric she'd left on Saengo's bed and shakes it out. The gown is in a much different style. The neckline is cut lower, the waist higher, and the sleeves are long and billowing, spilling down over the full length of the dress.

"Since you've made friends with Hlau Theyen, I had to find you something more appropriate to wear."

"I have *not* made friends with Theyen." I cringe at the idea. "And he hasn't even met Saengo yet."

She waves away my comment. "Even so. This color will look perfect with your skin tone."

"Where did you even find gowns like this in Spinner's End?" I head into the bathing chamber to wash my hands and clean up. It'd be a waste to wear them for someone like Theyen. He's not a friend, but at least he isn't an enemy.

My hands still, the water cupped in my palms sluicing between my fingers into the silver basin.

Not everyone stands to benefit from what you can do.

No. He wouldn't have dared. Sending a shadowblessed with powers not unlike his own would be too blatant. And yet the assassin had called me a weapon of the shamans, and Theyen made no secret of his dislike for me.

"They belonged to a previous guest," the maid calls from the bedroom.

I close my eyes and resume washing my face. There will be time enough later to consider whether the assassin had been working alone or if he'd been sent.

Back in the bedroom, I spot Saengo at the edge of her bed, expression guarded as she fingers the silk sleeves of the gown set out for her.

"Some guests who arrive here underestimate the journey through the Dead Wood," the maid continues. "Sometimes, in order to make the return journey more quickly, they abandon whatever they'd brought with them."

Still, the former owner would have been someone of great means to discard spidersilk.

With a glance at Saengo, I say, "Saengo and I can manage from here. Thank you so much."

The woman lifts one eyebrow but doesn't argue. She bobs a curtsy and leaves, shutting the door gently after her. I turn to Saengo, not even sure what to say. Her misery is my doing, and I don't know how to fix it other than to continue in my bargain with Ronin.

A beat before the silence between us grows awkward, Saengo pastes a smile on her face and rises from the bed. "These really are beautiful. My father promised me a spidersilk gown for my wedding one day. I guess that's unlikely now."

"Saengo," I begin, but she cuts me off.

"I like seeing how happy you get over pretty things." She crosses the room to the gown on my bed. "Come on. I'll help you try it on."

Reluctantly, I tug off my nightgown. Without the layers common in Evewynian fashion, dressing is a much quicker affair.

As she helps me into the gown's thin chemise, I say, "Do you think it was a Spinner back in that garden maze?"

The evidence all around the castle makes it plain that there are Spinners within the grounds. Although that's likely what I heard last night, the press of that strange power does give me pause. The mere memory of it is like a tug at my navel, urging me to brush away Saengo's hands and rush back to the garden. It takes more effort than it should to force my thoughts away from that nameless sensation.

"I should like to see a Spinner." Saengo tilts her head thoughtfully. She holds out the gown for me to slip my arms through.

"I don't. After the sorts of things Kendara made me hunt, I'd rather not meet any eight-legged creatures larger than a drake in shadowy garden mazes."

Saengo tucks one side of the sleek fabric beneath the other, securing the bodice with tiny pearl buttons. I've never worn anything so exquisite in my life. The only gown I possess—pale-pink satin robes Saengo gifted me when we graduated from the Prince's Company—sits at the bottom of my trunk in the barracks.

The gown has likely already been confiscated by the officits with all my other possessions: a worn volume of Evewynian myths and folktales, a dried plum blossom pressed between the pages; a doll I'd bought with my first month's stipend at the Queen's Company; a cloth square embroidered with mountain orchards in bloom, purchased from a festival; ticket stubs to plays I'd attended with Saengo at the theater; the very first message Kendara wrote me, a single sentence indicating a time and place to meet, meaningless to all but me.

They were few in number and yet the physical sum of all my years in Vos Talwyn. A pang of longing strikes swiftly, making my chest ache with the knowledge of lost things, lost time, lost dreams. Every moment I'm here feels like I'm careening further and further away from the life I'd chosen.

Saengo makes a face and ties the scarlet sash around my waist. "You know I respect Kendara, but I don't like her 'tests.' You always come back looking a little less like yourself." Her voice grows quiet. "Like how you looked when you stabbed that shadowblessed. Everything about you goes cold."

"He was trying to kill me," I say dryly. I slip my bare arms through the sleeves of the robes, which cascade down my form. In a gown like this, I would have fit right into one of the queen's lavish balls or dinner parties.

On those evenings, Saengo and I would sneak from the barracks and hide within the gardens, watching the court in their resplendent silks beneath the glow of hundreds of painted lanterns. Being a lord's daughter and heir, Saengo of course was taught to dance. So we pranced in circles around ylang-ylang trees, swinging our arms in dramatic swan poses between rows of hibiscus and plumeria, each dreaming our impossible dreams.

Saengo shakes her head. "I know. You didn't have a choice. But you're also one of the most compassionate people I know. Stop rolling your eyes. It's true. I worry when you're forced to do things like that. Kendara didn't like seeing any softness in you."

I sigh. "She would absolutely disapprove of this gown." She disapproves of anything too conspicuous, like silks and jewelry and smiling and pretty much anything that isn't dour and boring.

Still, she taught me to survive. Saengo doesn't understand that I've rarely had the luxury to *be* soft. I didn't have the protection of a powerful family. Or *any* family. I didn't have wealth, status, and comfort.

All things she's lost because of me.

"All right, your turn." I reach for the laces at Saengo's collar. She jerks away, but not before my fingers pull down the fabric, just enough to reveal spidery blue lines climbing over her collarbones. "Saengo!"

"Don't." She backs away. Her hands clutch the laces at her throat, hiding the blue lines. "I didn't want to tell you."

"Why?" I ask, incredulous.

"Because I didn't want to worry you any further." Slowly, she releases her grip on her collar and tugs down the material. "I thought maybe it was a side effect of the familiar bond, but . . . I don't think it is."

My heart pounds as I look more closely. The lines are thin but bright and ominous, radiating outward from the center of her chest. I swallow, dread settling thick as oil at the back of my throat.

"Wait here." I turn and rush through the sitting room before flinging open the door. Out in the hall, Phaut reclines on a chair, arms crossed. The other guard is gone.

I must look somewhat frantic because she immediately grasps her sword and straightens out of her chair. "What is it?"

Without a word, I turn on my heel and lead her back into our bedroom. Phaut's fierce expression transforms into confusion as she takes in the space, free of intruders, and then me, dressed like I'm about to have tea with the queen.

"Are you in danger?" she asks warily.

"Tell me what this is," I say as I cross to Saengo.

Saengo looks resigned as she unlaces the collar of her

nightgown and pulls it open to reveal the blue lines spidering her skin. Phaut's face goes white, the age lines around her mouth deepening. Her hand falls from the pommel of her sword.

"The rot," she whispers. "How is this possible?"

Saengo sways on her feet. I guide her to a chair. Even with the window in my mind shut against the flame of Saengo's emotions, her fear pushes through me. My pulse pounds at my temples, drowning out everything but the harsh sound of my breathing.

The rot is incurable. A sickness of the soul.

"Get Ronin," I say. Phaut doesn't even argue. She all but flees the room.

"I've arranged for a healer." Ronin stands beside the door, watching me pace the length of the sitting room.

Saengo sits nearby, hands clenched tight in her lap. She's changed into simple pants and a tunic, the blue lines of infection covered up again. Phaut lingers behind Ronin, her gaze darting from me to Saengo in bewilderment. She's still reeling from the news that Saengo is a human familiar.

Ronin says, "If I'd known she was your familiar, I wouldn't have sent for the both of you. But once it became apparent, the fact she survived the journey without signs of sickness left me hopeful she would be immune. The rot usually settles in far more quickly. Perhaps a human soul is more resistant."

The detached tone of his voice irritates me. I make another agitated turn around the room. The airy layers of spidersilk flutter around me.

"What if I took her away from the Dead Wood? Somewhere far."

He shakes his head. His hands are clasped behind his back. Although he wears an unassuming gray tunic and robes, his presence commands the room. "It's no use. Once the disease has taken root, distance makes no difference."

I want to rage and scream and cry. But Saengo sits quiet and pale, as if frozen with shock, so instead I ask, "Then what can a light stitcher do for her?"

A light stitcher is a lightwender who can summon light and heal wounds and illnesses. Some years ago, Saengo and I jokingly made a list of ailments we wondered if a stitcher could cure: warts, laziness, incontinence, and acute idiocy.

But even the greatest shaman healers have been unable to cure the rot. I pause beside the table. Our breakfast has been cleared away, leaving only a bowl filled with clusters of longan. At a festival last year, we'd bought a bucket of the small, round fruit and hidden ourselves on a rooftop overlooking a street choked with revelers. When Jonyah and his friends passed beneath our roof, we flung the seeds at his head and then laughed at his confusion.

My eyes squeeze shut against the stinging sensation behind my lids.

"The healer isn't a light stitcher. She's a shadowblessed. Hlau Theyen sent for his own personal healer. She'll be here by tonight."

I turn to frown at Ronin. "Tonight?"

The sooner, the better, of course, but how can a shadow-blessed travel from Kazahyn to Spinner's End in half a day? That shouldn't be possible unless she meant to arrive by wyvern. I'd read about how the Kazan rode wyverns into battle against the shamans in wars past. That the Kazan have found a way to coexist with such fearsome creatures, one of Thiy's deadliest predators and the inspiration behind many a story, is truly a marvel.

"Yes," Ronin says, without explanation.

"If I die," Saengo says abruptly, "will Sirscha lose her magic forever?"

My fingers dig into my thighs. "You're *not* dying."

Her voice is soft but insistent. "But if I do—"

"But you won't."

"No," Ronin says, interrupting us. "Shamans who lose their familiar need only bond with a new one. Don't think on that now. Given how resilient you've been and the early stage of the disease, you should be in no immediate danger. Phaut will alert you when the healer arrives tonight."

Phaut opens the door for him. She gives us both a troubled look and then follows him into the hall.

"I'd wondered about the rot," Saengo says. "But it hadn't felt real. Not until now."

I press my fist to my stomach, against the knot there that makes me wish for my swords. It's a stupid impulse. The rot isn't something I can fight.

Or can I? The rot is a sickness of the soul. If I can supposedly shepherd souls back to the living, maybe I could heal one.

"I want to try something." I kneel in front of her. My gown gathers around me in golden layers.

She doesn't react when I take her hands in mine. Unfortunately, I haven't the faintest idea what I'm doing. I can't even summon my craft yet. But if there's the slightest chance I can heal her, I have to try.

I close my eyes and recall that searing heat at the moment my craft awakened—but I twitch my head, discarding the memory as the pain of that night floods my senses. I can't yet bring myself to examine the details of Saengo's death, a moment dipped in bronze, immortalized in my thoughts.

Instead, I return to the Dead Wood, when the trees closed around us and I thought our deaths imminent. I squeeze my eyes tighter, searching for that spark of magic and the memory of those twinkling orbs. Everything goes silent, as if even the flames crackling in the fireplace are waiting for . . .

Nothing. Nothing happens.

I dampen my dry lips. Saengo's despair swells through me. Flecks of heat dance beneath my skin, but I can't hold on to them. All I can feel is the inevitability of failure, again and again and again.

With a hiss, I release her hands and lurch to my feet. Covering my face, I resume pacing. An apology lodges in my throat.

"It was worth a try." Saengo draws a deep breath that seems to straighten her spine, despite the weight of it all trying to pull her back down. "What else can we do?"

Her words give me strength. Neither of us are giving up. I turn to face her, my gown sweeping around me. "Like I said yesterday, we have to tear it out by its roots. We stop the infection at its source."

Her lips twist to one side. "What does that mean? You're going to destroy the entire Dead Wood?"

My hands fist around the spidersilk. "Yes. It's infecting you. As long as it exists, you're at risk."

Her gaze slides away from mine. She's skeptical, and I don't blame her. It's an outrageous declaration. Fear, guilt, self-doubt— all these things eat at my resolve. But I push them away.

"I'll learn how to free the souls in the Dead Wood. Once that's done and you're healed, we'll get a pardon from the queen. Then you'll be able to do whatever you want. You can go back to the Company or travel the kingdom or go home and be with your family. I'll make sure to come see you every few weeks to renew our bond. Other than that, you can live your life however you choose."

Saengo's eyes soften. She stands and pulls me into a hug. "You're going to make the finest Shadow Evewyn has ever known. Kendara would be a fool not to have you, and we both know she's no fool. But if that isn't what you want anymore, then I expect you to come back to me. We'll travel Evewyn first and then the world."

I hug her back. Through the vise squeezing my throat, I whisper, "It's a promise."

FOURTEEN

I t takes less coaxing than I anticipated to convince Phaut that
I need to venture into the Dead Wood. Ronin never forbade
me from going in there, so although she's wary, her curiosity over
my craft wins out.

Ronin won't be happy about my decision to destroy the trees
rather than control them, but he doesn't need to know. Not just
yet. And maybe Thiy shouldn't need the Dead Wood anyway.
Maybe what Thiy needs isn't a wall to divide its peoples but a
bridge.

But the first step is to learn how to summon my craft. Theyen
said only genuine danger might invoke my magic, and the most
dangerous things here are the trees.

Phaut and I garner quite the attention passing through the
gate. Servants stare and the soldiers watch, perplexed, but nobody
stops us for questioning. I'll bet this is the first time they've seen

anyone willingly step out of the gates without Ronin. They don't even know how they should react.

Saengo waits in the courtyard, practicing her archery. She wanted a more physical means of exorcising her anxiety. We have that in common. With Ronin's permission, the soldiers have set up a wooden dummy for her. She's already loosed arrows into the dummy's head and chest by the time I even step past the troll-bone palisade.

As we reach the white drapes, it takes every bit of courage I possess to lift aside the veil and keep walking. The first gnarled tree stands less than ten paces away. Its branches press against Ronin's webbing, which snares around its knots and angles.

My breaths quicken. I reach for my swords.

"I'll be right here," Phaut says softly, as if afraid to draw the attention of the trees.

My fingers flex around the hilts of my swords. I take several deep breaths as I recall the sting of Kendara's stick against my legs, raising welts. One strike for every flinch, every wince. One strike for every time my face gave away a moment's pain or indecision. She repeated the lesson for weeks until my legs were bruised and swollen, until I could end a fight without betraying a single emotion.

When my heart has calmed, I take a purposeful step into the trees. Then another. I count my paces, but I don't get far before the trees rustle. My skin prickles with rising fear. I stop twenty-five paces into the Dead Wood. I can still glimpse the white veil of Spinner's End. Swords at my sides, I wait.

The awareness of something ancient and angry stirs around me. I suddenly realize why the presence in the garden maze felt familiar—it had felt a little like this. Whatever's back there is tied somehow to the Dead Wood, although I've no idea how that's possible, unless the gardens are closer to the trees than I thought. But then what about the creature I'd heard scuttling over the cobblestones?

Now is no time to let my thoughts wander. Although I know what to expect, the sight of faces surfacing from within the decaying trunks still spills ice down my spine. Knobby, fractured fingers press outward, stretching gray-green bark that flakes off like dead skin. The burls of their eyes squint and weep sticky sap.

My hands shake. I grip my swords so hard that my fingers go numb. To keep my legs in motion, I turn in a slow circle. That warmth of magic sparks in my chest. I try to focus on it, but my breaths come faster and my heartbeat resounds in my ears.

Their mouths stretch wide, but there's nothing inside except the aged whorls and rivets of the bark. My attention snags on those lips formed of wood and rot. They're moving in sync, and I realize with a sinking dread that they're all mouthing the same thing. A single word, again and again: *Run.*

My breath sticks in my throat, and I nearly do just that. But through the haze of fear, my instincts latch onto a single thought, which keeps me in place—can the spirits *talk*?

The roots behind me lift. I whirl to face them, watching as they shake off a crust of earth. Dirt scatters across my boots.

Pulse racing, I ask through clenched teeth, "Why are you telling me to run?"

If the spirits can somehow communicate with me, then they can tell me what's keeping them tethered here.

But there's no answer as the faces retreat and the trees shamble closer. A single tentacle-like appendage snags my foot. I slash at it. It recoils, thrashing like a snake.

Something stains my blade. At first, I think it's sap. It laces the roots and clings in viscous strings to the branches over my head. Another root snares my leg as something sharp rakes down my back. My swords blur through the air as I cut myself free. The branch drops at my feet, something wet and viscid sliding from its fingerlike ends.

More branches snatch at my hair. All thoughts of trying to communicate vanish. I can't focus. I can't think or see anything but those horrible eyes, clammy fingers, and ragged nails shredding at me, mouths screaming as the roots crawl from their throats and rip their faces in two. My swords move purely on reflex, because my mind is paralyzed with terror, screaming at me to obey the trees and run.

Something like a hoarse rasp disrupts the trees' wails. I seek out the sound, which seems to have come from a thick trunk, misshapen like the rest but unusually swollen. The molding wood leaks black sap, as if bloated or waterlogged. Bark fractures and then peels away as the tree buckles. Something reaches out from within.

Like my nightmares made real, blackened, shriveled arms elbow away the dead bark as the creature hauls itself from the recesses of the tree. What was once a head strains next through the gap, followed by a collapsed torso, ribs protruding at all angles.

Sisters, protect me, I think with a terror that pins me in place and crushes my lungs. As the creature's wrecked hands touch the ground, clumps of hair fall from its shoulders. The hair is white.

This creature—and the slime that coats the trees—is what's left of my shadowblessed assassin.

He is a ruin of bone and gristle. Even as his body drops to the ground with a wet *thud*, he is clearly still a part of the Dead Wood. What remains of his skin and muscles stretches from his raw skull and shoulders to the tree's innards in fleshy strips like gruesome puppet strings. His face is gone, the pit of his mouth the only indication of something once human.

The stump of his torso ends abruptly, the tail of his spine enveloped in thick gray vines. As his fingers dig into the earth and his broken body slides toward me, I release a horrified cry and slash my swords at his limbs. Blood gone black and thick spills onto the dirt. His throat makes a croaking sound as the tree tries to reel him back, pulling the strings taut. He flops like a caught fish, and I can't bear it a moment longer.

I kick viciously at a root and run, almost tripping as another root shoots into my path. My swords flash at even the slightest movement as I dart through the trees that contort and quake. My breaths are thin and uneven, my lungs refusing to function. His hatred gropes at my retreating back as the souls howl at my intrusion.

Bursting from the woods, I slam straight into Phaut.

"Whoa, whoa!" She grabs my shoulders.

I shove past her, unable to think or breathe until the white veil closes behind us and the path returns beneath our feet.

I angle my face away from the guards who watch us with renewed curiosity. My cheeks burn with shame, and my chest heaves with each breath. Saengo calls my name, but I'm shaking so hard I can barely focus on anything except putting one foot in front of the other. I don't even remember walking through the castle, but suddenly I'm in front of my door, and all I want is a scalding bath to scrub away the feel of those dead branches and the shadowblessed's remains.

I push inside, slamming the door shut behind me. Phaut's hand shoots out, catching it.

"May I come in?" she asks.

A refusal catches in my throat. It was kind of her to go out there with me when she could have said no. I'm pretty sure her orders to remain at my side at all times exclude my stupid impulses to go into the Dead Wood. I gesture for her to enter. Nodding in thanks, she slips inside a moment before Saengo appears at the threshold as well, breathless from running. Saengo's guard hovers behind her in the hallway.

"What happened?" Saengo shuts the door with more care than I had.

Phaut stands awkwardly in the middle of the sitting room. "It didn't go very well."

I fling my swords onto the sofa. "Must you gloat about it?"

"It's not gloating if I'm stating a fact. Still," Phaut says, voice softening, "it took great courage for you to even step foot into the Dead Wood. And you remained there for longer than I had expected."

I slump onto the sofa and begin yanking my boots off. "I don't need your flattery."

Phaut's brows dip and the lines around her mouth go taut. With a curt bow, she turns to leave.

I wince, feeling like an ass even without the weight of Saengo's glare. "Wait."

Phaut pauses with her fingers on the doorknob. I rub my hands over my face and then down my braid before tugging angrily at the ends. I glare at my trembling arms, unnerved by how rattled I am. It will be a long while before I'm able to silence the memory of that shadowblessed hauling his mutilated body out of the tree.

"I'm sorry for snapping at you. I just . . ." I squeeze my eyes shut. "Something . . . some*one* was . . . it was fresh. It came out. It was . . . terrible." I know my words make little sense, but Phaut seems to understand because her eyes go wide.

"There was someone new in the trees?" she asks, surprised.

"I think so," I say carefully.

Saengo stiffens and then goes very still.

Phaut looks uncomfortable as she rubs her thumb over the pommel of her sword. "I suppose that explains why no one's been able to find Kamryne today. Poor fool."

I look away, rubbing my arm. "A member of the staff?"

"A squire, actually. He's been with us for over a year, so he should have known well enough to stay away from the trees.

I don't think this has ever happened before. Lord Ronin will want to know as soon as possible."

So my attacker *was* a castle servant, and an old one at that. Curious. If staff members or soldiers have wound up in the trees in the past, Ronin wouldn't very well spread the knowledge. It would set a deadly precedent—that Spinner's End isn't safe even with Ronin here.

"I regret that you had to experience that," Phaut continues. "Those taken by the trees become . . . well, I needn't explain it to you. The trees devour the bodies over time, and it's only because he was newly taken that he wasn't yet . . . fully absorbed. Their souls remain trapped as well. The older the soul, the more a part of the Dead Wood they become until they are no more than wood, rot, and rage."

I shudder. The shadowblessed, Kamryne, is beyond any help save what my craft could provide, and instead of standing my ground and calling my magic, I let fear consume me. "I shouldn't have run."

"I admit I was prepared to dislike you when you first arrived. In my experience, lightwenders can't always be trusted to handle something as sacred as the source of another shaman's life and magic. But you're much braver and tougher than I expected. And you fight as fiercely as any Nuvali sun warrior."

I angle her a curious look. "Thanks?"

"Come on." Saengo holds out her hand. "You can help me stab things with sharp objects. That always makes me feel better."

The sun has set by the time Theyen's healer arrives. To my annoyance, the healer insists on working with Saengo alone.

Phaut sits with me in the waiting room. She drapes her long, lean body over the sofa and pokes at the pile of books resting on the end table.

Since Saengo has been through enough today, I didn't tell her my suspicions about who might have sent that assassin after me. It makes me uneasy having to trust Theyen's own healer to care for her, but the woman had seemed genuinely concerned with Saengo's condition. It's the only reason I'd relented and left them alone, Ronin's orders or not.

If that shadowblessed assassin was working for Theyen, it begs the question of how my death would benefit him specifically. Saengo said that a soulguide would be significant for the shamans. Maybe Theyen thinks that if I'm killed by a shadowblessed, it would infuriate the Empire enough to nullify his engagement.

But it could also lead to war. Would Theyen really go that far?

While Phaut pages through a book about the mythologies of the Nuvalyn Empire's western provinces, the ones that border the Dead Wood, I open a compendium of the Shamanic Callings. I flip past the first four: fire, water, earth, and wind. I'll read them more thoroughly later. Right now, my interest is in the Calling of Light.

I skim the first two: lightgivers, shamans who can transfer

the energy, or light, of one person to another; and light stitchers.

I turn to the last craft. Soulguides. The section begins with a preface that all the knowledge therein should be read with the understanding that only one soulguide has ever existed and so it couldn't be verified against any other sources. Not the most confident of texts, but I'll take what I can get.

The section goes on to cover the few things I already know, like how a soulguide's power can resonate with other spirits, and how if Sury were present at someone's death, she could guide the soul safely into the afterlife. Or depending on the type of death and the condition of the body, she could ensnare the departing soul and coax it back, restoring the person to life.

The next paragraph talks about how Sury could disarm shamans by choking their bonds with their familiars, rendering them temporarily powerless. Or she could sever those bonds entirely. That would be handy against other shamans.

Unfortunately, that's the end of the section. Hardly anything at all. I need to locate a proper biography on Sury, one that isn't based on legend and speculation. If such a thing exists.

Turning the page, I discover the next two are missing. At first, I think they might have fallen out due to the book's age and the broken binding. But a quick examination confirms the pages were torn hastily and messily. The inner margin of the first page is still intact, including part of the heading: Soulrender. Calling of Light.

I stare at the words. Then I flip back to count the crafts, even though I know I've read through all three already. But there aren't three. There are four.

I press down the ragged edges of the torn page. Very little text is left, and all I can glean is that soulrenders were efficient game hunters, capable of instantly killing their prey from a distance by ripping . . .

The line ends there. But I know what the rest of that sentence would say: Soulrenders could instantly kill their prey from a distance by ripping out their souls.

My fingers tighten around the edges of the book. The Soulless was a soulrender. A lightwender.

Footsteps in the bedroom startle me from my thoughts. I stare at the door, stiff with expectation, but it doesn't open.

"Don't worry," Phaut says. "She's in good hands. I've heard that Kazan healers are extraordinary. It's only the prejudices between the shamans and the shadowblessed that keep them from sharing their knowledge."

I rub my temples. "What's the difference between a light stitcher and a shadowblessed healer?"

She closes her book and considers an answer. "A light stitcher repairs the soul energy of a person. The body heals once a person's soul energy is in balance. But a shadowblessed healer works differently. They're called flesh workers, which can be a little intimidating."

My stomach turns. I'd left Saengo alone in a room with someone whose craft was called flesh worker?

"They repair the body—the blood and bone. They can keep the physical symptoms of the rot at bay to slow the spread of the disease."

I suspect that a flesh worker's ability to manipulate blood and bone could be used in other, less beneficial ways. "You've seen this done before?"

She nods. "A small fox familiar once found its way into Spinner's End. It'd been hiding among Lord Ronin's supplies."

"How long did the fox live?"

She looks down, and I brace for her answer. "Almost two weeks."

When I release my breath, it comes out thin and uneven. I feel like I've been stabbed in the gut. I half expect to find myself bleeding out all over the sofa. The whole world goes quiet until all that remains is the pounding of my heart and the familiar warmth of Saengo's candle. It's flickering, fearful but strong.

When I can't stand it any longer, I shove to my feet. She's been in there long enough. Just as Phaut jumps up to block my path, the bedroom door swings open.

The shadowblessed healer steps out. She's a short woman with dark gray skin. Her white hair is pulled up into a braided bun at the crown of her head. She wears a simple but finely made tunic along with the crimson flame of the Fireborn Queens pinned beneath her collar.

"I'll need to see her every evening to repeat the treatment," the woman says.

I thank her and then rush past into the bedroom. Saengo sits up in bed, sipping water. Neither of us speak, but she scoots over and lifts the edge of the blanket.

I slide in beside her. We lie down, face to face and hands

clasped the way we used to when we were children in the Prince's Company. The officits of the Prince's Company hadn't been as strict about our sleeping arrangements, especially for the heir of a powerful House. It took a long time for Saengo to grow accustomed to the austere barracks. Sharing a bed had helped her homesickness.

The talisman bumps against my wrist bone. It had protected me against that firewender's magic. I unclasp the talisman from my wrist and secure it around hers. The rot is a magical disease. Maybe the troll bone will help slow its spread. Saengo's other hand falls over the bracelet, learning its shape in the dim light of the dying fireplace.

"When you were dueling Theyen yesterday morning, Millie arrived at our balcony."

At this, I rise onto my elbow. We haven't seen the falcon since the night of the teahouse attack. "What? How in the Sisters did she find you?"

Her voice softens as she says, "She's special. I think she could find me anywhere. She bore a message from my father."

I slowly sink into the mattress again. When Saengo shares memories of her childhood, they're so beyond the scope of my own experience they sound more like fairy tales, filled with lessons and tutors, dancing and gifts, festivals and dresses. It's no wonder Saengo took so long to adjust to life at the Company.

Although she missed her family and her home, she knew what awaited her there. As heir, she'll one day assume control over Falcons Ridge and all their lands. Her father is eager to begin shifting over responsibilities to prepare her. She's been running from those responsibilities for years.

"He received a message from the Company informing him of my desertion and that I'm now in Ronin's custody. He . . ." Her breath hitches, and her voice grows thick with tears. "He asked if I needed him to send a party to fetch me and take me home."

I squeeze her hand. No wonder she hadn't told me. No doubt she dearly wishes to see her parents, and it's a testament to her father that he would defy the Spider King to try.

But there's far too much standing in the way of their reunion. The guilt rips me open once again.

Her parents love her, but they've always disapproved of her decision to join the Queen's Company. They blame me, of course. They'd rather believe I dragged Saengo into service with me instead of accepting their daughter wants a life that's hers to choose. I have little affection for them, but I will do everything in my power to see Saengo home.

"Did you reply?"

"No," she whispers. "I sent Millie off, but she'll be back. I'll reply then. I don't know what to tell them."

I'm sorry, I think for the thousandth time. This is my fault. I'll fix this somehow. But hope is hard to find and harder still to hold on to.

"You should rest," I say.

"You too. You haven't slept well since we got here."

My eyes find the shape of the bedpost behind her head, faintly outlined in silver from the balcony. "It's my dreams. The spirits in the Dead Wood won't leave me alone."

Her fingers tighten around mine. "Have they ever spoken in your dreams? Like how they did today?"

I'd told her earlier about the strange moment in the trees. "No. Do you think I should try to talk to them?"

"It'd be safer than going back into the trees. They can't hurt you in your dreams."

I burrow deeper into the warmth of the blanket as I remember the sensation of decaying fingers trying to worm into my mouth and gouge my eyes. The pain always feels real enough.

After what happened today in the Dead Wood, the last thing I want is to be confronted again by those horrifying spirits in my head. But for Saengo, I'll try.

FIFTEEN

*H*ands emerge from the dark. I suck in my breath as the clammy cold of their dead skin closes around mine. Ragged nails tear into me.

"Stop," I whisper. I have to fight the urge to curl into myself and hide from their grasping hands. That familiar dark awareness settles in my gut. Claws of ice wrap around my spine, tugging me somewhere I don't want to go. Back into the depths of that garden maze. "I need to speak to you."

Faces appear next, broken beyond recognition. Their necks swell and roil as roots push up their throats. One mouth opens wide, black sap spilling down its chin. Panic seizes me, and all I want is to scream or run. But I'd done that in the Dead Wood, and I owe it to Saengo to swallow my fear.

Broken fingers wrap painfully in my hair. Before I lose my nerve, I shout, "Why do you stay in the Dead Wood?"

The hands clawing at me seem to recoil, if only for a moment. The faces snarl and gnash their teeth. "Trapped," they whisper in raw, overlapping voices. "Trapped, trapped, trapped."

"How are you trapped? What keeps you here?"

But they only repeat the word, as if no longer capable of anything more than that.

Then another face emerges, pushing out from the side of a swollen, twisted neck. Everything inside me turns to ice. There's enough of her left that I recognize the thin lips, the gaunt cheeks, the small but slightly crooked nose. Where her bright emerald eyes had been, there are only black, weeping burls.

It's the healer from the Valley of Cranes.

She opens her mouth and whispers in a harsh, broken voice, "Suryali."

I awaken with a scream lodged in my throat.

Saengo is leaning over me, calling my name. With a deep breath, I relax into the bed and throw an arm over my face. Enough light presses through the drapes that it must be well past dawn.

"The spirits?" she asks softly.

I nod and tell her about the dream and the earthwender girl who'd treated me at the Valley of Cranes. What could have happened? Had Evewyn's soldiers thrown her to the trees?

"Do you think they meant Ronin trapped them?" Saengo asks.

"Who else could they mean?" And why would she say Suryali? It's a Nuvali word and the name of Kendara's sword.

If, somehow, Ronin bound the souls to the Dead Wood, then Ronin's problem isn't that he's losing control over the trees; he's losing control over his own powers. That would explain why he deflected my questions. Maybe that loss of control led to the emergence of the rot. The rot, like the ever-increasing spread of the Dead Wood, is a symptom of a deeper problem.

As I wash up, the earthwender girl's face surfaces again behind my closed eyes. She must have been newly taken. To be able to speak to me, some part of who she'd been must remain intact. But the longer she's trapped there, the more her soul will wither until, as Phaut said, she will become nothing but rage.

Would Ronin know what happened to her? Would he even tell me? I'd probably have more luck asking Theyen. He's informed of what goes on beyond Spinner's End.

Given the way our duel ended and my suspicions about the shadowblessed assassin, the idea of reaching out to him makes my stomach curdle. But I have questions, and not just about what's going on in Evewyn. Theyen might have answers.

Before I change my mind, I draft an invitation to dinner this evening as thanks for his healer's services and send it off with our maid. To my surprise, Theyen responds promptly.

"He says he'd prefer we join him in his rooms for lunch, and he will see us at noon," I say, reading the message he sent back with the maid.

"That was quick." Saengo rubs her chest, wincing a bit.

The echo of her pain tightens behind my ribs. "Maybe—"

"Don't you dare suggest I stay in bed." She drops her hand from her chest. "When's the next time I'll get to dine with a Kazan prince? I'm going."

"Fine. But I warn you he's completely unbearable."

I'm wary of him, but I doubt he'd try anything in his own rooms. Besides, Theyen is well informed and in a position of considerable influence. If he weren't my enemy, then a Kazan Hlau would be a powerful ally.

Theyen and his many attendants occupy an entire wing of the castle. Kazan guards are posted at nearly every entrance and stairwell. Their uniforms—ink-black armor over midnight-blue tunics and curved blades tucked into matching sashes—mark them as soldiers from Penumbria.

Eventually, we come to a huge door with metal cuffs at the corners and a knocker in the shape of a wyvern's head at its center. I knock once. No more than a second passes before the door opens to reveal a Kazan servant who ushers Saengo and me inside. Our guards remain in the corridor with Theyen's.

We step into a small foyer, to the right of which is a dining room. Theyen is already waiting at a low table, sitting cross-legged on a plush cushion with lavender tassels. In the brilliant light of multiple lanterns, his skin is the pale gray of river stones. He's dressed in a teal tunic with silver embroidery. He wears a matching jacket and a darker gray sash knotted around his waist. At our arrival, he stands.

I decide it's best to stick to diplomacy. "Hlau Theyen, may I introduce you to my dearest friend, Saengo Phang."

They both bow respectfully and exchange greetings. He waits until Saengo and I lower onto large beaded cushions and then finds his seat again.

His civility surprises me. But then he shakes his head and casts a critical eye at my appearance. "You look haggard."

I glance at Saengo with an "I told you so" look. I can tell she's calling on every ounce of her good breeding to keep from glowering at him.

Passing a hand down my splendorous attire, I affect a mock frown. "Do I not meet your approval?"

"No one meets my approval," he says easily. I suspect he isn't entirely joking. "Did you not sleep well last night?"

Ghostly hands scratch at my arms. But I smile and say, "I slept fine. And you?"

"Perfectly. The Kazan need very little sleep in general."

His servants finish serving our lunch, a sumptuous offering of roast smothered in plum sauce, fragrant herbed rice, pickled vegetables, and bite-size slices of fresh fruit.

"Hlau Theyen, thank you for the services of your healer. I'm deeply grateful," Saengo says.

He nods. "I was sorry to hear of your condition."

He does sound genuinely sorry, but I can't help searching his face for anything that might betray an ulterior motive.

Saengo murmurs something noncommittal and then says more brightly, "I once read something about how the Fireborn Queens acquired their name. Is it true that Penumbria is protected by inferni?"

Theyen smiles, a secretive curve of his mouth. "That isn't an answer that's mine to give."

"You're a Hlau," I point out. "Penumbria's secrets are all but yours."

He shakes his head. "I'll say this and nothing more—the inferni like the dark places of the earth, and our chroniclers tell of how our ancestors formed a blood pact with them for mutual protection. But storytellers do like to embellish."

"What would the inferni need protection from?" Saengo's gaze flicks to mine, and I know she's recalling the time I nearly crossed paths with one.

Kendara had sent me into a mineshaft in search of some crystal buried deep in the Coral Mountains. The inferni had been a creature of shadows and embers, its edges distorted and shimmery with smokeless heat. The mere sight of it had been terrifying. Like most Evewynians, I hadn't believed such creatures still existed.

"Firewenders," he says. "There's an old Nuvali custom for firewenders to hunt the inferni to prove their mastery over their element."

I make a face at this and hope the custom is long dead.

"Now that we've finished with the pleasantries, what's the true purpose of this gathering?" he asks me as I shovel rice into my mouth. His lip curls, and I resist the urge to chew with my mouth open just to irritate him.

Saengo's cheeks go pink, but I only swallow my food and say, "I have questions I was hoping you'd be able to answer."

He looks amused. "Well then, I'll try not to disappoint. What sort of questions?"

"Did you know that the Calling of Light has four crafts?"

"Yes," he says, like it should be obvious. "Please tell me you didn't come here just to ask that."

I ignore the remark. "But how did you know? The craft of soulrender was torn from the compendium I was reading last night."

"The Soulless was a soulrender," he says in that condescending tone. "There obviously had to be a fourth craft, even if knowledge of it is no longer taught to the Nuvali. Nor to anyone in Thiy."

"Why is that?" Saengo leans over her plate in interest.

"As game hunters, soulrenders used their craft primarily on beasts, but—"

"But when a shaman reaches a certain level of power," I say, remembering what Ronin had told me, "the limitations of shamanic crafts begin to bend."

Theyen nods. "Exactly. The Soulless continued to push until those limitations broke, until he could rip the souls not just from beasts but from other people."

Even if the Soulless hadn't gone mad with power, shamans with the ability to strip away souls—even if only those of animals—would be a strange and terrifying power indeed.

"Souls are the source of all our magic. To steal them was desecration. So soulrenders were hunted into extinction."

I rub the spidersilk of my robes between two fingers, remembering the ragged edges of the torn pages. The Soulless couldn't be erased from Thiy's history—his mark still scars the land—but his power had been so dark and so hated that those who came after tore what knowledge they could from that book. And likely from other books as well.

"That's terrible," Saengo says.

Theyen lifts one elegant shoulder in a slight shrug. "Crafts aren't strictly hereditary, but they can be more common within families, so when one was found, the entire house was executed to prevent the bloodline from producing more soulrenders. It was an effective, if archaic, solution."

The fear of him and his legacy infected Thiy so deeply that every soulrender since has paid for his crimes. Generations of families massacred, all because of a single shaman.

"You don't disapprove?" I ask.

He lifts his gaze from his plate. Those bright eyes are cold. "I don't care how the shamans choose to kill one another. If they want to hunt their own, let them."

I tap one finger against the edge of my plate and consider his words. Would that callousness extend to sending an assassin after me?

Saengo pokes her fork into her food, like she no longer wants to eat it. "I must say, Hlau Theyen. You're not endearing me to the Nuvali."

"Not at all deliberate, I assure you. But one positive thing that can be said for them," he says, shredding a piece of succulent meat with his fork, "is that they know their culinary skills."

"Not much variety in the mountains?" I ask.

"Some. From imports, mainly. The Kazan sleep during the

morning hours, and they dislike daylight, so there aren't enough people willing to till and plant the mountainsides."

"You don't seem to mind daylight."

He casts a reproachful look at the window. "I'm trying to get used to it. If I'm to live in the Nuvalyn Empire, then there will be little shelter. The Nuvali worship Suryal, the sun god, creator of all spirits. Mirrim is filled with towers of glass and open roofs."

"Don't the Yalaeng royals have eight children? Lots of contenders." I twirl my spoon in a frothy sauce that smells of lemongrass. "Maybe you'll get lucky, and your intended will be killed before there's even a wedding."

"Sirscha," Saengo says, incensed.

Theyen only laughs, low and quiet. "Unfortunately, barring outright war, I'm honor bound to unite our Houses, one way or another."

My brows lift a fraction at the admission that only war would sever his engagement. A slip due to arrogance, or a deliberate remark?

"Is that so?" I ask. "And, in your opinion, how likely is outright war?"

"Are you worried?"

"Should I be?"

A beat passes between us, something indefinite and guarded.

But then it passes, and Theyen smiles mockingly. "No one welcomes war, but we must always be prepared for it."

It's a diplomatic answer, which annoys me. "So if the Ember

Princess died, what would happen?"

"It's as much a symbolic marriage as it is a political one. Bearing my child to seal the alliance would, of course, be ideal, but in desperate situations—as, for example, when war is a tangible threat—the Yalaengs would select one of her siblings to take her place. A union with a prince would work just as well. Possibly even preferably, since I doubt they want any half-Kazan children becoming potential threats to the throne."

"I see." As much good as the union might bring to Thiy, a royal marriage can't erase past wrongs. Just as a peace treaty can't hold forever. Words on paper, signed by kings and queens long dead. Signing a contract agreeing not to act on standing hatreds is not a promise to stop hating.

I hadn't understood until I arrived here how fragile Ronin's grip is on the peace. He's holding the kingdoms together by a gossamer spider's thread.

Theyen insists on finishing his meal before answering any other questions, so I allow him to change the subject. Since he seems to enjoy hearing himself talk, I let him carry the conversation as I construct a mental layout of his suite in case I ever get the opportunity to rifle through his rooms in his absence.

After we finish eating, we move into the sitting room as servants clear the table. A few patches of white mar the walls in here, but the room is otherwise in superb condition. Silk dressings adorn the walls, framing a tapestry of a landscape constructed from thousands of perfect little stitches.

Random musical notes puncture the room as Theyen plucks

at a long horizontal string instrument tucked into the corner. I've always envied those with musical talent.

"Have you been by that maze of gardens at the back of the castle?" I ask Theyen. The memory of scurrying legs and the density of an unnameable power sends a shiver through me. Saengo and I move to the window, drawn by a warm draft of air.

"I've seen them in passing. The area is restricted to everyone but a few guards. The staff whisper that Ronin keeps his familiar back there."

"His Spinner?" I knew that had been a Spinner lurking in the maze, but Ronin's own familiar? "What about the rot? How can his familiar survive in the middle of the Dead Wood?"

Saengo looks to Theyen, clearly keen on the answer as well.

Theyen smiles with false benevolence. "I understand why you would think that I know everything, Sirscha, but—prepare yourself now—shockingly, that isn't the case." As I roll my eyes, he continues, "Ronin's magic is intact. I've seen him use it to heal some sagging crops in the vegetable gardens. So clearly he must have a familiar stowed somewhere nearby."

"Ronin is a sower," I say quietly, surprised. Sowers use their water magic to nurture the earth. They're architects of nature, the most powerful of whom can make crops flourish even in times of drought.

I suppose Ronin's familiar, connected to his considerable power through their bond, could account for the presence that had crawled inside my chest and made room against my spine, demanding my attention.

"What?" Theyen says distractedly as he tunes his instrument, strings stretched over a long resonant cavity made of lacquered wood.

"What do you think he's hiding back there?" I ask.

He pauses and looks down his nose at me. "You're going to have to be less dim-witted if you expect to keep my company. We just discussed the existence of a Spinner."

"Kindly stop insulting my friend," Saengo says with an arch of her brows that I'm certain she learned from her father.

Theyen is unimpressed. "That was your idea of an insult? I wasn't even trying."

"It's fine," I say. "He doesn't pretend to like me. I'm used to it."

"Just because I don't like you doesn't mean I dislike you."

"Well, that's flattering," I say dryly.

"You should be flattered. My attention is hard to keep."

Any more time in Theyen's company, and I'll be at risk of injuring myself from repeatedly rolling my eyes. "Anyway, I don't mean just a Spinner."

Whatever power lurks in the garden maze sank hooks into my skin, and it's been trying to reel me back ever since. If his familiar is back there, then it must be powerful indeed to not only resist the rot but to maintain Ronin's control—

The thought jolts through me. Ronin's familiar is the key to his power. It's so stupidly obvious now that I've realized it. Shamans can't perform magic without familiars. Ronin is no different. His loss of control over the Dead Wood and whatever's keeping the spirits tied here is connected as well to his familiar. Something must be wrong with it.

"Do you think you could help me get into that maze?" I ask.

"Why would I do that?" His fingers hover over the strings, waiting.

"Because I know you want Ronin to dissolve your engagement with the Ember Princess. Maybe we'll find something back there to help you negotiate."

A slow smile twists his mouth as he withdraws a fingerpick from beneath the instrument. "I think I'm beginning to like you."

I turn a triumphant look at Saengo. She mouths, "I don't trust him."

Neither do I. But I mean to take advantage of whatever assistance he's willing to offer.

"There's one more thing I was hoping you could tell me. Have you heard any news from Evewyn? Anything about the shamanborn?"

"Why would I have news from the human kingdom?" he asks as he begins to play. His long gray fingers glide across the strings with mesmerizing grace.

I consider a lie. But then the earthwender's face appears in my thoughts. Somewhere in the Dead Wood, she's suffering. Trapped. My heart twinges at the memory of her eyes, bright with defiance. Anger heats through me. She deserved so much better.

"I had a dream. I saw a girl I knew from the Valley of Cranes. She was taken by the trees."

"Ah. I suppose between Ronin and me, I was the easier option for seeking out answers." Theyen doesn't look up, his hands continuing to move as each note shivers through the air.

Saengo winces, but I only lean my shoulder against the wall and cross my arms. "Does that mean you don't know anything?"

He glances at me, eyes bright with amusement. "When your queen outlawed shamans, she also restricted the shadowblessed to Evewyn's port cities. I've been informed that Vos Gillis's notice boards are filled with posters warning of shamanborn hiding in the city. The result of an escape from the prison camp."

The words lance through me like a bolt of lightning. An escape.

He finishes his song and then shifts in his seat to face us. "Rumor has it, someone within the queen's circle is helping the shamanborn stow aboard ships to escape the country, but no one's been able to catch more than a glimpse of a shadow."

"Sirscha, you can't do this," Saengo says once we're back in our rooms.

I'd have thought by now that she would know better than to tell me I can't do something. It only makes me want to try harder.

"It's Kendara," I say. "It has to be. She's always hated the prison camp, and who else would have the means to help those shamanborn without getting caught?" Not to mention the word the earthwender healer said in my dream also connects to Kendara. It can't be a coincidence.

"You can't leave on little more than a guess. What if the queen catches you? It's too dangerous."

"It's worth the risk," I insist. "I have to speak to her, and there's no better opportunity. Vos Gillis is a big port city and as far from the capital and the queen as you can get in Evewyn. If I can find her, I know she'll help us."

Kendara is the most intelligent person I know. As the queen's Shadow, she's also one of the most informed. She'll be able to tell me more about Ronin and his familiar, and what might be going on with the Dead Wood.

"But would she really betray the queen by helping the shaman-born? Even if she hates the prison, she's also a loyal subject."

Kendara once sent me into the home of a minor lord to re-trieve copies of the man's ledgers. The lord in question had been in Vos Talwyn at the time, and his estate was barely guarded. When I'd questioned the morality of stealing from the queen's own lords, she'd said that sometimes one had to work around the law in order to best serve it.

"She is a loyal subject," I say. She'll do what she thinks is best for the kingdom. "Besides, it's only treason if you're caught."

"Then I'll come with you."

"You can't. You can't risk missing any treatments with the healer."

She tosses up her hands and storms over to the balcony where she braces both palms against the glass. "If the rot doesn't kill me, this confinement will. I can't breathe here. I need to do something. To be useful."

The set of her shoulders tells me she's not looking to be comforted, so I remain where I am by my bed. I've changed out of my gown, which lies in a pool of spidersilk in front of the armoire.

"As soon as I have the information I need to destroy the Dead Wood, you won't ever have to come back here again."

Saengo's hands curl into fists against the glass. "We used to be a team." Her voice is soft, but the words still cut. "Now all I am is a piece of you. A shadow tethered to your soles, looking at your back."

Her pain is a hard knot at the center of me. My nails dig into my stomach, like I might be able to tear the feeling away. "I'm sorry," I whisper. "I'm sorry I did this to you."

She looks back at me. Sadness sharpens her eyes and the lines of her mouth. "I don't blame you. You didn't know what you were doing. But maybe you're right that I should stay. I think I need to be alone."

With Phaut's help, I'm given an audience with Ronin later that afternoon. Leaving Spinner's End would be impossible without his assistance.

She takes me again to what had once been the throne room. I approach the broad, sweeping stairs leading up to the dais where Ronin stands. The doors shut behind me with a resonating clank. A fire burns low at his back. A hazy heat ripples the air around his tall figure. He's dressed in a plain gray shirt tucked into loose black pants and a matching jacket. The table from the last time I was here is gone.

"You seem troubled," Ronin says. He speaks in that same soft voice that's much too difficult to read.

Why wouldn't I be troubled? Learning my craft is still necessary, but it won't be enough to destroy the Dead Wood before the rot takes my best friend.

"I think . . . I think the best way to restore control over the Dead Wood is to find out what's keeping the spirits rooted to the trees. We need to undo whatever curse keeps them here."

Without moving a single muscle, Ronin cuts me a look that makes my tongue shrink back in my mouth. His eyes narrow into thin chips of sapphire. "It's no wonder you've made so little progress summoning your craft when you squander your time on useless pursuits. We already have a solution to the problem—your power, which you're meant to be developing. Instead, you dawdle over questions I've already exhausted."

I bite the inside of my cheeks and force a small, acquiescent bow. His response only confirms that I won't find any answers with him. I'll have to seek them elsewhere.

"Of course," I agree, schooling my voice into something neutral.

"You'll be glad to know that the shaman who attacked your friend was captured three nights ago."

And you're only telling me now? "I'm relieved to hear that. What were his motives?"

"I sent soldiers to collect him for interrogation. But before they could, the shaman escaped. Evidently, there was a prison break at the Valley of Cranes, and the shaman took advantage."

Frustration pinches at my temples. Of course he escaped. Could nothing go right? "I see. But you'll recover him?"

"As soon as I can. But in the meantime, some of the escaped shamanborn have arrived at my western encampment. I'm leaving to meet them in the morning."

Surprised, I smother my rising anger. "You're going to help them?"

"I won't return them to Queen Meilyr, but as a neutral entity, I'm unable to do anything for them."

In the firelight, the hard angles of his face soften. I don't know how to interpret his expression, but I imagine it's not one he wears often. As the ruler of the Dead Wood, softness or vulnerability are indulgences that are not available to him. He must always be in control, and for the first time, I wonder at the burden he must carry.

"But you wish you could?" I ask quietly.

Any shred of softness in him vanishes. He links his fingers together, once again the picture of calm. I can't tell if it's an act. How many years, decades, lifetimes even, would it take for someone to become unmoved by tragedy?

When he responds, it's without inflection. "I do what I must to keep the peace."

I shouldn't have overstepped. Straightening my shoulders, I say as firmly as I dare, "I'd like to accompany you to your encampment."

He regards me for an excruciatingly long second. "For what reason?"

I clasp my hands behind my back, gripping my fingers tight, and speak a half-truth. "I believe the shamanborn might have information that will help me find someone—a former mentor. I haven't yet been able to summon my craft, and I think she can help me." In case he doubts my intentions, I add, "Saengo will stay here with the shadowblessed healer."

He appears to genuinely consider my request. My heart thunders, and my palms grow slick with anticipation.

At last, he says, "Very well. You may accompany me to Sab Hlee and speak to the shamanborn. I intend to remain there for three days. After that, I will return to Spinner's End. If you haven't located your mentor and returned by that time, you'll have to find your own way."

He means to make this into another test. Without Ronin as an escort, getting back to Spinner's End on my own would be all but impossible. Still, I nod, my thoughts already racing to the challenge ahead.

SIXTEEN

The next morning, I'm given an hour to pull together a satchel of necessities. There are only five of us leaving—Ronin, two soldiers, Phaut, and myself.

Saengo waves from the front steps of the castle, her face pale and worried. I whisper a prayer to the Falcon Warrior to keep watch over her safety until I return. As we pass beneath the white drape and enter the Dead Wood, everyone in our party seems to hold their breaths. Even the soldiers look nervous, tugging their cloaks closer. We follow Ronin's path through the trees, thankfully away from where I encountered Kamryne.

Ronin walks purposefully, his steps never faltering. He's the only one in our party who isn't wearing a spidersilk cloak, choosing instead a simple jacket and sash over leather armor. The woods shrink before him, clearing his path.

Every creak of the trees sends magic coiling beneath my skin, magic that I'm not at all confident I can call upon. The roots rustle and spasm but never quite complete the threat of tripping us. Withered bark splits, baring black rot. Those burl eyes track us as we pass.

The soldiers try not to look afraid in Ronin's presence, but their body language gives them away. Their hands never leave their swords. What conversations they manage are short and stilted.

A face rises through the decayed bark, its mouth screaming soundlessly. I look away. They can't tear free of the trees. They've been dead so long that their bodies have long merged with the Dead Wood, the branches becoming their arms and the roots their legs.

My gaze searches for somewhere to rest that isn't pitted and rotten, and it finds the ornate pommel of Phaut's sword. I gesture to it. "Where did you get your sword?"

She doesn't look away from her scrutiny of the trees. "I made it."

I consider her eyes. They're jewel green, bright against the drab gray of the woods. "What kind of earthwender are you?"

"Forger."

That would explain it. Forgers can shape and bend metals with more ease and precision than any blacksmith.

"My master, the one who taught me how to refine my craft, learned under a Kazan weaponsmith," she says. "Kazan weapons are superior to our own. They're forged from rare metals mined from the hearts of their mountains and imbued with shadow crafts unique to each clan."

Our attempts at conversation grow infrequent as the day slips by. The constant tension exhausts everyone. We gnaw on strips of dried meat and rice balls to assuage our hunger, but we don't stop to rest. What feels like an eternity later, Ronin speaks for the first time since leaving Spinner's End.

"The encampment isn't far now."

Relief courses through me just as the soldier behind me screams. I turn, drawing my swords even before I spot the trouble. A pair of distinctly human arms thrust out from a tree. Jagged bone tears through the black-blue skin of the corpse that's taken hold of one of the soldiers—Audri's her name, I think. Its mangled fingers score her throat and grip the edges of her breastplate to drag her into the tree. The other soldier grabs hold of Audri's waist, his neck muscles straining as he pulls with little effect.

Phaut immediately jumps forward to help, but Audri's frantic screams rouse the other trees. My swords strike the corpse's arms. It releases her as another body rears out from the recesses of the tree. I recoil, gasping. The new creature's skull is crushed on one side and its head hangs awkwardly, as if its neck is broken. A rattle issues from its mouth as it wrenches Audri hard, tearing her from both Phaut's and the other soldier's grasps.

Phaut nearly tumbles into the tree with her. I dive for Phaut's legs, knocking her into the dirt. Audri's screams grow muffled, her upper body buried within bark as we try to get a hold of her kicking feet.

"Help!" I scream at Ronin, who isn't even watching us. His sharp eyes dart from tree to tree.

All around us, chunks of bark litter the roots as corpses twist and yank their emaciated limbs out from their wooden prisons.

"Oh, Sisters," I breathe, redoubling my efforts to free Audri. Panic sprints through my chest as the bodies move in my peripheral vision. My magic builds, bright and thrilling. My skin feels like it's been set aflame, heat shooting through my shoulders, down my arms.

Then Audri's shrieks abruptly stop and her lower body goes limp. I gasp, shock dousing my craft.

The other soldier makes a sound like a sob and a scream. Half crawling to get away, he draws his sword. Phaut helps me to my feet. I try to recover my magic, desperate to do something other than gape in horror as the rest of Audri's body is devoured by the shriveled black stump.

"Run," Ronin orders curtly. None of us need any more urging than that.

We run, terror lending speed to our flight. The trees fly by in a gray-green blur. We slash and jump and kick. Phaut is nearly dragged down twice before, at last, the branches thin and the afternoon sky appears. We burst from the trees and collapse to the ground.

The grass cools my flushed skin. Incongruously, the sun shines brightly overhead. Phaut is on her hands and knees beside me. Her short hair falls messily over her cheekbones. Her breaths come hard, as labored as mine. We must have sprinted a mile in record time.

"There were so many," she whispers.

I nod mutely, still numb with shock. We remain there a moment, silent, reliving the last few minutes; our minds remain trapped in the trees with Audri. I should have tried harder to help her, to help them all. But all I did was run. My fingers curl into the earth, grounding myself in the present. Clumps of grass tear free as I rise. I assist Phaut to her feet before noticing the other soldier has staggered ahead.

We've emerged near the path where I first entered the Dead Wood almost a week ago. Sab Hlee lies a short ride away.

"Where's Ronin?" I turn in a circle to scan the area. Phaut copies me, her hands combing roughly through her tousled hair. He told us to run but did not run with us. Was he still in there?

Phaut's legs jolt haltingly toward the trees, as if intending to go after him. But then Ronin's tall figure materializes from the shadowy boughs.

"What happened?" I ask, returning my swords to their sheaths.

"The souls have been silenced," Ronin says without further explanation.

And what about Audri? I want to shout, despite that the question would be pointless.

We follow him toward the encampment, the silence wrought with fear unabated by Ronin's reassurance. Those had been newly taken souls. Why would they go into the trees, knowing what awaited them?

After the horror of the Dead Wood, I'm caught off guard by the distant sprawl of the mountains far to the west. My breath catches unexpectedly at the awareness of how close Evewyn is. This strip of land outside the Dead Wood is still Ronin's territory but beyond . . . just beyond that is home. Yearning throbs inside me.

Soon. Once Saengo is healed and our safety assured.

When we arrive at Sab Hlee, soldiers line up to receive Ronin. The soldier who'd gone ahead, looking hollow-eyed but composed, rejoins us. Ronin's soldiers swore their oaths knowing the risks, but still . . . my stomach churns.

At the center of the encampment, a group of bedraggled shamans occupy an array of dinner tables. There must be more than twenty, from elderly to children, enough to fill nearly every seat. Their eyes inspect our approach, especially Ronin's.

I can imagine how he must appear, mysterious and intimidating, his tall figure resplendent in the afternoon light. And there is clearly cause to fear his power after he alone quelled those newly taken souls while the rest of us ran. I bite the inside of my cheek, the pain muting my shame.

Some of the shamans shift uneasily. Their thin bodies shrink into the shadows. For others, their sallow faces come alive, their bodies straining from their seats. I remain with Phaut, content to blend in with the soldiers.

Ronin pauses before the tables. Dirty dishes stacked along the ends indicate a recent meal. A much-needed one by the looks of them. Their clothes are threadbare, holes patched and then patched again. How had they managed to escape the Valley?

"How many others?" Ronin asks a soldier in a slightly different uniform from the rest.

The officit, a windwender, says in a low voice, "They don't

know. But they say some went south instead. This is what's left of the survivors."

"And those who did not survive?" Ronin asks. His words are a chill breeze in the warm afternoon that raises the recent memory of corpses strung to trees by remnants of flesh.

"We couldn't recover very many," the officit says, voice heavy. "But the ones we did . . ." She nods to the north side of the camp.

I squint in that direction and make out plots of freshly turned dirt. They must have been truly desperate to enter the Dead Wood. Maybe they were fleeing pursuers? The earthwender healer must have been among them.

"What should we do about . . ." The officit's voice trails off, but she's looking at the Dead Wood.

"Nothing can be done for them," Ronin says, and I know the disappointed flick of his eyes in my direction isn't imagined.

I wince and lower my gaze. His feet whisper over the hard-packed dirt, his jacket dusting the earth as he circles the tables.

"I cannot give you sanctuary," he says to the shamanborn.

Instantly, several crumple to the tabletops in despair. A more daring shaman cries out, "We were told you accept the services of any who will swear allegiance to you."

Ronin nods at this, to the mumbled confusion of the shamanborn. "I welcome the service of all who are free to make such pledges. You are not. You are Evewynian prisoners. To shelter you would violate standing peace treaties. You must leave for the north at nightfall."

North. They mean to cross the grasslands into the Nuvalyn

Empire then. It seems the surest route to safety, but the queen's soldiers will know that as well. If the group travels at night, keeping close enough to the edge of the Dead Wood where Evewyn's patrols aren't permitted, they might stand a chance.

But what about Vos Gillis? Theyen said the shamanborn were being smuggled onto ships to escape Evewyn.

"What about south?" I say. All eyes turn to me, but I focus on Ronin.

He doesn't appear to mind my interruption. "Even if they reach the coast, a ship can't be guaranteed. In Vos Gillis, several shamanborn have already been captured and await transport to the prison."

My shoulders tense. Theyen hadn't mentioned that. I suppose even Kendara can't protect every shamanborn who sneaks into the port city.

Ronin addresses the shamanborn. "Queen Meilyr has issued a decree that if any of you are caught, you're to be returned to the Valley of Cranes for execution. Her soldiers have been given leave to take any means necessary to subdue you." He lets his words settle, lets the fresh horror of their reality sink into their wearied bones. Then he repeats, "You must go north at nightfall."

My hands ball into fists. Perhaps sensing my urge to argue with Ronin's refusal to protect them, Phaut rests a hand on my shoulder.

A small voice says, "Suryali?"

My head jerks, seeking out the speaker. The girl looks no more than ten years old. Unlike the older shamans, her eyes are still gray. She's gaunt, little more than flesh stretched over bone.

She looks fragile like a baby bird, the likeness made more striking when she cocks her head and tugs on the sleeve of the man beside her. "Is it her?"

"That's just a lightwender, little one," the man says. But now that it's been spoken, the shamanborn pass the word around in a flurry of whispers, the same word the earthwender healer uttered in my dream.

Beside me, Phaut gives a light cough and translates in a whisper, "Little Sun God."

I stiffen. Are they referring to *me*?

Their murmurs grow in volume as some are quicker than others to realize who I might be. Those farther back stand to get a better look, as if I'm a performer at a spectacle. I step back as their gazes flit from me to Ronin. I'm surprised when Ronin does nothing other than nod once. A confirmation.

My nostrils flare. Is this another test? The little girl stands from the table. Others follow, their steps shuffling and hesitant as they approach. The urge to shrink into the shadows and disappear as Kendara taught me is nearly overwhelming.

"Suryali," they repeat in hushed voices. One reaches out. I stumble back, alarmed, and yank my cloak away from his outstretched hands.

Phaut steps in to shield me. She has somehow transformed from guard to protector. But she is only one person. They swarm us, expressions fierce and eager.

"Is it true?" a voice shouts out above the rest. A shaman with uneven hair cut close to her scalp eyes me with distrust. She hangs back with the more cautious of the group, most of whom have half risen from their seats.

"Are you the soulguide?" another shaman asks.

"It can't be true," someone mutters.

"You're shamanborn. One of us. We thought we'd have to travel all the way to Mirrim to find you."

"She's just a child," whispers someone else. Irritation blossoms in my chest.

"We escaped for you," says a small voice. The little girl with the gray eyes gazes up at me, awe brimming from her smile.

I shake my head. *What?*

Behind the girl stands a man with shining amber eyes, a shade paler than mine but still jewel bright. He touches the center of his chest. "Six nights ago, every lightwender in the camp felt a surge of magic within us. I haven't felt the heat of magic in years." His voice wavers. "It only lasted a moment. Most of us hold faith with the Five Sisters, but we also know the old shaman tales."

My lips compress. They had felt the awakening of my craft and suspected what it might mean. And if they believed, like Ronin, that the appearance of a soulguide was an omen, maybe . . . just maybe, that could have been enough to rally them, to stage a revolt big enough to allow some to escape.

Suddenly, I can't draw a full breath. The weight of those gazes presses around me, their hopes and expectations deposited in my arms while they await miracles I can't perform. They escaped for me—did that make their protection my responsibility? It's not a responsibility I want, and yet I wish I could help them. That I could be what they so fervently want.

At the back of the group, a man rises from his seat. He's taller than the others, but he stoops, as if trying to appear small. When he glances up at me, the glint of purple catches my attention. He's disheveled and dirty, fidgeting restlessly as his gaze darts uneasily around the encampment. My eyes widen.

It's the windwender from the night of the attack. The shaman who killed Saengo.

He realizes the moment I recognize him because he turns and runs.

"Stop!" I shove past the shamanborn gathered around me, costing me precious seconds before I'm free.

Phaut is close beside me as we sprint through the encampment, around tables and tents, following the frantic flight of the windwender.

Ronin's soldiers draw their weapons but hesitate, uncertain whom to assist. I don't pay them any attention, my gaze fixed on my quarry. Fury burns through me, chasing away any remnants of fear from the Dead Wood and the shock of discovering why the shamanborn had escaped. My teeth are clenched tight. The wind screams in my ears as my boots devour the distance between us.

We're nearing the edge of the encampment when an arrow sings past me. It pierces the windwender's back, sending him sprawling into the dirt.

"No," I gasp, digging in my heels.

In seconds, I'm on top of him, dragging him up by his collar.

His eyes roll back in his head, but I give him a violent shake.

"No! You're not dying until you tell me why you attacked us at the teahouse. Who sent you to kill the queen's Shadow? Speak!"

"Sirscha," Phaut says, horrified.

"Tell me!" I demand.

The windwender coughs. Blood spatters his chin. "B-betrayed," he manages to say in a garbled whisper. "P-promised . . . safe . . . ty."

"Who promised you safety?" My knuckles are as white as his face. Anger pushes my breaths out in quick, thin pants.

"The q-queen," he says thickly.

"The queen?" I echo, confused. "Queen Meilyr?"

He nods, eyes fluttering shut.

I shake him again. "What are you talking about?"

But it's no use. The man's bright eyes don't open again. A moment later, he goes slack.

"No!" I slam his limp body to the ground, then shove to my feet, brushing off Phaut's quiet murmur of confusion. My fingers furrow through my hair. My legs are unable to remain still as I prowl around the dead windwender, nearly giving into the urge to kick his corpse.

Ronin's soldiers close in on the body. I have no idea which one shot him, but I want to punch something. What did he mean that the queen had promised them safety? He had to have been lying. The queen wouldn't have promised them such a thing unless she'd been the one to send them, which is ludicrous.

She wouldn't have sent assassins after her own Shadow.

It didn't make any sense.

Yet, what reason would a dying man have to lie?

Ronin puts me in a tent to calm down so that I don't upset the other shamanborn. The tent is sparse, with nothing but a cot to fill the small space.

Phaut hovers near the entrance, one hand braced on the tent flap as if preparing to leave. She doesn't, though.

"You all right?" she asks uncertainly.

It's just too much. All I have are questions piled upon questions. How can I believe that Queen Meilyr sent shamans after her own Shadow? How am I supposed to help Saengo or the shamanborn when I couldn't even save Audri from the trees?

"Do you believe what they say about soulguides?" I demand, perhaps more harshly than she deserves.

Her lips twist to one side, like she's deliberating how best to answer without making me angry. "I'd never given it much thought before you arrived, to be honest. I've not had the best experience with lightwenders."

"You mentioned something like that before. What happened?"

She shifts on her feet and lowers her eyes.

I shake my head. "Never mind. I shouldn't have asked. Can I just—" I tug at my braid. "Can I be alone for a minute?"

She nods at the exit. "I'll be right outside."

The sunlight knifes across the ground as she leaves, before the tent is once again immersed in shadows. The low murmur of the shamanborn penetrates the tent. I push loose hair roughly behind my ears, my fingers once again finding those thin scars, proof that what and who I am cannot be so easily erased. Maybe Ronin is right. Maybe I should've been practicing my craft instead of wasting time trying to unearth the Dead Wood's secrets.

If I'd practiced more, dared the dangers of the Dead Wood more, fought Theyen more, maybe I could have saved Audri. Maybe I could heal Saengo. Maybe I would actually deserve the faith these shamanborn have placed in me.

With a groan, I cover my face and listen only to the sounds of my breaths. In and out.

Facts, Sirscha, I tell myself. Focus on the facts.

Audri's death is a grim reminder that the Dead Wood must be dealt with. I could free Audri and the other trapped souls. I need only learn how. And to save Saengo, I must remove the source of the disease. I need to find Kendara and learn what she knows about Ronin and the Dead Wood.

The crush of so many expectations is matched only by the fear of not measuring up. I press my palms to my temples. Fear is not a wall. It is a whip at my back, driving me onward.

I might not be a proper soulguide, but I am not helpless. Kendara made sure of that. I already possess every skill I'll need to reach her in Vos Gillis. But what about the shamanborn imprisoned there? They'll be executed if they're returned to the Valley.

Once, I might have helped to imprison them if the queen had ordered it—what sort of monster did that make me? Knowing what she does to her enemies, looking the other way becomes terribly easy. But no longer. I won't leave the imprisoned shamanborn to the queen's vengeance.

They risked their lives to escape the Valley of Cranes on little more than hope. Many plunged recklessly into the Dead Wood as a result of that hope. After all they have suffered—which is far more than what even I have had to endure—the ferocity in all their eyes says the same thing: *We are not broken.*

SEVENTEEN

Ronin looks the other way as I gather provisions. This means convincing his soldiers that I have permission to rummage through Sab Hlee's larder, located in one of the collapsible thatch buildings.

Fortunately, Phaut is quick to corroborate my story. Ronin must have briefed her on my search for Kendara while I was in the tent, because she doesn't ask questions as she saddles her own drake. She's changed into a worn-looking black shirt tucked into loose black pants and a yellow sash. It's the first time I've seen her in anything but the drab gray of Ronin's soldiers.

It's not until we've left Sab Hlee that I inform her of my intentions to free the shamanborn in Vos Gillis. Curiously, she doesn't argue except to assert that whatever we do, Ronin can't be connected to it.

Time is against us if we're to make it to the southern coast and back again in three days, so we mutually agree to continue through the night. If we don't return before Ronin leaves, we'll be left to travel the Dead Wood on our own.

We grab a few hours of sleep before dawn to rest the drakes, then keep to the trees when we can. Our eyes are conspicuous. Neither of us is likely to forget what would happen if we're caught, especially as Ronin would offer no protection.

It's well after sunset when we reach Vos Gillis. As expected, guards watch every road into the city and sentinels patrol its limits. There's a small fishing village not far to the west of Vos Gillis, where we steal a rowboat off the quay and return east along the coast. Any shamanborn attempting to get into the city wouldn't be doing so by boat; that's how they'd be leaving.

My main goal is to find Kendara, but I can do that while focusing on the shamanborn. If she's helping them escape the city, then freeing the imprisoned shamanborn might force her to reveal herself. But I don't want them stowing away on a cargo ship. If discovered, they'll either be returned to Evewyn or thrown overboard. Depending on their numbers, we have to find ships willing to take them as passengers or extra hands.

There are far fewer guards watching the waterways. We steer our boat toward a narrow canal that passes under a wooden bridge. The bridge is dimly lit by a single lantern suspended on a hooked post. Two sentinels stand watch, illuminated by the little sphere of yellow light.

I'm about to suggest a distraction when Phaut extends one hand. The metal hook holding the lantern aloft snaps. The light goes out as the lantern tips and lands with a clatter on the bridge.

Swearing, the sentinels scramble to right it as Phaut and I row quietly and quickly into the murk beneath the bridge. We're gliding into the city's main waterway by the time the sentinels get the lantern lit again.

"How did you do that?" I ask.

"Simple magic," Phaut says.

"No, I mean, don't you need a familiar?"

"I have one. Back in the Empire, away from the Dead Wood. I was there a couple of weeks ago, well before you arrived at Spinner's End."

"I didn't know that." I tilt my head at her.

"You didn't ask."

I'd like to ask now. There's so much I don't know about this woman who's shadowed my steps from the moment I arrived at Spinner's End—a fact that I no longer resent. However, such questions will have to wait.

"I assume you have a plan," she says as we cut through the water.

"I do," I say, but there are far too many variables for my liking. "I'll need to get a better view of the city." From the roofs, it'll be easier to spot the guardhouse and get a lay of the streets in case we need a quick escape. Which I'm sure we will. It might also give me a better idea of where Kendara might be hiding.

She has to be here. In a city teeming with guards, no one else would have her resources to get the shamanborn safely stowed away on ships. Please let her be here.

Despite the late hour, once we enter the city's market district,

Vos Gillis's waterways are far from quiet. Merchants crowd the canals, ferrying their wares up and down the riverfront. Houses sit on stilts, jutting out over the water like the prows of ships. Sleek little boats shoot past our slower one, the sharp blades of their sails extended like fins.

Bridges arch over our heads, some with railings fashioned into slithering zaj serpents and others with no railing at all. We steer our boat toward a dock and pull up beside an elaborate vessel with a canopy draped in airy silks. A woman's laugh issues from beneath.

Phaut and I adjust our plain wool cloaks as we climb from our stolen boat and anchor it to one of the many lantern posts lining the waterfront. The head of this particular post is in the shape of a phoenix, its flaming tail and magnificent wings raised high. The lantern hangs from its curved beak. Oddly enchanted, I push into the busy streets.

The buildings are tall and cramped, homes stacked one on top of another. A haphazard tiered roof caps each level. They look to be held upright only by virtue of the buildings beside them, which are equally off center. Suspension bridges stretch overhead, connecting the higher levels. They swing precariously at every gust off the sea.

The streets are more mud than dirt. My boots make a squelching sound with each step. Despite this and the overcrowding, Vos Gillis is a colorful city.

Paper lanterns hang from nearly every roof and awning. They're strung from bridges and windows in every shape and color, from cream cylinders capped in green to crimson spheres accented with golden tassels, so that the lines of the city seem drawn in lights. Painted signs hang over the swinging doors of taverns, teahouses, and shops selling trinkets and sweets. Streamers flutter and twine in the air, and beneath the chaotic hum of the crowds is the tinkling of windchimes.

We've wandered directly into Vos Gillis's night market. Perfect. A thriving market means an abundance of purses to pickpocket. Phaut tries to direct me toward a quieter street, but I pull away, plunging into the heart of the Market District.

"Sirscha," she hisses, tugging at her hood. I wonder if she's ever been in Evewyn without the protection of Ronin's name.

"It's fine." I skirt around bodies to peer at the market stalls, my fingers deft and silent. I pause to admire one stall that carries bolts of sandsilk, weever lace, and other imported fabrics. The next stall drips with necklaces and charms that flare copper and amber in the firelight.

All I can see of Phaut's face is her pinched lips. I laugh as I move on to inspect a stack of polished teakettles and dainty hand-painted fans. I scan the crowds, searching as well for any hint of Kendara. A couple of years ago, Saengo had visited this city with her parents. She hadn't been allowed to explore the market, but she'd still returned with stories of massive ships as tall as the Temple of the Sisters. We'd promised to travel the country together someday, and I mean to keep that promise.

After some time, Phaut jabs my shoulder blade. Sighing, I gesture with my chin toward a quieter side street. As we leave the market behind, we pass several inns, common enough in a port city where people are always coming and going. Loitering on a street corner between two inns, we pretend like we're considering which might have vacancies as we discuss our next move.

"I'm going up," I say, indicating the roofs. "You head down to the docks. See if you can find out which ships are leaving tomorrow evening and which might be friendly to shamanborn passengers." Many ships fly the colors of their country in addition to their own banners. It should be simple enough to avoid Evewynian vessels. "I've heard it said that folk from across the sea are fascinated by our crafts. Use that if you have to."

Phaut frowns as she glances up and down the street. Although people still mill about, it's far less crowded here. Some have foregone an inn entirely, instead finding a narrow alley to sleep off their drink. "And how do you propose I buy their passage?"

I dig into my pockets and emerge with fistfuls of coin purses, which I shove beneath Phaut's cloak into her stunned hands. She gawks at no less than a half-dozen purses, one so heavy that she nearly drops the lot.

"What . . . did you steal these?" she hisses, stuffing the incriminating items into her own pockets.

"You didn't think I was just browsing the market, did you?" I ask, smiling. Phaut's nose wrinkles, and she does a terrible job of not looking like she's carrying pockets full of stolen coins. I almost feel sorry for her. "There were a lot of soldiers patrolling the market and elsewhere. So stay alert and don't get caught. Meet back here at sunrise."

If Vos Gillis at night is magnificent, it becomes an even more glorious jumble by daylight.

The buildings are almost entirely constructed of wood. Their various roofs once might have been a handsome green but have aged into the color of mildew. The mood of the city is so different from Vos Talwyn, which is suffused in history. Everything here feels transient, ever changing, as if the buildings might pick themselves up and shuffle around when you aren't looking.

The only buildings that aren't made of wood are the temple and the four watchtowers. The towers teem with soldiers. Guards patrol at every level on balconies that wrap around the entire structure. Attached to the westernmost tower is the guardhouse, a two-story building with an elaborate series of roofs that resemble the blooming petals of a lotus.

Once I understand the layout of the city, I spend the rest of the night making discreet inquiries about Kendara. No luck there, though. I can only hope she'll make herself known. More than likely, she'll find me well before I find her.

At sunrise, Phaut and I reconvene to discuss our next steps. I'll spend the day preparing the shamanborn so that when she creates a distraction at sunset, they'll be ready to run. That should leave us a full day to make it back to Sab Hlee before Ronin returns to Spinner's End.

Once we're agreed, Phaut returns to the docks to barter with the only captain willing to take passengers. She hasn't outright stated the passengers would be shamanborn, but she'd spotted shamans among the crew, tucked safely aboard their ship and off Evewynian soil.

I'm happy to leave the bartering to Phaut. As she explained it, she spent much of her childhood haggling over the prices of her father's vegetables at their local market. While she's busy ensuring the shamanborn have a means of travel, I return to the night market, which transitions seamlessly with the dawn.

The streets fill with waves of new customers, many of them having only disembarked that morning. I steal a pair of hairpins off a table and push them into the lining of my drawers where the additional fabric should conceal them.

If I'm to help the shamanborn escape, I'll first need access to them. There's no better way than to join them in the guardhouse.

In the market, I can't take two steps without spotting a guard. Some scan the crowd for the flash of jeweled eyes, but most loiter in clusters of three or four. As I draw near one such group, I duck my head sharply and tug jerkily at my hood. I wring my hands and hunch my shoulders, crossing and uncrossing my arms. I walk too fast and then make an abrupt turn, shuffling my feet.

Part of me hopes Kendara will notice and swoop in to assure me she already has a plan.

But while my behavior is certainly noticed, it's not by Kendara. One of the guards breaks away from the others, his hand going to the sword at his hip. I lift my head in a quick glance. Our eyes meet for the briefest of moments.

It's enough. He sees the glimmer of amber. "You! Stop there!"

I turn and run, straight into the corner of a stall. My cloak tangles around my legs as I crash into the dirt. Others around me exclaim in surprise, backing away. Scrambling with the folds of my cloak, I try to stand, but by then, the guards are on me. Two grab my arms and haul me to my feet. My hood falls back. The people nearest us gasp as my eyes are revealed to the sunlight.

One guard has drawn his sword, and the other has notched an arrow, bowstring stretched taut. They watch, prepared to strike, as the two restraining me search me for weapons. They're waiting to see if I use a craft, I realize. Best not to make any sudden movements in case that archer gets twitchy. For effect, my bottom lip wobbles.

Once they're satisfied I'm unarmed, both physically and magically, they lead me through the streets, following the path I predicted they'd take to the guardhouse.

Curious, I observe the guards escorting me under the pretense of fearful glances. They don't seem overly hostile, not like Eyebrow Tattoos. But neither are they gentle as they pull me through the door. Directly past the front desk is a hallway ending in a barred metal door that presumably leads to the cells.

They don't deliver me there, though. I take mental stock of where everything is as they guide me instead toward an office door that's slightly ajar. The guard in front pushes it open and then steps aside. My feet stall, and all my careful planning crashes around me. Sitting behind the desk is Prince Meilek.

I blink slowly. This is a complication.

"We found another one, Your Highness." The guard gives me a hard shake so that I remember my manners. Gathering my wits, I dip into a bow as low as my captors will allow me.

Prince Meilek, for his part, hides his surprise well. He gives nothing away other than a slight twitch of his eyebrow.

He stands. "Thank you for your efforts. You may leave."

The guards glance at each other, their hands yet to loosen around my arms. "Are you sure that's wise?"

"I'll be fine. You may remain in the hall if that will put your minds at ease, but lightwenders are rarely much trouble."

Reluctantly, they release me. When the door shuts behind them, Prince Meilek gestures to the chair opposite his. I don't sit. What is he doing here?

His clothes suggest he's here more as a prince than as a captain. He wears a fusion of leather and plate armor over green silk brocade. The high collar is finely detailed with golden thread. His cloak's gleaming clasp bears the triple-horned stag of his House. His hair has been pulled back, secured at the crown of his head with a hairpiece that resembles jagged antlers.

"Does Ronin know he's missing a soulguide?" he asks, clasping his hands behind his back.

I shrug one shoulder.

"I was glad to hear you'd made it safely to Spinner's End. But how did you manage to escape?"

"You're aware of my training," I say. Better that he believes I left of my own accord. Anything else might incriminate Ronin.

"Sirscha, we both know you haven't done anything to deserve

imprisonment. At least not yet," he says, a warning in his tone. Those brown eyes are much too perceptive. "And, as you say, with your training, I somehow doubt you would be here if this weren't exactly where you wished to be."

A bead of sweat slides down the back of my neck. If Prince Meilek suspects my purpose here, he could ruin everything. And yet, what can I possibly say in my defense? Vos Gillis's guards are well trained, but they're not Blades, and they're certainly not a match for one of Kendara's pupils. Prince Meilek knows that as well as I do.

In this instance, the truth will serve me best. "I'm here to find Kendara."

His brows furrow. "Why would you think she's in Vos Gillis?"

"I heard a rumor. I need to speak to her. It's urgent."

"I'm sorry, but I highly doubt she's here."

"She has to be."

I'm not sure he's being truthful, but I don't see why he'd lie. He knows what Kendara means to me—we share that in common, at least. He wouldn't deliberately shield me from her if he knows anything, would he?

A pit opens up in my stomach. What if I'm wrong? What if Theyen had been lying or misinformed?

"It was foolish to risk coming here. Hasn't Ronin told you that the queen has declared you a Nuvali spy?"

His words pull me out of my dismal thoughts. "That's ridiculous."

"She's decided that you infiltrated our military to send its secrets back to the Empire and that your friend Saengo may have collaborated with you."

My mouth opens and closes, not even sure how to respond to such absurd allegations.

"Will House Phang be punished for this?" The thought of Saengo and her family suffering even more for my mistakes sends dread skittering through me.

"No," he says, sensing my alarm. "House Phang has been a longtime ally of House Sancor, and she wouldn't risk losing their support. She believes Saengo was coerced." He winces apologetically.

What a load of drake dung. The queen knows I was Kendara's apprentice. If anyone can verify I'm not a spy, it's the queen's own Shadow.

"It isn't true," I say, just in case Prince Meilek has doubts.

"Of course it isn't. But I expected you to be at Spinner's End, out of my sister's reach."

Why would the queen fabricate such a story about me? Once we go north and Ronin proclaims my role as soulguide, I can tell my side of the story.

But if I expose Queen Meilyr for a liar, it might enrage the Nuvali and make me the queen's eternal enemy. Saengo and I could never hope to find a home in Evewyn again.

I have to believe that Kendara might yet be here—she wouldn't share her intent to commit treason with the prince, after all. But since she isn't here at this very moment to reveal what she knows of Ronin and the Dead Wood, Prince Meilek will have to do.

"Well, maybe you can help me instead?"

He gestures for me to continue. I tell him about the task Ronin has given me to cull the Dead Wood and bring it back under control. "Ronin wants me to practice my craft, but I think the best way to handle the trees is to find out what's keeping them there."

With a heavy sigh, he rubs the back of his neck. "I'm sorry. I don't know more than what we discussed when Ronin summoned you. He can be a bit of a recluse."

I grind my teeth together. "My best friend is sick. She's dying, in fact. I can't save her unless I know why and how the trees are cursed."

"Why would her life depend on the Dead Wood?"

"It's a long story, and it's not important right now. What's important is that I succeed."

His gaze is steady as he says, "I wish I knew more. Truly. Kendara would certainly be of more help, but I don't think she's here. She's been missing for days."

"What do you mean 'missing'? She does tend to come and go a lot."

"But only on my sister's orders. Speaking of which, I never got the chance to apologize about the apprenticeship. Mei and I were both convinced she'd choose you."

His words sting, but only briefly and not as badly as I expect. Sometime over the last several days, my concerns have grown far beyond me becoming Kendara's apprentice.

I lift my chin. "That doesn't prove she's not here."

He reaches into a hidden pocket and withdraws a folded slip of paper. "She left a note. For you, in fact. I meant to send it by falcon as soon as I deciphered it, but seeing as you're here . . ."

He holds it out. The longer I stare at it, the larger that pit inside me grows. But I will my hand to reach out and take it from him.

My name is scrawled along the back in Kendara's handwriting. Slowly, so that my hands don't shake, I unfold the message. The paper slides across my fingertips with a dry hiss.

Inside, she's written:

Death and rebirth. Aisle 15. Case 34. Bottom right corner. My brows crash together.

"Judging by your expression, I gather you've no idea what it means," Prince Meilek says. "We've checked all the storerooms in Vos Talwyn, and I'm working through the warehouses in our port cities that might fit the description. We've turned up nothing of significance yet."

Case 34. Perhaps it's only because I've spent the last several days cooped up in a library that I wonder if perhaps she means a bookcase. Prince Meilek might have considered that already, but he'll have disregarded it because Vos Talwyn doesn't have a library that large.

But Spinner's End does.

My pulse drums beneath my skin, but when I speak, my words are mild. "Since you've shared this with me, I should inform you of something as well. I found the shaman from the attack at the teahouse."

He frowns. "And where is he now?"

"Dead of an arrow. Couldn't be helped. I'm just as frustrated. But before he died, he did say something rather confusing."

It might be foolish to tell him, but I want to see his reaction. As the queen's brother, he might be the one person who knows her best.

"He implied that the person who sent him to attack the queen's Shadow at the teahouse was the queen herself."

Prince Meilek's eyes flicker with something I can't quite name. It only lasts half a second before his gaze hardens, not long enough to draw any conclusions but long enough to make the connection between the shaman's claim and Kendara's sudden disappearance.

"That's not possible," he says firmly. "Kendara is too vital."

"She also knows all of Evewyn's secrets," I point out.

His jaw tightens. "What you're suggesting is impossible. Mei wouldn't have sent shamans to attack Kendara, because she knew that Kendara wouldn't be there. Kendara had planned to send her chosen apprentice instead, and she doesn't do anything without Mei's approval. My sister hasn't always made the best choices, but—"

"Like deciding I'm a Nuvali spy?" I ask before I can leash my tongue.

His lips compress. His tone, when he speaks, is harsher than I've heard it before. "I will hear no more of this. You will be held with the other shamanborn while I write to Ronin to have you escorted back to Spinner's End."

"The other shamanborn? The ones who escaped from the Valley of Cranes? Are they to be executed?"

Although I think he means to ignore the question, after a moment of indecision, he does answer. "I'm escorting the shamanborn back to the Valley of Cranes, but I won't allow them to be executed. Unfortunately, that's the most I can do at the moment."

He sounds unhappy, but I'm unable to summon any sympathy. In fact, his tone annoys me.

"You're the prince of Evewyn. You're the only one who can do something." I don't know what's gotten hold of my tongue, but the shamanborn don't deserve any of this. Prince Meilek is the queen's brother, and yet he claims to be powerless?

"It would mean breaking laws that I swore an oath to uphold," he says.

I clench my teeth to try to keep from spitting out, "Laws that are wrong."

"Mei is my queen. Do you think she'd suffer my interference just because I'm her brother? Any power I have to help them would be taken from me."

I've always admired Prince Meilek's sense of honor. He values his duty to his queen and sister. But what about his duty to his people? To the shamanborn cast into the Valley of Cranes? What about their honor? Their dignity? They respect him because he eases their time in the camp, but what is he doing to release them?

His fingers flex against the tabletop before he straightens again, hands falling to his sides with the faint rustle of silk. "You are changed since I saw you last. You haven't lowered your eyes once."

My shoulders tense, and I look away. Then I infuse my spine with steel and lift my gaze again to meet his brown eyes. "Spinner's End doesn't hold to such customs."

He nods faintly. "They're silly customs, anyway. I prefer to see a person's eyes when they're speaking to me. Tell me, Sirscha, have your loyalties shifted?"

"Of course not. I am Evewynian."

"Good. One of my guards will see you to your cell."

Not only does his guard see me to my cell, but Prince Meilek instructs her on exactly where to find my hairpins. Evidently, he'd also gotten that particular lesson from Kendara.

I guess I'll be finding another way to escape. In the cell adjacent to mine, four shamanborn huddle on a bench in the corner. I'm surprised by how few there are. I'd been expecting more. But then I recall Ronin saying the queen's soldiers would use any means necessary to subdue the shamanborn, and my anger rekindles.

My thoughts tumble back to that day with the monks when they'd forced us to watch the execution of two shamanborn. If the queen can commit such atrocities against her own people, I can easily imagine she'd send shamans after her Shadow. Except if Prince Meilek spoke the truth, then she hadn't sent them after Kendara. She'd sent them after Kendara's apprentice. Which doesn't make any sense.

Unless . . . those assassins were meant for me? Prince Meilek said it himself—they'd been convinced that Kendara would select me, and his sister had known Kendara would send her chosen pupil on that mission. Only it hadn't been me. Kendara had inadvertently spared me from walking into a trap, and I'd walked right into it anyway.

But why in the Sisters would the queen send assassins after me? The only reason I can fathom is if she'd known I'm shamanborn.

It's . . . improbable. But, I grudgingly allow, not impossible.

So assuming she knows about me, what would she gain from having me attacked? She's made me into a traitor and a spy, and she's all but set to go to war with the Empire.

But there has to be more to it than that. There are better ways to start a war than to target one lowly wyvern in the Queen's Company. And the fact I've learned all this since leaving Spinner's End makes me realize Ronin is either keeping the information from me—highly likely—or he isn't doing as much as he can to investigate the matter.

Four pairs of eyes watch as I lean against the wall, and I realize I'll have to figure this out later. Right now, my focus needs to be on the shamanborn.

Their appraising looks take in my general state. Although I'm tired from the journey south and I've barely slept in days,

I'm obviously not a former prisoner. I'm lean, but that's from rigorous training, not malnutrition. My clothes are wrinkled and dusty but not threadbare. These four wear clean but ill-fitting clothes, either stolen during their escape or provided after their capture.

"Hello." I pitch my voice low so that the guards down the hall won't hear us.

The keys to the cells currently hang on the other side of the barred door separating the offices from the cell area. I have no idea how I'm going to get them. It's a pity Phaut isn't here. Her craft could bend these locks easily enough.

"You're not from the Valley," one says, a woman with brown skin and sapphire eyes.

I explain in hushed words why I've allowed myself to be captured. They look increasingly skeptical, bordering on pitying. They probably think I've lost my mind, and I can't blame them. Prince Meilek has already put a dent in my plans by taking my pins, and if even he can't help them, what good will a random stranger possibly be?

"I'm Kudera," the waterwender says. She nods at another shaman with light skin and black curls that tangle around her shoulders. Her eyes are purple amethysts. "This is Maiya. The little one is Morun, my brother." She touches the shoulder of the boy, who doesn't look much older than eight. His eyes are still gray.

"I'm Nong," says an older man with graying hair. Deep lines bracket his mouth and carve the skin around his eyes. "How have you avoided being imprisoned in the labor camp?"

Their trust has been broken enough without me lying to them as well. But the truth isn't yet something I want to reveal. "I'm sort of new to all this."

Kudera's head tilts, and she gets that look on her face, the same one the earthwender wore back at the Valley of Cranes, like she suspects who I might be but doesn't quite accept the possibility. Just because these shamanborn escaped during the prison break doesn't mean they believe in anything about a soulguide.

Footsteps approach the door to the cell area. Keys jangle, and the door swings open. A guard enters with our meals. I'm surprised by the hearty fare—warm rice porridge and a boiled chicken-leg quarter, fragrant with lemongrass. Prince Meilek is to thank for this.

I eat quickly, mostly to keep my strength. But the other shamanborn eat as if ravenous, licking their bowls and fingers clean.

"Which of you can fight?" I hate to ask, given that they've faced so much already. But I have to take stock of all possible assets.

Kudera regards me with a thoughtful tilt of her head. She must be their leader.

"We're not soldiers," she says cautiously. "But I have my craft. My familiar can fly, so I've ordered him far from the Dead Wood."

I blink, surprised. "What about the others?"

"We only came across the one spirit. Spirits are drawn to the use of magic. There used to be more in Evewyn, before we were all put in the Valley."

I nod and pretend like I already knew that. Still, a waterwender might be useful, and it's more than I thought we had a moment ago. "Did no one try to bond with a familiar to escape the camp?"

"Some." She looks down. "It always ended in the familiar dying of the rot or being killed by soldiers. We eventually stopped trying. It seemed cruel to risk subjecting them to a painful death just for our sake."

"Familiars are sacred to us," Nong says, cutting in. "Souls are the source of all our magic, and only they can access them. Without them, we would be magicless. To harm another shaman's familiar is unforgiveable."

As the day passes, they gradually open up about their former lives. Before her imprisonment, Maiya had been a teacher, preparing children with the skills they'd need for the Prince's Company when they turned eleven. I marvel that shamanborn had once attended the Prince's Company and even the Queen's— then called the King's Company, under Prince Meilek's father. Apparently, the Royal Army once had a battalion comprised solely of shamanborn.

Even if war between the kingdoms can be prevented, what of the war within Evewyn against its own people? The shamanborn will remember this injustice for generations to come.

Nong, being a medium, had helped young shamans bond with their first familiars. His ability to communicate directly with spirits isn't a craft reliant upon a familiar. It's simply a gift some shamans are born with, regardless of their Calling.

Kudera had been in the Prince's Company when the edict

against shamanborn went out. All shamanborn students were taken into custody without explanation and imprisoned in the dungeons of the Grand Palace until the mountain prison was established. Later, she'd found her brother in the labor camp through sheer chance. Their father had died years before, but the camp had taken their mother. Morun hasn't spoken since.

Maiya tells me that when they fled south, they were a group of twenty-three. They'd split once they hit the coast, most choosing to try their luck among the scatter of fishing villages. Stealing a small boat would be far easier than stowing aboard a ship. But Kudera's group of ten hadn't wanted to risk a small vessel on the open water.

They regretted it now, of course. The density of Vos Gillis's population hadn't concealed them as they'd hoped. Now they'd never know what became of the others.

After our evening meal, I grow restless with anticipation. As the hours stretch on, I worry that something has gone wrong with Phaut.

I glower at the darkness beyond the window slit just as the door to the guardhouse bursts open, slamming into the wall with a bang. I jolt upright.

"Fire!" a voice shouts. "The Queen's Wharf is on fire!"

EIGHTEEN

There's a confusion of sounds: the heavy clomping of hurried feet, the shuffling of hands snatching up coats and weapons, and then another slam of the door, followed by a ringing silence.

I wait, breath held, listening. Before long, I hear the scrape of chair legs as a seat is pulled out and then the low grumble of the guard left behind to keep watch over the prisoners.

The Queen's Wharf is a section of the coast restricted to the queen's ships and visiting dignitaries. It's rarely used. The queen's most impressive vessels are docked south of Vos Talwyn within a series of royal berths in Needle Bay. Though she does keep several ships here. I spotted them this morning from the rooftops. Huge, majestic ghosts well separated from the bustling docks.

Phaut is a genius. I didn't know what she had planned, but she'd seemed confident. Now I see why. It's the perfect spot to set a fire and avoid causing serious injury, especially in a city as cramped and overcrowded as this one.

I turn to the shamanborn, who watch me with pale, expectant faces. I hiss at Nong, "Faint!"

His wrinkles crease in puzzlement.

"Pretend to faint."

His mouth forms a quick "Oh!" and then he enacts an impressive swoon.

"Help!" I shout. "Please, we need help!"

Despite the urgency in my voice, the guard takes his time coming to check on us. My fingers tighten around the bars, imagining his neck.

"What is it?" he grumbles when he at last comes into view.

"Please." I gesture to where Nong lies on the floor. Kudera and Morun fuss over him. I wince a little at Kudera's dramatics and hope the guard doesn't notice. "He needs water. Fresh air. Something."

The guard scowls and turns away. I shout after him, but he does return a moment later with a cup of water. He takes the keys from the wall and unlocks the door leading into the cells. As he passes, my arm darts out. I seize the collar of his uniform and slam him headfirst into the bars of my cell. He cries out, dazed, so I do it again before he can recover.

Groaning, he slumps to the floor. To my frustration, the keys fall just out of reach. I strain against the bars, nails scraping over stone, but I can't reach them.

"Sisters," I mutter. I search the guard for a weapon, a dagger, anything that will extend my reach by a few finger lengths.

All he has is a belt. With a grunt, I heave his dead weight closer so I can reach the buckle. The shamanborn watch in taut silence, hands wringing and eyes shining with uncertain hope.

I glance at the window, where the wild energy of the distant fire rises on the wind. I curse loudly. I'm wasting so much time.

At last, my fingers grasp the belt buckle. I begin to work it free when the pool of spilled water suddenly wobbles and lifts. I gasp, startling back. Kudera has her hands braced against the bars. She's focused intently on the water, which transforms into a long, thin stream. The liquid glides through the air and loops around the fallen keys like a length of rope. I release my breath as the water carries the keys the short distance into Kudera's waiting hand.

The grin she gives me is magnificent. Quickly she opens first her door and then mine. I shove the unconscious guard into my cell and lock him inside.

"Where to?" Kudera asks, Maiya at her elbow. Nong lifts Morun onto his back, and all four await my instructions.

"We're to meet a friend at the docks," I say as we head into the front of the guardhouse. Off to the side there's a mini armory, where I locate a set of dual swords. They're plain and unadorned, soldier's weapons.

"Do you know how to use those?" Kudera asks. She selects a short dagger for herself and shoves it into the waist of her pants.

"Well enough," I say.

Cracking open the door, I peer outside. The street is deserted. Everyone's gone to either help with the fire or watch the spectacle. I gesture for them to follow as I dart outside, crossing the street into a darkened alley. The southwest sky glows orange as the queen's ships burn.

Although I pause at every street to assess how exposed we'll be, the only other people are a stray drunk and a couple searching for a quiet space where they won't have to pay for a room.

This part of Vos Gillis is more subdued than the night market. Lanterns shine from street corners and the occasional roof, but they're for function, not decoration. My shadow stretches long and stark over the dirt before I duck into another alley.

The others follow closely just as two guards appear at the end of the alley, blocking our path.

"Sirscha." Kudera grasps my elbow.

I raise my swords as they bear down on us. From behind me comes the distinct sound of an arrow being loosed.

There's a gasp and a grunt. *No!* My mind screams as the first guard reaches me. I slam the hilt of my sword into his temple and then turn, my mind racing back to the horror of Talon's Teahouse.

Nong lies half on top of Maiya, an arrow embedded in his back. He must have shielded her with his body. Morun clings to Kudera's waist, wide-eyed with terror.

I can tell with a glance that the arrow punctured something vital. Nong doesn't move. Maiya's mouth is open on a soundless scream, her entire body trembling as she squirms out from under Nong's weight.

With a furious cry, I knock aside the second guard's sword. I kick him in the face, sending him crashing into the dirt. Then

I shift my attention to the archer.

Kudera pulls Maiya and Morun against the wall, eyes frantic, pleading for help.

Why did you come for them, Sirscha? A voice inside me asks. *Why would you try?*

I came to Vos Gillis to find Kendara and to save Saengo, but why risk helping the shamanborn?

The answer is clear and quick: because I was afraid.

Not for my life. I was afraid of being invisible, a fear I've held close from the moment I was old enough to understand that I'd been abandoned with no true name. It's why I so desperately sought Kendara's approval. She is the only person besides Saengo who's ever truly seen me. It's why I couldn't allow myself to be beaten in the sparring circle despite that it would have better served me to be underestimated, to be dismissed.

I'd hoped once I secured Kendara's and the queen's approval, that irrational part of myself—that childish need to be seen, to be acknowledged—would be appeased.

Standing in the tent at Sab Hlee, at last understanding the enormity of what being a soulguide meant and how I could never hope to measure up, I'd felt an echo of that familiar fear. And I could not bear it.

I step past Nong's body, sprawled gracelessly in the dirt. My nostrils flare. A cool stillness settles over me as I slash at the archer's next arrow, snapping it in half.

The archer scrambles back, reaching for another arrow. I rush him, forcing him to draw his sword instead. Our blades meet, his one against my two. My heart beats steadily, my breaths slow, my body given over to the battle calm.

The archer staggers beneath my onslaught, panic in the whites of his eyes. With a flourish, my swords rip his own from his hands. It clatters against the alley wall. I plant my foot in his gut. He falls to his knees, his chest heaving as I rest my swords at either side of his neck.

I could kill him. I could dig my blades into the tender flesh of his neck and let him bleed. His life for Nong's.

This violence, this capacity to hurt—what was it Saengo had said? This is what Kendara had seen in me all those years ago.

Danger makes you deadly. She'd misunderstood. It had never been danger. It was fear.

The guard pitches backward as my blades close around his neck. Twin lines of red form against the skin beneath his jaw as he rolls away, gasping. He turns to flee, but I fling one sword. It stabs into the back of his thigh. He cries out and collapses. I bend over to yank my sword from his flesh and then lift my other one.

A sword cuts into my path. Our blades meet with a sharp *clang*. Instantly, I redirect my strike and then pull up short when my eyes meet Prince Meilek's. Before I've even made the decision, I back away, putting space between us.

His gaze flits between me and the shamanborn, assessing the situation. There will be no talking this time. No bids for understanding or kindness. There are only our swords.

A week ago, I'd balked at the mere idea of raising my sword to the prince of Evewyn.

Have your loyalties shifted? I wasn't lying when I said they haven't. My loyalty remains with Evewyn. With its people. Human and shamanborn alike, those forsaken by our queen. My loyalties have not shifted—they have simply grown beyond myself.

I raise my swords into the third stance of the Wyvern's Dance. I can hardly believe my audacity as Prince Meilek frowns and lifts his own sword, copying my stance. Behind him, the injured archer drags himself away.

Kudera whispers a curse. One of the guards I'd knocked out is rising to his feet, his palm pressed against his temple. Kudera pushes Morun into Maiya's arms as she draws the dagger from her waist. Nearby, water streams down from a gutter, catching the glow of a lantern so that it appears almost like a ribbon of light.

"Are you sure about this?" Prince Meilek says, reclaiming my attention.

"I have no desire to fight you." But he's given me no choice. "You claim to care about the shamanborn, and yet they continue to die because you lack the conviction to defy your sister." He worries more about upholding his family's power than about the lives of his own citizens, who naively thank him for helping them with one hand while holding their chains with the other.

Prince Meilek's eyes narrow, but he doesn't respond to my accusations. I suppose because there's nothing to be said.

We regard each other. I draw a deep breath of air that smells of damp earth, mildew, and salt. I've never seen him fight seriously, but it would be a mistake to underestimate the captain of the Queen's Guard.

I strike out, not with any real speed. I just want to see how he responds. His reaction is immediate as he knocks aside my blade, looking almost languid. He's quick, his reflexes excellent. But no matter. The dual swords might have a shorter reach, but they're lighter and faster, like me.

He swings his sword in a quick attack. I block with both blades and then kick out. He jumps away. I follow, my swords dipping and twirling, moving as one. He deflects my strikes with impressive efficiency, and even though the speed of my attacks should allow for little retaliation, his blade manages to whisper past my side before I knock it away.

We move down the alley, using the limited space to our advantage as the low buzz of the city and the fire fade into background noise. This is not a fight; it is a dance. I dart forward, and Prince Meilek moves with me. He spins away, and I turn with him. I slip seamlessly into a more advanced sword form—Kendara's, one which she's never named. Our swords meet in a clang of sharp notes, music to our strange choreography, each strike answered with a perfectly timed block.

I push him back only for him to maneuver a quick reversal, confirming that he isn't just mimicking my form. He knows the stances, each move skillfully executed. Our bodies flow with the same effortless grace, our swords with the same lethal precision, for one simple reason that I've long suspected—because Kendara wasn't just a mother figure to him. She was his sword master.

Somewhere behind me, Kudera cries out. Water splashes against the alley wall, misting the backs of my legs. I duck beneath the swipe of Prince Meilek's sword arm, reversing our positions so I can check on Kudera. The guard has her cornered. Her dagger lies in the dirt, out of her reach. She flings a stream of water into his face. He staggers briefly and then swings his sword in a wide arc for her head.

I parry Prince Meilek's next attack with one sword and then hurl the other. The move leaves me exposed, but the tip finds its mark, clanging into the guard's blade. He gasps as the sword flies from his hand. Immediately, Prince Meilek pulls his next strike, which would have sliced open my side. Before I can retaliate, though, he steps in close and slides his blade beneath my chin.

Kudera makes a broad sweeping motion with her arms. The water snaps across the guard's face. With a grunt, his head lolls, and he crumples to the dirt. She's breathing hard as she turns, stricken, to me and Prince Meilek.

Silence settles in the alley. Prince Meilek's sword hand doesn't waver. His blade is cold against my skin. My mind races for a way to get out of this, but it comes up short. His skill matches mine. I mentally curse. My only option now is to distract him long enough to allow Kudera and the others to make a run for it. They might have a chance of reaching the ship unscathed.

I open my mouth to tell them to run when the sword drops from my neck. I instantly pull away, raising my remaining sword between us.

Prince Meilek's face is all sharp angles in the shadowy light, his eyes like flint and his mouth an angry slash. He jerks his head toward the mouth of the alley. "Get these shamanborn out of here.

That guard won't be out for long, and there are more coming."

Warily, my body poised for a trap, I wave at Kudera and the others to hurry ahead. They don't argue, scurrying quickly toward the next street. As I make to follow, my gaze falls on Nong's body. I pause. My throat works as I try to swallow the lump that forms there.

"I will have him seen to," Prince Meilek says.

What does that mean? Will he be given a proper burial? Who will sing his lifestory to the Sisters? Who will walk with his spirit, retracing the path he'd taken in life until he reaches the gates into the spirit realm?

But there's no time for questions. I pray that the Sisters allow his spirit a place among them even without the funeral rituals. Then, keeping my gaze on Prince Meilek, I retrieve my other sword and dart out of the alley after the others.

We rush past rows of ships to Berth 15, far from the Queen's Wharf. Phaut's lean form is pacing on the dock, the anxious set of her shoulders outlined in soft yellow lantern light. When she spots us, she waves and sprints to meet us.

"About time," she hisses and then draws up short when she sees the shamanborn. "Is this it? Only three?"

I nod grimly, and she doesn't ask any further questions. She gestures toward the waiting ship. The figures of the crew scurry aboard the deck.

The ship is small in comparison to the others, but it'll suffice. Phaut ushers Maiya and Morun up the gangplank, and I trust by the way someone readies to cast off the lines that she has settled their passage and they've agreed to a hasty departure. Only the captain pays the shamanborn any attention, greeting them curtly.

"Hurry." I gesture for Kudera to follow the others.

She hesitates, twisting the hem of her shirt around her fingers. Then, to my surprise, she hugs me. "Thank you," she whispers.

"I only guided you to a ship," I say.

Her arms tighten around my shoulders, her bony joints digging into me. "If you ever have need of us, send word, and we will come."

Her promise makes my throat go tight. Because it's suddenly difficult to speak, I can only nod. Phaut and I stand watch until the darkness claims the ship's figure and they're in no danger of being intercepted by the Royal Army that patrols the coast.

I wait to feel something like joy or relief. Instead, I feel hollow. Kendara never appeared. I am no closer to saving Saengo than I was a few days ago. On top of that, we saved three shamanborn out of the ten who entered Vos Gillis with Kudera, out of the twenty-three who came south with her. This is not a victory.

"My sister," Phaut says abruptly. I look at her, but her gaze remains fixed on the dark waves. "We came across a lightwender once who'd been attacked by a beast. He was a lightgiver, and he would have died, but he used his ability to transfer the life energy within my sister into himself, prolonging his life long enough for help to arrive."

"That's why you dislike lightwenders," I say. No wonder she'd been determined to distrust me when I arrived.

She nods. "He didn't even ask her permission. She almost died."

"That was a cowardly thing to do. I hope he paid for it."

"Some people simply can't be trusted to wield that kind of power." She turns from the sea to meet my eyes. "But risking your life to help these shamans . . . that was good of you, Sirscha. I'm sorry you didn't find your mentor, but I'm glad we did this."

A bit of that hollowness within me fades. "I couldn't have done this without you."

"You there!" a guard shouts.

"Damn it," I mutter.

Phaut and I sprint back into the streets to make our own escape. We lead the guards through twisting alleys and stacks of crates; over bridges that rattle beneath our boots, a board coming loose and splashing into the river below; past merchants thrusting their wares at passersby and chickens pecking for bugs. The chickens squawk and startle, flapping madly and spitting feathers into the guards' faces as their owners shout in protest.

I don't chance more than a quick glance over my shoulder. There are too many guards. We won't be able to lose them long enough to reach our drakes, not without heading onto the roofs, and I don't know how well Phaut can climb.

We head east, skirting the southern edge of the night market, where the strains of a reed pipe haunt the dirt-packed paths despite the night's activity. Seconds later, we hit a wall of bodies—spectators who've crammed into the streets to watch the blaze of the Queen's Wharf. The fire rages on, setting the night sky aflame. We elbow our way through the crowd, earning a few curses.

"Make way!" the guards shout from behind us. Their

command is drowned out by the commotion.

A manic laugh escapes me when I see that Phaut had set fire to all four of the queen's ships. Efforts to put them out have subsided. Instead, the fire crew watches along with everyone else as the ships burn, collapsing into the sea.

Within moments, we break free of the crush and dive back into the shadows of an alley. An arrow strikes the wall beside my head with a loud *thwack*.

At the next intersection, Phaut veers left in the direction of our drakes, but I clutch her sleeve and drag her with me to the right. We rush past a pile of refuse, and then the cramped towers of buildings abruptly end. We plunge into thigh-high grass. The field ripples under a sharp sea breeze, each blade of grass brushed gold from the glow of fire.

"Hurry," I shout as Phaut stumbles to a stop.

She drags in two wheezing breaths, then jumps into a run again when an arrow lands near her feet. "Our drakes?"

"We'll never make it!"

We cut a line straight through the field, heading directly for the twisted black shape of the Dead Wood.

"Are you sure about this?" she shouts. Another arrow sings through the air.

"No other choice!"

Taking the rowboat we'd stolen would be too slow, the canals too congested for swift movement. Even were that an option, the waters between Kazahyn and Evewyn are closely patrolled. If all shadowblessed have eyesight as sharp as Theyen's, our boat would be easily spotted. We can't risk returning to our drakes and being chased north, either. We might lead them straight to Sab Hlee.

It's dire indeed when the Dead Wood is our best option. This far south, the Dead Wood is at its narrowest. If we're quick, we can cross in fewer than two hours. Once we're in Kazahyn, we'll make our way north to Sab Hnou. Ronin's eastern encampment, the sister camp to Sab Hlee, sits between the borders of Kazahyn and the Nuvalyn Empire.

The Dead Wood looms ahead, a silent menace. Phaut begins to falter, her pace slowing. There's no going back now, so I pull ahead and plunge first into the darkness.

We don't go far. Once we're concealed, we crouch low to the earth and watch the soldiers who linger just beyond the reach of the trees. There are almost a dozen, arguing loudly. Most seem opposed to following us, insisting the Dead Wood will finish us off. Prince Meilek arrives a moment later. His dragule cuts a large swath through the grass.

The soldiers spread out to watch the perimeter, but Prince Meilek remains nearby, glowering into the gloom. Despite our fight in the alley, the sight of him makes guilt rattle around my ribs. I know, reasonably, that he doesn't have the power to free the shamanborn, even as the queen's brother. But that doesn't mean he's powerless, and he knows that.

I frown, struck by a sudden realization.

Kendara isn't in Vos Gillis. She never was. The person in the queen's circle helping the shamanborn escape is Prince Meilek. He would have the resources. He's so loyal to his sister and to his duty that it didn't even occur to me.

But as soon as his guards were either gone or knocked out, he let us go. Sisters, I'm such an idiot.

Something rustles to our left. Phaut hisses my name. Her voice quavers.

"Right," I whisper. "Let's go."

We run. This far from the heart of the Dead Wood, the trees stand farther apart, their limbs not quite so tangled. Moonlight brightens our path. I tune my ears to the crackle of dry bark and the hiss of the earth when the roots rise, sloughing dirt.

I tell myself that the hard part is already over. Kudera and the others are freed. But Phaut draws a thin, high breath, reminding me I still have someone else to keep safe before this night is through.

"Once we're in Kazahyn, how far to Sab Hnou?" I ask.

"Hard to say. Three or four days? I've never been this far south before." She sounds distracted, her focus on the trees.

I recall what she said about her familiar yesterday. Guilt pricks at my conscience because it's true that I haven't asked much about her. Of course, that was because Phaut wanted nothing to do with me, but I'd like to think it's different between us now.

"What do you miss most about your home country?"

"Why are you asking me this now?" she asks, voice breathy with barely leashed panic. She ducks a tree branch that is nowhere near her head.

"Because you're going to start hyperventilating if you don't calm down," I say.

She scowls, but she also draws slower, deeper breaths. Long seconds later, she replies, "The sunflower fields."

"They must be a common sight in an Empire that worships the sun." I speak steadily, despite the racing of my pulse. I don't want my fear to infect Phaut.

"They weren't yet blooming when I was last in the Empire. Have you ever seen them?"

I shake my head. "I've only seen sunflowers in the markets in Vos Talwyn. How long have you served Ronin?"

"Countless decades. The golden fields are a rare sight now." The furrow between her brows deepens. "My sisters and I used to sit in the oak tree that grew in front of our house, eating sunflower seeds until our fingers went numb from the late-autumn chill."

Behind the nervous energy in her voice, I hear the melancholy, an ache of yearning that never really goes away. It tugs at my own. Although Phaut seems happy to be in Ronin's service, I can't help but think that Spinner's End has been her prison for far longer than it's been mine.

Although the conversation helps to distract her, Phaut isn't a runner. Eventually, she has to stop speaking in order to breathe.

We run until her legs give out. She collapses, palms scraping over dirt, her chest heaving.

"I can't," she wheezes. "I can't . . . keep . . . running." She drags in lungfuls of air as I haul her back to her feet. It's dangerous to allow the roots such easy purchase. "Give me . . . a moment."

"We have to be near the Kazahyn border by now. We should be able to slow down, but we can't stop."

Phaut groans but doesn't argue. We trudge on, much too slowly for my comfort, but Phaut just barely keeps up. Before long, the crackle of bark grows louder, more frequent. Her breaths come even thinner, weighted by both exhaustion and fear, but she can't seem to make her body move any quicker, even with my help. I eye her height and weight, wondering if I could carry her the rest of the way. But with her on my back, I don't think I'd be fast enough to outrun a determined root.

I stop. Phaut wavers, her legs nearly folding again before I can steady her.

"I'm sorry," she says. Her hand squeezes the hilt of her sword.

"We can't rely on steel." I remember the disaster of my last foray into the trees. My craft is my most effective weapon here. Heart thundering, I look up through the twitching branches to the velvet black sky beyond and whisper a prayer to the Falcon Warrior.

"Sirscha." Phaut breathes my name, barely audible, as a tree shudders nearby. I shush her.

I close my eyes and roll my shoulders. My boots slide through the loose earth. My fingers flex as I search for that spark within me, waiting to be roused into heat and light. It's the same light that exists at the glowing core of all people—their souls, the source of their magic.

Something heavy drags across the ground to our right. It's joined by the snap of splitting bark and the high whine of air sliding through crevices. Something scratches my shoulder. I inhale sharply but don't move.

The trees creak. The wailing grows louder. My palms feel clammy, but there's nowhere to run this time. A root tightens around my ankle. A branch tears through my sleeve. I hiss as something whips across my cheek, breaking skin. Phaut draws her sword, breathing heavily, muttering words under her breath. Prayers to her gods.

Magic stirs in my blood. The warmth is a gentle and reassuring counterpoint to the chill of battle that finally settles over my nerves. This is as much a fight as our scrape with the guards had been, because I can fight the souls here. I am not helpless.

The heat within me sharpens, a burning coal trapped beneath my ribs. Branches gouge the backs of my hands as the light of my craft scorches through me, brilliant and painful and perfect.

I open my eyes and gasp. All around me are lights.

They are innumerable, a forest of souls so ancient that their original forms, whoever they might have been once, have long since withered. They are shapeless beings now, warped by the magic that binds them here, by the decay of long years and their own nurtured wrath.

I turn my palms. The branches clawing at Phaut crumble. The roots trying to drag me into the earth shrivel into dust. Only the souls remain, orbs of light that waver like the slightest draft might blow them out. My heart squeezes with unexpected emotion. Then, at last, they vanish.

NINETEEN

Without drakes, it takes us three and a half days to reach Sab Hnou. We avoid Kazan patrols by keeping as close to the trees as we dare.

I manage to summon my craft twice more when the branches over our heads grow bold, but each time leaves me exhausted. I don't trust my burgeoning skills to keep us safe if we try heading directly to Spinner's End.

We send word to Ronin once we're safe, and to my relief, he agrees to retrieve us from Sab Hnou. From there to Spinner's End is a four-hour walk. After the last few days, we're exhausted and hungry. But we're also eager for a bath, a warm meal, and a soft bed, so we march the last leg of the journey through the Dead Wood in tense silence.

Saengo greets us inside the gates. She looks pale and anxious. When she sees me, she releases a long exhale. The same relief rushes through me, easing muscles I hadn't realized were clenched tight.

She's trimmed her short hair so that the ends are now even. I hope it means she's feeling more optimistic. She's dressed plainly, with a high-collared tunic and loose pants, but the sash around her waist is knotted in the distinguished style of a reiwyn lady.

The moment we're back in our rooms, Saengo claps a hand over her mouth and mumbles, "I went snooping."

I pause in shucking off my travel-worn shirt. "Don't leave me in suspense."

She lowers her hands, looking quite pleased with herself. There's a giddy sort of energy to her that fills that pit in my gut. "I sneaked out through the library window and found my way back to Ronin's study."

My brows rise. "Are you vying for the job of Shadow?"

She gives me a sly grin. "Are you frightened?"

"Terrified. Go on, then."

She sits on her bed while I finish undressing. "Apparently, if I'm wearing a spidersilk gown and rushing about the castle like I belong here, no one questions me."

"It's also the way you walk," I say.

"What's wrong with the way I walk?"

"Nothing's wrong with it. It's just that you carry yourself the way all the stuffy reiwyn ladies do. Like you know you're more important than everyone else." I duck into the bathing chamber, laughing, as she throws a pillow at my head.

"Anyway," she calls out, louder so I can hear her as I fill the tub. "Ronin is an excessively organized man. Finding his ledgers was rather easy."

"Anything important in them?" I lower myself into the tub. The hot water is pure bliss on my aching muscles. I lather up a wedge of soap and begin the work of washing off nearly a week's worth of dirt and sweat.

"The usual stuff, like the expenses of running multiple estates. Apparently, he earns quite a bit of income from the spidersilk he exports all over the world. He absolutely has a Spinner or two. That's the only explanation for where he gets his supply of spidersilk."

Confirmation that Ronin is in possession of a Spinner. That's something, I guess.

"Also, I found a piece of correspondence with the Evewynian seal. It wasn't signed, but it must have been from Queen Meilyr. All it said was: 'Arrangements have been made. Please ensure accommodations for the additional staff.'"

I frown, watching water sluice over my knuckles. "It sounds like preparations for the gathering in the north."

Ronin had said that leaders from all over Thiy are journeying to his northern holding. If every leader brings their own soldiers, drakes, and staff, then it makes sense Ronin would supplement his own staff to ensure everything runs smoothly.

After a time, I rise from the water and pull the drain. As I dry off and change into a clean set of clothes, I tell Saengo everything that happened in Vos Gillis.

"Can't Ronin do anything to help them?" Saengo asks as I

emerge from the bathing chamber. She gestures me over to the chair and picks up the brush.

"Ronin can't interfere with how the queen runs her own kingdom, no matter how unjust her laws are."

Saengo's lips purse. Her hands work gently but efficiently, smoothing out the tangles in my hair. "Millie came back last night. I put her in the aviary so she wouldn't fly off. I've decided on what to tell my father. I plan to send the letter this evening, but I'll amend it to ask if he knows anything about what the queen might be planning."

Aside from providing the kingdom's best falcons, Saengo's father also oversees much of the northern orchards. A considerable portion of the Royal Army resides on his lands as well. If he's willing to share whatever information he might have with his heir, it can only help.

But in truth, I'm not convinced her parents won't use the queen's claims for their own benefit. They've never approved of Saengo's friendship with me, and they'd welcome the chance to rid me from their daughter's life for good.

But I don't tell Saengo this.

"Will your father be upset with you for not writing sooner?" I ask.

Saengo weaves my hair into a thick braid. At the Company, we'd been accustomed to braiding each other's hair every morning. Her hands linger in my hair where she would have secured the feathers if we'd still been wyverns.

With a sigh, she says, "Maybe. But he'll be glad to hear from me as well." Her mouth twists in amusement. "I'll include reassurance that you haven't coerced me into being your accomplice."

"Or have I?" I ask, turning to waggle my brows at her.

"If only he knew you'd been Kendara's pupil," she says, before suddenly growing somber. She reaches up to tug at the short ends of her hair. "I'm sorry you didn't find Kendara in Vos Gillis."

"She's missing," I say, frowning. "Look at this message she left me."

I rummage around in the pocket of the pants I'd discarded and pull out the folded slip of paper. I hand it to Saengo, who quickly reads the odd message.

"What does it mean?" she asks, handing it back.

"Let's find out."

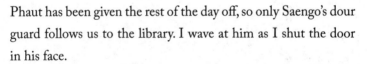

Phaut has been given the rest of the day off, so only Saengo's dour guard follows us to the library. I wave at him as I shut the door in his face.

Death and rebirth. Aisle 15. Case 34. Bottom right corner.

Spinner's End is a place of death and rebirth. The castle had been long abandoned when Ronin claimed it and gave it new life.

We count the aisles first and then the number of bookcases. When we're standing in front of aisle fifteen and bookcase thirty-four, I crouch to peer at the spines on the bottom shelf.

The last book on the right reads: *A Matter of Soulcraft.*

My heart skips a little as I pull it out. When I flip it open, a letter tumbles to the floor.

Tentative, I reach down. The old parchment feels brittle. The wax seal is stamped with an unfamiliar symbol: a pair of crossed swords against a sun.

Saengo gives a reassuring smile. I break the seal and unfold the parchment.

The writing is Kendara's. Tucked into the crease is a smaller square of paper, thicker than the parchment. On it, my name is written in an unfamiliar hand.

I stare at the card, a rushing sound filling my head as the walls of the library fall away. Something wrenches inside me. It feels almost like I'm observing the moment, looking down at myself as I hold up the same card tucked into my pocket the day my parents abandoned me to the monks, when I was two.

"Sirscha, what is that?" Saengo asks.

Wordlessly, I hand the card to her. My lips can't seem to form any words. My fingers tremble as they smooth over the letter to read what's written inside.

If you're reading this, then you are exactly where you shouldn't be. Still, I expect you're prepared to face the challenges ahead. I made a promise to your mother that you would be taken care of, which means ensuring you're equipped to take care of yourself. Trust no one, especially those who would use your magic. Whatever you decide, know that your mother loved you. As do I.

"What does it mean?" Saengo asks quietly. When I don't respond, she touches my shoulder.

The words blur on the page. The parchment slips from my fingers. I draw a slow, uneven breath and press my shaking hands to my face.

Kendara has always known what I am. In my earliest memory of her, I'd been practicing my sword forms, unaware that she'd been watching from the shadows until she made herself known. I'd always believed it to be a chance encounter, but it couldn't have been. Everything she'd fed me about potential and greatness—had it all been a lie?

She hadn't selected me as a pupil because she believed I could do great things. She chose me because she'd made a promise to my mother. Had she ever intended to make me Shadow? If she's always known what I am, then it seems unlikely.

Saengo brushes the letter aside as her arms circle my shoulders. I feel hollow, everything I am and everything I was scraped out.

The pathetic part is that I still miss her. I miss her so terribly that I ache with it. She is the closest thing to a mother I have ever known.

Sometime later, when I've gathered up the broken pieces of myself, I swipe the back of my hand over my eyes and pick up the letter again.

"We don't have to do this now," Saengo says softly.

"Yes, we do." I can't waste any more time feeling sorry for myself.

I turn the letter over to look at the wax seal again. Who had

Kendara been before she became Shadow? How had she known my mother? Had my mother been a soulguide as well? They must have suspected what my craft might be; otherwise, how else would she have guessed I'd end up here at Spinner's End?

"It sounds like she thought Ronin would try to use you to maintain his power," Saengo says. "'Whatever you decide.' She wanted you to choose."

I shake my head. "There's no choice to make, and what Ronin wants doesn't matter. I have to destroy the Dead Wood. That's the only way to save you. At least now we know why Queen Meilyr would send assassins after me. She must have known what I am."

"But the only person who could have told her is Kendara."

"We don't know that for sure." I rub my temple. Kendara is a master of secrets, including her own. As much as I love her, I know so little about her. How can she claim to love me and then betray me? How very like her to leave me so unbalanced.

With this revelation, there is little chance that I'll ever be allowed to return to Evewyn. If I'm honest with myself, I suppose there had never been much of a chance. If the queen has been plotting against me since even before I discovered what I am, nothing I do will sway her. But if I can destroy the Dead Wood, then at least Saengo might still have a home.

"Who else could it have been?" Saengo asks.

"There's no way to know anything for certain. If Kendara revealed my identity to the queen, then why would she be missing now?" Until I hear confirmation from Kendara's own lips, I have to trust that it wasn't her. "What would the queen hope to gain from having me attacked?"

"Maybe she wanted you to awaken your magic?" Saengo suggests.

My fingers trace over the wax seal, following the shape of the swords. "Ronin said that moments of high stress force a shaman to awaken their craft if a spirit is nearby. But it might not have worked. I might have been killed instead. Why take such a gamble?"

"It is a peculiar way to go about things," she agrees. "If Queen Meilyr wants war, she could hire shamans to attack her borders and claim they were under the Empire's orders. And if she knew that you're shamanborn and wanted you to awaken your craft, then why not send you to Ronin to help you do it the normal way?"

"She wouldn't do that. She'd never appear to help shamanborn."

Saengo's nose wrinkles. "A fair point. But still, it's all rather roundabout."

"Maybe it's intentional? She wouldn't want any of it tracing back to her. If I died in the attack, she could claim the Empire targeted her future Shadow and go to war with them. But since I awakened my craft instead, then she gets to claim I was planted by the Nuvali as a spy."

"And go to war with them," she finishes for me.

"It's stupid, but I'd thought stopping a war would win me her favor. A war would devastate the kingdom and cost thousands of Eveywnian lives. I hadn't considered that war could be what she wants."

"It's not the first conclusion I would have drawn, either."

"But why me?" I say, frustrated that I'm missing some vital piece of information. "Hiring shamans to kill any of Kendara's pupils would have been enough to claim a threat to her future Shadow. Was it for the convenience of getting rid of me as well?"

"She must not have known about you for long, or why would she have allowed Kendara to take you on as a pupil?" She frees the letter from my grip and tucks the card with my name on it back inside.

I shake my head, suddenly realizing that we've strayed from our immediate problem, which is the Dead Wood. "I'm sorry. It doesn't matter. What's done is done. Since I didn't learn anything about Ronin in Vos Gillis, I'm going to have to sneak back into that maze and see what he's hiding. It's bound to reveal something about his secrets."

"Like a giant spider?"

I cringe. "Possibly. But there's something back there, something that feels a lot like the Dead Wood. Whatever that is, it must be tied to the trees. Maybe it's tied to Ronin's power, too, and if it is, then it might be what's causing him to lose control now."

"I have a theory," says a low voice.

I leap to my feet, hands reaching for weapons that aren't there. Saengo quietly slips Kendara's letter into her tunic. At the end of the bookcase, shoulder propped against the corner, stands Theyen.

"How long have you been there?" I demand. Sisters, I allowed myself to become so distracted by the letter that I hadn't heard him approach.

"Not long," he assures with a knowing smile that makes me itch to duel him again. "Long enough to overhear you're planning to enter that maze. I thought you'd want my help with that."

He doesn't even have the decency to look ashamed for eavesdropping. Although I'd like to tell him to go away, I'm curious, despite myself. "What sort of theory?"

He straightens off the bookcase and holds up the book in his hand. "Specifically, I have a theory about Ronin's power. Do you remember this? I was reading these fables the day we met."

My eyes narrow on the familiar cover. "What's your point?"

"In 'The Tale of the Woodcutter', he tries to claim the power of the gods by ordering shamans to consume their familiars. Now look at this."

He flips through the pages, then holds up an ink drawing of a creature that's part man and part wolf. I have to get closer to see the details. The creature on the page is bent over, his hindquarters that of a wolf but ending in human feet. His face is a hideous mixture of wolf and man, long fangs gouging through torn cheeks.

Theyen says, "It's a story about a shaman who sought the power of the gods by forging an unnatural bond with his familiar. He drained the spirit blood of his wolf familiar and drank it, combining with the creature. Although misshapen beyond recognition, he thought himself the most powerful of beings. But the transformation was too much, and it soon killed him."

He flips the book shut, but the image remains branded in my mind. I glance back at Saengo. She looks unsettled, her fist pressed against the base of her throat.

"You think Ronin did the same as this shaman? That he . . . consumed his Spinner?"

Theyen lowers the book at his side. "The practice was banned and fell into obscurity, but some time before the Yalaeng Conquest, there were accounts of shamans who tried to do this. None survived. But if Ronin actually succeeded?" He pushes snowy hair off his forehead, his expression somber. "It would explain why he has magic here in the heart of the Dead Wood when no other shaman would risk bringing their familiar within a day's ride of the trees."

I lean my back against the bookcase, arms crossed. What Theyen suggests would explain a great many things about the Spider King. Although the notion that it was Ronin skittering through the gardens that night I ventured into the maze makes my skin crawl.

If he was already a powerful sower, pursuing an unnatural union with his familiar might have been enough to defeat the Soulless and win him control of the Dead Wood. Sowers likely control plants by manipulating the liquid within them. It seems a shame that Ronin should rule over the one place where he cannot use his craft as it was intended.

But the explanation doesn't quite fit. Even now, a phantom power wills me to return to the garden maze. Something is back there, and given the evidence, it can only be Ronin's familiar.

Saengo makes a quiet gasping sound, suddenly collapsing against the bookcase. My breath catches as I rush to her.

Her face is ashen, the skin around her mouth tight with pain. A sheen of sweat slicks her brow.

Theyen drops at her other side. He scoops her into his arms and lifts her easily from the floor. "Let's get her to your rooms. Quickly."

The rush to our rooms passes in a panicked blur. Theyen heads straight for the bedroom and places her on the sheets. His movements are gentle, but she still winces in pain and tugs at her collar.

"Sirscha," she says between gasps.

I grasp her hand tightly between mine as Theyen backs away to give us space. Fear churns in my gut. "Saengo, tell me what you need. Should I send for the healer?"

She grimaces. "It wouldn't do any good. She left yesterday."

I rear back a bit, first in surprise and then outrage. I turn on Theyen. "Why would she leave? Did you send her away?"

Saengo places a hand on my forearm. "Calm down. She left because there wasn't anything else she could do. The rot can no longer be contained. It's too far gone."

I shake my head and reach for the connection between us, which is when I realize . . . it's not there. Or rather, it's weakened enough that although I still sense Saengo, her emotions barely reach me now.

I suck in a sharp, panicked breath. For a dizzying moment, the room blurs and the floor tips. But then I dig my fingers into my thighs, finding a bruise I hadn't realized was even there, and the pain helps recenter me. For her sake, I can't break down. Saengo needs me to be strong and to come through on my promise to her.

"Sirscha." Her fingers tighten around my hand until it's nearly painful. I don't pull away. Instead, I grip her back. "There's a lot I would die for. My country. My family. My best friend. But I'm not going to die like this."

Her words are a spark. Determination burns through me. "I'm not going to let you."

TWENTY

Theyen gestures to the library's broken window, now cleared of glass. "No one's noticed?"

"I'm sure it's been noticed," I say, shrugging, "but no one's come to me about it."

I feel terrible deceiving Phaut by sneaking off, especially after what we endured together. But she'd never let me get anywhere close to the gardens, and we're leaving for the north in the morning. There's no time to waste.

"How exactly are you planning to get there from here?" Theyen asks.

"Over the roof," I say, which earns me a raised brow. "If the guards spot me without Phaut, they'll be suspicious. Once we're in the garden maze, you can use your shadow magic to"—I wiggle my fingers—"conceal us. We need to get as close as—"

Theyen's sharp eyes narrow. "My craft is not available for your illicit activities."

I frown. "But—"

"No magic. Or whatever"—he mimics the motion I just made with my hand—"that is."

"You're being unreasonable. You saw what's happening to Saengo. Shadow magic is perfect for this."

I tried to heal her again now that I can summon my craft, but it didn't work. Whatever's causing the rot is too strong.

"Don't try to guilt me. My personal healer cared for her, and now I've agreed to risk Ronin's trust by accompanying you."

I nearly snap at him, but he's right. He's already done more than expected. When I speak again, it's through clenched teeth. "Fine. Then consider it an opportunity to flaunt your magical superiority."

"Sirscha, every moment in your company is an opportunity to flaunt my superiority, magical or otherwise."

"Maybe I'll just bind and gag you and leave you back there as a diversion."

"I would make irresistible bait."

I rub my temple. "You do realize we might actually run into a Spinner? We could avoid being seen if you'd—"

"No. Magic."

I huff angrily. "Fine. If we're attacked by a giant spider, I'm tripping you and making a run for it. I'll meet you out back."

Without waiting for his response, I climb out the window and land silently on my feet. I'm far less confident now that

Theyen refuses to use his magic, but there's nothing for it. It doesn't take long to scale the castle and make my way to the walled garden maze. Within minutes, Theyen joins me. Once we've ensured we're alone, we enter through the arched doorway.

"This is charming," he mutters under his breath.

We walk slowly, alert for any guards who might patrol back here. We haven't gone far when Theyen says, "I heard a story this morning."

"Not one about woodcutters, I hope."

"There was a fire in Vos Gillis some days ago. Apparently, a handful of shamanborn used the diversion to escape from a guardhouse."

My stomach tenses, the only outward indication of my surprise. "Is that so?"

"Indeed. It wasn't the best test of your skills."

"I'm not sure what you mean."

"Don't insult me," he says, with a slow roll of his eyes.

I suppose it doesn't matter if he knows. I'm already a criminal in Evewyn. "If I'd done nothing, those shamanborn might be dead now."

The cobbled path takes us beneath the same stone arches I passed the last time, branching into more walled gardens.

"Don't pretend as if you went for them. You went for yourself."

I turn sharply to face him. "Haven't I already told you not to speak as if you know me?"

"But I do." He crosses his arms. "Oh sure, part of you went

for those shamans. You're surprisingly softhearted. But you went mainly because you had something to prove."

"To whom exactly?" I ask.

"To yourself." His voice would have been almost kind if not for the patronizing tilt of his nose. "And to the shamanborn who escaped the Valley of Cranes for you."

My irritation diffuses. There isn't any single, simple reason for why I chose to free the shamanborn. For them, for myself. Afraid of being nothing, but equally afraid that I might not be worthy of anything more.

"Don't claim ownership over their choices," he says. "Breaking from prison, entering the Dead Wood, escaping to Vos Gillis—they did those things for themselves, not for you."

I've no intention of discussing this with him. However, he does have a point. Most of the shamanborn who escaped likely didn't care whether I exist or not, only that an organized prison break meant freedom. Taking responsibility for what happened would be stripping from them the choices they'd made and the courage it had taken to make them. Still, that doesn't mean I should have done nothing.

He doesn't wait for my response. Instead, he steps ahead of me. "Shall we?"

The path forks and then forks again, taking us deeper into the odd maze of walls, arches, and weeds. Before long, we reach the garden with three paths. Prickling awareness skitters over my skin as a pressure builds inside my chest. I rub my hands, which are suddenly cold.

"That way," I whisper. My feet step carefully, my boots silent against the dusty cobblestones. Beside me, Theyen is a little less quiet. Dead weeds crackle underfoot, the sound uncomfortably loud.

"How can you be certain?" he says.

The pressure increases with every step, spreading through me, my whole body feeling stiff and unwieldy. I'm overcome by the same dread that grips me when I'm in the Dead Wood.

"Can't you feel it?" I shake my head as a slow ache begins to throb at the back of my head. Steady and rhythmic like a heartbeat.

Theyen tilts his head back, observing the stone arches that bridge the passageways leading from one garden into the next. "I feel nothing."

"Well, at least you admit it," I mumble, which earns me an amused glance.

The path curves sharply to the left between high brick walls and then abruptly opens into yet another enclosed garden. This one is larger than the others and more elaborate. The length stretches thrice the width, framed by tall columns. Webbing stretches between columns, wispy and tattered like old lace. Instead of weeds, there are empty beds of dry, fissured soil.

The path ends at a large structure hidden behind more webbing. It's an abandoned section of the castle, and the only way in appears to be a single wooden door.

I press my palms against the sides of my dark tunic. The sensation of clammy hands groping at my skin washes over me, and I barely keep from shuddering. Looking at Theyen, who appears unaffected, I ask, "What do you think?"

His lip curls. "How appropriately morbid."

He really can't feel it, whatever this is. I dig in my heels as the power presses ever closer, imaginary claws raking against my mind. Beckoning.

From somewhere beyond the door comes the sound of something moving. Something heavy. *Click. Click.*

I go rigid. Beside me, Theyen stiffens as well. Whatever power rests here swells against me. It stings my nostrils and coats my tongue in a bitter aftertaste. I fight the urge to gag. The magic is strong, old enough to have soaked into the surrounding maze like an oil slick. It feels tainted. Unnatural like the Dead Wood.

Something rustles beyond the wall at our left. Through a crack, I glimpse a large white creature scuttle past. *Click. Click. Click.*

Fear sinks into my stomach even as my curiosity heightens. My instincts urge me to run, but that twisted power coaxes me closer. It feels like claws teasing at my throat, even as it whispers of dark promises. I clench my fingers around the fabric of my pants, disturbed by the sudden desire to rush toward that closed wooden door even as the familiar fear of the Dead Wood closes around my lungs.

A shadow passes over the cobbled path behind us. It's brief, fast for a creature of that size, but I'm left with the impression of something massive, with multiple legs. Theyen's face pales. He grabs my wrist, his fingers squeezing. Our gazes meet. A moment of understanding passes between us.

We stand our ground, facing the only exit, and await the beast.

Ronin appears from around the curved path. I suck in a sharp breath and scan the empty space behind him, but nothing appears. Whatever else had been there is gone. He's alone.

Ronin's glare impales me like ice between my ribs. He asks in a cold, quiet voice, "What are you doing here?"

Each word is clearly articulated, his glacial rage as oppressive as the magic emanating from the door at the opposite end of the garden.

Somehow, I manage to speak. "Exploring. The castle grounds are fascinating and speak well of its many years."

"Is that so?" he asks with that same deadly calm.

"It is. Do you make a habit of sneaking up on your guests and scaring the wits out of them?"

He steps forward until we're mere paces apart. "I have a feeling that you are not so easily undone."

My throat is so dry that my tongue feels like sand against the roof of my mouth. But I force my lips into a smile.

He tilts his head at Theyen. "Hlau Theyen. It would be in your best interest to avoid this part of the castle from now on. Both of you."

Back in my rooms, I fill in Saengo on what happened. If I'd been uncertain before, there's no longer any doubt that Ronin keeps his familiar back there. But no familiar should be able to exist in the Dead Wood without contracting the rot, so how is he doing it?

Standing directly beside me, Theyen couldn't sense the power there. As my dreams remind me on a nightly basis, I am attuned to souls, including those trapped in the Dead Wood. It's the specific nature of my craft—like a song only souls can hear.

"What if his familiar doesn't connect him just to his magic?" I twirl my spoon through the thick meat stew we've been given for dinner. I'm hungry, but my stomach is still in knots. "What if his Spinner is connected to the spirits in the Dead Wood as well, and that's what keeps them tied here? And since the Spinner is his conduit, Ronin also gets access to the combined power of all those souls?"

"Is that even possible?" Saengo is still much too pale, and her hand trembles as she reaches for her cup. She insisted on getting out of bed to eat, though. She's doing what she needs to feel normal.

"The Soulless did it. He made himself more powerful by taking human souls. Maybe Ronin decided to do the same after defeating him."

"But the Soulless was a . . . what was it again?"

"Soulrender."

"Right. That. Ronin is a sower. He's not even a lightwender."

"But if he's using his familiar, then maybe it doesn't matter. Familiars channel magic, and they're spirits themselves." I immediately wince at my poor choice of words, but Saengo doesn't react. "I don't know how it'd work, but he must have figured out a way. That Spinner is the key. If I can break Ronin's bond with his familiar, it might free the spirits that it's anchoring here."

"We're leaving in the morning," she points out. I'd expressed concern over her traveling, but there will be many skilled healers among the various camps in the north. None will have ever seen a human familiar, but with so many medically gifted minds, surely someone will have a suggestion for how to help her.

"Yeah, but so is Ronin. Once we're settled up north, I'll sneak away and come back here."

Clearly torn, she chews the corner of her lip. "Should we ask Hlau Theyen for help?"

Theyen is going north as well, although he and his retinue plan to travel by a different means.

"I don't think he'd approve." Not after we were caught by Ronin today. "Besides, I'm still not sure how much we can trust him. We don't know who sent that shadowblessed after me." Whether Theyen wants war or not between the shamans and the shadow-blessed, it can't be ignored that he would benefit from one.

"But how are you going to make it through the Dead Wood without Ronin's protection?"

"I've done it once already."

"That was only a few hours. It's a much longer journey to get from the north to here."

"We don't have any other choice. I'll have to do it."

She leans back in her seat, her hand lifting to touch the base of her throat. Beneath her collar, the lines have spread nearly to her jaw. She doesn't need to voice her worry—I'll have my magic so long as I have a familiar.

"You're not dying, remember? As soon as I break Ronin's familiar bond, the magic holding the spirits trapped here will be broken, and you should be able to heal." I hope.

Maybe it's a fool's hope, but it's all I have.

TWENTY-ONE

I would have tried slipping out in the middle of the night, but the guards in sight of my balcony remained diligent. Instead, I slept fitfully, trying to dispel the sensation of claws scratching at my mental walls, insisting on my attention.

Our maid has our things packed before we're even finished with our breakfast. She's tucked several spidersilk gowns into our bags in case the clothing up north doesn't suit our tastes. I hug her goodbye.

As we set out, I worry about how Saengo will fare in the Dead Wood, but at least Ronin is leading us. Although she's slower than usual and her jaw tenses with pain, she never falters.

We travel in taut awareness of the trees. I walk slightly behind Saengo so I can catch her in case she falls. After a while, the silence becomes oppressive. I glance at Phaut.

"Will you know anyone once we reach the north?" I ask

quietly. "Anyone you might want to see again?"

"My friends are not so high up," she says with a crooked smile. "Rumor has it an emissary of the Nuvali Crown will be there."

"And the Kazan. Theyen will be there as representative for the Fireborn Queens."

"Someone from all the major clans will be there, I expect. And the Merchants Guild as well."

With most land routes between the kingdoms obstructed by the Dead Wood, nearly all imports and exports are conducted by ship. The sea merchants have made an empire off the needs of the countries. They would probably not look kindly on me coming along and ruining their business by clearing out the Dead Wood.

"Isn't it dangerous to have so many rivalries in one place?" One wrong word, one unforgivable slight, and the Kazan and Nuvali could go to war right there on the grasslands. Or the Evewynians and the Nuvali. Or all three.

"Any time Lord Ronin has need to discuss matters with the kingdoms, they meet in the north. This will not be the first time they'll be forced to share company, nor will it be the last. Besides, the camps will be well separated, and Lord Ronin will have soldiers patrolling the grasslands."

"Well," I say. "I suppose if they all kill one another, we'll have an excellent seat from which to watch."

She snorts. "That we will."

We trudge on, magic tingling through me every time the roots shift. But as with our return journey from Sab Hnou, we reach the border within hours without incident. I'm surprised, however, to find that we haven't emerged outside Sab Hnou. Instead, we must be north of it, well into the Empire.

Saengo and I gawk at the sight that greets us. A road runs parallel to the trees, where a dozen mounted and armed soldiers dressed in Ronin's livery await us, holding the banner of the Spider King. They've brought enough drakes for our party. But it's what's behind them that catches my breath.

Swaths of bright sunflowers blanket the rolling hills, their stalks taller than a grown man. Not all are in full bloom, but it seems we've arrived just in time. Farther off, the sunflowers turn red, a fuchsia ribbon dressing the sky. The scent of them, heady and sweet, overpowers the decay of the Dead Wood.

Once everyone's mounted, Ronin leads the charge, setting a brisk pace. As soon as Saengo's drake takes off, her face pales alarmingly, but she somehow holds on. Her pain echoes dully in my own chest. When I suggest asking Ronin to slow our party, Saengo refuses. The sooner we reach our destination, the better.

Phaut's gaze barely strays from the yellow fields. The other Nuvali soldiers breathe deeply the sweet air and turn their faces toward the sky like young sunflowers tracking the light.

Will the same joy lift me if I'm someday allowed back in Evewyn? I used to escape the Company for a few hours by sneaking out to Vos Talwyn's southern watchtower. I would sit at the lip of the roof, where the wind broke wildly against the cliffs and the briny air was thick enough to taste. Watching the frothing waves of Needle Bay, speckled with cargo ships, while my hair grew stiff with salt, always helped to soothe away my frustrations.

Will I be able to return to that watchtower and that feeling, or has everything been forever changed?

"How long has it been since you've seen them in bloom?" I ask Phaut.

Fields like these must exist all over the Empire. Sunflowers are one of the country's most prized exports. Every part of the flower serves a function, from food and medicine to clothing and ornamentation.

"Years." Her voice grows faint as she murmurs, "My father didn't grow sunflowers, but we were close enough that on a clear day their scent would carry all the way to our little farm."

"Sounds wonderful." I might have slept out in the fields if this had surrounded the orphanage.

"It was. I didn't want to be a farmer, though. I taught myself all I could about swordplay. My father was kindhearted. He didn't tell me until I was much older that only those of the Imperial Court can become sun warriors."

I frown. Evewyn's customs are rigid and its social etiquette stringent, but even so, any soldier of the Royal Army may rise to become a Blade regardless of their station. Up until Queen Meilyr, that had included shamanborn.

"You did even better." I throw back my shoulders and lift my chin. "You're the personal guard of the Little Sun God."

Phaut laughs and sits a bit taller in her saddle.

Over the next two days, we travel alongside the Dead Wood. We spot several small villages with squat houses lining dusty streets. This close to the trees, there isn't a familiar in sight.

Likely, these villages were here long before they learned the trees crept outward. One day, unless something is done, the Dead Wood will overtake them and kill those unable or unwilling to leave their homes behind.

As the sky transforms into a fiery gradient, the ground slopes upward. When we reach the crest, the road descends into the northern grasslands, which unfold before us in green waves. Normally, herds of beasts big and small roam the vast expanse, numbering in the thousands. During a migration, the earth rumbles from one end of the grasslands to the other.

Today, the sunset gilds the crowns of thousands of tents. Rainbows of banners catch in the wind, bearing so many emblems I hardly recognize any. Drakes and people navigate between tents, trampling the grass and carving pathways.

"Wow," Saengo whispers.

Phaut releases a low whistle. "This is incredible. I was expecting a dozen leaders, two dozen at the very most, like in the past. This looks like all of Thiy has gathered."

My heart flutters at that. All these people, leaders from every corner of Thiy, here for a single purpose.

Although it looks a bit like arriving at a war camp, as we pass through the first cluster of tents, the atmosphere is jovial. Noise assaults us from every direction: the slew of chatter in various languages, the clang of weapons, and the rhythm of music, several tunes at once blending into a cacophony of sound. The tangled aromas from dozens of cooking fires infuse the air.

Servants and soldiers alike pause to incline their heads as we pass. Whether out of respect or fear, no one wants to insult the Spider King.

This morning, Saengo and I donned spare uniforms to blend in with Ronin's soldiers. He doesn't want anyone knowing who I am until I can be officially introduced. In a company made up of shadow-blessed, shamans, and humans, no one gives us a second glance.

A troupe of five colorfully dressed musicians steps aside to make way for Ronin's retinue. They bow low, blowing notes into their reed pipes and jaw harps as we pass.

The Dead Wood remains always at our left. Ahead, the road veers into the trees. Ronin leads us through, the path wide enough for a couple of wagons driving abreast. The boisterous sounds die off quickly. Our group presses tight in the middle of the road.

Within minutes, the path leads to the gates of a bone palisade. Unlike the one at Spinner's End, there is no additional webbing to shield against the trees.

Ronin's manor house is an ornate, four-story behemoth, with the extravagant tiered roofs and intricate sculptural accessories that were lacking at Spinner's End. I suspect the house's white-washed walls and golden traceries are more for the benefit of its guests than for Ronin. Additional buildings stand perpendicular to the main house, extending farther back into the property. Staff rush in and out of the open front doors, hauling luggage from newly arrived dignitaries and directing drakes to the inner stables.

"You've been here before?" I ask Phaut.

"Twice. Each time, the trees have moved a little farther out. Once, long before I came into Lord Ronin's service, the manor stood well outside the Dead Wood."

As we pass through the gate, my body grows slack and weak, as if I've spent the entire day training with Kendara. I glance at the others, but they appear unaffected. Saengo gives me a concerned look. Is this an echo of her discomfort or something else? I grip the saddle with faintly trembling arms as I dismount, although it's more like a controlled fall. When my feet touch the ground, my legs nearly fold.

"Welcome to Vienth Manor. I'll show you to your room," a servant says after handing my drake off to a stable hand.

"What's wrong?" Saengo whispers as we link arms and cross the yard. We lean against each other, keeping the other upright.

"I don't know." My knees waver as I cross the threshold. I grab the door frame to keep from dragging Saengo down with me.

"My lady?" The servant's hand hovers over my arm, uncertain.

Phaut nudges the servant aside. She puts her arm around my waist, gathering my weight against her. "Tired?"

"You know me better than that," I snap.

"It's the troll bones," Ronin says, appearing in the foyer. Servants stream around us in an efficient sort of organized chaos, with Ronin at their center, an unflappable fixed point.

"What?" I look down at Saengo's wrist where the talisman is hidden beneath her sleeve.

"I desecrated the only troll graveyard in Thiy to build this structure. The masons mixed the crushed bones into the mortar. The house weakens all magic users who enter."

So that's why the manor house is the ideal place for the kingdoms' most powerful to gather. Here, we are all rendered equals.

"The strongest among us feel its effects more acutely," he says, eyes appraising. Does it surprise him to count me among those strongest? "You'll become accustomed to it soon." He turns away, his tunic rustling as he ascends the grand staircase.

Willing my legs to obey, I release the door frame. Phaut helps by shouldering my weight as the servant guides us to my room. Saengo grips my other hand. Once we're settled, maids arrive to help us wash, but I send them away. Saengo and I bathe alone so that no one else will see the startling lines of infection that spider Saengo's chest.

The maids have left me gorgeous plum-colored silks in the Nuvali style of flowing layers and intricately embroidered hems. But I regretfully pass on the gown. Instead, I put on formfitting pants and a loose top, belted with a simple red sash. I'll need the freedom of movement.

Once we're both washed and dressed, I empty my satchel of everything save my swords and then sling the bag over my shoulder. Saengo gives me a firm nod, her eyes dark and serious. The hot water has returned some much-needed warmth to her cheeks.

"Be careful," she says.

"I will." My plan is simple. After consulting some maps in the library, I learned that a creek runs through the rear of Vienth Manor. It flows directly south through the Dead Wood and cuts close to the western border of Spinner's End. It's the most direct route and should take a full night and day's ride. If the trees cooperate.

Once I'm missed, Saengo will say I went to meet her father to explain his daughter's circumstances in person. Falcons Ridge is only a couple of days' ride west of here. I'd be back in no time. Ronin will still be furious, and Phaut will probably go after me. She won't realize the deception until she arrives at Falcons Ridge and learns I'm not there.

It genuinely pains me to deceive Phaut. She's my friend, and I have so few of those. But she's also loyal to Ronin. Breaking his bond with his familiar is as much an attack on him as it is on the Dead Wood. I can't be certain Phaut would believe my theories or that she wouldn't report my intentions back to him.

Something rustles at our window. Saengo's eyes light up. "Millie!"

The falcon perches on the sill, watching us with a slight tilt of her head. Sometimes I'm convinced she understands what we're saying.

"I asked my father to send his response here instead of Spinner's End. She's probably been waiting for me." She coos at the falcon before retrieving the message attached to her leg. Since Millie only allows Saengo and her parents to handle her, they don't have to worry about anyone else getting a hold of their correspondence.

As Saengo reads the message, her joy at seeing Millie quickly fades. After a moment, she silently hands me the slip of paper.

I read quickly, my stomach in knots. According to her father, nearly the whole of the Royal Army stationed at Falcons Ridge marched east over a week ago with the queen. He remained behind, citing the queen's orders that her own generals would lead the troops. The lords and ladies of neighboring properties all report the same. He ends his letter with a request that Saengo prepare for whatever might happen.

I close the note, my thoughts buzzing with questions. If it's been well over a week since the army left Falcons Ridge, then they should have arrived by now. Even slowed by their numbers, an army of that size marching through the grasslands wouldn't go unnoticed.

So where are they?

"I have a bad feeling about this," Saengo says. What color the bath gave her has faded into a slightly green pallor. Even with the high collar of her shirt, I glimpse the lines of infection that have spread beneath her jaw.

Urgency presses around my lungs, making it hard to draw a full breath. She's running out of time. "We have to get you a healer."

I turn for the door, but she grabs my wrist. Even though she looks like a slight breeze might knock her over, her grip is strong.

"Promise me you'll do something about this news," she says. "This is more important, Sirscha."

"As soon as I find you a healer or five." The shamanborn called me Suryali. If the shamans here share the sentiment, then they won't hesitate to help me. And if they refuse, then I don't have to ask nicely. I'll—

"Stop it," Saengo chides softly, pulling me from my dark thoughts. "I think we need to tell Ronin. The people here have to be prepared in case . . ."

In case Queen Meilyr turns a gathering to discuss peace into a battlefield. But I shake my head. "Ronin's first priority is his own power. I don't trust that he won't twist the information to his advantage, especially to avoid admitting he can't keep the peace. I have a different idea."

Out in the hall, Phaut awaits us, looking freshly washed. Her short hair is only partly dry, black and gray curling around her ears. Her dusty uniform has been changed for a clean one.

"Can you find Ronin and ask him to send a healer for Saengo? Please."

Phaut opens her mouth, like she means to argue. But then she glimpses Saengo over my shoulder, and her jaw tightens. "Very well. What about you?"

My body thrums with restless frustration. I want to flee this instant for Spinner's End. Saengo's life is not less important, and the longer I delay, the less time she has.

But she's right that something has to be done first. "I need to find a prince."

As soon as I'm outside, the draining effect of the manor's walls begins to fade. My strength returns with every step.

A servant brings me a drake. I secure my satchel to the saddle and leave through the gate. Coming up the path in single file are a group of armored warriors. In the fading sunlight, I make out the symbols emblazoned on their breast-plates: two crossed swords over a sun.

I suck in my breath. Although I've never seen Nuvali sun warriors, there's nothing else they could be.

Sisters, does this mean Kendara had been a sun warrior? But that would mean she's Nuvali. Was my mother Nuvali as well? I'd assumed I was shamanborn.

The sun warriors ride a species of drakonys I've only read about—dragokin, native to the Empire. Dragokin are taller and larger than drakes, more suitable for bearing the weight of their riders' armor. The first one's scales are a slick crimson. Four black horns curl from its head. The sun warrior riding it wears black armor so exquisitely detailed that my eyes don't know where to rest.

Whorls and panels of complex filigree ornament the metal—a forger's skill. Gorgets rise like tiered fans around her neck. Her sash is a vivid yellow, tied around her waist in a series of knots I'm not familiar with, presumably a Nuvali style that denotes her rank. Her hair is as black as her dragokin's horns, but her eyes are a bright, hard ruby. They catch my scrutiny, and a smirk paints her lips. What I wouldn't give to test my skill against a sun warrior.

The path emerges onto the grasslands. I follow the perimeter of several camps, searching until I spot the familiar silver moon against a white banner. To reach the Evewynian camp, I cut through what appears to be a makeshift market.

Merchants have set up tables offering the usual fare—pottery, charms, bejeweled mirrors. There are also less common wares I wouldn't find in Vos Talwyn's market, like powdered zaj scales and bottled storms. The merchant waves one at us, claiming they're good to have on hand during the dry season.

I don't even know if Prince Meilek is here. Maybe he's with his sister. Though after what happened in Vos Gillis, I'd like to believe he wouldn't sit idly by if he knew his sister was planning something dangerous.

I'm nearly through the market when a voice calls, "Sirscha?"

I turn. Prince Meilek has risen from a group of soldiers eating noodles beneath a pavilion. Someone has set up wooden tables and benches to serve customers fresh food. At the sight of him, conflicting emotions clash within me—relief but also wariness. We didn't part on very good terms, and I don't know how I'll be received.

Rather than royal attire or even his captain's armor, he's dressed in the same uniform as the other soldiers—a leather breastplate fitted over the thick fabric of his green undershirt. A matching sash is tied around his waist, the ends hanging over an apron-like leather faulds. Silver vambraces gird his wrists. Loose pants tucked into fitted knee-high boots speckled in mud complete the illusion of an Evewynian soldier. Even his jewel-studded weapons have been traded for a simple sword.

He steps out from beneath the pavilion. His dark hair has been pulled back and knotted at the nape of his neck. Despite the disguise, the proper thing to do would be to dismount and bow. But I don't waste time on pleasantries or protocols.

"I need your help. It's urgent."

Prince Meilek's brows rise. Behind him, two other soldiers stand. I recognize them as his Blades, although they're also dressed as regular soldiers.

He gestures for them to keep their distance and gives me a warm smile. "Shall we walk?"

I dismount and shove the reins at another of his soldiers. The soldier looks confused but grudgingly accepts responsibility over the drake.

"I'm glad to see you've been well treated since we last met," Prince Meilek says, his words ending in a question. There is genuine concern in the way his eyes sweep over my face.

"I have." I gesture around us. "Can we speak somewhere more private?"

"It'll be dinner soon." Torches have already been lit throughout the camps. "We're to dine with Ronin tonight to welcome the lord's return to his manor. There's a stream down that way to wash up. It should be quiet enough."

Despite my impatience, I nod and allow him to lead us. His two Blades keep a respectful distance.

"Is your sister here yet?" I ask lightly.

"Not yet, but I left her to ride ahead two days ago. She should arrive by morning."

"Is she bringing a large entourage?"

If he finds the question strange, he doesn't show it. "Larger than I would have recommended, but not so many that we won't have enough tents."

I school my expression into blankness. This doesn't make sense. If the queen isn't bringing her entire army, then where are all her soldiers?

As we weave through the crowd, Prince Meilek's body language doesn't betray any awkwardness or resentment, despite what happened in Vos Gillis.

I stuff my hands into my pockets and blurt, "I need to apologize. For the last time we met. I shouldn't have raised my swords to you."

He gives me a crooked smile. "You shouldn't have, no. But I understand why you did."

"I wouldn't have killed you." I cringe at how that sounds, but he only laughs. How he can forgive me so easily baffles me. In his place, I'm not sure I'd be as understanding.

"You couldn't have, anyway," he says. "But you're a natural warrior. Kendara used to say that you try too hard, that you're too afraid to fail. I don't think that's it, though. You simply fight with all the fire in your being."

I flush a bit at his praise. What does one say when the prince of Evewyn compliments your skill after you've committed treason?

"You only won because I gave up one of my swords to save Kudera," I point out. "Otherwise, the fight could have gone either way. We do share the same sword master."

Prince Meilek doesn't look surprised. "Of course you'd notice. You were her star pupil, after all."

That's not true. Sadness and anger surges within me. She

never meant for me to be Shadow. She only trained me because of a promise she made to my mother.

"Back in the Prince's Company, you always attacked first. That doesn't seem to have changed."

"There's no point letting my opponent make the first move. If I attack quickly, I can end it quickly."

"Kendara always cautioned me to attack only when absolutely necessary."

"That's because you're you," I say. Still, I consider the implications. Prince Meilek must exercise caution because his loss would devastate the kingdom. I need no such restrictions. Because I am expendable.

I shake my head. I have to stop thinking this way. Kendara pushed me to fight my hardest so I would have the skills to survive.

As we pass the last few stalls in the market, something catches my eye. Nearly hidden by the growing gloom and a stack of small crates is a man washing dishes. It's not him I notice; it's the distinctive tattoos stretching from the ends of his eyebrows and into his hairline.

Confusion washes over me. "What's he doing here?"

Prince Meilek follows my gaze. His feet slow and then stop.

The wounds I'd given Eyebrow Tattoos are gone. He's dressed in common clothing, sleeves pushed up to his elbows as he dunks dishes into a tub of soapy water. A lightwender must have tended to his hands, although I can't imagine him allowing a shaman to perform magic on him.

"Was he dismissed from the Valley of Cranes?" Maybe he'd been fired for allowing the prison break.

"He wasn't dismissed," Prince Meilek says.

I follow his long strides as he cuts between two stalls. At the sounds of our approach, Eyebrow Tattoos looks up. His expression when he recognizes Prince Meilek is almost comical. The plate in his hand slips into the tub, splashing his shirt. His face goes ruddy as his expression twists into panic.

Then he turns and runs.

"Blades," Prince Meilek snaps. The two Blades at our backs bolt after him.

I'm not about to be left behind, so I take off as well. I follow closely as they sprint around people and tents, drakes and campfires. Eyebrow Tattoos is surprisingly fast. He knocks over a pot, spilling stew and hot embers. Smoke billows into the darkening sky. People shout and dash into our path.

I leap over a man crouched over the spilled stew. Prince Meilek is right beside me, a focused predatory glint in his eyes. I'm suddenly glad I didn't try to run when he caught Saengo and me those weeks ago.

The tents end as the ground slopes gradually downward toward a stream filled with splashing children and people bathing shamelessly in the torchlight. Eyebrow Tattoos has nearly reached a small copse of trees when one of the Blades finally tackles him. They go down in a crush of limbs and armor.

The Blade ends up on top, pinning Eyebrow Tattoos. In an instant, the other Blade has his sword drawn and pointed at the man's throat. He stops struggling immediately, his chest heaving from exertion.

Prince Meilek and I catch up a second later. In a clipped voice, Prince Meilek asks, "What are you doing here? Why aren't you at your post in the Valley?"

Eyebrow Tattoos shakes his head frantically. "I'm sorry, Your Highness. I didn't mean to run. I just—I panicked. I-I wasn't supposed to be seen."

"Seen by whom?"

"By you." His eyes are huge. His forehead is shiny with sweat. Is he scared of Prince Meilek?

Granted, the prince looks rather forbidding at the moment, with no trace of his usual kindness. "Who gave you this order?"

"Th—the queen, Your Highness."

Ah. Eyebrow Tattoos is terrified of what the queen will do to him now that he's broken her orders.

"And why would she do that?" Prince Meilek asks calmly, a threat beneath his words. This isn't just the prince of Evewyn. This is the captain of the Queen's Guard, and he doesn't tolerate lies.

"I don't question my queen's orders, Your Highness." His gaze darts frantically past the prince and his Blades, seeking escape.

So an Evewynian army marched east more than a week ago, before mysteriously vanishing, and now we find an Evewynian soldier hidden among the camps. The implications make my skin prickle.

"Are you the only soldier stationed here?" I ask.

Eyebrow Tattoos notices me for the first time. Disgust curls his lip. "You. Don't speak to me, shaman filth—"

"Answer the question," Prince Meilek says.

Eyebrow Tattoos swallows delicately against the sword at his throat. "I . . . I can't possibly know—"

"You're lying." My fists clench, imagining the grips of my swords. "How many others are there?"

The Blade holding the sword moves the edge against Eyebrow Tattoos's neck. Blood beads against the steel. With a whimper, he tries to wiggle out from beneath the weapon but stops when the other Blade presses a foot to his chest.

"You will answer the question, or I will leave you in the shaman's care for questioning," Prince Meilek says. "I trust you recall how your last meeting with her went."

I bare my teeth in a grin, impressed that the prince's expression doesn't give away the bluff. At least I think it's a bluff.

"I don't know!" Eyebrow Tattoos shouts, squeezing his eyes shut. "I swear! I just know they're spread out. Through the camps and the manor house."

My thoughts race. Why would Queen Meilyr include soldiers among Ronin's house staff? What could they hope to do in a manor house filled with Thiy's most powerful shamans and shadowblessed? In a manor house . . . made of troll bones.

"Why?" Prince Meilek repeats.

"I know why," I breathe as all the pieces suddenly click together.

It's a trap. Queen Meilyr plans to ambush the leaders inside the manor house, where they won't be able to fight back at their full strength. I press my palm to my chest, feeling the frantic flutter of my heart.

Ronin has to be warned. He has to—

And then I remember. The letter Saengo had found in Ronin's study. The arrangements the queen had mentioned. Ensuring preparations were made for additional staff.

No. I sway on my feet. Ronin can't have agreed to such a plan. His purpose has always been to keep the peace.

And yet, this at last answers the question I couldn't solve at Spinner's End: Why me?

Only a soulguide could have brought so many leaders together in one place. Phaut said there's never been a gathering like this one. Queen Meilyr gambled on me awakening as a soulguide, and it had paid off.

A plan involving the placement of so many hidden soldiers could never have been guaranteed without Ronin's help. What a perfect fool I've been. I knew that Ronin's priority was his own power, and yet I didn't see this coming.

Does Ronin even believe the things he's said about soul-guides? There's a pang at my center, in that dark, still place where my old fears crouch in wait—that I am destined for nothing. That I am nothing.

Prince Meilek gives me an expectant look, but how do I even begin to explain? Once Ronin and Queen Meilyr have won themselves all of Thiy, the only threat remaining will be the Dead Wood. A threat they can control, so long as they have me.

TWENTY-TWO

"R onin and Queen Meilyr are planning to ambush the leaders in the manor house."

The corners of Prince Meilek's lips tighten, but he doesn't otherwise react. "That seems unlikely."

I gesture to the man on the ground. "Your proof is right here."

His eyebrow twitches, a sign of his skepticism. But he addresses Eyebrow Tattoos. "Is this true?"

The man moans miserably, like he's already been condemned. Prince Meilek repeats the question. Hands clasped for mercy, Eyebrow Tattoos nods.

Prince Meilek steps back, his jaw set. "Take him to the camp for further questioning. Learn everything you can, but speak of this to no one. I'll meet you there shortly."

Once the Blades have gone, he turns on his heel, stalking into the nearby trees. His fingers clench and unclench at his side.

I sympathize that he needs to process, but we can't wait to act. I follow after him. "Prince Meilek, we need to warn everyone."

He ignores me as we move deeper into the trees. They're lush and green, the tall grass undisturbed and scattered with blue wildflowers. The sun has disappeared beneath the horizon, but full dark hasn't yet settled. Beneath the branches, the remaining light is a diffused glow.

He goes only far enough that the sound of rushing water drowns out the noise of those downstream. "Do you know what will happen if we share this information on the word of a single unreliable source?"

"I know what will happen if we don't. Saengo's father, the head of House Phang, has already confirmed the queen emptied northern Evewyn of its troops and led them east. I can produce proof of his message if you insist, but we're wasting time by arguing."

He prowls along the water's edge, his agitation feeding my own. "I have to speak to Mei and find out for myself what's going on. Maybe I can stop her."

"You can't. Who knows how long she's had this planned? Whatever you say now won't change anything."

Queen Meilyr must be as adept as Ronin at constructing webs, because she's woven so many lies and secrets around her brother, her own captain, that he hadn't even been aware of her plotting.

"And even if, by some miracle, you do manage to change your sister's mind, what about Ronin?" I say. "Whether she's there or not, Ronin might continue with their plan and kill everyone, anyway. We have to warn them."

A muscle works in his jaw. Although his expression is hard, there's a wounded look in his eyes. His sister's betrayal cuts deep. But will he betray her in turn? I can't claim to understand how difficult this must be for him. Despite everything she's done, he must still love her.

"The news needs to come from you. As Evewyn's prince, you might be able to convince the other leaders that your people aren't their enemy. But if you won't do it, then I will."

I turn on my heel only to jolt back again. A small knife pierces the shore shy of where my foot would have been.

A man with ribbons in his braids emerges from the trees, along with four others. I recognize them as the music troupe from only a few hours ago. In place of instruments, their hands grip swords. One wears a belt lined with small throwing knives.

Eyebrow Tattoos might not have run in this direction at random. I silently curse myself for leaving my weapons in my satchel, which is back in the market with my drake.

How long before Prince Meilek's Blades come searching for him? As Prince Meilek and I shift closer to each other, a sixth figure breaks from the trees. In the dark, I don't immediately recognize him. But when I do, my stomach clenches in renewed fury.

"Jonyah," I hiss.

Thick scars marble much of his face, the flesh shiny and taut. His head has been shaved, but the fuzz of new growth stops above his temple. The scars continue down his neck, disappearing beneath his collar.

"Sirscha, Sirscha. That's twice now I've sneaked up on you." The fire destroyed his lips, slurring his words. "Are you sure Kendara trained you?" His physical appearance is all that's changed. He still walks with a swagger, still puffs out his chest to emphasize his size.

"What's the meaning of this?" Prince Meilek asks. The cool edge to his voice makes me shiver.

But Jonyah's flinty eyes pass over him, dismissive. His instincts were never very sharp. "Keep quiet, Your Highness. This doesn't concern you."

"You will lower your weapons at once."

"My orders come from someone above you, so no." Jonyah stomps down into the strip of patchy grass that lies between the trees and the bank of the stream. His large boots make a squelching sound, crushing the water reeds that push through the mud. Gesturing to his face, he asks me, "What do you think? It was the best the healers could do without magic, but I kind of like it."

He's not looking for sympathy. He wants fear.

"I think your soul hasn't changed much, still shriveled and foul, like a ripe plum left in the sun to rot."

He barks laughter, loud enough to startle awake birds sleeping in the branches. Frantic wings snap leaves as they take flight. "You're always good for laughing at, Tshauv Taws. Should have been a court fool."

I smile sweetly. "And you're always good for mindless

obedience. Should have been a dog."

"You think you're so important? You're just another shaman who needs to be put down. I'd kill you now, but the queen wants you alive."

"Lucky me."

"As her Shadow, the duty of bringing you in fell to me. You made yourself pathetically easy to find."

It rubs me that he's right. I didn't try very hard to conceal myself, but neither did I expect Jonyah to be here, or that any Evewynian would attack me in Prince Meilek's presence.

"And we found you conspiring with the prince no less." He turns that vicious smile to Prince Meilek, who merely lifts one eyebrow. "Take them."

I dig my heel into the loose dirt just as one of the men makes a gurgling sound and falls facedown into the grass. A knife protrudes from the back of his neck. Some distance behind him, shrouded by the dark, stands Phaut with her sword drawn.

Everyone bursts into movement. I dive at the nearest musician's feet. He tumbles, hitting the ground hard. My hand finds two of his throwing knives. I tug them free before backing away to avoid a wild swipe of his sword. Over his shoulder, Phaut's blade flashes in the moonlight as she fends off Jonyah and a second musician.

I duck another strike and smash the heel of my palm into the man's nose. He cries out and staggers back, blood spilling down his face. I rush past him, flinging the knives. They both find their mark in Jonyah's and the musician's backs. The musician falters, falling to his knees, but Jonyah doesn't. He was trained by Kendara, after all.

He knocks aside Phaut's sword and drives his blade through her chest. Everything inside me turns to ice. Her gaze finds mine, startled and pained. Then she falls.

"No!" I scream, charging at him. My chest heaves with great gasping breaths. Tears burn my eyes. My heart has become a war hammer, smashing against my ribs.

The musician rises from the ground, lunging for me. He's already clawed the knife from his back. I barely keep my feet as he grabs me around my waist and aims the weapon for my side. I twist around, smashing my elbow into his face. He drops the knife. I catch the blade between two fingers, flip it, and drive it beneath his chin. He makes a choking sound as red foams at his lips.

Another knife sings through the air. I yank him in front of me. He spasms as the blade impales his chest.

Dropping my shield, I yank the knife from the man's throat and fling it, but not at the knife thrower. The blade buries in the back of one of Prince Meilek's opponents, allowing him to steal her sword. Then I lunge for the knife thrower who stands between Phaut and me. She lies just beyond, the shape of her indistinct in the deepening night.

I twist to the side as the point of a small blade narrowly misses my shoulder. Neither of us breaks stride as I dive for his legs and his fingers find his last throwing knife. I'm too close, with too much momentum to properly dodge.

Pain spears my leg as I barrel into him. We tumble into the

underbrush and crash against the base of a tree. He jams his fingers against the knife in my thigh. The pain makes me gasp. I smash my fist into his bloodied face. Sticky warmth coats my fingers. I need to reach Phaut. Why won't he just die?

Tears blot my vision. I punch him again. He catches my wrist, but I rotate my shoulder and smash my elbow into his jaw. We roll, stones digging into my spine. The knife thrower, at least twice my weight, ends up on top.

I grope for the knife in my thigh and rip it free, hissing through the pain before stabbing the blade into the man's side. He roars, but instead of falling off me, his hands close around my throat. I slam my knuckles into the hole in his side again and again, but his eyes grow crazed. He doesn't relent. His fingers crush my neck with the ferocity of a dying man.

I claw at his wrists and forearms. Black spots dance in my vision, and my blood roars in my ears.

"If I die, you die, too." The knife thrower spits into my face.

I rake my nails down his cheeks and his neck until my hands find his chest. The burning heat of my craft razes through me. A glow forms behind my fingers, like sunlight searing through clouds. Something pulses against my palm. My hand closes around it, and the grip around my neck loosens.

I throw my head back, air rushing into my lungs in long, wheezing gasps. Each breath is like razor blades down my throat, but I don't release the light in my hand. I know exactly what I'm holding. Above me, the knife thrower has gone immobile. When I regain enough breath to meet his gaze, the soul cupped in my palm illuminates his eyes, stark with fear.

I see Phaut's eyes, *her* fear. The regret in her face for failing to protect me, when I'm the one who failed her.

My fingers tighten, and I wrench free his soul. He convulses once. I heave him off me as he goes limp, dead before his body strikes the ground. Coughing raggedly, I turn my head to examine the orb of light clutched within my fingers. It lingers for a moment. Then I close my fist, and it dissipates.

Nearby, Prince Meilek has dispatched the others and disarmed Jonyah. They're both frozen now, staring at me and the dead knife thrower. I struggle to my feet and wonder why my leg won't hold me. Blood oozes from my thigh. I swear, slapping my palms over the wound and applying pressure. A wave of nausea washes over me.

Stumbling over the uneven ground, I collapse beside Phaut. Her shirt is saturated. A sob builds in my chest, but I swallow it down. Pressing my hands to her shoulders, I close my eyes.

Please. Please please please.

My magic stirs within me, but it's weak. Pain sharpens beneath my ribs, and my thoughts immediately go to Saengo. She's hurting. I have to save her before it's too late. Like I should have saved Phaut. Tears blur my eyes, and I dash angrily at them.

I slam my palms into the ground. I'm supposed to be able to restore a soul to life, aren't I? Work, damn it!

But nothing happens. I had gripped the bright warmth of the knife thrower's soul in my palm, and yet I can't save Phaut. Dirt slides beneath my nails as I sink my fingers into the earth, seeking purchase. I curl over Phaut's side. I can't breathe. The world tilts into a dizzying spiral.

I can't break down. Not now. Not with Saengo still depending on me.

"Are you all right?" Prince Meilek asks softly.

Although everything hurts, I force myself to look up. He's still standing by the shore, his sword pointed at Jonyah's chest.

"I think you're bleeding."

My thigh throbs in agreement. With a groan, I reach for the throwing knife still embedded in one of the musicians lying nearby. I wrench it free and wipe it off in the grass. Then I tug off my sash and cut into the fabric. With a few sharp motions, I tear the sash into several long strips.

As I bandage my thigh, hands shaking and stained, magic thrums beneath my skin. I can touch souls, so why can't I—

My fingers go still. Oh, Sisters. I hadn't just touched that knife thrower's soul. I had ripped his soul from his body. A single word rings through my ears.

Soulrender.

Soulguides shepherd those who've already passed, but soulrenders steal from the living. They can't help souls pass on. They can only manipulate and destroy them. It's a small but significant distinction. They are a blight to shamanic magic, a legacy of fear that remains even now in the existence of the Dead Wood.

I swallow thickly, the truth pushing the air from my chest as I knot off my bandage. Then I tuck the throwing knife into my belt and rise unsteadily to my feet.

Ahead of me, Jonyah suddenly turns, allowing Prince Meilek's blade to slice into his shoulder so he can slam the back of his fist into the prince's jaw. Prince Meilek staggers, the distraction just enough for Jonyah to plant a knee in his gut and steal his sword.

Fury sends energy coursing through me, chasing away the fatigue and confusion.

"I've always wanted to do that." Jonyah shakes out his hand. He grimaces as the movement strains the cut in his back. He does nothing to stop the bleeding.

When Prince Meilek's head lifts, his eyes have gone flat, the promise of death in that gaze. It's a promise he won't be able to keep, because I'm going to kill Jonyah first.

"Don't," I say. The word is meant for them both. Prince Meilek doesn't look at me, but he doesn't attack Jonyah, either.

Jonyah smirks and stalks toward me. "Finally you show some sense."

When he's near enough to grab for me, I snatch the throwing knife from my belt and stab his arm.

With a shout, he drops the sword. I lunge for it, but he kicks it into the shadows. I narrowly dodge his knee as I jump back, putting space between us.

Cursing loudly, he pulls the small knife from his arm. "You can never make anything easy, can you, Tshauv Taws?"

"I'm going to kill you," I say, limping backward. It hurts to move my entire left side, but I grit my teeth and bear it. I've endured worse. Kendara made sure of that.

I catch sight of Phaut's body. Anger crystalizes inside me.

I draw a slow, deep breath, relishing the pain in my throat, in my leg, in my heart—a reminder of what I will bestow tenfold on Jonyah. Already, calm sweeps through me, a cool breath of frost that numbs the worst of my pain.

Jonyah scoffs. "You're going to kill me after you saved my life at the teahouse? I wouldn't have done the same."

"I regret it daily."

The retort I'm expecting doesn't come. Instead, the mockery slips away, a peculiar solemnity taking its place as he considers the new wound in his arm. "Sometimes I envy you. Your existence is so . . . simple. You've never known family. You've never had to shoulder the duty of your elders. No one expects anything of you."

I laugh, a harsh sound. "You don't know anything about me."

"You have nothing to lose because you've always had nothing," he says, although his words lack their usual bite. "People like me, who are too low to hold a title but too high for drudgery? We have to fight for any scrap of power we get, no matter who we have to take it from."

Is he actually trying to justify the way he's bullied and terrorized me from the moment we met?

I speak softly, a promise in my voice. "Queen Meilyr claims I'm a traitor, which means I don't have to follow her rules anymore. I don't have to bite my tongue and suffer your pathetic inferiority complex. So why don't you come here and show me how you plan to keep whatever power you think you have?"

Jonyah sneers, all traces of gravity wiped away. "You've always talked big, but we both know it's all bluster. You don't have any power I would want. I already won the position of Shadow."

"Who cares about being Shadow anymore? Haven't you heard? I'm the Soul of Thiy, the Little Sun God. I'm the savior who's going to destroy the Dead Wood. Queen Meilyr needs me. You? You're just her pet. Easily replaced."

His face tightens with every word. It's so easy to bait him. If only my tongue had been allowed this freedom at the Company. He takes a step toward me and, like a complete idiot, tosses the small knife into the pockets of blackness beneath the trees.

He doesn't think he needs a weapon. I'm injured, and I've lost enough blood to make me light-headed. Besides, he can't kill me without risking his queen's wrath. He only wants to break me.

But even though he nearly died at the hands of shamanic magic, he still underestimates them. Still thinks himself better. And even though I'm in pain, whether by my anticipation or the shaman blood inside me, I'm not nearly as weak as he thinks I am.

Behind him, Prince Meilek watches with a fierce glint in his eyes. "Sirscha," he says. I hear the order in his voice: kill him.

Between one breath and the next, Jonyah attacks.

I duck his punch and jab his gut. The impact jars through my leg. His strength would quickly overpower me, so I can't risk getting caught. He kicks out. I leap back, but my injury makes me clumsy. My foot slides out from under me. I land on my side with an *oomph*. Pain jolts through my thigh.

He tries to get on top of me, but I bring up my knee, jabbing him in the side. He falls onto his back, groaning from the impact against the cut in his shoulder. I flip to my feet and drive my knee toward his neck. He rolls away, and my knee strikes dirt. As he climbs to his feet, I spy the dark sash of one of the dead musicians, half undone from the man's waist. I wrap one end of the rough cloth around my fist and stand as well.

Before Jonyah can attack, I land a punch on his jaw. He dodges the next punch. For his size, he's fast, and he's a competent fighter. More than competent. A bitter reminder that we share the same teacher.

He goes for my injured thigh, and I swing my other leg into his jaw. He collapses against a tree. Leaping onto his back, I dig my arm into the cut on his shoulder, making him stagger from the pain. Then I hook the sash around his neck, gripping the ends tight with one hand as my other presses to his chest.

Magic flares inside me. Jonyah goes rigid as his soul pulses against my fingers. Then agony spears my chest. My magic vanishes like a doused candle. Jonyah's elbow crashes into my temple. My grip loosens and I fall, landing hard on my back. Lights flicker behind my eyelids. Jonyah clutches the tree trunk, coughing and swearing as he pulls in air.

I roll onto my side, struggling to focus my vision. Saengo. Dread splits open my chest. She's dying. I have to defeat Jonyah and get to Spinner's End. But the weaker she grows, the less I'm able to access my magic.

Jonyah swipes for my head as I regain my feet. Blocking his fist, I slam my forehead into his face. He cries out, falling back.

I don't need magic to defeat him. I never have. The Company trained me to be a soldier, but Kendara trained me to survive. From the moment she took us both on as pupils, it was always meant to come to this: him or me. And I don't mean to lose.

I rush Jonyah as he's still clutching his face, slamming us both back into the tree and shaking the branches overhead. Leaves flutter down around us. Jonyah's fingers dig into my thigh as mine claw at his shoulder. Pain sears my leg and up my side, but it only enrages me as I wrap the sash again around his neck.

His eyes bulge. His legs kick, but I hook my feet behind his knees, using my body weight to bear down on him. His face turns bright red and then purple, made more livid by his scars. For a moment, the cold fury inside me wants to do worse to him, to make him suffer. He doesn't deserve such an easy end. But then Jonyah convulses, and his enormous body goes slack.

Slowly, I release the sash. His body slides clumsily to the ground, his vacant eyes gazing up at the night sky. I breathe hard. My limbs tremble from the exertion. Then everything goes fuzzy, and the darkness closes in.

When I wake, Prince Meilek is leaning over me. Beyond his shoulder, the moon sits high in the clouds.

"How do you feel?" he asks.

In an instant, I remember everything. I bolt upright. He backs away to avoid getting bashed in the head.

"How long was I out?" We're still beside the stream, but he's moved us away from the carnage.

"Only long enough for me to sneak supplies from my medic's tent."

I reach up and touch my neck. It's wrapped in bandages, although the strong smell of medicinal paste seeps through. Fresh bandages also cover my thigh, which aches dully.

He helps me to my feet. "I wanted to find you a healer, but the only person to ask would have been Ronin, and we can't trust him."

"Does this mean you're ready to warn the leaders in the manor house of your sister's attack?"

There's a moment of tense silence. Then, voice rough with emotion, he says, "Enough Evewynians have suffered because of her hatred. And now she wants to spread that hatred across all of Thiy." He nods at the darkness ahead. "Come on. I have a surprise for you."

After everything that's just happened, I'm not keen on surprises. "Where are your Blades?"

"It's best they remain uninvolved. I won't have Mei punishing them for my actions."

The branches over our heads grow thinner as we leave the trees. "What about Phaut?" The pain of her loss is still fresh. I have to force down the knot in my throat. At his confused look, I clarify. "Ronin's soldier. The woman Jonyah killed. She was my friend."

"I'm sorry. We'll go back for her as soon as there's time."

Something moves behind the shadows, and there's a quiet snuffling sound. I pause, but Prince Meilek tugs me along. As we near the source of the noise, I make out the silhouettes of two drakes waiting just outside the trees. I recognize instantly the sleek head and dark green scales of the drake sniffing around the dirt.

"Yandor," I whisper.

Yandor's head whips in my direction. He gives a joyous shake as I throw my arms around him. I press my face into his smooth scales. He rests his heavy head against my shoulder, his hot breaths blowing against my hair.

"I missed you." My voice catches.

"I spotted him when I went back for those healing herbs," Prince Meilek says. "Thought you might be pleased."

"Thank you," I whisper.

We mount our drakes in silence and head back through the camps toward Ronin's manor house. Torchlight speckles the grasslands as if to mirror the starlit sky above. The camps are quieter now, but no less crowded.

"I need to ask you to do something for me," I say as we near the Dead Wood. "Saengo is still in the manor house under Ronin's care. Will you get her out for me? I don't trust her with him once he learns we've discovered his plan."

He frowns. "Where will you be?"

"I have to go to Spinner's End."

By the tone of his voice, I can guess that he's scowling when he asks, "What for?"

"Warning everyone of the attack will lose Queen Meilyr the element of surprise. But the only way any of them will stand a chance is if we remove Ronin. And to do that, I have to go back to his castle."

Destroying Ronin's familiar bond should save Saengo, but it should also render him powerless. And I think, even if Saengo's life didn't depend on its destruction, even if Ronin hadn't chosen power over peace, I would still choose to destroy the Dead Wood. It is a disease on the land, infecting the kingdoms with its twisted power. It is a relic of an ancient war, a monument to hatred. It must be brought down.

"You'll never make it in time," he says.

"I know. But this is the only way to ensure victory in the long run."

As long as the leaders are warned, there's little else I can do in the grasslands. If there's a battle, it might very well be over before I even reach Spinner's End, but so long as I can sever Ronin's power, then I can end the war before it spreads.

"Once you've warned those in the manor house and retrieved Saengo," I say, "maybe you can reach your sister before she attacks. If she knows her plan with Ronin has been exposed, then she might listen to reason and retreat."

"I'll try. If we can avoid bloodshed, we might yet be able to salvage the peace."

Our drakes carry us down the path to the manor house and into the front yard. Prince Meilek waves away the servants who rush out to greet us. I lead the prince around the back of the manor to a narrow trickle of water that cuts through the property. The water isn't safe to drink, but it'll lead me to Spinner's End. All I have to do is survive a full day in the Dead Wood. My stomach turns.

I rub my palms down Yandor's neck. I don't want to take him into the Dead Wood, but there's no other choice. If the Falcon Warrior sees fit to protect us, I'm confident we can outrun the grasp of the trees. My connection to Saengo might be weak, but it's still there. Although I don't have the strength to grasp any living souls, I might have enough to fend off dead ones.

"You're sure about this?" he asks.

"I have to try. Please look after Saengo. I'm trusting her to you."

He reaches out, clasping my shoulder. "You have my word that I'll take care of her. Good luck, Sirscha."

"I'm going to need it."

"We'll see each other again. When this is over, we'll go to Byrth. We'll watch the ships make port, ride in a drake race, and eat sugared plum blossoms until we're sick."

I smile, and I'm glad that it's too dark for him to see the sadness in it. I don't have his capacity for hope; my victories have always been hard-won.

"May the Falcon Warrior protect you," I say.

"May the Demon Crone guide you," he replies, reciting the old prayer of the Five Sisters. I haven't spoken it since childhood, but I join him now, and our voices murmur together in the dark: "May the Serpent Mother provide. May the Twins lend you favor.

Carry with you the faith of the Sisters, and be blessed."

I lift my hand in farewell and then guide Yandor toward the abyss of the Dead Wood. Yandor growls and backs away in objection. "Please, my friend. I need you to be brave. I wouldn't ask this of you if it weren't of the utmost importance."

With an indignant shake and a few angry huffs, he lowers his head and charges into the embrace of the trees. I turn to see Prince Meilek vanish into the shadows of the property. I have to trust that Saengo will be okay, that the prince will do all within his ability to stop his sister from igniting war.

Then I face forward, focusing my full attention on the darkness that engulfs us. We head south, riding close along the right bank of the brook. The water is murky but allows for a narrow break in the branches overhead, providing enough moonlight to illuminate our path.

For a while, the trees are silent. I wonder if they can sense what I am and if they're as wary of me as I am of them. Fortunately, we travel too quickly for the branches to snag us, and the roots are thin so close to the bank. But it's not a pace Yandor can keep up indefinitely.

We've made good distance, several hours into the woods, before the hairs rise on the backs of my arms.

The trees groan, the snap of bark echoing in our wake. Yandor makes an alarmed sound. I do my best to settle him, to encourage us both to be brave. The shadows seem to grow, racing from branch to branch, obscuring their movement. Surely a trick of the moonlight and our haste.

Yandor pants loudly. We slow down so he can drink from my waterskin, but then the roots circle his legs, and he takes off again in a panic. With every passing hour, the trees press closer, slowly eliminating the narrow bank that brackets the rocky waterbed.

A branch drops into our path. I cry out, but Yandor roars, snapping razor-sharp teeth at the offending limb. Jaw tight, I cling to the reins as Yandor bravely charges on. I ride low on his back, my cheek pressed to the smooth scales of his neck. We tear through grasping branches that scratch at my face.

"We're going to survive this," I tell him, even as his foot slips briefly, nearly pitching me from the saddle. "We're not going to die here. I won't allow it." I cannot let my fears gain control again, even though they've been gnawing at me from the moment I realized what I did to that knife thrower.

Despite the odds, despite that I never quite believed what Ronin said about my craft, some desperate part of me wanted it to be true. So that I could make a difference. So that I could be someone. And for what? Recognition? Prestige? I tell myself I want these things, but my heart knows the truth.

It is not from the world that I need acknowledgment of my worth.

Pressure rises in my chest, dangerously close to a sob, but I swallow it down. I have not cried for myself in years, and now seems a foolish time to give in.

Yandor makes a pained, wheezing sound as he leaps high over a nest of roots converging on the bank. I kick one aside and tear at another with my hands, snapping it free before flinging it into the water. Then Yandor's leg is dragged out from under him. I gasp as we go down.

Pain wraps me in thorny arms as I collide with the earth and barely avoid being crushed under Yandor. He's on his feet almost instantly, claws ripping and teeth flashing. I'm slower to rise, lashing out at the nearest root and shouting with fury at the trees and at myself for leading us into this death trap.

Why do you keep trying, Sirscha? You're nothing special. You always fail. Why would this time be any different?

I haul myself into the saddle, fighting against the roots that try to drag me back down. If I die, then Saengo dies as well. Prince Meilek will have betrayed his queen and sacrificed his birthright for nothing. What did the shamanborn in the Valley of Cranes escape for if not the hope of something beyond death and imprisonment, the very things Queen Meilyr and Ronin would gift to Thiy should I fail here?

I might be a soulrender, but I am not the Soulless, and his legacy isn't mine. I have done things no other shaman can claim. I turned a human spirit into a familiar. I freed souls trapped within the Dead Wood. And now I'm going to stop Ronin and save Saengo from the rot. Me, Sirscha Ashwyn, a girl with no true name.

And I am not nothing.

TWENTY-THREE

The moment I'm situated again, Yandor leaps into the water. His claws shred through the roots. The rocks underfoot look unwieldy and treacherously slick, but he somehow keeps his footing. I press my lips to his neck and murmur my thanks for his bravery.

Shadows explode in our path. I gasp, yanking on the reins. Water splashes my legs as we skid to a stop. The shadows amass into a blackness so impenetrable that even the surrounding trees look hospitable in comparison. I turn Yandor, heels kicking into his sides, although he needs no encouragement to run. A figure with snowy hair emerges from the darkness.

Startled, I shout for Yandor to stop on the bank. Around his feet, shadows leap into the night, shielding us from the trees' attacks.

I whisper, uncertain, "Theyen?"

"About time," his voice snaps as he steps into the moonlight. "I've been trying to get your attention for hours now. I almost resorted to knocking you off your damned beast."

"Sisters, save me," I mutter, breathless with relief.

"No, that was me," he says, gesturing to the black doorway.

"How are you here?" The roots rustle underneath despite Theyen's shadows. Yandor dances to the side, snorting impatiently to get moving again.

"Shadow gate. It's how I'm able to travel to and from Spinner's End without needing to pass through the Dead Wood."

At that, I study the shadows anew. The very center of the gate is solid black, absorbing all light. The edges tumble and simmer in liquid black motion.

"What are you doing here?" I ask, wary again.

"Enjoying the scenery." He glares at me. "I'm helping you. Why else would I be here?"

"I don't know if I can trust you."

His lip curls, but he says in a clipped tone, "I saw you ride out from a seclusion of trees with the Evewynian prince. Thought it was a tryst, but too many dead bodies. Unless you're hiding some bizarre tendencies, in which case, keep them to yourself."

"Theyen," I begin, impatient, but he continues.

"I overheard something about an attack and figured you were in trouble, so I followed. Does that satisfy you, or would you like a full itinerary of my day?"

"I don't have time for your condescension right now."

"Then you'll have to trust me. I don't offer my help to just anyone. By the way, you look even more atrocious than normal. Were you strangled?"

I throw up my hands. "You're impossible."

"You must know that you'll never make it to Spinner's End before the trees find a way to grab your beast."

The branches scour through his shadows, splintering the amorphous beings. They re-form quick as lightning, but even Theyen looks nervous.

"You can take us directly to the castle?"

"Yes, but not more than one at a time."

I dismount. "Yandor first."

He opens his mouth to argue and then changes his mind. "Fine. Hand me your pack mule."

Yandor huffs and stomps as I give Theyen the reins. Within moments, they disappear into the gate. The shadowy doorway disperses in their wake.

One thick root shoots past Theyen's shadows. I slam my boot down on it. It recoils, sinking into the earth with the dry hiss of shifting soil. A boulder sits a few paces into the water. Gripping the stone, I climb onto its rough surface.

The shadows break apart, too far from Theyen now for him to maintain control over them. Roots lift like legs, shedding layers of papery skin. My breath comes shallow and quick. The trees moan as their crooked trunks warp, stretching skeletal branches at my head.

Something tugs at my sleeve. I spin around, but the boulder doesn't allow much room to maneuver. I don't want to use my craft unless absolutely necessary. Doing so could hurt Saengo.

The trees crowd ever closer. Fingers protrude from their innards, stretching the bark like a wet membrane ready to rupture. I imagine them breaking free, decomposed bodies clawing out from their earthen prisons. I immediately regret the thought. Something thin and cold scratches my forearm. I swipe out, breathing hard, and try to make myself as small a target as possible.

Where in the names of the Sisters is Theyen?

Roots slide through the water, circling the boulder like riverfiends converging on their prey. I hop onto another boulder, a larger one, but that brings me too close to a waiting knot of branches. They clamp onto my arms like barbs.

Magic races along my skin, eager to be used, but I hold back. Faces surface from every tree, screaming noiselessly. It takes a moment for me to realize they're all moving in terrifying unison: *Run.*

Shadows burst between us. A swirling black mass materializes before me, blocking out the trees.

Theyen leans out, hand extended. "Let's go!"

I rip my arms free, wincing as the branches tear through clothes and skin. He catches my hand and drags me through the gate.

Silence encloses us. The darkness is absolute. My body feels suspended, like I'm floating or flying. Theyen's arms encircle me, my only anchor in this sightless, soundless nightmare. My fingers dig into his back, terrified of being lost within the emptiness.

Something shimmers ahead, and he tugs me forward. I take a step, and my foot suddenly finds the ground. Gasping, I clutch at him until the world rights itself and the shock of the shadow gate fades.

"That was horrible," I croak as I uncurl my fingers from his tunic.

He makes a patronizing sound. Although we're still in the Dead Wood, we've emerged near the white curtain of webbing that surrounds Spinner's End.

It isn't until we're clear of the trees and just shy of the webbing that I allow myself to breathe easy.

"What took you so long?" I ask, peeking past the curtain to check for the night patrol. The gates are empty. I learned from my time here that the soldiers don't take guard duty very seriously, and why should they? The Dead Wood does all their work for them.

"The shadow gate scared your dim beast worse than the trees did. It took off the moment we emerged. I had to chase after it and then get it secured inside the castle grounds before coming back for you."

"But he's okay?"

"Yes, yes. Left him with a servant and orders to get him fed and cleaned up."

"Thank you." I push aside the white curtain and step past its shield. With most everyone in bed, the castle is still. Low burning torches illuminate the entrances. Moonlight edges the roofs in silver and bleaches the bone palisade ivory.

We stop first in the armory, which is simple enough to break into. I'm not going to kill any of Ronin's soldiers, but I'd rather not face a giant spider with only my fists. I locate a pair of dual swords and strap them to my back. The weight of the weapons improves my mood immensely.

On our way out, Theyen says, "Whatever you mean to do next, I can't go with you. I won't be any more involved than I already am."

I'm disappointed but not surprised. "You saved me just now. I can't ask anything more of you." I squint at his head and the shining circlet adorning his white hair. "Except for a hairpin."

His pale eyebrows pull together as he removes a slim silver hairpin. Thank the Sisters for his vanity.

"Sirscha," he says sharply, gripping my arm as I slide the pin into my own hair. "You must understand that I helped you as your friend, not as a Hlau of Penumbria. I don't quite know what's going on, but it's better that way. I won't have the Fireborn Queens dragged into war."

The word *friend* surprises me. Guilt pricks me for suspecting him of trying to kill me. I don't want his clan forced into a war, either. I don't want anyone getting caught between Queen Mei-lyr's hatred and Ronin's machinations.

"You should know this at least," I say. "Your people are in danger of attack. Prince Meilek should have already begun warning everyone, but the camps might be better convinced to hear it from you as well."

Although I can tell he's uncertain, he only nods. "I'll come back for you. Good luck." He crosses the courtyard and adds, "Try not to do anything too foolish."

I creep from shadow to shadow, my feet a whisper over stone. Rather than go through the gardens, I scale the surrounding wall, which gives me a better vantage point. There isn't a single soldier in sight now that Spinner's End has been emptied of its guests, but I remain up high, shrouded by the castle towers that lend their shadows to the deeper regions of the maze.

Before long, my boots fall on the arches dressed in webbing, and the pull of that dark magic squeezes around me. Here, I grip the edge of the stone and swing myself down onto the curved path. The power of Ronin's familiar weighs against my shoulders, a cloak woven of iron. It sinks hooks into my skin, reeling me toward the columns where webbing brushes ghostly fingers over the top of my head.

More webbing clings to the wooden door at the end of the garden. I tear away the bits of white. A heavy padlock secures the door shut. Brandishing Theyen's hairpin, I crouch and take the padlock in hand. The lock clicks in less than five seconds. I silently thank Kendara's obsessive training.

My eyes scan the courtyard again, ears straining for anything unusual. There's only silence. I draw the blades at my back, slowly, so that the sound of metal sliding from its sheath is no more than the wind whispering through the old castle stones. I nudge the door open with my foot. It doesn't creak.

There must be a separate entrance for the Spinner. Nothing larger than a person could get through this one. I cross the threshold into a wall of white. My feet touch stone, but I can't see where it leads because webbing stretches in thick layers from ceiling to floor.

Fear prickles my skin as I pierce the webbing with both swords and then slash downward to cut a hole wide enough for me to pass through. The hole reveals the collapsed wall of a small foyer. Dust clings to the heels of my boots. Broken boards and bits of wood lie piled in the corners.

That weighty power beckons to me. I move slowly, every part of me hyperaware that somewhere ahead, a giant spider awaits. I've fought all manner of beasts, from serpents to rock scorpions and spiny boars, with their half-dozen tusks. I pray it's prepared me to face a Spinner.

Beyond the wreckage are the ruins of an immense greenhouse. The ceiling soars high above, but very little glass remains. Instead, all the windows are completely sealed over with webbing. Columns marbled by age and decay stand in two lines at either side.

A series of lit lanterns adorn each column, illuminating the space and the enormous spiderweb that stretches floor to ceiling across the back wall. My stomach drops at the sight.

Caught within the web is a large cocoon.

I grip my swords tighter. Has the Spinner been feeding? What, exactly, does a spider twice the size of a drake even eat?

But the condition of the cocoon doesn't look new. The web is patchy and old, shriveled gray overlapped in white as if it's been repaired countless times over countless years. Moss climbs the taut strands, startlingly green, and encases half the cocoon like the speckled shell of a large egg. The entire structure is strangely beautiful, completely at odds with the magic emanating from within.

Nothing else but a Spinner could have woven the massive web, but why would its power be inside a cocoon?

Standing before it, the wrongness of this magic is impossible to ignore. Compared to the blazing purity of my craft, this strange magic is like oil spilling over water. It pulls at me. I have to know what's inside.

Sheathing my swords, I cross the greenhouse until my hands close around the thick threads of the spiderweb that span the height of the room. I climb. The moss provides a gentle cushion for my palms. Each strand of webbing is sturdy and taut. I'm nearly thirty paces off the ground when I at last reach the enormous cocoon.

I draw one sword and carefully pierce the thick webbing. Dragging the blade downward, slowly, I slice through the first few layers. I tear away what I can and then repeat the process. At length, I sheathe the sword and dig my fingers into the last layers, wrenching the webbing roughly aside.

Within the cocoon is a face. I recoil and almost lose my grip. My fingers seize the web, hanging on as my heart pounds. I stare, dumbstruck. It's a body.

Perplexed, I shred away more webbing, tilting my head as more of him is revealed.

He's . . . bizarrely beautiful, with high cheekbones and a regal nose. Long black hair twines around his neck and shoulders. His equally dark lashes cast shadows against his cheeks. His ears taper into a sharp point, like all highborn shamans.

There's a greenish tint to his skin, but not the foul green of decay. The body is perfectly preserved. The green adds an almost vibrant sheen to his pale skin, as if he has become a part of the moss that's overtaken his tomb. A small puncture wound darkens the skin at the base of his neck, like from a spider's bite. A clear liquid seeps from the wound.

This shaman has been here a very long time.

Swallowing uneasily, I lean in so that his mouth almost touches my cheek and then hold utterly still. Not a hint of breath. He's dead.

And yet, his power continues to press around me, a distorted oiliness that wants to catch in the flame of my magic. What kind of shaman could possess a power so immense that even death can't silence it?

One who has been blackened by unnatural magic, whose soul was so shattered that he defied death by living off the souls of others. I shake my head, reeling.

The Soulless.

TWENTY-FOUR

Impossible. How can I be staring into the face of the most powerful and terrible soulrender Thiy has ever known? He lived six hundred years ago, as old as Ronin.

I've had it all so unbelievably wrong. Ronin's familiar isn't anchoring the spirits to the Dead Wood. The Soulless is, along with the same dark magic that created this place—a magic that has continued to distort and corrode until it's become a poison, a rot seeping into the trees and the spirits. And infecting other spirits as well, including familiars.

I release a slow, tremulous breath. How could Ronin have done this?

Then again, Ronin desecrated an entire troll graveyard to build his manor house. I suppose it's not so unlikely that he would have preserved the Soulless's corpse in order to possess the magic that remained in his bones. I don't know how he's doing it, but he's using the Soulless like a human talisman, amplifying his power.

But also corrupting it. Could this be why Ronin is losing control of the Dead Wood?

"Someone has wandered into my web," says a soft voice.

I stiffen and look over my shoulder. Ronin stands at the other end of the greenhouse. Every muscle in my body tenses as I scan the room for his familiar. But still, there is nothing. Quickly, I climb back down.

Ronin, his gaze steady, lets me. When I'm on the ground, I turn to face him. His shadow stretches slowly around his feet, inky arms extending across the floor until the shape of an enormous spider rests at his back.

I swallow thickly, suddenly remembering "The Tale of the Woodcutter" and Theyen's theory. Maybe Ronin doesn't need a familiar because he devoured his Spinner. A sensation like hundreds of insect legs skitters down my spine. I draw my swords.

"You're supposed to be up north." Thankfully, my voice doesn't waver.

He takes a leisurely step forward. The spider's shadow follows, furred legs moving in time with his. I back away to maintain the space between us, but there's no way out of this greenhouse except through the door he's blocking.

"You're not the only one with friends who can open shadow gates. Although such friends should exercise better caution when using such abilities."

My lips tighten at the blatant threat. "Don't you have an ambush to prepare for?"

"Among other plans. I'd meant to introduce you at dinner. When I sent for you, my servants reported you missing and your friend escaping with the prince of Evewyn. I thought it prudent to return here to check on things." His gaze lifts to the cocoon behind me. "Just in case."

Anger surges through me. "You're going to let her kill all those people. Your own guests. Inside the manor, they'll be powerless."

"What would you have me do?" he asks, voice soft. "I am weary, Sirscha. Why shouldn't it all end?"

"Because you're supposed to keep the peace."

His eyes unfocus as his gaze turns inward, pensive. "And I will. Once all the kingdoms have been dismantled."

"So Queen Meilyr is as much your pawn as the rest of us?"

"I'm doing what I must."

"And that justifies it? Genocide isn't peace!" My shouted words reverberate through the large space.

"I didn't take you for an idealist."

I sneer. "I'm not. I'm just not a monster."

At last, a reaction. One corner of his mouth quirks upward. "Aren't you, though? Soulrender."

I tense. *Your powers are a question that must be addressed. Much relies on the answer.*

"You suspected from the beginning," I say. "That's the real reason why you wanted Theyen to invoke my craft." Every moment since I arrived at Spinner's End suddenly sharpens into focus. "Allowing me to go to Vos Gillis—you wanted me to slip up. And Kamryne. You sent him, didn't you? He killed himself because he knew you'd do the same when you learned he failed." I point both my swords at him, my voice vibrating with fury. "He's trapped now in those horrible trees."

He doesn't react to my words. "When you free the souls from the Dead Wood, do you even realize what you're doing? Soulrenders don't shepherd souls. You weren't sending those spirits into the afterlife. You were destroying them."

His quiet words hit me like a punch to my gut. I have to blink away the daze. Could it be true?

"You are a danger to yourself and everyone you touch. Your awakening allowed our plans to come together, but I hoped you'd reveal your true nature so that I could kill you and be done with it."

I shake my head. I came here with a purpose, and I still mean to finish it. "But you couldn't. Not without proof. Because every shaman and shadowblessed in Thiy believes I'm a soulguide, and killing me would turn them against you."

He releases a soft breath, all the long years of his life condensed into that single sound. "How quickly they forget that Thiy would have fallen without me. It was my power that saved it."

I try to imagine him as he might have once been—merely a man trying to protect his home. "You devoured your familiar so you could become powerful enough to fight the Soulless."

"And still, peace couldn't be found. The kingdoms insisted on their conflicts, their petty grievances, their bids for power." He shakes his head, and when he speaks again, it isn't with anger or regret. He sounds resolved. "I did what was necessary, just as I will do so now."

In a twisted way, I understand him. He sacrificed everything, even his humanity, to bring peace to Thiy, and the kingdoms gave that peace so little regard. But now he means to wipe them all away. This is far from a solution.

"The Soulless is poisoning you. You know that, don't you? His magic is twisting you the way it twisted him."

His gaze flicks away, just enough to confirm that he knows very well what the Soulless's magic is doing to him. But it doesn't seem to matter. He's chosen his path. Whatever decency he once possessed has long since been corrupted.

I slowly shift my weight to my injured leg, testing its strength. It doesn't hurt as much as it should, whether from the medicine or the energy coursing through me.

"How do you plan to control the Dead Wood?"

"I will find a way, as I always have. But if none can be found, then perhaps that is the ending Thiy deserves." At his back, his spider's shadow grows impossibly larger. "For what it's worth, I hoped that you might truly be a soulguide."

His head jerks to the side as his body stretches and contorts. I back away, horrified as his lower body swells grotesquely. His clothes rip away to reveal the bulbous abdomen of a white Spinner. Six enormous legs erupt from the Spinner's body, dusted with wiry white hairs. His upper body remains human, the transition between spider and human torso a mottled stretch of armor and skin. He brushes away the remnants of his tunic. Lines crease his forehead as if the transformation pains him.

I edge to my left. His monstrous body moves with me. The

greenhouse is large but bare. There is nothing to place between me and the creature Ronin has become.

The whole of his eyes, whites and all, darken to glistening black and then fracture into the unsettling impression of multiple eyes. The roots of his hair bleed into red, the color spreading across his temples like veins. Thick crimson stripes streak the Spinner's abdomen up through the sides of his human chest.

He towers over me, his Spinner legs lifting him to more than twice my height. Each of his fingers extends into a clawed point, tinted the same dark red as if dipped in paint. Every instinct I possess demands that I flee. I cannot win this fight. How could I ever hope to defeat this?

But I am the only person who knows Ronin's secret—that he's using the Soulless as a talisman to amplify and alter his own magic. If I don't stop him here, if I die, then Ronin will destroy everything and everyone I hold dear. Peace at the cost of utter destruction.

I twirl my swords, an invitation that Ronin doesn't hesitate to accept. He strikes fast, claws slashing. I deflect with my swords, momentarily surprised when his transformed fingers scrape against my blade like steel.

Diving low, I block the deadly jab of his claws and skid beneath his abdomen. My blades cut across his underbelly. He staggers, but his Spinner's armored skin is too thick. He turns with the agility of a spider a tenth his size, exposing me. His claws rake down my arm, drawing blood, as I roll away and dash for the columns.

The columns are tall and thick. I slide behind one, Ronin on my heels. His legs slam against the floor-to-ceiling windows. What panels remain on this side of the greenhouse shudder dangerously, cracks shooting through the glass. The space between the wall and column is too narrow for his body, but his claws hack at the stone. Dust and debris shower the musty air.

I allow myself a few heartbeats to gather my breath. Then I leap into the open, blades slicing across the claws that protect his vulnerable human torso. My body spins and dips, my feet and swords in constant motion as I dodge his many-legged reach.

Ducking another attack, I return my swords smoothly into their sheaths as I drop into a roll. My hands clutch one of his furred legs. The spider hairs are thick and coarse. My boots slam into his side for more momentum as I flip onto the Spinner's back.

He whirls violently, nearly throwing me off, but I wrap an arm around his human waist. I reach over my shoulder and slide one sword free, angling the blade to stab his exposed side.

Something yanks my arm back. I can't move. I twist around to find my hand and sword hilt snagged in a stream of web. More webbing shoots from his spinneret, coating my whole arm. I draw my other sword, hacking at the thick, sticky mass, but there's too much.

His human body rotates, his spine twisting in a way that should snap it in two. Red claws clamp around my leg and rip me off his back. Layers of webbing trap both my arms and swords as he hefts me up before him. One clawed hand wraps around my throat.

Each fragment of his many eyes stares back at me, unblinking.

I struggle against his hold, even as his claws bite into the skin beneath my jaw. Each small movement works my blades against the webbing.

"If only you'd been a soulguide instead." The regret in his voice makes my skin burn with anger.

"So you could use me? What does it matter, anyway? You'd still kill everyone."

He hauls me close. I gasp as his face hovers a breath from mine, his snarling mouth stretching with crowded, too-large fangs. "You've seen more death than others twice your age, and still, you know so little of sacrifice."

I struggle harder, moving more easily as my swords saw away at the webbing. Suddenly, the Soulless's dark power slithers around me, as if to replace my loosening bonds. It hooks into my skin, probing for weaknesses.

Ronin's mouth gapes open, impossibly wide. His jaws unhinge and his lips tear in a way no human mouth ever should. His enormous fangs unfurl.

That dark magic scratches at my ribs, demanding to be allowed in. I fear that power, wicked temptation wrapped in venom and thorns. But in this moment, I fear Ronin more.

I seize the Soulless's power. Instantly, magic rages through me, igniting my craft like a breath against kindling. Liquid fire burns in my veins, imbuing me with blazing, scorching magic that's almost too much for me to contain.

And then I see it—Ronin's souls. There are two, one human form and the other Spinner, both transposed against the abomination he has become. I don't need my hands to grip his souls tight. I need only to will it.

He goes rigid. His mouth slowly closes, fangs sinking back into the depths of his jaw. His magic heaves against mine. It takes all my concentration to hold him immobile.

The black drains from his eyes. Suddenly, his face is human again, brimming with an emotion so intense, so bleak, I hesitate. "You don't understand what you're doing. Only my power can keep Thiy safe."

"Thiy doesn't need you anymore, not once the Dead Wood is destroyed."

With an inhuman snarl, he wrenches free of my magic. His mouth snaps wide, fangs flashing.

My arms rip from my slackened restraints. I bury both swords hilt deep beneath his ribs.

He rears back, eyes wide with surprise. His claws drop me. I jerk my swords free as I fall. I land on my feet and shuffle back. Ronin stumbles. His legs fold. His huge body sinks to the dusty floor of the greenhouse. His eyes find mine, the knowledge of his death creeping into his face.

"Soulrender," he whispers. Then he slumps forward, and his legs go still.

I stab both of my blades into the stone and sink to my knees, panting and aching. My thigh feels like it's been set aflame, and I've bled through the bandages. I'll deal with it later. Weariness drags at my limbs, bone deep. But I draw a deep breath and force myself to stand.

The Soulless's magic continues to course through me, leaving an acrid scent in my nostrils. Even in death, he is more powerful than I am. It's hard to imagine how he must have been in life, a shaman so formidable it required an abomination like Ronin to stop him. Ronin must have been a great man once to make such a sacrifice for Thiy. But all the years of using the Soulless's perverse magic corrupted him.

I won't make that mistake. I'm going to end this, here and now.

Beneath the slick of the Soulless's magic, I can sense that even without Ronin, he remains connected to the Dead Wood. It's his magic that first trapped the souls here, after all. A clear venom was leaking from that puncture wound in his neck. That must be how Ronin kept him so well preserved.

With a beam of wood from the debris in the foyer and one of the lit lanterns, I manage to create a makeshift torch. Then I touch the flaming beam to the base of the spiderweb. The moss smolders, and the webbing instantly shrivels. The dust catches fire, spreading quickly along the thick strands. Smoke plumes upward, stinging my eyes.

Coughing, I shield my face and toss the flaming chunk of wood into the growing blaze. Then, with one last look up at the Soulless's cocoon, now indistinct through the haze of heat, I turn and flee.

TWENTY-FIVE

I make my way out as silently as I entered.

The greenhouse is so far removed from the occupied sections of the castle that I'm not worried the fire will spread beyond control. It'll be some time before the blaze is even noticed, but I'd better be quick either way. Every injury I've acquired in the last day makes itself known as I pick my way through the gardens. Most of the sky is still dark, but the sun will rise within hours. The crust of the eastern horizon has already brightened from black to dusky blue.

Questions plague me as I scale the walls and climb over sloping roofs, making my way up to Theyen's room, where I hope he's returned. Where is Kendara? Did the Nuvali and Kazan leaders listen to Prince Meilek? What will happen once word spreads that Ronin is missing?

And Saengo. Without the Soulless holding the spirits to

the Dead Wood, will she be able to heal? The flickering light of Saengo's candle still burns, so I know she's alive. But she grows weaker with every passing hour.

I wasn't sure what would happen once Ronin's power was gone, but I expected to feel something. And yet the trees beyond the white drape surrounding Spinner's End don't seem any different. Maybe magic as powerful as the Soulless's needs time to fade.

Within minutes, my fingers grasp the ledge of Theyen's sitting-room window. It's much too narrow for me to fit through, but I peek inside. A lantern on the mantel illuminates the room with a soft yellow glow. Theyen sits with one hand cupped over his forehead and the other wrinkling the hem of his sleeve. He's trying to read.

"Theyen," I whisper.

He starts and then rushes over to the window. "How in the— are all Evewynians as suicidal as you are?"

I roll my eyes. "Were you able to warn your clansmen?"

"Yes. They were preparing to leave when I returned for you."

"Good. I'm ready when you are. The quicker the better."

He rubs his temple. "This friendship business is a lot more troublesome than I was led to believe."

"Theyen—"

"Yes, yes. I'll meet you out front. Get down before you fall and break your neck."

I reach the courtyard mere seconds before Theyen bursts out the doors, a sword strapped to his waist. His feet pause on the stairs when he gets a full look at me.

"Why do you look like you were wrestling a Spinner?"

"I sort of was," I mumble. "Ronin was back there."

Smoke has begun to rise from the rear of the castle grounds, but against the night and with most of the soldiers and staff still abed, no one seems to have noticed yet.

For long seconds, Theyen stares at me, terrible realization growing behind his eyes. When he speaks, there's an icy tremor in his voice I've never heard before. "Did you kill him?"

"I had no choice."

A muscle ticks in his cheek as he clenches and unclenches his jaw. He descends the stairs, but his steps are slow, deliberate. Predatory.

I square my shoulders. "Theyen. He was going to—"

"I told you not to do anything foolish. You killed the Spider King? Have you lost your mind?"

"He meant to kill everyone," I say evenly. "I had to stop him."

"Ronin was the only person standing in the way of the Empire and Kazahyn going to war. He's kept the peace for longer than most anyone in Thiy can remember. But you," he says, sneering. "You think you know better? Less than a month ago, you didn't even know you were a shaman."

I rub my thumb over my knuckles, trying not to let Theyen's insults hurt me. "He wanted the kingdoms to go to war. He's been conspiring to destroy Thiy, starting with helping Queen Meilyr massacre everyone in the north. She'll reach the camps by dawn, if she isn't there already, and you want to stand here throwing accusations when you don't even know half of the things I've learned?"

"Don't you get it?" he hisses. "It doesn't matter. If House Yalaeng invades Kazahyn, the clans will have no choice but to retaliate. The Fireborn Queens won't be able to claim neutrality, especially if it's discovered I had a hand in helping you kill Ronin."

My arm shakes from my restraint. I want very much to punch the sense into him, but that would only make things worse. "You're not hearing me. Ronin was going to betray everyone. He was going to let Queen Meilyr kill all of his guests in his manor house today, including you since you had plans to be there."

"And who will corroborate such a story? Queen Meilyr? If she's truly marching on the grasslands, then no one would trust her word. No one will trust the word of any Evewynian." Theyen, suddenly weary, rubs a hand over his face. "Whether what you say is true or not, the fact remains that without Ronin, there is no one to enforce the peace treaty."

"You're wrong. There's me."

"Only a fool overestimates their own ability," he says, echoing something he'd said to me once before.

I stiffen my spine, chin lifting. "I did what I had to do, whether you understand or not."

Tension braids the space between us, a tangible thing that tugs on all my senses. At last, he brushes past me toward the bone palisade.

"Come on," he says curtly. "I can't open a gate on the castle grounds. Something to do with the webbing that keeps the trees at bay, although it may no longer hold without Ronin."

"Yandor is still—"

"I'll come back for your beast tomorrow night. There's no time."

I follow wordlessly and only hesitate a moment when he reaches for my hand and pulls me through the shadow gate.

We arrive to chaos. Queen Meilyr attacked early.

The grasslands are alight with burning tents and the clamor of flashing weapons. I immediately draw my swords.

"I must find my clansmen and ensure they escaped this madness," Theyen says. He extends his hand. "If you truly believe you can stop this war, then do it. But I can no longer offer my help, either as your friend or as a Kazan Hlau."

Throat tight, I take his hand and shake firmly. "Thank you, Theyen."

His bright multicolored eyes linger on our hands for a moment, his expression indecipherable. Then his gaze lifts to mine. "For as brief as it was, I enjoyed your friendship. Goodbye, Sirscha Ashwyn."

He sets off through the mayhem, his tall figure disappearing behind black smoke billowing from a burning caravan.

Screams ring out behind me. A figure of roiling flame hurtles through the battle, blasting soldiers off their feet. Crackling grass and a streak of black mars the ground in its wake. The fire fuses into a human form with brilliant red armor. A Nuvali sun warrior.

I head in a different direction, where the faint tether connecting me to Saengo leads. Dread sinks its teeth into my heels. Her candle continues to sputter and fail. With the source of the rot gone, why isn't she getting stronger?

My feet pound over scorched grass. Leaping into the midst of soldiers, I disarm one after another. If they're lucky, these poor fools will remain unconscious for the remainder of the battle and survive.

Smoke stings my eyes as I reach the ruined sprawl of the Evewynian camp. The fighting is sparse here, the thick of the battle farther west, where teeming bodies scream and stab and fall. But even here, I'm surrounded by the sounds of the dying, the screech of weapons, and the roar of drakes. Magic stirs in the distance as a violent tempest flings soldiers high into the air before sending them crashing to the earth.

At least fighting directly outside the Dead Wood means the shamans won't have access to their familiars. How long is it supposed to take before the trees wither? By now, the Soulless's body should be ash and embers. The souls are no longer tethered.

The flash of a captain's armor catches my eye. I cover my nose as I hurry past two burning tents. Prince Meilek is mounted on a drake, fending off a swordsman. He's no longer wearing a soldier's uniform.

His drake snarls, sharp teeth flashing as it snaps around the swordsman's arm, crushing the bone between its powerful jaws.

The swordsman screams, flopping into the grass. Prince Meilek spots me an instant later.

"What are you doing here?" he shouts, riding over. "Did you turn back?"

I shake my head. "I made it to the castle."

Confusion knits his brow, but he doesn't question me. "I warned everyone I could, but my sister arrived earlier than expected." He squints through the melee. "She attacked before everyone could rally their forces. I haven't seen Ronin yet, though."

"And you won't. I killed him."

He shakes his head as if he misheard. His brown eyes quickly take in the state of me, like Theyen did—the fresh blood streaking my arm and leaking from my thigh, as well as Ronin's blood, which stains the front of my shirt.

"You're not going to reprimand me as well, are you?" I ask.

"I haven't said a word," he says without inflection.

"Please just . . . wait to do so. I'll tell you everything later. Where's Saengo?"

Prince Meilek jerks his head for me to follow and then steers his drake away. He doesn't go far. A wagon lies on its side nearby. Upended barrels and crates rest in piles, their contents scattered across the grass. Hidden behind the crates, curled into the corner of the wagon, is Saengo.

A soldier hurtles from the haze of smoke, weapon swinging. I raise my swords, but he stops when he recognizes his prince as my companion.

"Soldier." Prince Meilek stares him down until the soldier

lowers his sword. "Gather who you can and return to Evewyn."

I leave the soldier to the prince and rush to Saengo's side. Her face is flushed red with fever, her hair soaked through. The blue veins have spread over her jaw and up her cheeks, bright and menacing.

"No," I whisper, smoothing away strands of dark hair from her forehead.

Behind me, the soldier stutters, "Y—Your Highness."

Something glints at the edge of my vision. I look up to see the soldier bow deep just as an arrow pierces clean through his throat.

A second arrowhead flashes in the smoky dawn light. I leap in front of Prince Meilek, my swords snapping the second arrow in half before it can pierce his chest. Prince Meilek jerks back, watching the soldier slump into the earth. A Nuvali sun warrior thunders up on a dragokin, another arrow nocked and pointed directly into Prince Meilek's furious face.

"Stop," I shout, pointing my swords at her. "He isn't your enemy."

Jewel-blue eyes narrow in distrust. She regards me first, the unmistakable evidence that I'm a shaman. Then she studies Prince Meilek and the gold circlet fitted against his dark hair. "The Evewynian prince who warned us?"

"Yes," I breathe, lowering my swords. "He—"

A low groan interrupts me. Abandoning the sun warrior, I return to Saengo's side. I gently cup her face. Her eyes are unfocused, her pupils tiny pinpricks. Her breaths are thin and hoarse. Tremors of anguish rock through me.

She can't die now. I defeated Ronin. I burned the Soulless's body to extinguish whatever power still connected him to the Dead Wood.

"How can this be?" the sun warrior asks. She's dismounted and is now peering over my shoulder. "She has the rot."

"She's not going to die," I say out loud, but the sun warrior gives a curt, pitying shake of her head.

"There is no cure for a broken soul."

I gather Saengo against my chest, clutching her body as my magic clings to her fragile soul, fighting to hold on. Pain wrenches beneath my ribs, a hollow echo of what she must be feeling. Tears slip down my cheeks, spattering against her flushed skin.

I wasn't able to heal her before, not with the Dead Wood still steeped in the Soulless's poisonous magic. But with the source of the rot gone, it would have to work now, wouldn't it?

I won't let her die. Not again. Closing my eyes, I touch my forehead to her burning one as my craft awakens. The Soulless's power still courses through me, a wildfire burning through my bones. It fuels my magic as I take hold of her soul.

Saengo gasps, back arching, her nails gouging my arms. I barely feel it. My magic traces the cracked edges of her soul, learning its warmth, its strength, its will to live. Her soul responds, reaching for me through our connection. She is my familiar, my conduit, which means she has access to my magic. I throw that connection wide, letting my magic pour into her, sinking into all the little fractures of her soul, sealing the splinters like mortar over stone.

Light explodes between us, so bright it sears through my

closed lids. The torrent surging through Saengo glows radiant, her body shining like sunlight trapped beneath her skin.

Then warm fingers touch my face. I startle back. Saengo smooths away my tears, but more fall as I shake in disbelief. I open the collar of her tunic. The rot isn't gone, but it has diminished into a tiny bundle of thin blue threads at the center of her chest.

It's a temporary fix. She isn't healed, maybe because I'm not a proper healer. But for now, it's enough. She'll live.

"The soulguide," the sun warrior whispers behind me. Her face goes slack with awe. Others have gathered behind her, shamans and shadowblessed alike, drawn by the beacon of our bond. "The soulguide! She's here! She stopped the rot!"

The words ripple across the battlefield, carried on columns of smoke and blades of grass, building from a series of whispers into a resounding chorus that rolls across the grasslands like a thundercloud.

The voices converge into a war cry as the Nuvali rage into battle once more. The earth trembles beneath the unleashing of crafts and the charge of their armored dragokin. Sellswords and soldiers flee before the renewed onslaught, terrified by the shamans' sudden fervor.

I look away, unable to bear the sight of Evewynians being cut down. Saengo pulls at my arm, and I help her sit up. She's weak, but the healthy flush of her skin has returned.

Smiling through my tears, I hug her to me and rest my forehead against her shoulder. I listen to her breathe against my hair, strong and sure, our connection shimmering between us like a lifeline.

"They're retreating," Prince Meilek says quietly. He watches his men flee, pain straining the skin around his eyes, his jaw clenched tight. To his sister, he is a traitor to his family, his friends, and his country: a prince without a kingdom, a truth that must rend him in two.

I suspect a part of him longs to join his men. Evewyn is where he belongs. And with Queen Meilyr's plans in ruins, her wrath will be devastating. His people will need him.

I want to say he did the right thing and that I will help him however I can, should he challenge his sister for the throne. But instead, I say nothing. There will be time later to consider what must come next.

His gaze lowers to mine then, and when our eyes meet, his face gentles. "You did it," he says.

The crowd around us grows as Prince Meilek helps Saengo and me to our feet. As I stand, the Nuvali and even many Kazan cheer. Their shouts of victory reverberate into the early morning sky. Some bow, words like "suryali" and "soulguide" passing their lips and settling uncomfortably over me.

I am not what they believe, and they can't know the truth. Not yet. History has proven what the fear of a single craft can yield. Although I'm still coming to terms with what my abilities might mean, I have proven to myself the measure of my worth. Someday, I will prove it to them as well.

TWENTY-SIX

When the dead have been seen to, Nuvali servants escort Saengo and me to a private tent at the eastern edge of the grasslands.

They mention something about their lord, but I don't recognize the name. Or if I do, I'm too mentally and physically exhausted to make the connection. All I want is to close my eyes and forget everything that's happened this day.

There've been questions about the conspicuous absence of a particular Spider King. His servants and soldiers have already been rounded up for questioning. No one has asked me anything directly yet, so I've offered no answers. But it's not something I can avoid for long.

By now, the fire will have been extinguished and Ronin's body discovered at Spinner's End. The staff is likely in a state of complete panic. Ronin must have had a steward to manage the castle in his absence, but how long would they wait before sending out falcons with news of their lord's death?

So far, the Dead Wood remains largely intact. Although I've spotted lights glimmering from within the dark of the trees, giving me hope that the souls might be breaking free, doubt continues to scratch at my thoughts.

Saengo is asleep the moment her head touches her pillow, and I'm glad. As soon as we're able, I'll have a light stitcher or flesh worker look at the remains of the infection and determine if it can be healed. For now, every healer still alive is too busy tending to the wounded, and I don't want to pull them away from their work.

I'd like nothing more than to follow Saengo into sleep, but the constant prickle of worry keeps me awake. The Soulless's magic lingers beneath my skin, molten fire as discomfiting as it is intriguing, and just as strong as when I first opened myself to it. It should have faded or weakened by now, surely. I don't know what it means that it hasn't.

There's a light cough outside my tent and then a tentative, "Sirscha?"

I rub my eyes and sit up on my cot. Most of the tents that weren't burned down had to be erected again. I glance at Saengo's prone form. Although the courtesy is unnecessary seeing as she's out cold, I leave the tent to speak outside.

Prince Meilek smiles faintly as I join him. It's well after dark, but hardly anyone has gone to bed. Too restless or too uneasy. Too haunted.

As promised, he'd gone back for Phaut. Her body is to be returned to her family for a proper burial. I recovered her sword as well, abandoned near the stream. Her loss is a splinter lodged in my heart, the pain sharpening when I consider that for all my supposed power, I could not save her.

"Are you well?" I ask quietly. He's spoken very little all day.

"I'll be fine. Am I keeping you up?" He drags his fingers roughly through his hair. The sweat and dirt from the day's labors make the already tousled strands stand on end.

"No. I've got a lot on my mind."

His gaze flickers downward, shadows and emotions playing about his mouth. "Let's sit."

I follow him to a nearby campfire. Two shadowblessed huddle in the grass near the fire. While they stare at us, they don't speak.

"Have you thought about what you'll do now?" he asks, voice soft to keep the shadowblessed from eavesdropping. I doubt they can hear us, anyway, over the low crackle of the flames and the murmur of other voices.

"Probably head to Mirrim." I sit with my knees pulled to my chest. The clothes I'm wearing are too big, but I couldn't stay in the shirt still stained with Ronin's blood. "We might even get an audience with the emperor."

The idea is intimidating. I'll have to be so careful with what I reveal about my craft. Once, I'd been convinced that to be anything of worth, I needed to be the queen's Shadow. I believed it so wholly that even now, even knowing that my worth will never be tied to what others make of me, it's difficult to completely silence the old fears.

I don't know that I'm ready to have every eye in Thiy focused on me, but I can't deny it's also a bit thrilling. Without Ronin or the Dead Wood, the kingdoms must learn to coexist without an intermediary. I could have a hand in helping to shape that future.

"Then I wish you safe travels," Prince Meilek says.

I stare at him. "I assumed you were coming with us. You can't be thinking of going back to Evewyn?"

"I haven't decided. But I can't go to Mirrim. I'm useless there, and my people need me."

"Your sister will kill you," I say.

He smiles gently and with such quiet confidence that I want to believe it isn't just a well-practiced facade. "I have no intention of allowing myself to be killed. But I can't protect my people from the other side of Thiy."

"Actually, you can. As far as I'm concerned, you are the voice of the Evewynian people. And their voices will be needed if the other countries decide to retaliate."

So far, the Kazan and Nuvali have remained civil in the aftermath of the attack, mostly ignoring each other. But I'll be glad when the camps disassemble and return to their own kingdoms. An alliance won't come easily, and Theyen's assertion that either country could attack the other is all too possible.

I wish I could speak to him, but Theyen has made clear his intent to avoid me. I can't blame him. But true to his word, once night fell, I found Yandor waiting for me outside my tent.

"I doubt my voice will be welcome in such discussions," he says. "Nor any Evewynian's."

"I'm Evewynian." My fingers tighten into a fist. "And they'll listen to me." At least, I hope they will.

Silence settles between us. In the distance, the lights within the Dead Wood have grown enough in number that people have gathered along its border, just beyond the reach of the branches. Relief begins to trickle through me.

Suddenly, unease seizes my insides. From within the Dead Wood, the souls flicker oddly. They wink in and out of existence, like candle flames lit and then smothered, one by one. Frowning, I begin to stand.

The ground quakes. I tumble sideways, grabbing Prince Meilek's shoulder as he braces himself on the ground. Conversations screech to a halt, silence descending on the camps. Power ripples over the grasslands like a physical blow, nearly knocking me backward. Sparks fly from the campfire, spilling smoke and cinders.

I know this power. It resonates inside me.

Prince Meilek stands, pulling me to my feet as well. All heads turn as one toward the Dead Wood. A great moaning rises from the dark mass, louder and louder as if all the souls are shrieking at once.

And suddenly, I understand what Ronin meant when he said it was only his power that could keep Thiy safe.

Ronin defeated the Soulless, but he hadn't killed him. Perhaps he'd been unable to. So instead, Ronin contained him within a cocoon, injecting him with venom not to preserve his body but to keep him asleep, trapped in a deathlike state for centuries.

Until I freed him when I killed Ronin.

Soulrender, he'd whispered with his dying breath. I thought it was an accusation, but it wasn't.

It was a warning.

END OF BOOK ONE

ACKNOWLEDGMENTS

This story has lived inside my head and on my hard drive for so long that it's almost unreal to know it'll at last be in the hands of readers.

Suzie Townsend, thank you for not giving up on Sirscha and for being an anchor in the hurricane that was writing and rewriting this book. I'm grateful for you beyond measure. Devin Ross, I can only wonder at how lucky I am to have you on my side. Thank you for your wisdom and humor and sharp editorial eye.

Ashley Hearn, I could never have discovered the heart of this book without your guidance. Thank you and the entire Page Street team for believing in Sirscha's story. Even more, thank you for your enthusiasm, support, and excellent use of caps lock.

I also dearly need to thank Mindee Arnett for reading so many drafts of this book that I've lost count. Not only that, but for always being there to brainstorm, commiserate, and cheer me on. I couldn't have asked for a better critique partner and friend.

Massive thanks to all the friends, colleagues, and kindhearted folks who read the book at different points in its many, many drafts: Lauren Teffeau, Carrie DiRisio, Heather Kassner, Cassandra Newbould, Christina Soontornvat, Erin Arkin, Jessica Rubinowski, Linda Canniff, and Lee Bross. I'm also forever grateful to my Fellowship, friends who've been there through crises and joys, through fandom and fanfic and publishing: Emily, Patricia, Audrey, Imaan, Aamyra, and Lyn.

Lastly, thank you to my family for never doubting me. For encouraging me to dream, and for always being proud no matter how small the accomplishment.

ABOUT THE AUTHOR

Lori M. Lee is the author of *Gates of Thread and Stone* and *The Infinite*. She's also a contributor to the anthologies *A Thousand Beginnings and Endings* and *Color outside the Lines*. She considers herself a unicorn aficionado, enjoys marathoning TV shows, and loves to write about magic, manipulation, and family. She lives in Wisconsin with her husband, kids, and an excitable shih tzu.

A sneak peak at

BROKEN WEB

the second book in the
Shamanborn trilogy

ONE

T he forest is still, the branches streaked in sunset. Weeds and shadows press at my heels.

The silence is a lie. I don't need my craft to catch the faint flutter of wings hidden behind broad summer leaves or the shuffle of small paws in the underbrush. But with my craft, every presence is amplified, like a dozen voices shouting at once.

My teeth clench. The souls are indistinct—I lack the control to separate them into individuals—and my fingers twitch restlessly. Magic burns through my veins, surging against my skin. With a frustrated exhale, I flatten my palms against my stomach and imagine compressing my craft into a burning ember of power at my core. It's like trying to stuff a storm into a cage. Still, my awareness of the souls dims enough that I can ignore them.

I draw a throwing knife from my belt, letting my other senses home in on the speckled hare digging for roots to my right. Before the blade leaves my hand, an arrow whizzes past my shoulder, finding my mark first.

Returning the knife to my belt, I face Saengo, who lowers her bow. "I had it," I say.

"You were taking ages, and I'm hungry." Her boots are silent as she moves past me through the deepening gloom to retrieve the hare. "No luck?"

"No," I say quietly. My gaze flicks in the direction she came from, toward camp where some three dozen Nuvali shamans and their familiars await.

Prince Meilek is there as well, having agreed to accompany us until the falcons he'd sent to Evewyn return. After betraying his sister, the queen, he's no longer safe in his own kingdom, not until he can confirm he still has allies.

For the last week, I've been trying to use my craft to hunt, as it was originally intended. But my first attempt ended in disaster when I ripped the souls of every creature within twenty paces. Since then, I've been trying to focus on individual souls, but it's been impossible without either physical contact or close proximity.

Heat flecks the tips of my fingers. It doesn't help that my magic seemingly *wants* to be used, straining toward every living thing within reach to loosen the tether between soul and body. It's disconcerting and keeps me on edge.

The Nuvali dislike that Saengo and I hunt on our own, but when they invited me to join them in the shaman capital, I made clear that I would keep my freedom to come and go as I wish. Thus far, they've tolerated it, but their grudging allowance is another reason to be cautious with my craft. I can't trust we won't be followed.

"You'll get it, Sirscha. You always do," Saengo says. Hare in hand, she wipes the arrowhead on some leaves and then returns it to her quiver.

I'm not so confident. My magic feels different, unruly. Before I fought Ronin at Spinner's End a fortnight ago, I struggled to even summon my craft. But to defeat him, I'd allowed the Soulless's power to flow through me and strengthen my magic. Even after the molten presence of his power faded, my craft never quite settled.

I haven't told Saengo. Hers is the only soul I can pick out without difficulty. She is always with me, a candle flame burning behind my ribs.

She hands me the hare and grimaces as I set about cleaning it. For all her training, she's surprisingly squeamish. I grin and consider flicking entrails at her.

"Don't you dare," she says, eyes narrowing as she backs away from me.

"What?" I say, laughing.

"Don't think I won't find something even more disgusting to leave in your bedroll."

I snort, grinning. "I would never underestimate you."

"I don't know how you can even see what you're doing." She indicates the quickening night.

"It's not fully dark yet. Besides, I'd make a lousy Shadow if I couldn't even do this. . . ." My voice trails off. I'd chased that ambition for so long—becoming Shadow to the queen of Evewyn, her royal spy and assassin. Sometimes I forget that, even if I still wanted it, it's now well beyond my reach.

Silence lingers for a beat, filled by the dull ache of old dreams. Then Saengo says, "We'll be to Mirrim soon."

I nod, crouched over my work. "Hopefully, we'll get some answers."

Mirrim, the capital of the Nuvalyn Empire, lies far to the east. Despite the risk, we agreed that going there was our best option. Posing as their soulguide is the best way to gain access to whatever information might be kept there about the Soulless. So long as my true craft stays hidden.

Besides Saengo, only Prince Meilek knows that I'm a soul-render, because he was present when I learned the truth. But we've another reason for venturing so deep into the Empire. Saengo is infected with the rot, and we've been promised Mirrim's best healers for her.

Part of me suspects, though, that she will never truly be healed until the Soulless is dealt with. His corrupted magic has infected her as surely as it's infected me, setting flame to my craft so that it burns beneath my skin. Always restless, always eager.

She fusses with the ends of her red sash, picking at frayed threads. "It's frightening, isn't it?" she asks softly.

"Me?" I fear my own craft, so why wouldn't Saengo? It was my power that turned her into a familiar. Now, she is bound to me—a spirit restored to shape and form in exchange for channeling my magic. Sometimes, I don't know how she can even bear to look at me, given what I've done to her.

"No, Sirscha," she says, exasperated. "Your magic."

"Me, my magic. It's all the same."

"Of course it isn't. You were you before you ever learned you were a soulrender."

I sigh. While I understand her meaning, it's not so simple. My powers are unsettling even to me. Souls are the source of shamanic magic. That a soulrender can grasp souls and destroy them is an attack against magic itself. Fear of what soulrenders can do—fear of what the Soulless did—is what drove the Empire to destroy them.

Aside from myself and the Soulless, no other soulrenders remain.

Finished with the hare, I stand and swing the carcass at

Saengo, who yelps and dashes out of reach.

"Get that thing to a cooking fire," she says, poking the air between us with one finger.

"At once, my lady."

She leads us back to camp, our boots whispering through the weeds. Somewhere overhead comes a sharp birdcall. Saengo looks up, grinning. Millie, her pet falcon, has been following us since we entered the Empire.

With her back to me, my smile fades. Holding the hare out at my side, I frown down at the faint spatter of blood on my pants. Although we're both in our old gray uniforms from the Queen's Company, there's little chance anyone would mistake us for fourth-years. Had I not discovered that I'm shaman-born, Saengo and I would have graduated from the Company a few weeks ago and been shipped off to some distant post to begin our years of military service. We probably would've been separated.

The person I was feels so far away that it might as well be a different lifetime.

Now, our uniforms are thoroughly travel-worn, washed and rewashed since we set out for Mirrim. I keep my hair in a braid for function, but Saengo's is short enough that the ends curl beneath her ears. She's a far cry from the reiwyn lady she's meant to be.

After the Soulless's awakening, no one had quite known

what to make of the surge of magic that swept from the Dead Wood. With no sign of the Spider King, no one was willing to enter a forest of vengeful souls to find out.

So the camps sent off their falcons and packed up. There'd been nothing else to do, and I wasn't about to risk Saengo's safety by volunteering the truth.

Sisters, this is hopeless. I draw a deep, slow breath and shake away the thought. The Soulless is just a man, same as Ronin. All shamans need familiars, something that bridges them with their magic. The Soulless can't be any different.

If we can find out what's connecting him to his magic, then we find the key to defeating him.

Two days later, we arrive in the trade city of Luam. Sitting at the confluence of two major rivers, the city sprawls around and above the water.

It is the largest city we've passed through. The previous towns were no more than a scattering of homes and buildings. I suspect our route was deliberate to keep word of my presence contained. There's no hiding here, though.

The sheer number of souls is overwhelming, and it takes several minutes for me to smother the surge of magic burning through my skin. I focus on the warm glow of Saengo's soul as she rides at my side. Exposing my craft wouldn't just put me and Saengo in danger. It would endanger Prince Meilek and the other Evewynians in our party. They only came this far at my request.

Boats pack the river from end to end. Some drift lazily along the banks and bridges, carrying goods to sell or trade. Others cut swiftly through the waves, a golden Nuvali sun painted along their sides and a uniformed waterwender at the helm. Broad bridges arch over the water. Buildings stand on thick stilts, crammed side to side, connected by wooden walkways.

Our procession is hard to miss as we enter the city, stalling foot traffic. At our lead is a lightwender priestess named Mia who met us on the road yesterday morning with a small party of lightwender guards. As everyone believes I'm a soulguide, the first to appear since the founding of the Empire, the Emperor had deemed it necessary to send an escort from the Temple of Light to ensure I reach Mirrim safely.

With the threat of war between the kingdoms, the Nuvali want me somewhere "safe." But I wouldn't have come if it didn't also serve my own purposes, and I'm only safe so long as they think I'm a soulguide.

After taking control of our group, Priestess Mia sent the Nuvali lord we'd been traveling with ahead to report to the Emperor. Aside from an awkward introduction, I've been doing my best to avoid them. I'm wary of questions I might not be able to answer.

Priestess Mia glances over her shoulder and gestures with one slick fingernail for me to join her at the head of our procession.

I smother my annoyance at being beckoned and nudge Yandor ahead. Yandor is a common drake with a sleek head and dark green scales. But Priestess Mia rides a snowy white dragokin, a species native to the Empire, with liquid black eyes and shining white horns swirled with gold paint. Like drakes, dragokins stand on two powerful legs but with shorter arms and claws, making them vicious companions in battle. Everything about Priestess Mia screams her status at the Temple of Light, where young lightwenders go to study and master their light crafts.

Priestess Mia herself is a petite woman with long black hair and warm copper skin. Her eyes are a luminous amber, the mark of a lightwender, and framed by sparse lashes accented with kohl. Gold dust streaks her lids. According to the murmurs in our party, she's a lightgiver. Lightgivers can transfer the light, or life, of one person to another—a power rarely used except in times of dire need.

White robes drape from her shoulders, the hem embroidered with golden sunbursts. A sheer golden sash cinches her waist, knotted elaborately to denote her rank.

"Priestess," I murmur as I join her and nod politely.

She returns the gesture. Her gaze passes over the two swords at my back and then to Yandor's saddle, where a third sword is wrapped within a long strip of cloth. She doesn't remark on why I'm carrying so many weapons.

Around us, people pause to watch as we pass. I fight the impulse to hide, to shrink into the shadows. Nearly everyone possesses the pointed ears and jewel-bright eyes of a shaman, although I've learned that even among the same Calling, the range of hues can vary. After two weeks on the road and numerous towns, I've seen lightwenders with every shade from the palest gold to vivid amber, and, in a trade city of this size, even some gray-eyed shamans who've never bonded with a familiar.

Familiars in the form of all manner of beasts accompany them. Birds flit from shoulders to rooftops, snakes and other smaller creatures curl around necks or ride tucked into satchels, their furred heads peering out from the openings. Lizards perch atop the brims of hats or burrow into the hoods of cloaks. Larger familiars—silver wolves, black foxes, and even a fire salamander—trot alongside their shamans. It's breathtaking to see so many creatures living naturally alongside people.

Among the boats that crowd the riverways, I glimpse the white hair and gray skin of the shadowblessed. I even spot brown-eyed humans with rounded ears like Saengo's. Like mine. To hide the truth of my parentage, whoever abandoned me to an orphanage cut my ears when I was a child.

"The governor of Luam is away on business, but he offered us the use of his home for the night," Priestess Mia says. Although her lips curve into a pleasant smile, there's a hardness in the way she observes me. Her luminous eyes lack warmth.

She must question the veracity of who I claim to be, and I don't blame her. I expect there will be others who feel the same in Mirrim.

"That was generous of him," I say awkwardly. I loathe making small talk and nearly glance back at Saengo for guidance. As the heir to House Phang, she is well versed in socializing with other reiwyn.

We cross a series of bridges, heading into the eastern part of the city. Beyond the bank of the river, built atop a rise half-covered in wild sunflowers, is a whitewashed mansion. It'll be a nice change from tents.

Priestess Mia runs her pale fingers along the reins of her dragokin. "There is one thing, however, about the Evewynian prince and his soldiers."

Her words steal my attention from the bustle around us. Prince Meilek and his small group of Eveywnians ride near the rear of our procession. A few days after setting out from the north, several of his Blades and servants caught up to our party, declaring their intent to remain with their prince. I recognized two of them from when Saengo and I were imprisoned at the Valley of Cranes.

After Prince Meilek warned the Nuvali and Kazan about his sister's attack in the north, no one objected to his presence. But while Prince Meilek agreed to remain with me until he's heard from his allies, I know he's restless. This deep into the Empire, the Evewynians have clung together, uncertain of their welcome and wary of a people their queen has fashioned into enemies.

"What about them?" I ask stiffly.

Priestess Mia speaks with a clipped matter-of-factness. "He and his soldiers are, of course, welcome in Luam. However, housing a fugitive prince within a government-issued home could be misconstrued. The Emperor has not decided how to respond to Evewyn's attack, and such a move might be seen as an escalation."

I was prepared to argue with whatever she said, but this is unexpected. It irks me that she has a point.

Still, Prince Meilek saved lives in the north. There's little doubt the Empire won't retaliate for Evewyn breaking the peace treaty long enforced by Ronin. But until the Emperor decides what that retaliation will be, they'll want to avoid anything that might imply the Emperor's approval.

Allowing Prince Meilek safe passage through the Empire

seems a clear enough stance to me, but what do I know of politics?

"Then I will find other accommodations with them," I say. Being able to speak with Prince Meilek away from the constant presence of our Nuvali escort will be welcome. There's too much we haven't discussed.

"You cannot," she says simply. "I have been entrusted with your safety."

"Not by me."

Her lips pinch, just the slightest. "By the High Priestess of the Temple of Light and the Emperor. Look at the manner of our arrival—within hours, everyone will know you're here. Luam is a city open to people from all over Thiy, including those historically at odds with the Empire."

I nearly snort. It's a delicate way of alluding to the ongoing hostility between the Nuvalyn Empire and Kazahyn.

"The governor's home is well protected. It's the safest place for you and your friend. But if you insist on remaining with the Evewynian prince, then my guards and I will have no choice but to join you," she says, her tone suggesting she'd rather dive into the river.

Saengo and I can take care of ourselves. As much as it would amuse me to inconvenience her, I wouldn't be able to speak freely with Prince Meilek, knowing she and her Light Temple guards are under the same roof. I can't trust them.

But there might still be a way.

"I'll speak with Prince Meilek," I say, and excuse myself with another bow.

Saengo lifts one eyebrow in question as I pass her. "Later," I mouth and make my way to Prince Meilek and the other Evewynians at the back of our party.

Prince Meilek rides flanked by two of his Blades, Evewyn's warrior elite and former members of the Queen's Guard. The rest of his group follow at his back, clustered together in this foreign city.

He has abandoned his pristine captain's look these last couple weeks. While the upper half of his hair is swept back into a ponytail at the crown of his head, the dark strands are mussed from a long day's ride, and a fine layer of dust coats his clothes. After the heat of the day, he's rolled back his sleeves and loosened the collar of his tunic. To blend in with the others, he's removed the golden hairpin that announces his royal blood, and the green sash at his waist is tied in a humble knot.

"Sirscha," he says, greeting me as I match Yandor to the pace of his dragule. His Blades make room for me.

I bow respectfully and quietly convey Priestess Mia's words. He doesn't seem surprised.

"I wondered how they planned to have me here without outright declaring their intent to oppose Evewyn. The attack in the north was an act of war. And now that the peace treaty is broken, the Empire will likely respond. But whatever they choose to reveal about their actions will be on their own terms."

"They owe you a debt," I mutter.

"She's right," one of his Blades murmurs, a tall thin man named Kou. "They disrespect you by—"

"They do what they must." Prince Meilek shrugs. "In truth, I'd planned to spend the night elsewhere anyway."

I frown. "You know someone in Luam?"

"A shamanborn acquaintance. There may be other shamanborn here as well. She'll be able to find us a room and a warm meal."

I don't like the idea of separating from my fellow Evewynians, who've offered a measure of comfort in their familiarity these last two weeks. Though I am loathe to admit it, Priestess Mia is right. As a soulguide, even a fake one, the Empire's enemies will view me as an enemy. If it were only me, I'd be willing to take the risk. But there's also Saengo's safety to consider.

Saengo falls back to join us, and we remain with them until we reach the path that winds through the sunflowers and up to the governor's mansion.

As we make our goodbyes, I pull Prince Meilek into a quick embrace and murmur in his ear, "We'll find you later."

"The Dancing Drake Inn," he replies promptly. He clearly knows more about the shamanborn in Luam than he initially let on.

I smile and bow. As Priestess Mia and the others continue ahead toward the mansion, Saengo and I linger on the road, watching as the flurry of traffic swallows Prince Meilek and the other Evewynians.